Lynda La Plante

CLEAN CUT

SIMON &
SCHUSTER

London · New York · Sydney · Toronto

First published in Great Britain by Simon & Schuster UK Ltd, 2004
This edition published 2011

Copyright © Lynda La Plante, 2004

7 9 10 8 6

Simon & Schuster UK Ltd
1st floor, 222 Gray's Inn Road
London WC1X 8HB

www.simonandschuster.co.uk

Simon & Schuster Australia
Sydney

A CIP catalogue record for this book
is available from the British Library

ISBN 978-1-84983-435-3

Printed and bound by CPI Group (UK) Ltd, Croydon, CR0 4YY

This book is dedicated to the memory of a truly special young man. The handsome, flame-haired Jason McCreight, I still mourn for him and perhaps I always will. Jason was a constant support, especially for my writing. During the first rough drafts of *Clean Cut* he was encouraging and played a very important role making notes and queries for me to answer. One paragraph he underlined, and when I asked him why, he smiled and said, 'because I liked it'. Whether this meant something special I will never know, but this was the paragraph:

Anna wept because deep down in her heart she knew, unlike her father, she would not be able to deal with it. If Langton did not recover, there would be a difficult transition and she doubted she had the strength to confront it, well not now, she would have to at some later date. In the meantime she intended to give him every possible incentive to be able to deal with whatever the future held. From now on, even though she did love him, she would take it day by day, and pray that she never had to walk away from him until he was strong enough to deal with it.

Acknowledgements

My gratitude to all those who gave their valuable time to help me with research on *Clean Cut*, in particular Lucy & Raff D'Orsi, Professor Ian Hill (pathology), Dr Liz Wilson (forensics), and Callum Sutherland for all their valuable police advice.

Thank you to my committed team at La Plante Productions; Liz Thorburn, Richard Dobbs, Pamela Wilson and Noel Farragher. For taking the weight off my shoulders to enable me to have the time to write and for running the La Plante Productions company. Thanks also go to Stephen Ross and Andrew Bennet-Smith and especially to Kara Manley.

To my literary agent Gill Coleridge and all at Rogers, Coleridge and White, I give great thanks. I give special thanks for their constant encouragement. To my publishers Ian Chapman, Suzanne Baboneau and to everyone at Simon & Schuster, especially Nigel Stoneman. I am very happy to be working with such a terrific company.

Chapter One

Anna was in a foul mood. He had not turned up for dinner. Work commitments sometimes took precedence, obviously – she knew that – but he only had to call and she would understand. In actual fact, she had put understanding of their profession right at the top of the pluses on her list. It was a Friday and she had a long weekend due; they had planned to drive out to the country and stay overnight at a lovely inn. It was unusual for them both to have time off, so it made it even more annoying that he had not phoned. She had left messages on his mobile but did not like to overkill, as it was possible he was on a call out; however, she knew that he was meant to be winding down the long and tedious enquiry he had been on for months.

Anna scraped the dried food off the plate into the bin. Tonight had not been the first time by any means and as she sat, tapping her teeth with a pencil, she tried to calculate just how often he had missed dinner. Sometimes he had not even turned up at all, but had gone to stay at his own flat. Although they did, to all intents and purposes, live together, he still kept his place in Kilburn; when he was on a particularly pressing case and working round the clock, he used it rather than disturb her. It was not a bone of contention; sometimes she had even been relieved, although she never admitted it. He also liked to spend quality time there with Kitty, his stepdaughter from his second marriage. All this she could take in her stride, especially if she was also up against it on a case of her own.

They did not work together; they had not, since they became an item. This was partly due to the Met's once unspoken rule that officers were not to fraternize, especially if assigned to the same case. It had bothered Langton more than Anna, but she had understood his reservations and was quietly relieved that, since the Red Dahlia case, they had been allocated to different enquiries. They had a tacit agreement not to bring work home to each other; she adhered to it, but Langton was often in such a fury that he started swearing and cursing as soon as the front door opened. She had never brought this up, but it had become very one-sided. As he ranted and railed about his team, about the press, about the CPS – about anything that had got under his skin that day – he rarely, if ever, asked what her day had been like. This went onto the list of minuses.

Anna went to stack the dishwasher; God forbid he ever considered moving his cereal bowl from the sink to the dishwasher. He was often in such a rush to get out in the morning that she would find coffee cups in the bedroom, the bathroom, as well as something she had grown to really detest: cigarette butts. If there wasn't an ashtray within arm's reach, he would stub his cigarettes out in his saucer or even in his cereal bowl; to her knowledge, he had never, since they had been together, ever emptied an ashtray. He had never taken the rubbish out to the bins either, or washed a milk bottle and put it out; in fact, he almost used her Maida Vale flat like a hotel. She was the one who sent the linen to the laundry, collected it and made up the beds with fresh sheets; then there was the washing and the ironing. He would leave their bedroom like a war zone: socks, underpants, shirts and pyjama bottoms strewn around the room, dropped where he had stepped out of them. There was also the slew of wet towels left on the floor in the bathroom after his morning shower, not to mention the toothpaste without its cap. She had brought up a few of these things and he apologized, promising he would mend his ways, but nothing had changed.

Anna poured herself a glass of wine. The list of minuses was now two sheets long; the pluses just a couple of lines. Now she got onto bills. He would, when she asked, open his wallet and pass over a couple of hundred pounds, but then often borrowed it back before the end of the week! It wasn't, she concluded, that he was tight-fisted; far from it. It was just that he never thought. This she knew: often he was complaining about his flat being cut off because he'd forgotten to pay his own bills. When he was at home, he ate like a starving man, but had never once accompanied her to do a grocery shop. The plus, if you could call it a plus, was that he did say anything she placed in front of him was good, when she knew her culinary expertise left a lot to be desired. He also downed wine at a rate of knots, and never went to bed without a whisky; this particular minus was underlined. Langton's drinking had always worried her. He had, on various occasions, gone on one of his drying-out periods; they usually lasted a week or so and were often done to prove that he was not, as she had implied, bordering on alcoholism. He could get into quite an angry mood if she brought it up, insisting he needed to wind down. She kept on writing, however; the drinking at home was one thing, but she knew he also hit the pub with his cohorts on a regular basis.

Anna emptied her wine glass and poured another; she was getting quite piddled herself, but was determined that when he did come home, it was time for a long talk about their relationship. She knew it was unsatisfactory: very obviously so, when she read through her list. What invariably happened when she had previously attempted to try to make him understand how she felt, was that the plus side of their life together made it never the right moment. He would draw her into his arms at night, so they lay wrapped around each other. She adored the way he would hold her in the curve of his body and nuzzle her neck. His hair was usually wet from the shower and he smelled of her shampoo and soap; many nights, he would shave before coming to bed, as his dark shadow was rough to her skin. His lovemaking left her breathless and adoring; he could be so gentle and yet passionate, and was caring and sensitive to her every whim — *in bed* . . .

Langton's presence filled her small flat from the moment he walked in the front door until the moment he left, and without him there was such an awful quiet emptiness. Sometimes she enjoyed it, but never for long; she missed him, and loved to hear him running up her front steps. She was always waiting as he let himself in, opened his arms and swung her round as if he'd been away weeks instead of a day. He then dropped his coat and briefcase, kicked off his shoes, and left a trail of discarded garments all over the place as he went into the bedroom to shower. He always showered before they had dinner; he hated the stink of cells, incident rooms and the stale cigarettes that clung to his clothes. After his shower, he would put on an old navy-blue and white dotted dressing-gown and, barefoot, go into the lounge to put the television on. He never settled down to watch any single programme, but would switch between news items and the various soaps that he hated with a vengeance. As she cooked, he would yell from the lounge what a load of crap was on TV, then join her to open the wine. Perched on a stool, he would talk about his day: the good, the bad and, sometimes, the hideous. He always had such energy and, in truth, when he did discuss his cases, she was always interested.

DCI Langton had a special gift; anyone who had ever worked with him knew it and, on the two occasions Anna had been assigned to work on his team, she had learned so much. In fact, living with him made her even more aware of just what a dedicated detective he was. He always looked out for his team and she, more than anyone, knew just how far he had gone to protect her when she had not obeyed the rules. Though he often bent them himself, he was a very clever operator; he had an intuitive mind, but his tendency to be obsessive made him tread a very dangerous line. During the eighteen months they had lived together, even when he had been hard at work all day, she had often seen him working into the early hours, going over and over the case files. He never missed a trick and his prowess at interrogation was notorious.

Anna sighed. Suddenly all her anger over him missing dinner and her urge to make lists evaporated; all she wanted was to hear his footsteps on the stairs and then his key turn in the lock. After all, she knew he was wrapping up a murder enquiry; doubtless he had just gone for a celebratory drink with the boys. She finished her wine and took a shower, getting ready for bed. She wondered, as it was so late, whether he had gone to his own flat. She rang, but there was no reply. She was about to call his mobile again when she heard footsteps on the stairs. She hurried to be there waiting for him, when she froze, listening. The steps were heavy and slow; instead of hearing the key in the front door, the bell rang. She hesitated; the bell rang again.

'Who is it?' she asked, listening at the door.

'It's Mike – Mike Lewis, Anna.'

She hurried to open the door. She knew instinctively something was wrong.

'Can I come in?'

'What is it,' she asked, opening the door wide.

DI Lewis was white-faced and tense. 'It's not good news.'

'What's happened?' She could hardly catch her breath.

'It's Jimmy. He's over at St Stephen's Hospital.'

Langton and his team had just charged the killer of a young woman. When the man had put in the frame two other members of his street gang, Langton, accompanied by Detectives Lewis and Barolli (close friends, as well as members of his murder team), had gone to investigate. As they approached the two men, one had knifed Langton in the chest, then slashed his thigh. He was in a very serious condition.

By the time the speeding patrol car reached the hospital, Anna had calmed herself down: no way did she want him to see her scared. As she hurried through the corridors leading to the Intensive Care Unit, she was met by Barolli.

'How is he?' Lewis asked.

'Holding his own, but it's touch and go.' Barolli reached out and squeezed Anna's hand. 'Bastard knifed him with a fucking machete.'

Anna swallowed. The three continued to the ICU.

Before Anna was allowed to see him, they met with the cardiothoracic surgeon. The weapon thankfully had missed Langton's heart, but had caused severe tissue damage; he also had a collapsed lung. She could hardly absorb the extent of the injuries: she felt faint from shock and had to continually take deep breaths. Both Lewis and Barolli were pale and silent. It was Lewis who asked if Langton would make it.

The surgeon repeated that he was in a very serious condition and, as yet, they could not estimate the full extent of his injuries. He was on a ventilator to assist his breathing; his pulse rate was of deep concern.

'Will I be allowed to see him?' Anna asked.

'You can, but only for a few moments. He's sedated, so obviously will not be able to talk. I must insist that you do not enter the Unit, but look through the viewing section. We cannot afford any contamination; he's obviously in a very vulnerable state.'

Langton was hardly visible among the tubes. The breathing apparatus made low hissing sounds as it pumped air into his lungs. Anna pressed her face close to the window; the tears she had tried so hard to contain flowed, yet she made no sound. Lewis had a protective arm around her shoulders, but she didn't want it. She wanted to be alone; she wanted to be closer to Langton – above all, she wanted to hold him.

Anna remained at the hospital all night; Lewis and Barolli returned to their homes.

The next morning, Langton went into relapse. Again, she could only watch helplessly as the medics worked to resuscitate his heart. Drained by anxiety, and both emotionally and physically exhausted, she finally returned home after being told he was stable.

DAY TWO

She was back again by mid-morning to sit and wait, in the hope she might be able to at least see him closer. The hours passed at a snail's pace; she constantly stood in the Intensive Care viewing room, watching the array of doctors and nurses tending to him. She hadn't cried again since first seeing him; she now felt as if she was suspended in a state of panic. Her head ached and she felt physically sick. It was Lewis who made her go and get something to eat; he would stay watching.

The hospital café was almost empty. She ordered a coffee, some soup and a roll. She hardly touched any of it, but picked at the bread, rolling it into small balls. She could hardly take it in: Langton might die. It was just so unthinkable that such an energy force could suddenly be terminated. Closing her eyes, she twisted her trembling hands in her lap, whispering over and over, 'Please don't let him die. Please don't let him die.'

When Anna returned to Lewis, he was sitting on a hard-backed chair, reading the *Daily Mail*. The headline read: *Top Detective Knifed*. Lewis had numerous other papers, all running the attack on the front page. It had created considerable political impact: the number of knife attacks in London had been escalating. Langton had become one of the first police officers to be wounded, and by an illegal immigrant; the list had mostly comprised murdered schoolkids until now. The news programmes all covered the knife amnesty arranged by the Met; the summation was that there were hundreds of thousands of armed kids in schools alone.

Lewis folded the paper, sighing. 'Makes me sick, reading these articles. What they don't say is that those two bastards are still being hunted, but with no luck tracing them. At least we got the bugger.'

'The man who attacked him?'

'No, the case we were working on – murder of a prostitute, Carly Ann North. He was picked up trying to slice her head off. A local cop caught him at it, rang for back-up and when they turned up, the two so-called pals did a runner.'

'Is that when you were brought in?'

'Yeah. Jimmy questioned him – he's a twenty-five-year-old Somali illegal immigrant called Idris Krasiniqe. He served six months in prison for robbery and was then released! Bloody mind-blowing, the fucker was let loose. He's now held at Islington station. Without Jimmy, I'll have to handle the trial.'

'These other men that were with him – have you got any trace on them at all?'

'No. We went to try to find them after we had a tip-off from Krasiniqe. That was when it happened.'

Anna could see Lewis was physically shaking; he kept swallowing, as if he was having trouble catching his breath.

'So, this tip-off?' she prompted.

Lewis stood up. 'That was when it happened. We were at this shithole in Brixton, walking up the stairs and . . .' He sighed and shook his head. 'Bastard's probably gone back to where he came from. It beggars belief, doesn't it? The one held in Islington was supposed to have been fucking deported, but the Home Office alleged that if he returned home, he'd be in danger – so they let him loose on our fucking streets! World is going crazy.'

Anna nodded. She knew about the massive media coverage of the issue of illegal immigrants, not just how many per se, but how many had been released from prison to disappear without trace, and not just robbers, but armed killers and rapists. It was, as Lewis said, beyond belief; now Langton was paying a terrible price. Lewis, she could see, was also suffering. She changed the subject.

'Why haven't they allowed any of us to see him?' she asked.

'Well, he was taken back down to surgery earlier, so I dunno what's happening, just that he's not doing too good.'

As if on cue, a surgeon approached them – one they had met previously. Hugh Huntingdon was a big, affable man and young, considering his qualifications. He drew up a chair to sit beside them.

'We've been working on your friend all day, and I think it's time to bring you up to date. Until now we've not been able to ascertain the extent of the damage. So, you want it straight?'

Anna nodded; he was so calm and easygoing, she felt relaxed. She noticed that both Lewis and Barolli were calmer, too.

'Okay. We have two ferocious machete wounds – one to the chest, and one to the front of the left thigh. The one to his chest sliced through his ribs, just above his nipple, thankfully avoiding, by some miracle, his heart.'

Huntingdon had a clipboard; he flipped over a couple of pages until he found one blank, and took out a felt-tip pen. 'Okay,' he said, rapidly sketching, 'this is the chest and lung area: his right lung is incised, and so are some of the blood vessels. This has caused a haemopneumothorax, which makes breathing very difficult, and that's why he's been on a ventilator since he was admitted. This situation can be fatal. One of the reasons we are keeping him in the ICU is to avoid any kind of possible contamination; if he were to get pneumonia, I doubt he'd have the strength to combat it.'

Huntingdon looked at his cell phone, on silent; he clicked the caller onto his voicemail and then returned it to his pocket. 'Sorry about that. Okay, I have no wish to sound such a doom courier, but you wanted it straight. Mr Langton lost a lot of blood, so he needed transfusions; he also had to have his chest drained. All this, combined with his leg injury . . . It's really very serious. The wound to his leg has affected the joint. He will need an operation but, due to the chest injury, we've got that on hold for the time being. The most important thing right now is we keep him clear of infection. Knee joints are buggers, and he'll be in a lot of pain, but now for the good news: he's one hell of a fighter and he is right now holding his own, so all I can say is: keep your fingers crossed.'

He smiled and flipped the pages back over to cover his drawing. 'You were lucky to have him brought here. We've got a great team working on him. I'm one of the best around!'

Huntingdon stood up and shook their hands. His cell

phone must have trembled again in his pocket; he took it out as he walked off down the corridor.

They remained silent for a moment. Then Anna stood up too.

'He's going to make it, I know. I liked that doctor a lot.'

'Me too,' said Lewis.

Barolli remained sitting, looking at the floor. 'Yeah, but that's his career down the tubes. He's never going to be able to get back to work.'

Anna turned on him angrily. 'Yes, he will, and don't even go there. He's going to be working and he won't need any kind of negative response; we keep his spirits up when we are allowed in to see him. Agreed?'

They all nodded, but there was a very uneasy feeling between them. They each, in their own way, adored their Gov. It was just unthinkable that he would not pull through.

SIX WEEKS LATER

It had been six frustrating weeks with still no result. Anna had been given special leave, and she had spent the time visiting Langton daily. There had been emotional moments that she had found difficult to deal with, not just because of her relationship with Langton: it brought back memories of visiting her beloved father when he was dying of cancer. They were similar in many respects, both such fighters, but her father was resigned to his death and, by the end, wanted to go quietly and peacefully. They had been so close; his love for her and his constant encouragement never faltered, and she adored him. There was never any need for any kind of reproach.

His intention was that she should be strong when he had gone. He worried that she would be on her own, but she assured him he had given her a backbone like his; she would be able to cope with life without him. He asked often if she was lonely; she had always insisted that she had lots of friends and had made many new ones at the Academy. This was not actually the truth; she did not have many close female friends and had no boyfriend at the time. Her father had died peacefully, holding her hand, but her loss felt all-consuming. She was glad he had never seen her distraught; never seen her grief become almost unbearable.

There was no such grief with Langton – he was going to survive. When she had at last been allowed near him, he often asked for her; sometimes when he dozed off, he woke saying her name. She would then grip hold of his hand and whisper that she was there beside him.

'Good; it's good to know you are here.' He had a rasp to his voice that sometimes made it difficult to understand what he was saying.

She had told him often how much she loved him, but he had never reciprocated by saying it back. She wished he would, but took as confirmation the way he smiled when she walked over to his bed. He complained about the food, so she often brought M&S sandwiches and chicken; however, he hardly touched it and it was usually Anna who polished off the grapes left by his many visitors from the murder team. Visiting hours were almost all day and she had to ask the nurses not to allow him to tire himself out.

Anna had just got home one evening when she received the call to return to the hospital. Just as it seemed Langton was on the road to recovery, they had a terrible setback. They had successfully operated on his knee joint, but he caught a chest infection, which developed into septicaemia. When she was told the news, she almost fainted. For two days and two nights, Langton's life hung in the balance. The time spent waiting to hear if he would survive was dreadful. Yet again though, he surprised the nursing staff: to their amazement, he pulled through.

SIX WEEKS AND FOUR DAYS

Eventually, Langton recovered enough to be sent to a police rehabilitation home. Glebe House nestled deep in the English countryside; its location was deliberately kept secret from the public by the Met. The atmosphere was ordered and yet very relaxed. The house had a fully equipped gym, spa and medical facilities, as well as a bar and a restaurant, and only 140 beds. In the previous year, almost 3,000 police officers had been there, mostly on a short-stay basis. Priority was given to injured officers; the staff were therefore well prepared for the amount of physiotherapy Langton would require. There were also a number of highly qualified psychiatric staff, as many officers arrived with stress-related issues and required counselling. Anna had been relieved when Langton agreed to be transferred; she knew she would be unable to deal with him in her small flat until he was physically recovered. He was a dreadful patient; even the nursing staff at St Stephen's were glad to see him leave. They didn't make Langton aware of it; quite the reverse. A few had written cards wishing him a speedy recovery, and two had brought flowers, but the way they gave encouragement to Anna, and warned Langton to behave himself, made her aware of how much trouble he must have caused. He even got angry about being helped into the wheelchair to take him down to her car; he had wanted to walk, but he was so unsteady that he had been forced to sit on the bed whilst she packed up his few belongings. He moaned and groaned, but did at least thank the staff, handing the boxes of chocolates that Anna had brought around to the nurses.

Wheeling him out of the ward and down to the car park, he carried on complaining about the bloody place and how glad he was to be getting the hell out of it. Next, she had the pleasure of helping him into her Mini; again, he muttered about her having such a small car, saying that was the reason he found it difficult to get from the wheelchair into the passenger seat. Anna could see how much it pained him to stand and then ease himself into the seat, his face twisting with agony and his breath rasping. She even had to help him with his seat-belt, as he was unable to turn his body to draw the strap around himself.

The drive down the M4 was just as hard going: he went into a rant about having to be shipped out to 'fucking no hopers' Glebe House'. Few, he maintained, were there as victims of injury. Most of the men there were time-wasters, he grumbled, or nutters who couldn't stand the strain, or had booze problems.

'Well, you'll get on well with them,' she tried to joke, but he wasn't amused. He snapped that he'd not had a drink in weeks, and that he was sick and tired of her insinuating that he had any kind of problem.

Changing the subject, she promised that, as soon as he felt stronger, he could come home and she would care for him there.

'Christ, I'll go mental in that small flat of yours.'

'Well, if we have to, we'll get a bigger place.'

He glared and then gave a derisive snort, muttering about where the money would come from. In case she'd forgotten, he only rented his flat.

Nothing she could say could make his dark mood lift; not once had he thanked her for arranging extended leave to be able to spend time with him at the hospital, nor acknowledged that she would now have to give up every weekend to drive back and forth to Glebe House.

He was rude to the staff who greeted him and helped him from the car into the waiting wheelchair. He was stony silent as they tried to make conversation, wheeling him through the reception area and towards the lift to the wing where he would be staying. His room over-looked the gardens; although small, it was bright and pleasant, but he glared around as if it was a prison cell.

After they had both been shown around, it was obvious that he was very tired, so they returned to his room. He had been asked to choose his dinner from a menu; he left it to Anna. He lay on the small bed, eyes closed.

'I'm going to go off now,' she said quietly. He made no response. She was sitting in an easy chair by the bed, and she took his hand. 'I have to get back.'

His fingers tightened on hers. 'When are you coming again?'

She leaned forwards to kiss his cheek. 'Tomorrow, and I'll be here as often as I can.'

'What time tomorrow?'

'Lunch; we'll have lunch together.'

'Okay.'

Still his eyes were closed, but his grip had not lessened on her hand. She waited; slowly, his fingers relaxed.

She inched open the door and crept out of the room, not wanting to wake him; then looked back towards him.

'I love you,' she said softly.

His eyes opened. In his gruff voice, he said, 'You want some advice? Don't come back. You get your own life on track. I'm just going to be a noose around your neck. I've wanted to tell you this for a long time. I've got no strength left, Anna, and I don't know if I am going to get out of this one. Maybe I am not going to make it back to work.'

She went back to his side and leaned over him, but he closed his eyes.

'Look at me,' she said. Then: 'Just you damned well look at me, Detective Chief Inspector James Langton!'

He looked up into her face.

'You *are* going to get well and you *are* going to get out of here! They won't have you here for more than a few weeks anyway, so just stop talking like some bloody loser. You make damned sure you are fit to come home to me, or I will move in here with you and make your life hell!'

'Can't be worse than it already is,' he muttered.

'Oh yes, it can. If you don't help yourself, nobody else will. It's up to you now. I just wish you could stop being in such a foul fucking mood and start trying to be a bit pleasant to people around you, because all they are trying to do is help you. They love you, they respect you – and they want you back!'

'Yeah, yeah, I hear you, but you have no idea what it feels like to be me. I hate being like this – I hate it! I can't get the strength up to even fucking walk by myself.'

'I'm going – I refuse to listen to you. Did you hear me? I'm off.'

'Go on then,' he snapped.

'No, I won't, not until you—'

'Until I what, Anna!? Get up and tango across the floor? I can't walk, I can't breathe properly and I've got pains in every part of my body. You tell me, what would *you* do?'

She leaned close again.

'I would fight every minute of every day to get my strength back, fight to get back to work so I could catch the son of a bitch that did this to me. That's what I would do.'

He reached out and drew her close, kissing her. 'You take care driving back, now. You were over the speed-limit more times than I could count.'

She could feel the tears welling up. 'Goodbye, see you tomorrow.'

'Thank you, Anna. I know I don't say it as much as I should do, but thank you.'

'I'd do anything for you, you know that.'

'Yeah, but I reckon you wouldn't change places with me.' He smiled.

It was the first time she had seen him smile since they had left the hospital – that smile of his that never ceased to touch her heart. She kissed him again. 'I love you.'

She was out quickly this time, not wanting to prolong it again; she didn't want him to see her getting upset. She left so quickly that she didn't see the tears well in his eyes as he began to weep.

Anna had no one she could confide in. The strain of the past weeks had taken its toll. She looked dreadful, and had lost a considerable amount of weight with worry. Often, two or three times a day, she had driven to the hospital and back, and would stay late into the night beside him. She had let everything else go. She had not cleaned her flat or done any washing, so that was all stacked up. She had not cooked for herself, but eaten at the hospital or ordered takeaways. When she got back from Glebe House that first day, she flopped down on her bed and lay there for ten minutes before forcing herself to get up and get organized.

Anna spent the next two hours hoovering, washing and making shopping lists. It was after eleven when she showered and finally got into bed with clean fresh sheets. She was asleep within minutes. It was the first night she had slept soundly for weeks. The fact that Jimmy was being cared for at Glebe House made her less stressed. She knew by the following week she would be back at work; on which murder enquiry, she didn't yet know, but it was strange to think she had not even thought about work during the entire time Langton had been hospitalized.

SIX WEEKS AND FIVE DAYS

Anna woke refreshed and was out very early doing a marathon grocery shop. She bought mounds of fruit to take to him, as well as stocking up her freezer and fridge. By ten, she had unpacked everything, eaten a good breakfast and arranged to have her hair cut and blow-dried. Having spent no time on herself over the past few weeks, she now enjoyed the luxury of having a pedicure and a manicure. She returned home at two, feeling so much better.

She tried on a couple of different outfits before she was satisfied; the weight loss was the only good thing about all this. She was only five feet four and was always intending to try to lose some weight; with the trauma of Langton's attack and the fear for his recovery, she had shed pounds. She decided she would start going to the gym for a workout a few mornings a week, or maybe visit the local swimming baths. She had always loved swimming, and remembered the day when her mother had suggested she cut off her long plaits so her hair didn't take up so much time to wash and dry. Anna had cried; she hadn't wanted to have her hair cut. Eleven years old, sitting in the salon, she had been heartbroken when her thick, wavy red hair was chopped and shaped into a bob. However, she had not been unhappy with the result – quite the reverse. The short hair had framed her heart-shaped face and the fringe accentuated her wide blue eyes. The smattering of freckles that, even now, were visible across her snub nose no haircut could hide, but she had hardly changed the style. She never wore much make-up, but she now made herself up with care, putting on a light-brown eye shadow and mascara, with a pale coral lipstick. Giving herself a good once-over in the bathroom mirror, she couldn't help but smile. She had lovely white even teeth; all the months she had worn braces as a child had paid off. Anna had come a long way from being the rather dumpy, red-haired, freckle-faced kid with glinting braces. She was very much a woman.

By two o'clock, she was driving back to Glebe House to see Langton, refreshed and feeling a whole lot more in control.

If he was pleased to see her, he didn't show it. He looked more morose than ever and said he'd had a terrible night: he'd hardly slept a wink. Instead of complimenting her on how she looked, he seemed almost petulant. 'You've had your hair cut.'

'Thank you – surprised you even noticed,' she said, making light of it, as she produced grapes, vine tomatoes and some smoked salmon.

'They do feed me here. I thought you were coming for lunch.'

'I know, but I had things to do and I just thought if you needed a snack . . .'

He plucked at one of the grapes; she saw that his hand was shaking.

'So, when do you go back to work?' he asked.

'I don't know. Probably next Monday.'

'Mmm, suppose you can't wait; give you an excuse not to have to drive out to this godforsaken place.'

'It isn't godforsaken. You know I only come because I want to see you, so it would be nice if you showed that you wanted to see me.'

He shrugged. 'Just seems a long schlep out here and I've nothing really to say – well, not as yet. I've not met any of the inmates, though I've heard them; you wouldn't believe how many of them are bawling their eyes out. Night nurse said they get a lot of it – call it post-traumatic stress syndrome now. Well, I've got a better word for it: nutters! It's not as if they've been out in Iraq, for Chrissakes.'

Anna listened as he ranted on; then there was a pause. He seemed to have exhausted himself.

'You know,' she said carefully, 'after a tragic event or, say, a particularly gruelling enquiry, some of our guys really suffer. It's actually called hyper-arousal or hyper-vigilance.'

'Oh, really! You been reading up on it, have you?'

'No. I was waiting for one of the nurses, to ask how you were getting on; she kept me waiting and when she did see me, she was a bit tensed up, so I asked her what was wrong. She said one of the patients had been very worrying; he would only sit with his back to the wall. All night, this was; he was in constant fear that something beyond his control was happening.'

'Seeing aliens next,' Langton said, like a grumpy old man.

Anna was able to change the subject by asking if she should go round to his place and see if there was any mail for him, or if there was anything he needed from there; she could then bring it in the next time she came to see him.

'Oh, ready to leave already, are you?'

She wanted to snap back at him; he was like a naughty child, trying anything he could to get her temper up. 'No, but I don't have a key, and if there is anything that might be important . . .'

'There won't be. I've nothing of any importance anyway.'

'Is there anyone you would like me to contact, to come and see you?'

'No.'

'How about Kitty?'

His face went red with anger. 'I don't want her anywhere near this place.'

'She might be worried about you; you've not seen her for so long.'

'I know exactly how long it's been, and no, I do *not* want to see her – nor anybody else for that matter.'

'Oh, I see. Does that include me?'

'Yes. You've no need to come out here; it's a long drive.'

'You don't mean that.'

'Yes, I do.'

There was an uneasy pause; he appeared more like a petulant child than ever. 'Well, you can come when you've nothing better to do,' he added eventually.

'Oh, thank you.'

'Sorry,' he muttered, not looking at her.

'I've made out a list of things you might need me to bring in.' She opened her bag and took out her notebook.

'God, you and your lists,' he said, but he sounded more like himself. Anna passed over her notes: books, pyjamas, shaving items.

'Yeah, I need all these.'

'Anything else?'

He closed his eyes. 'Yes, a miracle would be nice – one that will get me out of here fast, so I can track that bastard down who did this to me.'

'You might have used your quota up,' she said, smiling, and he gave a soft laugh. He knew just how close to death he had been; thankfully, he was at least able to see the funny side of his request.

Anna stayed for the rest of the afternoon. He talked about the amount of physio he was down to have for his knee, which pained him greatly. He was still unable to walk. The only good thing that had come out of the attack was that he could not smoke; he had been warned that, if he started again, it would create breathing problems, as his chest was still very weak.

By the time she left, he had added numerous items to her list, mostly books, and he had also given her his house keys. This was quite a big step as, although he had keys cut for her flat, he had never at any time suggested she have access to his. He had such a private and controlling nature, Anna had never even suggested it. To her astonishment, he even said that, given a week or so, maybe Kitty could be brought to see him by his ex-wife, but only when he was able to stand up straight and walk; he didn't want her to see him wheelchair bound. He wrote down their contact numbers. Again, this was a first; Anna had never even known where Kitty or his ex-wife lived. He sat scribbling in her notebook, before snapping it closed and handing it back to her.

It was not until she had driven home that she read what he had written. It was at the end of his list, and underlined. She burst into tears.

I'm a moody bastard, but I'll get better. Don't move anyone else into that box flat of yours. I will be coming home soon.

Beneath it, he had drawn a small heart with an arrow, and a small round smiley face. She had wanted to hear him say it to her so many times, but now he had written it: *I love you.* For all his bad temper and anger, those three words made up for it.

Anna had not applied for her special leave to continue, as she felt that she really needed her own space to be able to cope with him. She didn't know how she would deal with him coming home, especially if she was back at work, as she would be any day soon. She just hoped to God he would recover, because if he were a bad patient now, God knows how he would react if he had to quit the force.

Chapter Two

Anna was contacted early Monday morning: she was to join a new murder team in Brixton. The Senior Crime Officer was DCI John Sheldon, whom she knew nothing about and had never met. The murder team had taken over the second floor at the station and already shipped in were the obligatory computers and clerical staff. Sheldon had two officers who had worked with him many times, DI Frank Brandon and DS Harry Blunt; added to these were two more DIs, four more DSs, and fifteen Detective Constables. Anna was instructed to join Sheldon at the victim's flat.

Irene Phelps was thirty-nine years old and worked at the local public library. She was a quiet, studious woman with long blonde hair. She had been very pretty. The crime scene was still being worked over by the forensic teams; her body remained in the small study where she had been discovered. The room had been ransacked; there was overturned furniture, smashed ornaments and vases. She lay face down on the carpet. The wounds to her upper torso had left her blouse slashed and heavily bloodstained. Her skirt had been drawn up and her panties thrown to one side; she had terrible wounds to her throat and face. Irene had put up a fight for her life, but it had obviously been a very brutal and frenzied attack. Her twelve-year-old daughter had found her body.

Anna hovered in the doorway, not even entering the room to keep contamination down to the minimum. She looked over to the white-suited forensic officers; then physically jumped as a hand was placed on her shoulder.

'You must be DI Travis?'

'Yes, sir.'

'I'm the SIO on this one: DCI Sheldon.'

Sheldon had a soft Northern accent, blond hair thinning and swept back from a pleasant, pinkish face. He was wearing a cheap suit, white shirt and neat, unobtrusive tie. Anna gave a small smile and went to shake his hand but he turned away, gesturing to a big, square-shouldered officer.

'This is DI Frank Brandon. Frank!'

Brandon turned and walked over to be introduced. 'Hi, how's old Langton doing?'

Anna flushed. 'He's got a long way to go, but he's doing well.'

'That's good. I've heard he'll more than likely be invalided out, but knowing him – well, not personally, but he's got a hell of a reputation – he won't like it.'

Before Anna could reply, DS Harry Blunt called out from the kitchen; they all turned to look down the hallway.

Blunt was short and stocky, with a reddish crew cut and flushed cheeks.

'Getting a lot of prints; looks like the bastard washed up in here and made himself a sandwich. The knife found by her body may come from a set on the kitchen counter.'

'This is Anna Travis,' Sheldon said, indicating Anna.

She got a cool nod from Blunt, as he turned his attention back towards the kitchen and the forensic team working dusting for prints.

Sheldon pursed his lips and then looked at his wristwatch. 'Right, may as well get back to the station. Did you come in your own car?' he asked Anna.

'Yes, sir.'

'Okay, see you back there then.' He walked down the hall to the open front door.

'Would it be all right if I just stayed on for a while, to get the layout?' Anna asked Blunt.

The DS shrugged his shoulders and edged past her. He obviously suited his name: she felt as if he had little or no time to waste on small talk.

'You know where the station is?' This was Brandon; Anna said that she had checked it out before she arrived.

'Good – and mind if I give you a word of advice? The Gov is a stickler for time, so if he's going to give a briefing, I wouldn't be too long. We've all been here since early this morning.'

'Who's looking after her daughter?' Anna asked.

Brandon said she was with grandparents; then, like Sheldon, he walked off, leaving her standing by the kitchen door.

The incident room was silent. Anna was directed over to the Detective Inspectors' desks, which were in a small corner; due to the limited size of the station, they did not have their own offices. The incident board had already been set up; the victim's name and address were printed up, with little else. Anna could see Sheldon talking to Brandon in his office through the open blinds. There were three female and two male officers standing by a tea urn. None made any reaction to Anna or bothered to introduce themselves, but all parted as Sheldon came out of his office and crossed to the board. He didn't even need to ask for attention; everyone immediately returned to their desks and sat waiting.

'Okay, victim's name is Irene Phelps, works at the public library. She got divorced five years ago; ex-husband lives in Devon and is an estate agent. He's been contacted and will be travelling up to see his daughter. She's only twelve; very traumatized and staying with her grandparents. They live three streets away from the victim's flat. Okay, Frank, over to you.'

Sheldon nodded to Brandon, who flipped open his notebook. Brandon spoke rather loudly, unlike Sheldon. 'Right, Gov. We've so far gathered that Irene always left work at three; this was to make sure she was home by the time her daughter returned from school. The route to her home was by tube from Brixton, one stop; from there, she could walk home. On this particular day, she left work as usual, but her daughter Natalie went to see her grandmother after school; she arrived at four-thirty, then left to walk home at about five forty-five. She would have reached home at just after six, found the front door open and discovered the body of her mother. We therefore only have a short timeframe. Irene Phelps could have met her killer on the tube and walked with him to her flat; he killed her between the hours of four to five-thirty. That's it from me, Gov.'

Sheldon ran his fingers through his thinning hair, then continued in his soft Northern accent, hardly raising his voice, 'We need to ascertain whether she knew her killer or disturbed him inside her flat. The place looks ransacked, but she had little of value and very rarely kept any money there; the place had been turned over and the lady put up one hell of a fight. We found no visible signs of forced entry but we'll know for sure when the forensic teams give us their report. If she did know her killer and let him in, then we need to spread the net to question anyone that knew her, any ongoing relationships; so far, we've not had time to gather much evidence of who she knew, so that will be our first priority.'

Sheldon then gave a list to the duty manager of what he wanted the team to work on. He checked his watch and gave a strange low whistle. No one spoke. He sucked in his breath, gesturing at the photographs up on the incident board.

'She took a terrible beating. It was a vicious attack and we need to get this bastard fast, because there is carelessness about the murder scene. Eating a fucking sandwich, drinking a cup of tea – unless the victim made them for him, but I doubt it; there was too much blood in the kitchen. Whoever killed her would have heavily bloodstained clothes, so question neighbours, anyone around her flat: someone must have seen this son of a bitch, so let's not waste time. Get out there! Meanwhile, we wait for the PM and the forensic reports. That's it, everyone. Let's get moving, unless anyone has got anything to say?'

No one did; the briefing broke up as everyone got their marching orders. Frank Brandon came to Anna's desk.

'You and me, we've got the neighbours and work-place. You want to split it or work together?'

'Whatever suits,' Anna said.

'Okay, I'll do the neighbours, you get over to the library. May I call you Anna?'

She smiled. 'Yes, of course. I was just wondering, who is questioning her daughter?'

'That'll be Harry; he's good with kids, got a brood himself. She was in a right state, so maybe they'll delay talking to her until she's had some counselling.'

'Did she call the police?'

'Yeah – well, she ran to a neighbour and they called us for her.'

'And she's twelve?'

'Yeah, just a kid. Her dad's coming to see her; she'll be staying at the grandparents'. Why you interested in her?'

'Well, she found the body, and with the short time period, she might have even seen the killer – maybe she even knew him.'

'Yeah, well – leave that to Harry, okay?'

'Fine. I'll get over to the library.'

Brandon had a chiselled face, high cheekbones and, with his square shoulders, it was obvious he worked out. Although he had everything going for him in the looks department, there was something unattractive about him – at least, there was to Anna. He used a very heavy cologne, which she thought was Aramis; in any case, it was certainly very pungent, and he had this manner, as if he was an object of desire. Perhaps he was – in his own mirror.

The library had not been closed, but there were numerous bouquets of flowers left by the doors. They looked rather sad and bedraggled; a couple had cards written by children.

Anna was introduced to a pleasant-faced woman, who shook her hand firmly.

'I'm Deidre Lane; poor Irene worked alongside me in the children's department. I suppose you've seen a few of them have left flowers. I've more in my office and I'm not quite sure what to do with them. It's just so dreadful, none of us can believe it.'

They walked towards a small office, where Anna accepted a cup of lukewarm tea. The office was filled with posters advertising forthcoming children's activities and readings. Deidre's desk was piled high with books and files; she cleared a space for Anna to put down her cup. She then drew up a chair to sit beside her, rather than behind the desk.

'Was it a burglary or something like that?' she asked.

'We won't know that until we have had time to check, but I am here really to ask if you knew of anyone who had some kind of grudge against her.'

'Against Irene? No, no, good heavens, no. There wasn't a soul who had a bad word to say about her.'

'Could you list all the people employed here?'

'It wouldn't − it couldn't be connected to anyone from here.'

'But I do need to know everyone's name and address just for elimination purposes.'

'I see. Well, yes, of course.'

'That will include cleaners or janitors, anyone who has recently worked here, painting or redecorating, doing carpentry − any odd-job men who may have come into contact with Ms Phelps.'

Deidre went over to a filing cabinet and took out a large ledger. This time, she sat at her desk, and began to list for Anna everyone working at the library. She included a plumber who had been working on the drains recently and two boys who had helped clear the pathways around the library.

It became clear to Anna that most of the employees had been at the library for many years, even the odd-job men. Armed with names and addresses, she then turned her attention to asking for more details about Irene. She learned that Irene was a very diligent and loved member of the team, always on time in the morning, and always leaving promptly at three so she could be at home when her daughter returned from school.

'She worshipped her little girl; she is such a lovely pleasant child, always very well dressed. Her name is Natalie, but everyone calls her Natty; she often helps out with the Saturday-morning activities. Irene didn't get any extra money for this; to be honest, she wasn't paid that much, but I know she had a settlement after her divorce. I think her ex-husband paid the rent, so she was not kept short. Between you and me, I think it was a bitter divorce – he left her for someone else and went to live in Devon, I think, but I can't be too sure. Irene didn't like to talk about him and I never met him, or really knew her while they were together.'

Anna went through the usual queries, asking if anyone knew whether Irene had any boyfriends or was in any kind of relationship, but this also led nowhere.

'I didn't really socialize with her,' Deidre explained. 'I had never been to her flat, but working alongside her for so many years, we became quite good friends, and I never heard her mention that she was seeing anyone. I think she led a very quiet life, with just herself and Natty. On a few occasions, she mentioned that she had been to see a movie, usually with Natty at weekends; she had her parents quite close so would spend Sundays with them. I think she did a bit of shopping and cleaning for them, as they are quite elderly. Christmas-time, when we had our office party, we would all bring our husbands and partners, but Irene was always alone; in fact, I never saw her with anyone but her daughter.'

Anna spent another hour talking to the other librarians. In each case, they were very shocked and distraught at the brutality of the murder. She then contacted the plumber and arranged to see him later that same morning, plus the two young kids who had swept the pathways. It was becoming obvious that no one really knew Irene out of work time; nor had they ever seen her with anyone apart from her daughter. It was really very sad; Irene Phelps appeared to be a hardworking and caring woman whose life focused on her job, her daughter and her elderly parents.

The plumber turned out to be a short, ruddy faced man, who wasn't too sure if he had even met Irene. He had worked for the library virtually on a charity basis, he told Anna, as they were always short of finances; he would come in on Sundays to see to any jobs that needed doing. For the entire day of the murder, he had been working in Clerkenwell on a new housing estate. The two young lads were also unable to give any details about Irene; they had been paid in cash to sweep the pathway of leaves, and then both had gone to a gym straight after. They had seen no one lurking around and nothing suspicious.

Anna returned to the incident room just after three. She typed up her report and went over to discuss her interviews with the duty manager; together, they brought the board up to date with the lists of colleagues, part-time workers and alibis. She then returned to her desk and made herself look busy, as there was to be a briefing at five. She hoped it would not go on for too long, as she was planning to drive over to Glebe House.

At five o'clock sharp, Sheldon walked out of his office, just as Harry Blunt and Frank Brandon entered the incident room. None of them acknowledged Anna or, for that matter, anyone else; they sat at their desks checking over their notes. Sheldon stood for a moment, looking at the board and the results of the day's enquiries. He slowly loosened his tie and then turned to the room.

'We should get the lab reports in tomorrow; forensic are still at the murder site. So, in the meantime, let's hear how today progressed.'

There was a brief silence, then Harry Blunt stood up.

'Didn't get much for us from the grandparents – they're very elderly and very obviously shook up. I talked with Natalie, the daughter; she has a counsellor with her, but the outcome is again not too helpful. On the day of the murder, she returned home, a bit later than usual; she'd been to see her grandmother, as she's had a bout of flu. So it was nearer to five forty-five when she thinks she got home. Front door was ajar, so she called out—'

Sheldon wafted his hand. 'We know this. What else have you got?'

'Well, she saw her mother, then ran to a neighbour who called the police. They kept her with them until the locals arrived and then they took her to stay with her grandparents. As far as we can ascertain, she saw no one else inside the premises and no one outside; she also said she didn't know anyone who would want to hurt her mother, or of any new friend Irene had who she might have been seeing. I have suggested we maybe talk to her again in a proper audiovisual suite. From what I've gathered, the victim kept herself very much to herself and rarely, if ever, entertained, but was well-respected and liked by both sets of neighbours living in the same house. None, when questioned, had seen or heard anything and were all very shocked. There had been no workmen around lately, so no strangers in and out of the premises, which are quite secure; we've also got nothing from any CCTV cameras.'

Sheldon nodded and pulled at his tie again; he now looked to Frank Brandon.

'Coming up with much the same thing, Gov: well-respected, hard worker, did the same journey to school and work every morning, and returned around about the same time every day. This makes the timeframe for the murder to be from around four to when the daughter returned home.'

'Yes, yes, we know that,' Sheldon snapped, and then indicated Anna.

Anna went through her report in a little more detail than the others. Sheldon sat down in the middle of it. He yawned, checked his watch and, when Anna had completed her report, he stood up and gestured to the board.

'We got anything on the ex-husband?'

Frank remained seated as he flipped open his book. 'He's an estate agent, quite well off, remarried, has two young kids by his second wife. He was in Devon on the day that the victim was killed. He's travelling up to see his daughter, so we can talk to him then.'

Sheldon dug his hands in his pockets. 'Well, let's hope we get something from the PM and forensic, because we've got bugger all so far. I want the house-to-house to continue; see if anyone in the area saw or knows something.'

He turned to Anna, pointing. 'Yes?'

'Have they said the weapon used was from the victim's flat?'

'They have not verified it, but there is one carving knife missing from the block and one found in the kitchen sink; bastard probably used it to cut up his sandwich. We are hoping to get DNA and a match on fingerprints but, like I said, we wait to see what they come up with. In the meantime, I want a significant trawling of any possible CCTV footage in and around the murder site. That's it — reconvene at nine in the morning.'

Anna was surprised; she had never been on an enquiry that felt like a nine to five. She'd also never seen an incident room clear out so fast, leaving just clerical and the small night staff to run the enquiry.

Anna had intended to call in at Langton's apartment, to collect his mail, etc., but by the time she had returned home, showered and changed, it was already after six-thirty. She knew she wouldn't be able to avoid the rush-hour traffic on the M4 heading out of London and so accepted she wasn't going to get to see him until way after eight. She spent the time in the slow-moving traffic going over the case. She found it all very depressing: so different from working alongside Langton, whose energy and tireless pressure on everyone around him always paid dividends. There had been numerous other cases she had been involved in, before and after Langton; none of the SIOs ever matched him, or even came close.

Langton was waiting for her, sitting in a wheelchair in

the empty recreational room. He gave her a glum smile. 'I'd just about given up on you.'

'Well, I started on a new investigation this morning – victim murdered in her own flat. Her kid found the body.'

'Who's heading it up?' he asked moodily.

Anna listed Sheldon and co., and he snorted.

'That stuffed shirt! Can't stand him and that body-builder sidekick of his – thinks he's Burt Reynolds. If he spent less time in the gym and more time policing ... They're all a bunch of wankers.'

Anna grinned; he was always abusive about anyone else working on the murder teams, but he had actually summed up her own thoughts.

Langton gestured around the empty room. 'They're all watching a movie, creaking and groaning around a plasma screen.'

'What film?'

'I don't bloody know. I hate it; all they do is moan and groan or burst into tears all the time. It's like a wailing wall around here.'

He sighed and then asked if she'd got any mail for him. She apologized and said she would collect it tomorrow.

'Don't put yourself out.'

'Oh, just stop this. I didn't have the time this evening.'

'I bet Sheldon closed shop at five; he's a real nine-to-five copper.'

She laughed and agreed; however, until they had some results from the lab and forensics, they couldn't move in on anyone with a motive.

Langton ruffled his hair. 'You know, before the days of DNA and the white suits at forensic, we had maybe not as much to go on, but nobody ever clicked their heels; now, it's all down to waiting for scientific evidence. Sometimes, they come up with bugger all as well.'

Anna didn't really want to get into the details of the case, but he obviously did. After receiving a brief rundown, he remained silent, and then suggested that they check out all hostels and halfway houses in and around the area.

'Sounds like some nutter, some bastard that might have been able to monitor your victim's routine.'

'Yes, I've thought about that too; it's quite a tough area.'

He winced in pain and rubbed his knee.

'You okay?'

'No. This physio bloke massages my knee as if I was in a rugby scrum; it hurts like hell and yet I'm still not able to walk more than a couple of paces. They even brought me a fucking Zimmer frame. I said, the day you see me shuffling around on that, pal, is the day you can give me an OD of morphine.'

Anna remained with Langton for almost two hours; he then seemed to suddenly fade fast. He was hardly able to keep his eyes open, so she suggested she leave and see him the following evening. As she turned to go, he caught her hand.

'Eh, you don't have to make this schlep out here every day. If you're up to your eyes in this case, leave it – just call me.'

She kissed him, and he held onto her hand tightly. 'I'll pull through this. It's just going to take longer than I thought, but I'll make a promise – next time you see me, I'll be on my feet.'

She kissed him again and then left him, still sitting in his solitary position, surrounded by gym equipment he couldn't use. She didn't mention that she was going to talk to the head nurse for an update.

Anna was kept waiting for half an hour before she was able to discuss Langton's progress. The nurse was a pleasant six-foot-five giant with a big wide smile.

'Well, he's not an easy patient, and he's got one hell of a temper, but he is very determined. The reality is, this is going to take a lot longer than he thinks. The knee joint is very worrying and I know causes agony; sometimes it would be better for him to rest up, but he refuses and demands painkillers. He had a bad fall because he tried to stand and wanted to work out on weights, but after a chest injury as bad as the one he suffered, he has to be patient.'

'How long will he be staying here?'

'Well, we usually do a two-week stint, then patients can go home. If they need further treatment, they come back; we've got some that have been coming back and forth for months. I'd say James is going to be looking at the very least, six months.'

'Six months?!'

'Yes, and I can't guarantee that he will be able to walk unaided – but that is not the only problem. He can't unwind, or he won't; his desperation to get into the gym and work out is very common. They think if they exercise to excess, it'll block out their thoughts and then they won't have to consider their own feelings. Sadly, the support system network that used to exist for officers like James has virtually eroded in the last year. There used to be a much stronger camaraderie and humour. What I am concerned about is his isolation; he refuses to interact with any of the other patients and this will, I am sure, eventually lead to depression.'

Anna felt depressed herself, driving home. It was after one when she eventually got to bed and she was so tired, she crashed straight out. She also forgot to set her alarm, so was late getting up and got caught in the rush hour driving over to Brixton.

The briefing was already in progress when she quietly entered the incident room and sat at her desk. As she suspected, Sheldon had requested they check into all men on probation that were known in the area.

'I think, due to the ferocity of the attack, we could be looking at someone with a previous record of violence and assault, so get cracking and let's see if we can get a better result today.'

Anna said nothing. She noticed Blunt and Brandon huddle with Sheldon for a while before they broke up. Sheldon then gestured for her to come into his office.

'You were late,' he said curtly.

'Yes, I'm sorry – I got caught up in traffic.'

'Not a good enough excuse. I run a very tight unit.'

'I'm sorry.' She changed the subject fast. 'Have you heard anything from the PM report?'

'Nope. In fact, I'm just on my way over there if you'd like to join me.'

'Thank you.'

She sat in rather uneasy silence in the rear of the patrol car, while Sheldon had a lengthy call to someone she presumed was his dentist, as he was asking about root canals and the cost; then it went from root canals to implants. He again discussed the cost, and swore, before eventually agreeing to call back.

'Do you have toothache?' she asked.

'No, my wife, but it's private and costs a bloody fortune. She had four front teeth capped six months ago and it came to over three thousand quid.'

'It is expensive,' she murmured, not that interested.

'How is he doing?'

'Pardon?'

'Langton. I heard he was in a bloody no hope situation.'

She felt her hand tense. 'Well, he's far from that and is expected out of Glebe House soon,' she lied.

'Well, he's a fighter, I'll give him that, but not someone I've ever got on with – probably why he's never made Superintendent. Now, he might – if he's going to be kept on in some kind of desk job capacity.'

She bit her lip. 'I think he's very keen to get back to the murder team.'

'Yeah, they all say that, you know – but you don't get shipped out there for nothing.'

She wanted to punch the back of his red neck. 'He simply requires a lot of physio on his injured knee.'

Sheldon turned round, resting his arm along the back of the seat. 'Well, I suppose you'll be a regular visitor, so send him my regards when you next see him.'

'I will.' She was annoyed at the implication that she was on such close terms with Langton, as she had attempted to keep their private life just that – private.

'I knew his first wife,' the DCI went on. 'Indian, I think she was, very beautiful – had a tumour and died very suddenly.'

'Yes, I believe so.'

'He had a tough time dealing with it – well, I suppose one would. I think he was shipped out to Glebe House that time too, though I may be wrong.'

'Yes, you are. He has never been there before.'

'Ah well, you know how rumours spread.'

'Yes, I do.' She leaned back and stared out of the window, hoping the conversation was over.

'I worked with your father,' Sheldon continued. It was bad enough him talking about Langton, but now her father! 'Yeah, just in uniform. He was a character – scared the life out of everyone, had a right old temper on him, similar to Langton, in many ways. He never could tolerate all the paperwork. Well, he'd hate it even more now – fart and you've got to leave a bloody memo.'

She was saved from any further conversation as they drew up into the car park of the mortuary.

Unlike Langton, Sheldon was quite the gentleman, holding open the doors for her to walk in ahead of him; he also told her to gown up, as if she'd never been at a post mortem before.

Irene Phelps had really fought for her life. The defensive wounds to her hands and arms were like a patchwork quilt. The crisscross wounds also slashed her cheeks, neck and eyes, with one incision virtually slicing through her right eye. She had died from a single knife wound to her heart: the blade, a kitchen carving knife, had been thrust into her up to the hilt. She had been raped and sodomized after the attack. They had DNA from the assailant's semen and blood.

Returning back to base with Sheldon, Anna remained as silent as they had been while at the mortuary.

They drove for at least five minutes before he spoke. 'Well, what do you think?' he asked, not turning to look at her in the passenger seat directly behind him.

'Well, it was obviously a frenzied attack by a killer

who left his DNA and probably his fingerprints all over the weapon and the flat.'

'Yes, and . . .?'

'I don't think burglary was his initial motive; he may have ransacked the premises after the kill, but I think he was there to kill. He—'

She was interrupted. 'Why do you say that?'

'Because of the severity of the wounds. I think he must have been waiting for the opportunity rather than planning it.'

'Go on.'

'There are no signs of a break-in, which means he was possibly already holding our victim when she let herself in. From what I saw at the flat, it did not look as if he was a professional burglar. It's just as if he was in such a frenzy after the murder and the sexual gratification: he threw things around, searching for anything of immediate value. We know he must have bloodstained clothes; as we have not had anyone coming forwards, having seen the assailant either in or around the victim's home, he must have somewhere close that he could walk out to.'

Sheldon turned to face her. 'Very good observation.'

'Well, it's all rather obvious. I also think he will have a record of violence and mental instability; he may not have killed before but he will, I am sure, have done this before.'

'Done what exactly?'

'Attacked. The sex we know took place after the victim was dead, or in the throes of dying. Nothing looked premeditated, apart from the entry to the victim's flat, so there is a possibility that she knew him or had met him before. I don't mean she knew him well, but she may have seen him before, which again makes me think he lives close by. He could have been watching her, seen her arrive home and then moved to force her into allowing him to enter. As we know, the timeframe is short between Irene leaving work and her daughter discovering the body, so it must have all happened in less than an hour.'

'What about the sandwich he made for himself?'

Anna shrugged. 'He was hungry.'

At the briefing, Sheldon repeated almost word for word what Anna had said. She listened, taken aback; the way Sheldon talked, it was as if he had come up with the possible scenario. By now, they also had the forensic report: the killer had left fibres, two hairs and fingerprints in the kitchen, hall and the study where he had killed Irene Phelps.

By four-fifteen, they had a suspect who had a police record for assaults on women. Arthur George Murphy was forty-seven years old and had served fewer than thirteen years of a life sentence for a violent sex attack. In other words, he was on parole! Murphy also had a record of attacks on strangers dating back more than thirty years. This convicted sex attacker, whilst on parole and supposedly under supervision, had been free to kill Irene Phelps.

As the search went out for Murphy, more details of his past came in. The reports were astonishing. Despite his appalling history, Murphy had been considered a low risk, when he was clearly a serious danger to the public. Even a brief check of his file would have been enough to convince anyone that Murphy should not have been walking the streets. His criminal record stretched back to

1975, when he was first convicted for terrorizing women. In 1990, he had been handed a nine-year term for rape. He served six years, the Old Bailey heard how Murphy turned into a snarling animal when he spied his victims. This was when he was sentenced to life; his crime had been a knifepoint rape.

Within hours, the team had been given an address for Murphy, two streets away from Irene Phelps. There was a huge amount of press and TV coverage, warning the public that they should not approach Murphy but contact the police if he was seen. In the hostel that he had been allocated by the probation services, they found Murphy's possessions: bloodstained clothes, a pair of trainers that had blood on the soles and over the laces, stacks of pornography and a few items of no significant value that had belonged to Irene Phelps. There were also all his social services records and probation contacts, and twenty-two pounds in cash stuffed into an envelope. But there was no sign of Murphy himself; no one at the hostel had seen him for two days.

Sheldon was in a fury as the details came in. He was standing behind his desk, shaking his head. The fact that nobody from the probation service or the community management of offenders had reported the disappearance of Murphy to the police was disgusting. His face had gone puce with anger.

'It's fucking unbelievable; this bastard is released halfway through a life sentence for rape and manages to just walk out of his hostel to kill another woman without anyone knowing what was going on! The probation services just bleated on about lack of funds and serious staff shortages, especially here in London; well, that doesn't help us, that doesn't help us one fucking iota, because that son of a bitch is out there and we know he's going to do it again!'

Anna let Sheldon wind down, not that she disagreed with a word he was saying; the entire system was a farce. It was obvious there were serious deficiencies in the way Murphy had been managed.

'I was just wondering, sir, if we have any details on Murphy's parents, or any relatives? We know he left the hostel in a hurry, and with money left behind, so he has to be on the run somewhere. Maybe someone is hiding or protecting him.'

'What kind of person hides this animal? And don't give me mother love; if she is hiding him, then she's as bad as he is.'

'So do we have anything on his parents?'

'Some bitch spawned him, yeah.' He checked through a file. 'Father dead eight years ago. Mother is named as Beryl Dunn – God only knows where she is. Brother also dead, but younger sister, Gail Dunn, living at an undisclosed address. We can check her out, but I want you to get onto his probation department and get them to give us as many details as they can.'

Murphy's probation officer, one of a team allocated to him and numerous others, was surprisingly young. She was slim and neat with large rimless glasses, and very much on the defensive.

'You know we have two hundred thousand offenders under supervision at any one time.'

'But not in the specific area.' Anna tried not to sound angry.

'No, of course not, but we do have over a hundred. What I was going to say was that, out of that two hundred thousand, we know that only about a hundred will commit a further serious offence. That is a fraction of one per cent.'

Anna gritted her teeth. 'I am here about one specific offender, Arthur George Murphy.'

'Yes, yes, I know that, but I am trying to explain to you: we get so much pressure – blame, in reality – when we do not have the resources to monitor offenders, even those that we have been told are high or very high risk.'

Anna took a deep breath. 'That is irrelevant. The fact is Arthur Murphy was able to walk out of his hostel and kill a poor defenceless woman. I am not here to listen to the problems within the probation services; it sounds very sobering and appalling and for you, obviously, deeply distressing. I need from you any possible friend, relative, any previous known contact of his that he might have been able to get to, anyone who could be protecting him.'

'I am not allowed to divulge personal details.'

That was it. Anna jumped up and banged on the woman's desk with the flat of her hand. 'Irene Phelps was raped and sodomized, her throat cut, her body slashed, and she was found by her twelve-year-old daughter. Now, that child will live for the rest of her life with that nightmarish image of her mother. We need to bring this man in and charge him; we need to put him away and this time, for life, so if you have anything, and I mean *anything*, that might help us trace him, then would you please assist me to the best of your ability and not make excuses for the total failure of your department!'

Anna slammed the door of her Mini so hard the car rocked. She could not believe the amount of time it had taken to get three possible contacts that their killer might or might not have approached. His sister, Gail Dunn, had requested anonymity after her brother's last rape and prison sentence: she had moved away from London in the hope of losing all contact with him. The other two names were recently released prisoners who had spent time with Murphy. Both these men were installed in different hostels in London, one tagged, so they should not be too difficult to track down.

Anna reported back to the incident room. Blunt took the job of tracking down the two ex-prisoners; she and Brandon were to visit Murphy's sister. To be cooped up with Brandon and his cologne for a long drive to the New Forest was not a prospect Anna relished. She would have preferred to do it alone.

When she had suggested this, Sheldon had one of his nasty turns, pointing his finger at her. 'This man is dangerous. No way would I allow you to visit his sister alone; neither of you can take the risk if he's hiding out there, and it's a possibility. So, I've already contacted local police for back-up; you touch base with them as soon as you arrive and they'll be standing by. You are not working with risk-taker Langton now, Detective Inspector Travis – I look out for my team. Now get on out there!'

Anna made no reply. He'd made her feel two inches tall, and she was beginning to loathe him, but at the same time she knew he was right. Murphy could be anywhere, and he was dangerous.

Gail Dunn, Arthur Murphy's sister, had been traced to the New Forest. She had been using the surname Summers when she first moved, but now called herself Sickert. Gail was living in a rented bungalow with numerous outhouses used as a small market garden business and piggery. Judging by the state of the entire premises, it was none too successful. The gate hung off its hinges and there were deep puddles and potholes in the drive leading to the bungalow. Numerous wrecked cars littered the land, rusting and tyreless. Kids' bicycles and toys were left in profusion on a balding patch of lawn.

Brandon sniffed and pulled a face. 'Jesus Christ, what is that stench?'

'Pigs. There's some pens out the back.'

Brandon looked around uneasily. 'You know, the Gov was right. I don't like the look of this place. I'll call in for the back-up. If Murphy's hiding out in any of those outbuildings, he can just do a runner.'

'Maybe we should have just tipped them off to search and not waste time.' Anna followed his gaze. The place looked awash with mud. 'Or don't you want to get your shoes muddy?'

Brandon glared at her; he was not amused, but walked away from the front door to make a call. He gestured for her to go ahead and ring the doorbell. Anna pressed the bell, but it made no sound; she pressed again.

Brandon joined her. 'We got two cars on their way; not answering the door, huh?'

'Bell's not working.' Anna rapped with her knuckles on the door.

Brandon walked to a window and cupped his hands to peer inside, then rejoined Anna at the front door.

'I don't like this; let's wait for back-up to get here.'

Anna nodded, then checked her watch. 'Unless she's gone to pick up her kids from school ... Do we know if she's living with anyone? Changes her name often enough.'

'They didn't have any details.' Brandon walked over to look at the greenhouses and huts behind the bungalow then rejoined Anna. 'Bloody good place to hide out though, isn't it? Christ, this stench is disgusting. How can she live here with kids?'

She nodded; the place did have a desolate feel. Like Brandon, she now started to look through the windows.

'Let's go round the back,' she suggested.

Brandon shook his head. 'Nope, we wait.'

'No dog.'

'What?'

'I said, there's no dog. Usually in a place like this, they have some scraggy dog loose, or chained up. It's the silence that's freaky.'

'Yeah,' he sighed. 'Okay – I'll take a look round the back, you stay out front. They should be here any minute.'

Anna nodded, and couldn't help but smile as she saw Brandon roll up the bottom of his trousers to head down the muddy pathway. He was only just out of sight when Anna heard a soft mewing sound; at first, she thought it could be a cat, but listening harder, she was sure it was a child.

At the same time, two patrol cars headed into the drive. Anna hurried across and gestured for one car to head round the back to join Brandon and the second to come with her to the front door.

'There's been no answer at the front door, but some-one's inside. I think you need to give a big loud bang on the door and make yourselves obvious. If still no one opens up, break it down.'

Brandon was relieved to be accompanied by one officer; the other began sloshing through the mud towards the outhouses. Closer, the stench of the pigs made him feel sick. He heard the loud banging at the front door just as he reached the back one.

'Police! Open the door! Police!'

Brandon tried the back door; it too was locked. He stepped back, put his shoulder against it and gave a strong push, then another, but it took both him and the officer with him to burst it open.

At the same time, Anna, with her two officers, had broken down the front door and entered the hallway.

'Police! Come out and show yourself! Police!'

A terrified little girl wearing a pair of pyjamas toddled out of the back bedroom. Anna bent down and opened her arms.

'It's okay, little one. Come here – come on, come to me.'

The child seemed rooted to the spot, so Anna had to walk very slowly towards her. She turned to the officers and quietly told them to search the front room where she thought she had seen the curtain move.

Anna bent down to be on the child's level. 'Where's your mummy?'

She began to cry.

'What's your name? I'm not going to hurt you. Why don't you just come to me and tell me your name?'

The child started to scream as the officers came out from the front room. 'No one in there.'

Meanwhile, Brandon was looking around the kitchen; piled with dirty dishes and used pans, it looked as if a meal had been prepared and left on the table. He walked into the hall.

'Nobody's in the kitchen, but someone left in a hurry.'

Anna had by now calmed the little girl, and was carrying her in her arms. 'I don't know if she can talk, but she's soaking wet, and we've no one in the front room.'

Brandon nodded and then opened a bedroom door: dirty sheets and three unmade beds, plus a child's cot. Toys strewn everywhere.

'Empty; let's try this one.'

This was the only room they had not yet looked into. He eased the door open very quietly and then hung back, before he slowly pushed it wide open.

This was the main bedroom: a double bed, again with unmade sheets and very untidy, but no occupant.

'Where's your mummy?' Anna again asked the little girl who was now silent; she smelled strongly of urine and possibly more. 'Is your mummy outside?'

It was at this point that the officer who had been looking around the outhouses and huts appeared at the back door.

'Nobody out there, but we'd need more men to have a thorough search. Place is really run down; there's some hens in a pen and pigs and a goat, but nothing else moving.'

Brandon shrugged. 'What do you make of this?'

Anna carried the little girl into the children's room, and sat her down on a small child's armchair.

'Do you know where your mummy is?' she tried again.

No reply. Anna sighed; the child was totally mute, staring at her with wide, terrified eyes.

Brandon stood in the doorway. She looked at him.

'Listen, should I change her, put her in dry clothes? She's soaking wet and she stinks.'

'I wouldn't — it's up to you.'

'Can I get you some nice dry clothes?'

The child shrank back from her.

It was then they heard a jeep driving up, an old Shogun that sounded as if the exhaust had fallen off. By the time Brandon had reached the front door, a woman had jumped out of the Shogun and was running towards the bungalow, screaming.

'What's going on? What the hell is going on?'

She was tall and skinny, wearing jeans and Wellington boots, with a man's jacket tied round her waist over a stained T-shirt.

Brandon blocked her at the front door. 'Gail Sickert? I am Detective Inspector Brandon.'

'What the fuck has happened?' She tried to push past him, shouting out, 'Tina! Tina!'

'Just calm down, love. Is this your little girl?'

'What's happened? Let me in – get out the fucking way!'

Brandon blocked the door. 'Your kid's fine. Just stay calm. We need to talk to you.'

Anna carried out the little girl.

Gail was allowed to go to her. She held out her arms and hugged her tightly. 'Fucking coppers, you broke me door. What's this about?'

Brandon cleared the officers out and told them to wait in the patrol cars.

By now, Gail had changed Tina, and her other daughter, Sharon, had been brought out of the Shogun. Sharon was seven years old, a thin waif-like child with lank blonde hair and red-rimmed eyes.

'I only went to get her from school and take my Keith round to his mate's house to play. I weren't gone for longer than twenty minutes, for God's sake. You're not going to report this to the bloody social services, are you?'

Anna asked Brandon to give her some space as Gail was in such a state, rocking the still-silent Tina in her arms and keeping Sharon close to her.

'Gail, I'm really sorry we've frightened you.'

'You just bloody broke in here – you got no right to do that, she's terrified. You got no right to break into the place.'

'Gail, we do have every right. We're looking for your brother.'

'He's not fucking here. I wouldn't let him cross the bloody doorstep, he's a lunatic. I'm gonna make an official complaint about this.'

'Your brother is wanted in connection with a murder.'

'That's got nothing to do with me. You lot have had him in the nick more times than I've had hot fucking dinners and you just let him out; he's sick, sick in his head. I've not seen him for years and if he did come here, my bloke'd take a shotgun to him.'

Gail started to sob. This upset the little girl, Tina, and she began to cry. This started Sharon off and she clung to her mother, crying too.

Anna put the kettle on. It was greasy to touch and the sink was full of filthy dishes. The kitchen was disgusting.

'Where is your husband?' she asked.

Gail sniffed and wiped her face with the back of her hand. 'He left just after I moved in here; bastard just pissed off.'

'That would be Mr Summers?'

'Yeah. I changed me name to Sickert, as I'm livin' with someone else now.'

'And where is he?'

'He had to collect some pig food, went off early this morning. I have never left my kid on her own before, but I had to pick this one up.'

Anna emptied a cold teapot full of tea bags into the overflowing trash.

Brandon and the other officers did a thorough search of the property, but there was no sign of Murphy. The patrol cars left and Brandon came to the back door, but got a warning look from Anna to stay out. By now, she had made a cup of tea for Gail and warmed a bottle to give Tina some milk.

'She's deaf,' Gail said, rocking her.

Sharon was sitting eating biscuits, banging her heels against the side of a high stool. Anna sat opposite Gail, drinking from a nasty chipped mug.

'We need to find your brother,' she said softly.

'Well, I dunno where he is, and I don't want to know; if I did know I would tell you, and you have to believe me. I think they should have locked him away for life – meaning life – after what he done to those poor women, and now you say he's done it again.' Gail took a deep breath. 'Molested me when I was at home with me mum – I think he'd have raped his own granny if he could. Few drinks and he was a brute. I hated him; my mum didn't know how to handle him, now he's killed some poor woman and it's me you come to looking for him. I dunno what's wrong with you lot. I'd like to kill him myself.'

Anna listened and kept her voice calm and steady. 'We'll get both your doors repaired today, Gail.'

'So you bleedin' should. My man's gonna go apeshit when he comes back. You'd best make yourself scarce.

'Is there anywhere you think your brother would go to, to stay with someone who would be prepared to protect him?'

'I wouldn't know. I've not seen him for Christ knows how long.'

'No one you can think of?'

'No. Like I said, I've not been in contact with him since ...' She frowned, then put her mug of tea down and went over to an untidy sideboard. She opened one drawer after another, then took out a small photograph.

'The last time he was released, Arthur come by and he was with this horrible bloke, stank of booze; they wanted money and my husband kicked them out. He warned Arthur that if he ever came back, he'd beat the hell out of him. For all his bravado and macho thing with women, he's a wimp, but he had this guy with him and my kid Keith had this little throwaway camera ... I don't remember the other one's name even, just that they'd met in prison; he and Arthur were bragging about stuff, and I made Sharon go up an' stay in her room.' She passed the photograph to Anna. 'I remember him gloating about how he'd been living free of police supervision because of some legal loophole; he said something about the register. He and Arthur had had a fair amount to drink. That was when my husband had listened to enough and threw them out.'

Anna looked at the photograph. 'And this was how many years ago?'

'Two – no, longer. I dunno. I didn't even have Tina then, so it's a while back.'

'So it wouldn't have been here at the bungalow?'

'No, me other place.'

'Has he been here?'

Gail turned away and wiped her nose with her sleeve. 'No, thank God.'

'And this man with your brother, you don't recall his name?'

'No. Had a Newcastle accent though.'

Anna spent a while longer with Gail before she felt she was able to leave.

Brandon, sitting in the car, was impatient. He glared at her as she sat beside him. 'I hope you bloody got something. I know I did – fleas! What a shithole. She should be reported to the social services for leaving that little kid on her own.'

Anna said nothing as he started up the engine and they drove out; just as they turned into the road, an open lorry piled high with pig food turned into the drive.

Back at the station they used computer imagery to identify the man in the photograph as Vernon Kramer. 1976: he had convictions for dishonesty and served twelve months. 1980: convicted of bodily harm and theft; received a six-month sentence. 1984: acquitted of three rapes. 1986: sentenced to six years for the rape and indecent assault of two fourteen-year-old girls. He was released early in 1990, after serving just three years. Eight months later, Kramer was sentenced to five years for the false imprisonment of a thirteen-year-old girl he abducted at knifepoint. This sentence coincided with Murphy's conviction; the two men then served time in the same prison.

Anna sighed and turned to Brandon. 'He was released yet again in January 1997. This is maybe what Gail meant – he gloated about being out too early to be listed on the sex offenders' register.'

'Yeah, him and thousands of others, because their crimes took place before the register was created. It was, believe it or not, feared they would claim their inclusion was a breach of bloody human rights! Makes me want to throw up.'

Anna nodded in agreement, then she turned over a page and looked to Brandon.

'Last known address . . . you are not going to believe this, but it's in Brixton – and not far from where our victim was living.'

Brandon approached and leaned over the back of her chair; he'd refreshed his cologne and she had to take a deep breath.

'Let's check it out,' he said. 'If he's harbouring Murphy, we need to get in there – and fast.'

Not wanting to tip off Kramer, they used the old 'voting register' scam. Anna had agreed to act as a decoy; she would simply knock on the door of the hostel to ask whoever answered if they had the correct names listed for the voting register. The hostel was in a very rundown area of Brixton, and contained eight bedsits. The man who opened the front door was black, very muscular, and naked, down to a pair of boxer shorts; he also seemed stoned out of his head. He had a wide, gap-toothed smile, with two gold teeth beside the gap. He looked her up and down, then slammed the door shut, having told her to fuck off! Anna gasped – he had towered above her and smelt heavily of body odour. She reported back to the team. As the house was already staked out, they decided Anna could return to base and they would wait.

As luck would have it, before she even left, the front door opened again and Kramer walked out. Anna remained in the unmarked patrol car. He was tailed to an off-licence, where he bought twelve cans of beer and a bottle of vodka. He then walked to a fish and chip shop and was seen to buy two portions of fish and chips.

Totally unaware he was being tailed, Kramer walked casually back to the house. He stopped at one point to light a fresh cigarette from the stub in his mouth, tossing it aside. He then continued to the front door and fumbled with the keys. Just as he was letting himself in, Brandon and two back-up officers moved in. Kramer didn't put up any kind of resistance. He admitted that Murphy was in his flat, and said he was scared to kick him out. He was searched, handcuffed and taken to Anna's patrol car; he sat sullenly in the back, leaning his head against the window as they drove back to the station.

Kramer lived in bedsit 4B. Brandon, accompanied by the two uniformed officers, entered the house and knocked on the door. There was a pause, then it was unlocked.

'Did you remember to get them to put vinegar on mine?' said a voice.

Brandon shouldered his way in. There was a brief moment when Murphy thought of attempting to fight his way past, but he gave up fast.

Anna would have liked to have been in on the interrogation, but no way: this was Brandon and Sheldon's territory. As Murphy was intoxicated when he was brought in, they delayed questioning him until first thing the following morning. No one had mentioned the fact that it was Anna who had patiently questioned his sister and come up with the photograph that led them to capture him. She remained at the station until nine, writing up her report, before leaving for home. She was too tired to go and visit Langton, so called Glebe House to say she was working late. She spoke to the night nurse and was told that Langton had had a good day's physio and was watching a movie. Anna asked for him not to be interrupted, but to pass on the message that she would see him the following evening.

She felt guilty about being so relieved to get an early night. Tomorrow would be the interrogation, then Murphy would be taken to the magistrates. There was, she knew, no possibility of bail. She calculated that a trial date would be set quite quickly, then it would be down to preparation for the trial. That would be the end of the case.

Anna was back at the station by eight-fifteen the next day; Murphy was to be brought up from the holding cell at nine for the interrogation. By nine-fifteen, she was sitting alone in the small observation room adjacent to the interview room. Murphy had still not been brought up, as they were waiting for his solicitor to finish talking to him. It was just after ten when they took up their seats and she saw Murphy for the first time.

Murphy, wearing a white paper suit, was sullen-faced. He had cropped hair, big flat ears and a large nose. His thin mouth was drawn downwards, almost clownishly, at the sides. His eyes were dark and blank, giving hardly any expression at all. He sat with his hands cupped in front of him, big gnarled hands with dirty fingernails. Anna felt disgusted by the look of him, by his insolence and by the lack of any kind of remorse when shown the photographs of his victim.

He leaned forwards and then rested back. 'Yeah, that's her.'

It was chilling to hear him explain how he had seen Irene Phelps on a number of occasions walking back towards her flat. He said, without any emotion, how on that particular day he had followed her to her door and simply pushed her inside. At one point, when Brandon was discussing the DNA results from his attack, he had shrugged.

'You know, you people think rape is about sex. Of course, sex comes into it, but you know what it's really about? Power.' Murphy's thin clown mouth drew down in a sickening smirk. 'I had power over her. Sex is just an extension of that power. Afterwards, I was real hungry, so I made up a sandwich: tomatoes, lettuce, and there was some ham. It tasted good.'

Anna clenched her fists; it was so hard to believe what this man had done and, moreover, how he could sit there talking about making a ham sandwich with the blood of his victim still on his hideous hands.

'I can't help it.' He gestured wide, then continued. 'I got this determination, you see, deep down inside me, and it's really deepset, you know what I mean? And my problem has always been that I have to satisfy that anger. What did you say her name was?'

Brandon's face was taut. 'Irene Phelps.'

'Right, Irene; well, she was just in the wrong place at the wrong time. I suppose it was lucky her daughter wasn't home, because I'd thought about doing her.'

Anna walked out of the room. She couldn't stand to watch another second's gloating from that sickening man, who'd murdered a decent young woman and probably traumatized her twelve-year-old daughter for the rest of her life. Murphy's psychiatric reports from the time he had been in prison evaluated him as being very dangerous; the fact that he was released made it chilling to even contemplate the total ineptness of the probation departments. It exposed the terrifying weaknesses at the heart of the criminal justice system.

Anna returned to her desk as Harry Blunt passed with two mugs of coffee; he placed one down for her.

'Thank you,' she said, rather surprised.

'Good work – that photograph was a piece of luck. That animal could have hung out for weeks, maybe months; the filth he was living with, they could have started to kill together.'

Anna sipped her coffee. Harry seemed loath to move away. 'I've got a daughter the same age as Irene Phelps's little girl,' he told her.

'Did her father come and see her?' she asked.

'Yeah, she's going to be living with him. Won't be easy; he's got two kids with another wife and, at her age, moving schools, new environment ... Poor little soul.' He slurped his coffee and then sighed. 'You know, there are no excuses over this bastard. Everything that could go wrong did go wrong, and what makes me puke is that no one is going to take the blame, and they should. His effing so-called probation officers should be sacked. Whoever gave that son of a bitch a low-risk category should be fired; better still, be made to look at the dead woman's corpse – ask them then if they still think he's a low risk. Do you know how many murders last year were committed by low-risk bastards freed on parole?'

'Not right off, no, I don't.'

Harry leaned forwards. 'Nearly fifty. I dunno how they think we can do our job; we no sooner get them to trial and banged up than they let them loose again! Bloody frustrating. I tell you what, if that creature in there had killed my daughter, then I'd strangle him. Why not? Gimme twelve years – good behaviour, I'd be out in seven, probably less. I'm not kidding. The Home Secretary said there was a crisis – a fucking *crisis*? I'd say it's a lot more than that. My mate's a prison officer, and he says his pals have been warning the Prison Officers Association: there's overcrowded wings, riots and hostage taking – something he's gotta face every week, and you know what? The Home Office pays forces nearly four hundred quid for each prisoner, that's if you count it up; a bill to the tax payers of over ten bleedin' million, and are they building new prisons? Are they hell as like. That's how fucking pricks like Murphy get out early. And now you know they are giving inmates friggin' keys to their cells, so they gain respect? Jesus Christ, I dunno what the world is coming to.'

He drained his coffee and stood up. 'Sorry,' he said with a rueful smile. 'Just needed to get it off my chest.'

'Do you ever talk about your work with your wife?'

'No, I try to close down when I walk out of here, but on this, with my daughter being the same age . . . I kept on looking at her, then looking at my wife and thinking, what if it had happened here, in my house? My home invaded by that madman, and one that should never have been let out on the streets? Well, look at poor old Jimmy.'

'I'm sorry?'

'Langton. Fucking illegal immigrant got him and nearly killed him, and from what I've heard, he'd have been better off.'

'What do you mean by that?'

'Well, he's not going to walk again, is he?'

Anna flushed. 'Yes, of course he is. I don't know who you've been talking to, but he's making a remarkable recovery.'

'Just a bloke I knew who was at the rehabilitation home, released a few days ago; he told me. May have got it wrong, sorry.'

'Yes, you have got it wrong, Harry.'

'Well, I've said I'm sorry, love. I know you and he are – what exactly? Living together?'

Anna stood up, packing her files. 'I hope you will put your friend right. James is really hoping to get back to work soon.'

'Oh well, good on him.' Harry moved away, leaving her feeling tense and angry, but thankfully no longer thinking about Arthur George Murphy. She would not allow him to invade her life. Langton already had.

She felt so protective towards Jimmy and, moreover, so upset that rumours were spreading that he would never walk again.

Chapter Three

As soon as Anna had been released from duty, she called the rehabilitation home to see if she could speak to Langton to confirm that she would, unlike the previous night, be there to see him.

'Hi, how you doing?' He sounded unlike himself.

'Well, we caught the killer and he's admitted it. He couldn't really get out of it; we had enough evidence.' She listened. 'Hello, are you still there?'

'Yeah, but listen, I'm feeling really whacked out, been doing a lot of work in the gym. I'm just going to crash out and have an early night. Let's say you come tomorrow?'

'Well, it's up to you.'

'So, see you tomorrow. I'm glad you got a result. G'night.'

The phone went dead. She sat holding the receiver, feeling wretched. He really hadn't sounded like himself – not even his moody self. She waited a while and then called again, this time to speak to the nurse. By the time that call ended, she felt even worse.

Langton had not been working out in the gym – far from it. He had overstretched himself the day before and now had an infection in his knee joint; he was unable to walk and in great pain. The swelling was the size of a football and they were very concerned; having already had septicaemia once, they were worried there might be a recurrence. He had been given morphine to dull the pain and was, as they spoke, being taken back to his room to sleep.

Anna wanted to weep. Had this so-called friend of Harry Blunt's been right, and would Langton never walk again? She went over everything the nurse had said and was certain that if Langton did rest, did not push himself, the infection could be controlled and he would be able to return to exercising, in moderation.

She cooked herself an omelette but hardly touched it, and was about to go over to Langton's flat to collect his mail, when the doorbell rang. It was Mike Lewis; he apologized for not calling her and just turning up, but he had been to see Langton himself.

Anna passed Lewis a glass of wine; he sat, glum-faced, on her sofa.

'He's not in good shape, Anna.'

She said she'd called the night nurse and knew about the knee infection.

'Well, that's part of his problem.'

'What do you mean?'

'Well, it's all the other stuff, you know.'

'No, I don't. What do you mean?'

'His head; his mind is all confused, and he's so bloody angry.'

'Wouldn't you be?' she said defensively.

'Yeah yeah – of course, but I can't help him Anna. I can't do what he wants.'

'Which is what, exactly?'

'Track down this bloody illegal immigrant that knifed him.'

'Has he asked you to do that?'

'Christ, he's on the phone every day asking me how far I've got, what I've come up with, but you know there's been a dedicated team trying to locate the bastards. I'm already on another case and I don't have the time to do what he wants.'

'How far have you got?'

'Well, that's the point – I haven't. There's no trace of them. I reckon they've already skipped the country, but telling him that is like a red rag to a bull. He refuses to believe the bastard could just walk away, or fly, or whatever he's done, but we can't get a trace on either of them. The team handling the search have done no better.'

'Have you got any details with you?'

Lewis sighed and opened his briefcase. 'I've the original case file, which I should not have made copies of, but I did. The rest is all I've been able to get so far.'

'Can you leave this with me?'

Lewis nodded. 'Sure, but you won't get any help from anyone. I've just come across a brick wall. I don't know what else to do.'

Anna made Lewis a sandwich and changed the subject, asking him about his son and how Barolli was doing.

'Well, we're all missing having the boss as our SIO; no one comes up to him, have you found that? I know you've been working with that prick Sheldon.'

Anna smiled.

'Anna, there is nothing I wouldn't do for him, same with Barolli, but it's fruitless.' Lewis hesitated. 'You know, what *is* important is that he concentrates on getting fit. As it stands, he's never going to be able to work again; he'll have to go before a physical assessment board and no way will he come through it. I think he'll get signed off.'

Anna showed Lewis out. By this time, it was after eleven and she didn't feel like going through the files he had left. She had too much to think about, predominantly Langton's physical condition. She set her alarm for five o'clock, to give her time to read up on the file. She had no notion of what it contained, but if she could do anything to help, then she would make it her priority.

The file contained copies of all the murder enquiry paperwork: witness statements, documents from the arrest of the suspect, and numerous photographs. Added to these were Lewis's notes and, in a small black notebook, Langton's own private notes on the case. Langton had an expression: 'it's in the book'. He would tap the breast pocket where he kept it. Jokes about train spotting or 'one for the book, Gov' were often heard around the incident room. He would say it whenever anyone screwed up – that could even mean forgetting his morning coffee! When Anna had asked him about it, he had grinned and said it was common knowledge he had a terrible memory; he had started, when he was a rookie, just making notes of things he shouldn't forget – sometimes, it could be just to remind himself to collect his laundry. Over the years, it had become a habit and then a talking-point; then he noticed that he could make detectives very edgy if they saw him jotting something down whilst he was with them.

'Like to keep my team on their toes,' he laughed.

She said to him that she had never seen him use it.

'Ah. That's because what I jotted down about you had nothing to do with police work.'

'You're telling me you needed to be reminded of whether or not you fancied me?'

Again he had laughed, dismissing it with a waft of his hand. 'The date of your birthday? Now forget it. It's just a joke anyway; and besides, you constantly have your nose in your official notebook – more than any other officer I have ever worked with.'

It was true; in fact, her father had tipped her off. He always said to write everything down, because the memory can play tricks. If you are required to recall in detail an incident for the courtroom, your book becomes your security blanket.

Langton's notebook had a red elastic band wound tightly round it. It was slightly curved, as if it had taken the shape of his chest. Anna eased back the elastic band, and wrapped it round the palm of her hand before she opened the book. His small, tight handwriting covered every page, back and front, until three-quarters of the way through, when it stopped abruptly. The thin pages were stiff; a couple she had to blow apart, which made her think that no one had read the notes recently. Maybe Lewis hadn't bothered; if the notebook was such a joke, he might not have thought it of any value.

The writing was meticulously neat, but not that easy to read; she peered at page one.

The call out for the horrific murder of a teenage girl called Carly Ann North came in at 9 a.m. The body had been discovered on wasteground behind King's

Cross station. Although only sixteen years of age, North had already been convicted of prostitution and sent to a young offenders' institute. She was from a very dysfunctional background, both parents heroin addicts. She had been knifed and her wounds were horrific; the killer had attempted to decapitate her. He had also tried to remove her hands, to avoid fingerprints being taken. A police officer had disturbed the killer, having seen three men loitering near the wasteground. He caught him, but the others, obviously acting as lookouts, ran off, leaving their friend fighting with the officer. The killer was an illegal immigrant. The judge had ordered at his trial that, after serving a sentence for rape, he should be deported. Underlined was his name: *Idris Krasiniqe*, aged twenty-five.

Anna then turned from the notebook back to the case file. Krasiniqe had a string of offences, from possession of cannabis to common assault; he'd had community punishment when only eighteen years of age. His last offence was the robbery, when the judge had ordered his deportation after sentence; yet eight months after his release, he was still at large and this time had murdered Carly Ann North.

Anna sighed. It was just unbelievable, especially with the ongoing case against Arthur Murphy. How could this man have been allowed to stay in the country, after a judge's order for deportation!

In the same meticulous writing, Langton had made a few personal notes: one about Barolli being too over-weight; another, that Lewis was slacking, as his wife was expecting another child and, with a toddler, he was often tired and late for work.

Anna sat back. She wondered how many of these

private notes he had made about her, but she didn't have time to continue looking over the file. She had to get herself to work on time!

The day went slowly. Murphy was taken before a magistrate. Bail, as they knew it would be, was refused and he was shipped off to Wandsworth prison to await his trial.

Anna returned home to change and get ready to leave for Glebe House. First, she picked up Langton's keys and went round to his flat.

There was a stack of post, mostly junk mail, on the doormat. She picked it all up and took it to the dining-room table, to sift through it. There was a similar stack already on the table. The flat was quite tidy; she wondered if his ex-wife had been round. Anna knew she often stayed there with Kitty. If this was the case, she hadn't bothered to empty the laundry basket in the bathroom. Anna stuffed everything into a bin liner to take home to wash, and then went into his bedroom.

The bed had been made and the room looked reasonably neat. The only photograph on his bedside table was of Kitty, sitting on a pony and beaming into the camera. Anna checked for any unpaid bills on the dressing-table, but there were just some ten- and twenty-pound notes left with change on top. She opened a drawer to take out some fresh pyjamas and, as she did so, she found a photo album. Anna felt guilty about looking through it, but couldn't resist. It was of his wedding to his first wife. She was, as Anna had been told, very beautiful and they looked very much in love. At the end of the book was a small remembrance card from her funeral.

Anna replaced the album and shut the drawer. Just

as she turned away, she noticed a piece of newspaper sticking out of another drawer. She eased it open. It was crammed with newspaper articles, cut out and pinned together. Anna checked the time and reckoned she had better get a move on, or she would be later than ever to see Langton. Collecting them all, she put the cuttings into her briefcase.

Langton wheeled towards her in the reception area, beaming. 'I was just about to give up on you.'

'I'm sorry. I went over to your flat to collect some clean pyjamas.'

'Any mail for me?'

'Yes, I've brought it. Can we go somewhere and sit down?'

'I already am,' he laughed.

Langton spun round and headed towards a lounge area, banging the double doors open with his chair. Anna gave a rueful smile; even in his wheelchair, he still had the habit of forgetting she was behind him, barging through doors and letting them swing back in her face.

'As you can see, it's a hive of activity,' he said, gesturing to the empty room.

'Well, that's good, we can have some privacy.'

'They'll all be watching some crap on TV, or in the bar; you want a drink?'

'No, thanks. Have you had something to eat?'

'I think it was fish, but it could have been Christ only knows what; I could have used it as a table-tennis bat.'

She sat in a comfortable chair and placed her various bags on the coffee-table. Langton manoeuvred the chair to sit opposite; as she took out the mail, he glanced through it, muttering that it was all rubbish.

'I left a load of junk mail behind,' Anna told him. 'I think your ex-wife had been there and left even more. There's a few bills you need to pay.'

'Yeah yeah, leave them – I'll sort them.'

'Do you have your chequebook with you?'

'Yeah yeah, and my credit card, so no problem.'

She laid out his clean clothes. He kept twisting in his chair.

'You look well,' she said. He didn't. He was unshaven and he smelled of drink. 'Been in the bar, have you?'

'I have; there's nothing else to do, and don't ask about the conversation in there – load of fruits. Can't have a sane conversation with any one of them.'

'I'm sure that's not true.'

He suddenly went quiet. 'Nope. It's not, just making conversation.'

She leaned forwards. 'How's the physio going?'

He bowed his head. 'I can't walk yet and it's painful, but the bastards won't give me any more painkillers. They count them out like I was ten years old.'

'Well, they have to do that for a reason; you don't want to get addicted to them.'

'What would you know about it?'

'Well, I'm really glad I schlepped all the way here, if you can't be pleasant.'

'I hate this fucking chair.'

'You seem to be very adept at wheeling about in it.'

He shrugged. 'I might be in it for the rest of my life.'

'Of course you won't.'

'I hate it – hate being so dependent, you know? I can't even take a piss without falling over.'

'Well, you were told it would take time.'

'Oh, stop talking down to me as if I was mentally screwed up as well as physically.'

'You know, undergoing a life-threatening operation, and then—'

'I know what I went through. Sometimes I wish I'd never pulled through.'

'Well, I for one am glad that you did.'

'Are you?' He cocked his head to one side. 'You fancy being attached to a cripple, do you?'

She took a deep breath. 'Well, if you want a straight answer: as it is, you are pretty unpleasant, but—'

He interrupted her. 'Well, I've given this some thought, and I want you to know that I'm not coming back to your place. In fact, I think it's probably better if we call it quits right now.'

'Call what quits?'

'You and me, Anna – what do you think I'm talking about? I don't want you coming to see me any more. I mean it; you didn't bargain for this, nor did I. So, let's just be adult about my situation.'

'You think you are?'

'What?'

'Being adult about this!'

'I reckon I am.'

'Then why don't you take into consideration my feelings?'

'That's just what I am bloody doing!'

'No, you are not. You haven't even given me a chance to say what I think, what I feel—'

'I'm all ears.'

He was making her feel so frustrated, there was such anger in him.

'Maybe the fact that I love you should be considered.'

'Do you?'

'You know I do.'

He turned away.

'You don't show me any kind of affection whatsoever; you've not even touched me, let alone kissed me,' she said.

'Hard from this chair.'

'Oh stop it, please.'

He bowed his head and the tears streamed down his face. She was not expecting that. She got up and went to him, wanting to put her arms around him.

'For Chrissakes, leave me alone.'

She gripped the arms of his chair. 'Look at me. *Look at me!*'

He wouldn't and she felt such anguish; she was close enough to touch him and yet he was refusing to allow her near.

'Right, fuck you then.' She straightened, returned to her bag and started packing up her things. 'If this is the way you want it.'

'It is. Just go away, Anna. Leave me – I mean it.'

She made quite a show of putting aside the things she had brought for him and getting her car keys. He remained silent.

She really didn't have anything else she could say, apart from, 'Goodbye. Please don't bother to show me out.'

She had never heard his voice so soft and painful. 'I'm sorry.'

She chucked her keys onto the table and went to him, wrapping him in her arms. 'Please don't send me away.'

'I'm sorry; you are the only thing I have.'

75

'Then for God's sake, stop this nonsense and never, never do it again to me. You hurt me and I get all confused, because I love you so much.'

He said it – hardly audible, but he said it. 'I love you, Anna.'

They kissed. It wasn't a passionate embrace, but the kiss was sweet and gentle. He touched her face. 'I wait all day to see you, then I behave like a bastard.'

'I wait all day to be with you.' She drew up a chair to be able to sit close to him and hold his hand. He gripped it so tightly it hurt, but she didn't mind.

Anna eventually had to leave, but there was a quiet understanding between them that had never been there before. When he kissed her goodbye, he whispered that he would count the hours until he saw her again. He was tearful again; it was so poignant and heartbreaking.

Langton waved to her as she crossed the car park. He had gone by the time she was sitting inside her car. She waited for a few moments before she was able to cry. He had never been so vulnerable, so dependent and so scared of the future. She drove home with such mixed feelings churning up inside her. The reality was, she didn't honestly know how she would be able to cope with him coming home. If he remained as incapacitated as he was now, there was no way he could return to work. She knew her love would have to be very strong to deal with him and the probability that he would be an invalid for the rest of his life.

Anna was still deeply unsettled when she got home. She made some hot chocolate and sat up in bed, thinking about her parents. Isabella Travis had been like a child in many ways. She had been sexually assaulted as a young art student. Anna's father, Jack, had investigated the case, became her protector and subsequently her husband. Anna's entire childhood had been blissfully ignorant of any trauma; they had kept it so far removed from her that she had never known the truth until both parents were dead. Could she, like her father, take on Langton and love him, no matter what?

Anna continued to work on Murphy's forthcoming trial; at the same time, she made the daily visits to see Langton. She found it very exhausting to drive the distance every night there and back before going into the station the next morning. Some nights, the prognosis was good and he was cheerful; other nights, he was morose and in great pain. The injury to his knee was taking a long time to heal, but what made her really worried was the latest talk she had with the head nurse.

He described Langton's physical condition as 50 per cent better; however, he was not mentally coping with the injuries. He was, as she well knew, deeply angry, but what she had been unprepared for was to be told that he was suffering from deep depression. He was also drinking heavily and creating ill-feeling amongst the other patients.

It did not help for Anna to be told that, during these rehabilitation periods, many officers behaved in much the same way. They were so used to being in control: to lose it became so emotionally debilitating that often the nurses, physiotherapists and psychiatrists were unable to make any headway until they were about to be discharged. Anna could not bring herself to ask if it was conceivable that Langton would be able to return to work. It was looking highly unlikely, every visit.

It was not until the weekend, however, when she was checking through the bundle of newspaper clippings she had taken from Langton's flat, that she became most concerned.

1. *Hunt for child sex attacker who cut off his tag to flee bail hostel.* The suspect's photograph was ringed in pencil.
2. *Why was this rapist who butchered our beautiful daughter allowed to walk the streets unsupervised?* The article was underlined twice.
3. *This Latvian came to Britain after raping two women. Now he's accused of the murder of a schoolgirl here.* The suspect's photo had a black mark across his face.
4. *The one hundred year backlog on asylum.* This article was so heavily underlined that the pen had cut through the newspaper.
5. *UK passports for 200,000 foreigners.*
6. *Asylum seekers come first.* He'd underlined this in red.
7. *23 foreign offenders allowed to walk free.*
8. *Offenders.* Reoffenders convicted of fresh crimes including drugs, violent disorder, grievous and actual body harm, and two murders. The row of faces was again ringed, with odd dates jotted down beside them.
9. *Will no one pay for this fiasco? A thousand convicts lost in the system.* Again, Langton had underlined sections.
10. *Super hostels planned for free sex offenders.* This had a deep, thick pencil cross over it.
11. *Hunt for released killers.*

12. *One immigrant arrives in Britain EVERY minute.*
    The article went on to show migrants hiding
    their faces, as they prepared another bid to
    cross the Channel illegally.
13. *ILLEGAL IMMIGRANT who worked at the Old
    Bailey was twice deported.*
14. *Paedophile backlash: website identifying convicted
    offenders could drive them into hiding in fear of
    vigilantes, warns probation supremo.*
15. *TRAVESTY: asylum seeker raped a child and got an
    eight-year sentence, then chose to stay in jail rather
    than be deported. now we are paying him fifty
    thousand for his inconvenience.*
16. *Child rapists' rights were put before victims.*
17. *Life means six years: almost one hundred murders
    were committed by criminals supposedly under the
    supervision of probation officers in the past two years;
    chilling figures are a shocking indictment of
    Government failure across the board to protect the
    public . . .*
18. *DOSSIER reveals 50 dangerous convicts in our open
    prisons.*

There were over thirty more cuttings, all about the
Home Office's inept handling of the deportation of
illegal immigrants and the appalling situation that had
resulted. Why had Langton kept them? Not only had he
cut them out, but his handwriting was also scrawled
across them, and he had ringed photographs of suspects.

She wondered if any of them had any connection
to his own case, but they were all dated before he was
attacked. Anna packed them away in a folder; she would
bring it up next time she went to visit. Then she

worried: maybe she shouldn't ask him about them, as it would look as if she had been snooping around his flat. She decided she would contact Mike Lewis again.

Lewis agreed to drop by her place later that afternoon. It was almost three when he turned up and said he couldn't stay long as he was working. He seemed very uneasy.

'I've felt bad about not going to see him but you know, work pressures and with a wife and new kid on the way . . .' He trailed off, obviously feeling guilty.

'I see him most nights,' she said, placing his coffee down on the table in front of him.

'Word is he's not doing so well,' Lewis said, avoiding looking at her.

'It's going to take time.'

'Yeah, I guess so – that was what I was told.'

'Has Barolli been to see him?'

'I dunno, I've not spoken to him in a while. He's on another case. Life goes on!' Lewis paused. 'He's not going to get back to work, is he?'

Anna drew up a chair and smiled. 'Well, that's what they say, but you know him better than anyone. I don't think he's going to give up that easily.'

'It's not a question of giving up though, is it? If he's still unable to walk, then there's no hope of him coming back. I know he wouldn't take on any kind of pen-pushing job. Maybe that's why I can't face it, you know; I hate to see him this way.'

There was a long pause. Anna waited. Lewis suddenly bowed his head.

'I keep on thinking about that night – you know, when it happened. I've been put on sleeping tablets by my doc. I just keep on seeing the look on his face when that bastard slashed him and thinking, could I have done something to stop it happening? It all happened so quickly. I thought he would bleed to death. Barolli's the same; he was off for a few weeks, you know. Having worked with the old bastard for so long, we really felt bad. He was always so . . .' Lewis shook his head. 'I'm sorry.' He took out a handkerchief and wiped his eyes.

Anna picked up the file. 'I found these newspaper cuttings in his flat. Can you have a look at them for me?'

'Sure.'

She handed him the file and walked out to get some fresh coffee and to leave him alone for a few moments. When she returned, Lewis had them laid out on the coffee-table in front of him.

'More coffee?'

'No – no, thank you.' He leaned back, and then gestured to the cuttings. 'The case we were on: that girl was raped and murdered by an illegal immigrant, Idris Krasiniqe. He was supposed to have been deported, but slipped through the net.'

'I've read the case file.'

'I think all these are just the Gov's fury at what happened.'

'But all these cuttings are dated before that.'

'I suspect the Gov was going to really make a loud noise about it. As you can see, all this press, all these bastards walking around, but suddenly it's all gone quiet. Home Office have put their hands up and admitted they have screwed up, probation department ditto. Nobody is taking the flak for what has gone on – what is *still* going on – and the prison service is helpless to deal with the overcrowding.' He sighed. 'Which leaves us, the police, in a pretty pitiful state. We catch them; they are released or, as you can see from this article . . .' He picked it up. 'Bloke is put into a hostel, cuts off his tag, goes out and kills a thirteen-year-old girl! Beggars belief. Jimmy was getting fed up to the back teeth with it all.'

Anna nodded. 'I'm on a case with a guy let out early on parole who killed a woman; her twelve-year-old daughter found her.'

'There you go. I can tell you, there's an awful lot of us that are about to throw the towel in. If I was the Gov, I'd walk away, get my pension and live the rest of my life out of this bloody city. It's all out of control; without the money and the manpower, we're flailing around like idiots. What he ever thought he could do about it, only he can tell you.'

'Has he called you again? Last time you mentioned that he kept in touch.'

'Yes, he calls me, at work, at home. Yes, he bloody won't let up – but, like I said the last time I was here, there's not a lot I can do.'

'It's hard to believe they haven't arrested the man who attacked him.'

'No, they never found him. In reality, we should have had an armed operation, but the Gov was impatient.' Lewis drained his coffee and stood up. 'I've got to go.'

'But what about the attack on Langton?'

'You tell me, case left open . . .' Lewis rubbed his eyes wearily. 'I can't start hunting them down in my free time, for Chrissakes; besides, we don't even know where to start looking. We think the bastard is already out of the country – I told you that. The murder enquiry was over when we caught the killer and he got sent down for life.'

'But what if Langton's life sentence is him stuck in a fucking wheelchair?' she snapped.

'Look, don't do this. It's out of our hands. He's alive.'

'You mean there would be a bigger enquiry if he was dead – if he'd died from his wounds? Is that what you are saying?'

'No!'

'Then what is happening about tracking down the men who did this to him?'

Lewis sighed. 'There is a new division set up to deal with all the problems surrounding immigration, illegal immigrants, parole jumpers, et cetera. The Home Office are backing them, and—'

'That sounds like a big whitewash load of crap,' she said furiously.

'Maybe it is, but it's ongoing, and maybe you need to talk to them. But . . .' He hesitated.

'But what?'

'Well, word of warning. You are part of the murder squad; they are a different department, so you don't want to muddy the waters.'

'Muddy the waters?'

'Yeah. If you start making moves on them, they won't like it. As it is, they're keeping their heads down because of all the bad press.'

'Oh, I see. That's all Langton is – bad press? I don't believe what I am hearing, Mike. He almost died!'

Lewis turned angrily towards her. 'I know that, for Chrissakes – I was there, all right? But at the same time, I have my career to think about. I've got a toddler and a baby on the way and I can't afford to lose out by switching divisions. I've worked hard enough to get to where I am now.'

'You got there because of Langton and you know it.'

Lewis had to clench his fists, she was making him so angry; beneath it was his guilt, because he knew she was right.

'Listen, Anna, back off me. I'm keeping up to date with any new developments, but I am not going to become a vigilante trying to track down this bastard. We've already been told he is more than likely back in Somalia. They use fake passports; he could have switched his name a dozen times by now!'

'What about the others? There were other suspects, weren't there?'

'Yes,' he sighed again, looking unutterably weary.

'What about them?'

'We're trying to find them, but Krasiniqe, the guy we arrested for Carly Ann's murder, is in prison, terrified because he named them in the first place. He keeps on about voodoo and they had to place him in a segregation wing because he's so scared he's going to be killed. Don't think I just walked away from this, because I didn't. I tried; Barolli tried. Now we just have to get on with our lives.'

Anna closed the door behind him. She could hardly bring herself to be pleasant, or thank him for coming to see her. She found it so hard to believe that after what had happened to Langton, no one seemed to be mounting a full-scale operation to nail down his attacker.

She looked at all the cuttings Lewis had spread out over the coffee-table. No wonder Langton was depressed. Having almost died from his injuries, he was now trapped in a wheelchair with little hope of ever returning to work. He also must know that there appeared to be equally little hope of ever bringing to justice the man who had put him there.

Anna checked the time: it was now nearly four, so she decided she would buy some grapes and smoked salmon and bagels to take to Glebe House. She placed all the cuttings back into the folder and then picked up the case file Lewis had left on his previous visit.

The mortuary shots of Carly Ann North were horrific; she had suffered appalling injuries at the hands of her killer. Anna read and reread the way he had been arrested. A police officer on patrol had radioed in for assistance, after seeing the men with the body. He had arrested Idris Krasiniqe, who had really put up a fight, but the other two men had run for it as soon as the patrol car was visible. During Langton's interrogation, Idris admitted that he had killed Carly Ann but insisted that the other two men were also there when she was killed, holding her down. He also admitted that they had gang-raped her. They had DNA evidence to verify this. Idris's lawyers hoped to get a more lenient sentence for him, for helping the police by naming his friends. He had to give an address. Accompanied by Lewis and Barolli, Langton went to question them. The attack on Langton had taken place in the hallway of the residence. Both men escaped.

Anna suddenly realized the time. Abandoning her reading, she changed and hurried out, heading for the M4 via a deli. All the way there, her mind churned over and over her conversation with Lewis and her take on the case file. She had changed her mind about what to do with the newspaper cuttings: they were now in her briefcase.

Anna parked her Mini and bent into the back seat to

collect the groceries and the files; when she turned round, she nearly dropped them all.

Langton was standing on the steps of the Glebe House. Standing – and with a grin stretched from ear to ear. He waved.

Anna ran to him, overcome with emotion.

'Now don't you grab me, or I could fall over,' he said.

'I don't believe it!'

'You'd better. I've walked from the lounge to here unaided and now I am going to walk back in there.'

Anna watched as he turned slowly and walked, step-by-step, opening the door for her; then, a little unsteady, he kept on walking towards the lounge. She saw him wince in pain, but he was so determined to keep on his feet that he refused to even place a hand against the wall to steady himself.

He eventually got to a big comfortable wingback chair and eased his body down. Then he looked up at her. His face was glistening with sweat.

'I'm coming back, Anna! Gimme a few more days, I'll run out there to meet you.'

Anna put down her briefcase and groceries on a table as he raised his hand to her.

'Come here, you.' He drew her close and she bent down to kiss him, trying hard not to cry. He kissed her right back and then gave a long sigh. 'If I keep going at this rate, I'll be home by the end of next week.'

She drew up a chair to sit close to him.

'What do you think?' he asked.

'I think that would be wonderful,' she said, taking out the grapes and smoked salmon and bagels.

He had shaved and was wearing a shirt and trousers

rather than pyjamas, though he still had slippers on his feet.

'So,' he said, still with that smile on his face. 'How's your day been?'

had dominated her thoughts for the months they had been trying to trace him.

Anna sat in a bathrobe and began to rip at the pages and pages of her notes. She did not care if Idris Krasiniqe was awarded a new trial or not: she didn't want any more of the sickness to invade her life. She knew, without a doubt, that DCI Langton must have recognized Eugene Camorra, just as she was certain he had fed him the horror poison.

Camorra had died in terror; she could only imagine the terror of the poor little boy whose decapitated body was found, like floating rubbish, in the canal. She could also imagine the terror of Carly Ann North, of Gail Sickert, her little girl and her two other children.

Langton's physical and mental control both astonished and frightened her. He was a formidable man, and she had no desire to get on the wrong side of him. She now knew she held a secret – a very dangerous one.

they cared for Langton and how many times they had worked alongside each other; their lack of enthusiasm depressed her.

There was no mention of Sickert in the incident room as the case against Vernon Kramer went before the crown court. He was wearing a sober grey suit, white shirt and tie. It never ceased to amaze her how the legal teams cleaned up their clients. He pleaded guilty to harbouring Arthur Murphy, but claimed he was afraid of him, saying that Murphy had threatened him if he did not help. This lie was swiftly demolished, as they were able to report that Vernon was actually wandering around buying fish and chips and beer, and could at any time have contacted the police. It was pointed out that the newspapers had front-page photographs of Murphy and requests for the public to assist in tracing him. Vernon replied that he didn't read newspapers. In summation, he was found guilty and, as he was on parole, he was returned to Wandsworth prison with an extra eighteen months added onto the rest of his previous sentence. This time, he was to serve the full term with no leave to apply for parole.

Sheldon looked at Anna and shrugged. 'Should never have been on early release anyway, the sick bastard.'

'No wonder Gail was scared, her brother a killer and his best pal a paedophile.'

'Listen, both of them are sick fucks, but Murphy's going down for life. Another couple of years and Vernon here will be back in a hostel with more of his sicko friends. He'll probably meet even more in the nick: they get segregated for their own protection from the other cons; come out and they're at it again. He reckoned he was clever because he wasn't on the sex offenders' register; this time, I'm gonna make damned sure he is.'

Langton was sitting in the lounge, chatting to two other residents when she walked in. He waved, slowly stood up, and then walked towards her with his arms outstretched.

'Eh, take a look at me?' he grinned.

She wrapped her arms around him, almost in tears; he was a little unsteady and joked that she was pushing him over. They walked together to a vacant area, with two armchairs and a coffee-table. He sat down and she noticed that he winced in pain as he grasped the arms of the chair, easing himself down. He then blew out his breath.

'I've got some good and some bad news,' he smiled.

'Well, I'm all ears.'

'Tomorrow I'm having a physical assessment and if I pass, I'm coming home at the weekend.'

She was shocked: she hadn't expected him to be released for another week at least.

'They don't keep us here for long, you know – get 'em out fast is their motto! So, how do you feel about that?'

She forced a smile. 'It's wonderful! This weekend?'

'Yep. If I get under the weather, then I'll be back for another two weeks – it's the way they work it – but I reckon as soon as I'm out, that means out out.'

She leaned across to kiss his cheek.

'So what do you think?' he asked. 'Should I go back to my place or come and stay with you?'

'What do *you* think?' she said in mock anger.

'Well, I won't be much use, you know. I can't drive

yet, but I'll get compensation and that's dosh for a taxi back and forth to a gym and the physio. I'm going to need a lot of work done on my knee. You know what the nurse said to me? Said it's going to feel like housemaid's knee. I said to her: "Well, never having been one, I wouldn't know, so what does it feel like?" And she said: "Fucking painful!"' He laughed and she couldn't help but join in.

She brought out some fresh fruit. He winced, saying he couldn't face another grape, but ate the apples one after the other, munching through them like a kid. All the while, he gave her a running commentary about the other patients; he had her laughing as he mimicked them, using funny voices. It was a while before he calmed down and then reached over to take her hand.

'You sure about taking me on, sweetheart?'

'I have never been more sure about anything. Besides, your flat has a walk up four flights; I'm only two flights plus a lift and my flat is all on one floor, so it's obviously the better place. Added to that, you'll have me to cook and look after you.'

'I don't need mothering, Anna.'

'Who said I'd be doing that? I want you fit and back to work as soon as possible, because I know you are not going to be easy.'

He grinned, then frowned. 'Keep it quiet though. I don't want visitors. I don't want to see any of the old team, not until I'm ready.'

'Whatever you say.'

'I've made a list of stuff I'll need to be brought in for me to go out looking the business.'

He handed it over and she slipped it into her handbag. She did not open her briefcase, which still contained the case file and his own folder of press cuttings. The time passed very quickly as they kissed and hugged each other. She was very tearful when he whispered that he loved her.

'I love you too, and you are going to get back in shape, I know it.'

He cocked his head to one side. 'I have to, because no way am I going to be shoved into some desk job, not me. I'm coming out and I've got a lot of unsolved business to sort!'

She felt very uneasy, but he clasped her hand.

'Don't get that worried look on your face. I won't be doing anything dumb, but if you know me and I think you do, you know it's not over.'

She gave a sad smile. 'I know.'

Chapter Six

Anna had been called by Langton four times on the morning she was due to collect him. He wanted some chocolates for certain nurses; then he rang to say to bring some good bottles of wine. Next, had she got the right suit and tie? Then again, to make sure she remembered to bring the gifts. Anna could hear the excitement in his voice, like a kid, as he checked the time for the pick-up on every call, constantly reminding her not to tell anyone he was discharged.

She drove to Glebe House as instructed, to be there for two-thirty. She arrived slightly earlier, due to a traffic-free M4; she handed over his suitcase and said she would wait in the lounge. He did not appear until almost three. He looked fantastic, and very smart, taking the wine and chocolates from her to hand out like royalty to the staff.

A number of staff stood to wave him goodbye as he walked towards Anna's Mini. She carried the suitcase filled with his laundry and odds and ends. She opened the passenger door for him and then walked round to put the suitcase into the boot. By the time she stashed it and closed the boot, he was still standing, waving, and holding onto the edge of the door. He stood there until the staff had disappeared inside, then with a grimace he began to ease himself into the seat, which she had pulled back as far as possible, earlier on. It took quite some time, as his knee obviously pained him greatly. He swore at her for having such a bloody small car but eventually managed to flop down and haul his bad leg inside.

As they drove home, he sighed deeply, as if still in pain; every time she asked if he was all right, he said he was fine. By the time they reached home, he was rubbing his knee and wincing.

'It's because I'm so cramped,' he said.

'Well, let me get the case inside first, then I'll come back and help you out.'

'I don't need any help, just go on inside. I'll follow you in a second.'

Anna took his case up into the flat, and then returned to the car. He was still unable to get out of the seat. She bent down to suggest he swing his legs out first, and he swore at her.

'I'm just getting my breath! Don't tell me what to do.'

Anna stood back and watched as he painfully eased one leg round, and then used both hands to lift his right leg. He was forced to hold on to her to stand upright. The sweat rolled down his cheeks as he attempted to straighten up. It was a very slow walk to the lift, then, from there, the few paces into her flat; each step was obviously agony for him and, much against his will, he was still forced to cling to her.

As they went into the lounge, he almost fell onto the sofa, rubbing his leg and muttering how it was all because of being in such a cramped position in her car. She unpacked his case, and left him to cool down. She then asked if he was hungry, and would he like to go out to eat, or dine at home.

'Oh, let's run down to the local Italian!' he said sarcastically.

'I was joking! I've got steak and salad and a good bottle of wine.'

'Come here.' He held out his hand and clasped hers, drawing her down to sit beside him on the sofa. 'I'm a sourpuss and an ungrateful son of a bitch, but if you get the pills in the blue-labelled bottle, it'll help ease this housemaid's fucking knee. Christ only knows how housemaids deal with it; mind you, they're not on their hands and knees washing down steps any more, are they?'

She kissed his cheek; it felt cold and clammy. The pills were in a black leather shaving bag. She was surprised how many bottles of different prescriptions he had been given. After he'd taken two with a glass of wine (which she doubted was the best way to take them) the pain obviously lessened and when she served dinner, he ate hungrily and said it was the best dinner he'd had since he'd been injured. It was not until they had coffee (or she had one – he was still drinking) that he became quiet and serious.

'It's not going to be easy, is it?' he said.

'I never thought it would be, but then I never thought you'd be home this quickly. In fact, you just being here is a miracle.'

He smiled, and lifted his glass. 'To my sweet Anna!'

She blew him a kiss. 'Right, I'll going to clear up, and then we can watch TV – or have an early night; maybe you should do that. It's been a big day for you and you don't want to tire yourself out.'

'Let me tell you when I'm tired.'

'Fine, just sit then. I won't be long.'

She had just wiped down the kitchen counters and had put the dishwasher on when she heard him calling her. She went over to him.

'I can't get up,' he said quietly.

It wasn't easy getting him up onto his feet; he was like a dead weight. They had to walk very slowly towards the bedroom. He gasped for breath at each step; twice they had to pause whilst he gritted his teeth before being able to move another step forwards. He was embarrassed at being unable to take a piss without her helping him, but he was incapable of retaining his balance.

She helped him undress, ready to take a shower. He had grown silent; time and time again he winced with pain, but said nothing. She took his dirty clothes into the kitchen to put into the washing machine and to give him some privacy, but when she returned to the bedroom he was still sitting, naked apart from a towelling robe around his shoulders.

'I can't stand up again,' he said, head bowed.

'That's okay. For goodness' sake, it's your first day home.'

She leaned forwards to put her hands under his armpits to try and haul him up, but he was too heavy; she eventually managed it by letting him lean his weight forwards onto her and then very slowly standing.

He took the few steps towards the ensuite with one arm resting round her shoulders, his other hand groping the wall. He had lost a considerable amount of weight; his tall frame looked rake thin. Anna turned on the shower as he rested against the tiled sides, and she got a good soaking before she was able to help him stand beneath the water jets.

Only now had Anna the opportunity to see the terrible scars to his body. One ran from his right shoulder-blade, crossing his chest and reaching almost down to his waist. The other ran from the middle of his right thigh over his kneecap, almost down to his shinbone. He must have required hundreds of stitches.

'Bit like a patchwork quilt, aren't I?' he joked, as she soaped his back and helped him wash his hair.

They had quite a struggle to get him back to the bedroom and into his pyjamas, and he then lay back exhausted. She felt such compassion and such love that she wanted to weep, but she kept up a bright and steady chatter, setting the alarm and preparing to take her make-up off.

By the time Anna was ready to get into bed, he was asleep on top of the duvet. She had to ease one side open and slide in. She turned the lights out, feeling exhausted herself.

Twice during the night he had to have some more painkillers before she had him finally tucked up beside her. He had hardly said another word, as if even talking pained him. She lay awake beside him for a long time, assessing just what she had taken on. She had always known that it wouldn't be easy; however, it had never really dawned on her exactly how difficult it was going to be.

'This is going to put us to the test, isn't it?' he said softly, as if he knew what she was thinking. She was surprised; she had thought he was sleeping. He raised his arm for her to snuggle closer to him.

'I suppose a fuck is out of the question?' he asked, and she could hear him smiling.

'Right now it is, I'm too tired – but you won't get away with it for too long.'

He laughed. 'I won't wait for long; I need to see if everything is in working order. At least the bastard missed my dick!'

The following morning, Anna helped him dress before she went to work. She left him sitting in the lounge, watching breakfast TV with a tray of eggs and bacon. He seemed in a better frame of mind and smiled as she waved a kiss goodbye.

'I won't be late. Any special orders for dinner?'

'Blow job would be nice.'

She pulled a face and walked out.

At the station, Harry Blunt was having an argument with Frank Brandon, as usual. This time, it was a bet on what had been the fastest trial from the time of arrest. Blunt insisted it was thirty-six days, but Brandon was adamant it was forty-seven. After a few phone calls, Blunt held out his hand for a twenty-pound note.

Murphy had pleaded guilty at the plea and directions hearing. He was still held at Wandsworth; the trial date had been set and counsel appointed to represent him. Harry, as usual, went into a fury at the waste of public money, but the full show had to continue: it was the law. A law, Harry felt, that should be reviewed. With all the evidence and the admission of guilt from Murphy, he reckoned Murphy should just go before a judge and receive his sentence there and then. 'Better still, give the son of a bitch a lethal injection! Get rid of the dross of humanity, instead of allowing them to clog up every prison.'

He was about to launch into another favourite topic of conversation, the prison system, when Brandon told him to shut up; they'd all heard it before.

'How's Langton doing? I heard he's left Glebe House,' Brandon asked.

He'd be furious that news had got out already about his release, Anna thought. 'He's doing really well,' she said.

'He's a bloody marvel,' Harry interrupted, and then went into another tirade. 'Do you know how much my pal got, for being knocked out and kicked like a football? Poor bastard, he was on full pay for just six months; then they cut it down to half pay for a further six months, and then the fuckers cut the pay off altogether! All he could claim was twenty quid per week from the Police Federation. Twenty quid! You can't buy a week's groceries with that. It's fucking disgusting. Poor bastard can't even remember his own name.'

Brandon nodded – actually agreeing with Blunt! 'I've got private medical insurance, mate.'

Harry pursed his lips. 'Well, I bloody haven't – not with two kids and a mortgage.' He turned to Anna. 'Has Langton got private insurance?'

'I don't know.'

'Well, I hope so – he's gonna be out for months. Will he be claiming disability pension?'

'He's not disabled,' Anna said brusquely.

Brandon parked his backside on the edge of her desk. 'Friend of mine, he was a triathlete, right? Knocked off his motorbike, paralysed from the waist down. He went before the Chief Medical Officer. I mean, he was all right upstairs, understand? Just his legs got crushed. He's earning good if not better money now, doing a non-operational job over at Hammersmith.'

Anna chewed her lips; between the pair of them, she was beginning to get really furious. 'No way will he be disabled, nor, I can assure you, is he mentally screwed up either, so just shut up, the pair of you. You're like two old women.'

Brandon shrugged and returned to his own desk, but she caught the look between him and Harry, as if they knew she was lying.

Langton was sitting at the bar in the kitchen, as he found the high stool more comfortable. She had bought tuna steaks and microwave chips and was tossing the salad as he opened a bottle of wine.

'Do you have medical insurance?' she asked.

'Why do you ask?'

'Just Harry Blunt was talking about some friend of his.'

'What, hang-'em-all-Harry?' he said, grinning.

'He was saying today that there shouldn't be a trial if someone has pleaded guilty and there is strong evidence to prove it.'

'What, actually just hang them?' he said, taking out the cork.

She laughed. 'He's such a gossip – kept on about disability pay and how little an officer gets.'

'Talking about me, were you?'

She put down the salad tongs. 'Well, they asked how you were.'

'Oh yeah, and what did you tell them?'

'That you had made a remarkable recovery and no way would you be claiming any disability.'

'It's going to be a few months, you know,' he said, pouring the wine.

She sat beside him. 'So, do you have medical insurance?'

'Yes. I took it out after my first wife died, mainly because I loathed the bloody hospital she was taken to, though she didn't last long enough to see the place. I just thought to myself, if anything happened to me, no way was I going to end up in a bloody National Health ward; probably die of something I picked up from the floors.'

'That's good.'

He turned towards her. 'Don't talk about me, Anna.'

'I didn't; they just asked me how you were.'

'And you come back with all these queries about private medical insurance and disability pensions!'

'I just said that you were recovering!'

'Don't even say that, okay?'

'Yes, all right! So, you want salad?'

After dinner, they sat in the lounge and Langton brought out a notebook.

'I've got a driver and a car at my disposal,' he began by saying, 'so it's not going to inconvenience you.'

'I don't mind driving you around.'

'Well, you can't when you're at work, so this is what I've organized so far.'

Anna looked down his list. He had a personal trainer booked for every other day. He'd apparently wanted a session every day, but had been told that he needed a day in between, so the muscles could acclimatize to the workout. He had therefore arranged physio sessions on the days between the workouts, plus a massage three times a week, as well as swimming, saunas and steam baths.

'You are going to be doing all this every week?' she asked, astonished.

'Yep. It's taken me all day on the phone arranging it.'

'Good for you,' she said, and meant it. She was proud of him and said she would make sure he ate healthy foods to put some weight back on.

When she went into the bedroom, she had to step over a selection of weights and equipment. He'd evidently asked the delivery men to shift the furniture around and it made her bedroom look rather like a gymnasium. It irritated her slightly that he hadn't mentioned it to her, but she said nothing.

'I've got a rowing machine coming in tomorrow,' he said, rubbing his knee with a foul-smelling liniment.

'Where on earth are you going to put it?'

'In the hall – the only place with enough space. The rowing action will build up my shoulders and the knee action will strengthen the ligaments. Sorry about this stuff; it stinks.'

She wrinkled up her nose. 'My dad used something like it on an injured shoulder.'

'Yeah, it's good old-fashioned grease with a heat mix. The scars have healed well, but the skin is so taut around them and the muscles ache like hell on my knee.'

'Do you want me to do that for you?' she asked.

'Nope, better I do it – I've got a very low pain threshold,' he joked.

Anna kissed his cheek; he hadn't shaved and it was like a bristle brush. 'Would you like me to shave you?'

'No, I'm growing a beard. Day I shave it off is the day you know I'm back in shape.'

'Oh.'

'Does it bother you?'

'No. You'll look a bit like Rasputin.'

He grinned. 'Yeah, look how many shots the assassins fired into him before they could kill him, mean bastard. They even tried to drown him, then poison him as well.'

'I'm going to take a shower.'

'Fine, go ahead.' He was wrapping an elastic bandage around his knee.

She couldn't help feeling as if he had taken over her entire flat, as well as her life. She opened the bathroom door and was taken aback to see a walking frame. She went back in and asked him what it was in there for.

'Ah, it's just so you don't have to help me piss, or watch me crap. Makes me more independent – but it stays in there, I'm not using it anywhere else.'

Anna shut the door, easing herself around the bloody walking frame. Lined up in the bathroom were rows of vitamins, gels and tablets, crowding her make-up shelves. She couldn't find her toothbrush, and had to move his pills around to find it.

'This won't last for long. It's just temporary, so stay calm,' she muttered to herself, but she felt as if the walls of the bathroom were closing in on her.

Anna had yet to bring up the situation with Sickert, though it still concerned her. It never seemed to be the right time, as they were settling down to quite an amicable partnership. The fact that she ran her life around him, cooked and laundered, and was a constant support as he grew stronger, made him less demanding. Langton constantly impressed her with his total dedication to regaining his strength. They also started making love again; he was, as he had been before, a generous and exciting lover. They didn't exactly swing from the rafters, but if he was in any discomfort, he never showed it. His knee injury was still very obvious and she knew he depended on his painkillers to continue the rigorous training programme he had set for himself. He also had moments of deep depression and anxiety. These times she knew to leave him alone; that was not easy if she was at home, as the flat was so small.

As far as she knew, Langton made no contact with anyone apart from his trainer. He now had quite long hair and a beard; not exactly Rasputin, but it altered his appearance totally. He mostly wore tracksuits and trainers, so that if he did venture out, she doubted anyone would have recognized him. He seemed to have no desire to either take in a movie or dinner at a restaurant, but he did make one trip: she returned home from work one day to find his bicycle propped up in the hall. She knew he had always used one to work out at the track in Maida Vale, but she had no idea how the hell he had got it into the flat. With the rowing machine, and now the bicycle, circumnavigating the hall was hazardous. The bike pedals always caught her ankle and she had tripped over the rowing machine so many times that she had a permanent bruise on her leg.

A stack of mail he must have collected from his flat, all unopened, took up almost the entire space on the coffee-table. This was another irritation to her: everywhere he went, he left a trail of trainers and tracksuit tops. Newspapers he would buy every morning, so she had a stack of them in the kitchen. She tried to throw them out, but he insisted she keep them, as there were some articles he was interested in. It would have been an ideal opportunity for her to discuss the cuttings she had discovered at his flat all those weeks ago, but they were interrupted when the doorbell rang. It was his physio, come for a morning session.

Sometimes, just when she felt it was all too much for her, he would do something that made her melt. He would often return from his workouts with a bunch of flowers. A few times, he cooked dinner and made such an effort it touched her heart, as he was so boyish and eager for her to compliment his culinary efforts. He rarely asked about her work and never spoke of Lewis or Barolli — if Anna did refer to them, he would waft his hand as if to say 'don't go there' — but he was eager to talk about vitamins and minerals and physical therapy. He was now having extra massages and treatment from an acupuncturist.

Langton was obsessed with his recovery: it was his sole occupation and he would allow nothing to disrupt his regime. Anna knew it must be costing a fortune, since his personal trainer alone was a hundred pounds an hour. But the results were really astonishing: already his frame had filled out and he was almost back to his original weight. He was very proud of his six-pack and often stood admiring himself in the wardrobe mirror. He would be up and out with his bicycle before she showered. He'd cycle to the Maida Vale bike track and do five miles, then cycle home for his porridge and mound of vitamins. He was still often in pain and had been warned by everyone on his training programme not to push it too much, but he refused to listen.

The trial of Murphy was a week away. Vernon

Kramer had already been sentenced and sent back to Wandsworth prison, as he had requested to serve out his time close to family and friends.

This had caused Harry Blunt to deliver yet another tirade about the prison services. 'You know that bastard will be segregated on Rule 43 because he's a child molester; now he'll be back with his old cronies and probably swapping dirty pictures, the bastards! They don't call it that any more – Rule 43: seems it offended some of the arseholes. Mind you, now they'll have keys to their own fucking cells!'

Brandon looked at Anna and gave her a half-smile. She had grown to like him, especially now he had dispensed with his cologne. He came over to her desk and passed a note.

'Came in late afternoon yesterday, but you'd already left,' he said. 'She insists she wants to talk to you, but wouldn't say what it was about. That's her mobile number.'

'Thanks.' Anna glanced at the Post-it note. 'Beryl Dunn . . .?' She looked at the name, tried to think if she had ever heard it before and then it clicked: Beryl Dunn was Arthur Murphy's mother.

She dialled the number. 'Is this Mrs Dunn?' Anna asked.

'Yes.'

'I am Detective Inspector Anna Travis.'

'Oh, yes.'

'You left a message for me to call you?'

'Yes.'

'Would you like to tell me what it is a—'

'Not on the phone,' the woman interrupted.

'Well, that makes it rather difficult.'

'It's important I speak to you, but I'm not coming into no police station.' She had a strong Newcastle accent.

'If you could just tell me why you wished to see me, then I can arrange to meet you.'

There was a pause.

'Hello, Beryl? Are you still there?'

'Yes.'

'Why do you want to see me?'

'I need to talk to someone about something. It's important: you arrested my son.'

Anna waited; she could hear heavy breathing on the end of the line.

'I'm talking about Arthur Murphy,' said Beryl.

Anna hesitated, then agreed to meet her the following day in a café next to the old Peabody estate in Lilly Road. Then she went straight off to knock on Sheldon's office door, to inform him of this latest development.

'Whatever she has to say won't help him – he's going down for life. Take Brandon with you; give him something to do,' barked Sheldon.

Anna hesitated. 'I think he should just be in the background. She seemed very uneasy, and as she's coming all the way down from Newcastle, I don't want her to take fright and do a runner.'

'That's as may be, but take him with you anyway. It's a café – let him go in and get a cup of tea. Better to be safe than sorry. If she's as nuts as her son, you might need back-up.'

Brandon went into the seedy café fifteen minutes before Anna had agreed to meet Beryl Dunn. He was sitting in a corner with an order of eggs, bacon, sausage and chips swimming in grease, with a milky cup of tea and white bread and butter. He glanced up as Anna walked in. She looked around; apart from Brandon, there were only two other customers, who both wore painters' overalls and were tucking into plates of the same disgusting food.

Anna ordered a cup of coffee from the old man behind the glass counter. He dumped a thick-rimmed cup and saucer onto the flat counter. She handed over seventy pence, looked around and picked a table for two as far from the painting duo as possible, but reasonably close to Brandon.

Moments later, a woman walked in, waved over to the counter and asked for an espresso before looking round and making her way slowly to Anna's table. She was about five feet two and very overweight, with heavy swollen ankles in strappy sandals. She had a bright red coat and a large plastic handbag. Her hair was bleached yellowish-blonde and hung down to her shoulders, the black and grey roots just showing. She wore heavy make-up: thick black eyeliner and spiky mascara, rouged cheeks and dark red lipstick that ran in small rivulets up the lines around her mouth.

'You Detective Inspector Travis?' she said quietly.

'Yes.'

'I'm Beryl Dunn.'

She sat down in a waft of heavy, sweet perfume. She inched the coat off to rest on the back of her chair, revealing a white frilly lace blouse with a low neckline, showing off her cleavage and large breasts. Her small plump hands with red nail varnish had numerous rings; she wore a man's wristwatch. She said nothing else until her espresso was placed down in front of her, then reached over for the box of paper napkins and removed one, slipping it into the neck of her blouse.

'Don't want to drop coffee down meself,' she said, then lifted the thick cup to her lips and slurped. She placed it carefully down on the saucer. 'I said he was my son, but I disowned him years ago. He was always a nasty little bastard. I even feel sick to admit I give him birth. His father was a nasty bastard too, glad to be rid of him; cancer got him, but I'd have liked to shoot the bugger. Whatever our Arthur gets, he's got it coming to him. He's a disgusting pervert.'

She sipped her coffee again. Her lipstick left marks on the rim of her cup. 'I was in showbusiness.'

'Really?' Anna smiled, surprised.

'Stand-up comic; did the rounds of all the Northern clubs. Now standing is hard enough, never mind making the buggers laugh.' She gave a hoarse throaty laugh; her lipstick was smeared on her row of false teeth.

'You wanted to see me,' Anna prompted her.

'Yes. It's about our Gail.'

'Gail is your daughter?'

'Yes.' Beryl Dunn leaned back. 'She's been trouble as well, but she's a good girl, really – just stupid, know what I mean? She got involved with a man, who left her pregnant with her first kid, our Sharon, but she got a nice council flat out of it. Then she had another one, little Keith – he's a right tearaway, he is – a year or so later, but she got involved with drugs and they kicked her out with two kids, so she came back to live with me.'

Again she paused as she sipped her coffee. 'I couldn't keep her there for long. I got my private life, know what I mean? Anyways, that was several years ago, all water under the bridge.'

She licked her lips and sighed. 'I always forgave her, because of what Arthur done; she had to go to therapy for it. For a while she was safe from him down in London – Hackney, it was – 'cos he was banged up in prison, but they no sooner put the bugger away than he's out again and after her, so she went to the police – you know, to get protection, to keep him away from her.'

Anna nodded her head. She knew all this and was trying to fathom out why Beryl wanted to see her.

'Next thing, he gets out with this no-good bloke called Vernon something or other, and he bloody gets her pregnant! I mean, you'd have thought she'd have learned, but no. Like I said, she's a bit on the stupid side.'

'I saw the little girl,' Anna said. She wondered if this could possibly be Vernon Kramer's child.

'Yeah, Tina's a cute little thing, but Gail would have nothing more to do with Vernon because he was after her other daughter, sick bastard. So she kicked him out and said if he ever came near her again, or near her kids, she'd get him arrested.'

'Was his surname Kramer?'

Beryl tapped the teaspoon on the side of her cup. 'I dunno his surname, but he was a friend of that bugger Arthur. Now look, Detective Inspector, my Gail may be stupid, but she's always had a good heart and she's been a good mother to those kids. She calls me and writes, sends me photographs, and we have always kept in touch. I give her money when I can and see her Christmas-times, if I'm able to.'

She took out a handkerchief and wiped her mouth. 'Few months back, I got a postcard from her saying she was moving to the New Forest with her latest bloke: she was renting some place and said not to let Arthur know where she was, as she'd got this restrainin' order against him. I wouldn't have given him the time of day, let alone told him where she was. I bought her a mobile for her birthday so we could keep in touch; she'd had problems with her phone and not paid the bills. Anyways, next thing I hear, this new bloke has run off and she's living with someone else.'

Anna nodded.

'When I went to see her, I got a shock,' the woman continued. 'I'm no racist, but me, I've never gone with a darkie. He was all right, I suppose. He was clearing up the yard and gonna decorate the bungalow, but Gail said the stench from the pigs made her feel sick.'

'So you went to see her?'

'Yes – that's when I met *him* – called himself Joseph Sickert. Gail started using his surname. Stupid, but she wanted to do it, so . . .' Beryl blinked, and dabbed the corner of her eyes. 'I got a call from her and that's when she told me about you being there, about puttin' Vernon in it, and how they arrested Arthur. She says you was very nice.'

'So you think Vernon Kramer is Tina's father?'

'I'm guessing so. Like I said, I never knew his surname, just that he was some friend of Arthur's. She gets done up 'cos she won't use contraceptives. I wish to Christ *I* had, but we're good Catholics.'

'I liked her,' Anna said quietly. At the same time, she knew that Gail had lied about how well she had known Kramer. It was obvious that if he was the baby's father, he would have seen her more than just the once when he had turned up with Arthur Murphy.

Anna realized Mrs Dunn had been talking and apologized. 'I'm sorry, what did you say?'

'I said, I think something has happened to her. The phone is not turned on, she's not at the bungalow, I dunno where she is. I am worried sick.'

'How long has it been since you last talked to her?'

Beryl tried to remember the exact date. It was around the time Anna had been to see Gail about the photograph.

'She would never usually leave it this long, because I get stuff sent to me for her, you see. Because she was always moving around, I get sent her child support cheques and I post them on to her, but she's not been in touch. I dunno whether or not to report it, and I dunno which place I should go to, you know, to file a missing person. To be honest, I don't want anythin' to do with the police. No disrespect, but I've had a few run-ins in the past and I've just got meself sorted.'

'What do you want me to do?' Anna asked.

'Well, could you find her and tell her to contact me, just so I don't worry, and I can send on her money.'

'Yes, I'll do what I can.'

The plump hand clasped Anna's. 'Thanks, love.'

Beryl Dunn had been married three times and had a history of prostitution going back to the 1960s. She had also served six months for running a brothel and living off immoral earnings.

Anna and Brandon discussed with Sheldon what they should do about Beryl's request, plus the fact that the young child Tina was possibly Vernon Kramer's.

'Pass it over to social services and the local police station where she was last known to be in residence. That's all we can do,' Sheldon said. 'She could be any-where. They can file a missing persons report, or the mother will have to do it herself.'

Anna looked at Brandon. 'Her kids were on an at-risk list from the last place she lived – no wonder, if that bastard Kramer fathered a child with her. I am very concerned, especially as her DSS monies have not been cashed.'

Sheldon sighed. 'Travis, we are not a probation office, or a social service department. Like I said, just pass the report over to her local branch. If she's gone missing, she probably had reasons.'

Anna returned to her desk, wrote up her report for their files and then contacted Gail's local police station. She looked up as Harry Blunt leaned on her desk.

'You worried about her?'

'Yes, I am. It's hard to do a moonlight with three kids, isn't it? And it looked like they left in a big hurry.'

'She'll turn up when she needs money, they usually do; unless you're worried about that Rasta she was with?'

'I am more concerned about the Vernon Kramer link. I mean, she said she had been threatened.'

'But he's banged up and so is Murphy, so there's not a lot either can do now. If they were on the loose, yeah – but not now.'

As she drove home, Anna decided that she would discuss the whole episode with Langton; she'd put it off long enough.

She was surprised that he was not there. There was no note to say where he had gone. There were two suits in her wardrobe and more shirts. She showered and got into a dressing-gown, wondering about dinner; it was now after eight. She went into the kitchen and started emptying the dishwasher, a job she hated and one Langton never did. Just then, the front door banged open.

'You home?' he yelled.

'In the kitchen!' she called back.

He walked in, clean-shaven, hair cut, but still in a tracksuit.

'Here I am,' he said grinning.

'Good heavens, what brought this on?'

He walked out, calling back to her, 'I have my appointment with the police review board.'

She followed him out of the kitchen. 'When?'

'Tomorrow morning.'

'Tomorrow?'

'Yes, I applied last week.'

'Why didn't you tell me?'

'I didn't get a date until today, so there was no reason to tell you. It could have been another week or month.'

'But are you ready for it?'

Langton put his hands on his hips. 'I wouldn't have applied if I didn't think I was. Why, don't you think I'm fit enough?'

'Well, yes, I do, but surely you don't want to rush things?'

'I do. I want to get back to work; my insurance won't cover much more of the treatment.'

She smiled. 'Well, if you think it's the right time ... You are obviously the one who'd know.'

He cupped her face in his hands and kissed her. 'Don't get so worried. I know what I am doing. I wouldn't have applied if I didn't feel up to it.' He kissed her again, then went into the bedroom. 'Just got to decide on which suit, so I'll need your opinion.'

Anna returned to the kitchen. 'I'm going to cook some pasta,' she called, then listened as she heard the shower running. She shook her head, hardly able to believe that without ever mentioning it to her, he had applied for a fitness test. She knew it would be quite a tough one. He would have to be assessed both mentally and physically to remain in office. The Chief Medical Officer would have to certify him as ready to return to work.

She poured some water into a pan and set it on the stove to boil, then opened a packet of spaghetti and took out some tins of chopped tomatoes. She began to cut up an onion to fry with the tomatoes, slicing some garlic and herbs. By the time Langton joined her, fresh from his shower, the sauce was bubbling away and the pasta ready to be drained.

He kissed her neck. 'Smells good.'

She turned, smiling. 'You look good.'

'I feel good.'

He started to open a bottle of wine. She had almost forgotten how handsome he was. He'd looked rough for so long, with his straggling hair and unshaven face; now he really did look like the old Jimmy. In fact, she had to admit that he actually looked a lot better, as he had cut down on his drinking.

He placed two wine glasses down and poured; he passed her glass over. 'To me, for the test tomorrow!'

'To you,' she said, and they clinked glasses and drank. It was yet again not the right time to get into Sickert or discuss Langton's attack.

Chapter Seven

Anna waited until he had dressed. She knew she was going to be late for work, but this was more important. He had switched suits and changed his mind about the shirt and tie three times. As it was also to be a physical test, he packed a clean tracksuit and T-shirt. She offered to drive him but he had ordered a car and he insisted she leave, to give him time to calm down.

Langton waited until the door closed behind her before he took a double dose of painkillers. He had been upping the dosage for some considerable time; the excruciating pain that still lingered, especially in the mornings, made it necessary.

Anna waited all morning for a call; she had no idea how long the test would take. She rang his mobile, but it was turned off. She heard nothing all afternoon. She thought about contacting Lewis to see if he had heard anything, but decided against it. She eventually talked with Harry Blunt about the friend he had mentioned. She tried to sound nonchalant, wondering what kind of tests Langton would be put through if he were to go before the review board.

Harry shrugged; he wasn't too sure. 'Thing is, they're

pretty hot on testing the old brain cells. Basically, if an officer has been through the mill, shot or injured badly, it can do a lot of damage upstairs. They probably do running, jumping, and a few weights for the physical, but I honestly don't know. Is he recovered then?'

'Just wondering,' Anna shrugged.

'Want me to find out?' Harry asked.

'No, no. I was just thinking ahead really.' She did not want to tell any lies, but remembered her promise to Jimmy to stay silent about his progress.

'How's it going with him?'

'Oh, coming along well enough to make my life a misery,' she joked.

'My wife does that to me every day and night. One of my kids has bad asthma and she sometimes has to deal with his attacks solo. We've been in and out of A&E more times than I've had hot dinners.'

Harry continued to talk about his son's asthma and what a game little boy he was, and how frustrating it was because he was such a fighter. Anna smiled and nodded. Langton was a fighter all right; she just wished he would call. She, more than anyone else, knew how important it was for him to get past the police review board. The day dragged on and, driving home, she was unsure of how she would be able to deal with his rejection.

The massive bouquet of flowers was propped on his rowing machine. There was a large card attached to the stems, with her name scrawled in black felt-tipped pen. She opened the envelope. It was actually a birthday card, but he had scribbled over the message and written: *For my little red-headed nurse.* She bit her lip; it was such a simple gesture but so unexpected from him. There was a bottle of champagne on ice in the kitchen sink. He was taking a shower; she opened the bathroom door.

'Why didn't you call me?'

He turned, his hair filled with soapsuds, and grabbed her, drawing her under the water jets. She tried to struggle free, but he wouldn't let her go and he kissed her with such passion she relented and clung to him. She knew her suit would shrink and her shoes would be ruined, but it didn't matter.

Langton had passed the physical examination and spent the afternoon with the Chief Medical Officer, who turned out to be someone he had known for years. After the test, they had gone to a bar and had a few drinks.

'I'm back, Anna! I return to full operational duties next week!'

She couldn't chide him about not contacting her, he was so full of energy and enthusiasm. He told her a number of times about the questions and tests he'd been put through for the psychological part, and how he'd walked through it with ease.

'They didn't stand a hope in hell of catching me out,' he said. Anna caught him flick a glance towards her.

'What do you mean by that?' she asked.

'Nothing.' She could tell he wished he'd kept his mouth shut.

'Caught you out? That's what you said – that they didn't stand a hope in hell of catching you out.'

'For Chrissakes! I just meant they didn't suss that my knee is not in as good a shape as it should be.'

'What did they make you do?'

He sighed with impatience. 'Run on a treadmill, rowing machine, monitored my heart, et cetera, et cetera.'

'And it hurt?'

'Of course it bloody did! But you tell me how often I am gonna need to row over a river to catch someone.' He laughed.

She took a deep breath. 'I want to talk to you.'

'Just drop this, Anna, please. Let's finish the champagne and go to bed.'

'It's not about the review. It's something I should have told you about weeks ago, but I didn't. The time was never right, and then—'

'You want me to leave?'

The look on his face made her want to wrap him in her arms. 'No, of course I don't.'

'Well what is it? Is it something I've done?'

'*No.* Now just shut up for a minute and let me tell you. It's connected in a way to the case I've been on. It's about this guy called Sickert.'

'Who the hell is he?'

'Please don't interrupt me, just listen.'

Langton poured more champagne and then sat with the glass held loosely in his hands as Anna gave him a short summation of the reasons why they had interviewed Gail Sickert, about the photograph and how Anna had returned to the bungalow to see her again. At this point, she got up and opened a drawer, taking out her small tape recorder, and returned to sit opposite him. He put his feet up on the coffee-table and sipped the champagne. He was listening, but he also yawned.

Anna continued talking quietly, not looking at him. She described how she had hurried back to her car as Sickert drew up in his truck.

'This is what he shouted at me. It's quite hard to hear everything, but listen.'

She then pressed Play on the tape. Langton leaned

forwards. She watched him as it got to the point when Sickert threatened her. The tape stopped. He leaned back and gestured for her to replay it. She did; then he drained the glass of champagne and placed it down on the coffee-table.

'Describe him,' he said quietly.

Anna did so, and he nodded his head.

'Anyone in your team opened their mouths about us? Me?'

'No, I've asked, and neither Arthur Murphy nor Vernon Kramer could have known about our relationship.'

'This Sickert got a record?'

'No, I only just found out his Christian name yesterday – it's Joseph – but there's nothing on him on the database.'

'You tell me why you think he said what he said.'

Anna shrugged. 'Well, it could have just been a blind threat – you know, coincidence – and I would have sort of accepted it, until—'

'Until what?'

'Well, they've disappeared, and in a hurry – that's Gail, her three kids and Sickert. Yesterday her mother called and asked to speak to me; she wouldn't come into the station, so I met her in a café. She's worried about Gail and her kids as she's made no contact. We've reported it to the local cop shop, but whether or not social services will help trace her, we don't know. Her mother wanted me to file a missing person's report, which you know I can't do. She said she forwards on Gail's child-support cheques from Newcastle, where she herself lives, and as she's had no contact, she's been unable to send them.'

Langton remained silent.

'She had no money, the place was a shithole, and they owed rent. The kids had been on the risk-lists of a number of social services from Newcastle to London. Gail herself had taken out a restraining order against her brother Arthur Murphy; he had molested her when she was a kid.'

'But he's banged up, isn't he?'

'Yes, since his arrest. The trial's due and it's very unlikely he'll be out in under twelve years. Vernon got eighteen months for his part in hiding out Murphy and, as he broke his parole, he will serve out the rest of his sentence: maybe two years. It's all so murky. Vernon is the father of Gail's youngest child, but she found out he was going after her elder daughter, so she kicked him out. She must have met Vernon through her brother – he's got a record for being a sex offender, it's so sick – anyway, at some point after her husband had left her, she then met up with Sickert – maybe via them, I wouldn't know – but it had to be within the last year or so; the little girl is still in nappies and looks about eighteen months old. Obviously, the local cops will report back to us if they find any connection to our murder enquiry, because it is worrying that Gail has not contacted her mother for her money . . .'

Langton remained silent again as Anna trailed off. She reached over to touch his arm, but he withdrew it.

'I was going to tell you so many times, and then . . . You know, it could all be coincidence, what he said to me. What do you think?'

'Not sure,' he said flatly.

Anna got up and opened her briefcase; she took out the file of the newspaper clippings she'd taken from his flat.

'I also wanted to talk to you about these.' She placed the file down in front of him, but didn't open it; instead, she went on to tell him about her talks with both Lewis and Barolli.

'I tried to get them to explain a few things. They both took so long getting back to me, as they're on enquiries and pretty busy, but I got the feeling that they didn't really want to know: they felt you were putting pressure on them to trace your attacker, and ... They said they couldn't act like some kind of vigilantes, but I was stunned that, after what had happened to you, nothing seemed to be being done about trying to track the men down. Lewis was sure they would have got out of the country by now anyway.'

She wished Jimmy would say something, but he just remained silent, so she kept going.

'When I was at your flat looking for some clean clothes, I found these newspaper cuttings. I know you've been collecting more whilst you've been here with me.'

He glared at her.

'I wasn't snooping about; they were in the drawer with your pyjamas.' She waited, and then stood up. 'For Chrissake, why don't you say something?'

He suddenly hurled the champagne glass at the wall; it shattered, spraying the contents over the wallpaper.

'Well, that was a reaction!' she said angrily.

'What the fuck do you want me to say?' he grunted, and hauled himself to his feet, his face twisted with pain. 'You sneak around, acting as if I was some mental retard that couldn't deal with any of the shit you've just laid on me. These ... these!' He snatched up the file. 'Just my personal research, nothing ulterior, nothing weird, just information for me to store up because of the screw-up confronting the Met. Like Lewis, like fucking Barolli, I am not intending to act like some vigilante to get these sons of bitches, nor did I ever at any time ask them to do anything improper or against the law. All I did ask was for them to keep me updated, because it isn't over – not for me. I am *not* going to walk away and pretend this never happened. Why do you think I've been pushing myself to get back on the force? I want the fucker that sliced me open, and I'll find him – but I'm not hiring a mask and a cloak, for Chrissakes!'

'I never said you—'

'You never said – that is it, isn't it? You kept all this quiet, never opened your mouth about all this.' He wafted the file. 'Why in God's name didn't you talk to me?'

'Because the time was never right! You almost died!'

'You think I don't know that?'

'Maybe what you don't know was what the effect of your injuries did to me and to everyone who knew you. I was afraid for you.'

'Afraid?'

'Yes. I didn't want to upset you.'

'Upset me?'

'Yes! All I wanted was for you to get better; that was all I ever wanted and if I did wrong, then I'm sorry, all right? I'm sorry I tried to protect you.'

'Protect me from what?'

She burst into tears.

'What the hell are you crying for?'

'Because you make me feel as if I have done something wrong, when all I was doing, trying to do, was make sure you got well and fit.'

He stared at her, so angry that she could see the muscle in his cheek twitching. 'I'm never going to be fit; I'll have this for the rest of my life.' He pulled open his shirt to show the scar. 'I'll look at this every day for the rest of my life. I'll feel the ache in my knee just as a reminder. But they never slashed my brain, Anna; they never damaged my fucking head, and for you to tiptoe around, afraid I wouldn't be able to deal . . .'

Anna turned and slammed out of the room and went into the bedroom. She flung herself onto the bed face down.

He kicked open the door. 'I haven't finished. Don't you walk out on me like this!'

'*I've* finished!' she shouted.

'Have you? You mean, there isn't anything else you felt I couldn't cope with?'

She whipped round. 'I tell you what I am finding hard to cope with. You are a thankless, egotistical bastard, who never thinks of anyone but yourself. I have had to put up with all your shit for how many weeks? I can't move in my own flat, but have you heard me complain? Have you? And all I tried to do was care for you, protect you. I didn't want to bring up anything I've said tonight, for one reason. I didn't want it to worry you.'

He was about to interrupt, but she flung a pillow at him.

'Just for one second think about *me*; think about what *I* have gone through. I doubt that you can, because all you ever really think about is yourself!'

'Well, now I *am* thinking of you. The sooner I get out of your life is obviously going to be the best for both of us!'

'Fine – go ahead. You do exactly what you want, like you always do.'

Langton threw his clothes into a suitcase. She watched

him for a few minutes before she walked out into the kitchen. She made herself a cup of coffee and sat at her breakfast bar, listening to him banging around the bedroom. After about fifteen minutes, he appeared in the doorway.

'I'll get the rest of my stuff packed up tomorrow.'

'Whatever you want.'

He called a taxi and chucked his set of spare keys onto the coffee-table. She looked at him as he carried his case to the front door.

'Won't you need your keys to get into the flat to move all this crap out? Your bicycle, your rowing machine?'

'I'll let you know when I can get them moved out over to my place.'

Then he was gone.

All the shelves in the bathroom where he'd kept his rows of pills were empty. She was quite shocked, not at the available space, but how he had in such a rage remembered to take them all. He'd left some socks and a pair of shoes, his dirty laundry in the basket, a few shirts and one suit. She felt like taking a pair of scissors and cutting them to shreds; instead, she slammed the wardrobe door and went to clean up the broken champagne glass. Tipping it into the bin in the kitchen, she noticed a number of empty pill bottles. She took them out. They were all his painkillers but some of them, she noticed, had different strengths and, oddly enough, various labels, all from different chemists. She threw them back into the bin, tied up the plastic bag and placed it by the front door to take to the bins outside the next morning.

Anna had a terrible night. She couldn't sleep, yet she didn't feel like crying. The more she tossed and turned, the more angry she felt at the way he had behaved. She would not contact him; she was sure that, when he thought about the entire situation, he would apologize. She'd wait, because she did not feel she had in any way been at fault; all she had ever done was consider his recovery to be the most important thing. All *he* had very obviously done was selfishly make it his sole priority. Well, he had achieved what he was so determined to do: he had been reinstated as a leading detective in the Murder Squad. She would no doubt read about him in the *Police Gazette,* and by next week he would be attached to a murder enquiry.

Arthur Murphy's trial would soon be over and she would be onto another case, obviously not with Langton. If he went down on bended knee for her to join whatever team he was selecting, she would never work alongside him again. In fact, by four o'clock in the morning, she had worked herself up into such a fury that she dragged down one of her own suitcases and hurled into it everything she could find that he had left behind. She then went into the hall and chucked it onto his rowing machine.

When Anna returned to bed, she decided she would ask Harry to help her remove everything and leave it at Langton's flat. She punched her pillow with her fist and dragged the duvet cover around herself.

The next thing, she was jolted awake by her alarm clock. She reached over to slap it off with the flat of her hand and lay there for a moment, her heart thudding. The silence, the total silence, did it to her; she broke down and sobbed. It was over, he'd gone, and already she missed him.

★

Arthur George Murphy was sentenced to life with a minimum term of fifteen years for the murder of Irene Phelps. His mother, Beryl Dunn, sat almost hidden at the end of the gallery. Three of Irene's co-workers from the library sat in the centre of the gallery, staring at the smug gloating face of their friend's killer, unaware his mother was so close. Irene's parents wept, holding each other's hands. Murphy showed no remorse, and shrugged his shoulders in the dock as if the sentence meant nothing.

As Anna left the court, Beryl Dunn hurried towards her.

'Excuse me? Hello!'

Anna had seen Beryl but didn't really want to face her again.

'I've still not heard from our Gail,' she said loudly. She was wearing the same clothes she had worn in the café, and her make-up looked as if she'd just given it another layer. 'Did you do anything about it for me?'

Anna saw Brandon making a quick exit, and she hesitated.

Mrs Dunn continued. 'Like I said, I've not heard from her. Something's got to be done – I mean, she's not even called me.'

'I gave the local police near her bungalow the details, and they will have no doubt contacted social services.'

'Did you report her missing?'

'No. I told you that you would have to make a formal report.'

'But that's not right; she's never not kept in touch and I got her social cheques and her child support. I told you they get sent to me, now why wouldn't she want them?'

'Mrs Dunn, if you really think something is wrong then –'

'I know something is.'

'– then make a report.'

'Fuck off,' she said, and pushed past Anna.

It was then that Irene's ex-husband walked towards Anna. He introduced himself and thanked her, as Beryl banged out of the court. He was a tall, rather gaunt man, with thinning sandy hair and a dark navy suit.

'I am Kenneth Phelps,' he said, then hesitated, as if saying his name was somehow embarrassing.

'How is your daughter?' she asked.

'Natalie is gradually settling down with us in Devon, but it's very hard; she misses her mother, obviously. We have some help from a counsellor, but of course, she has nightmares. Her grandparents visit when they can. Eventually, she'll make new friends at the school, but right now, we just take it day by day.'

Anna watched him walk over to join Irene's mother and father; at least he was not alone.

Outside, Harry Blunt made Anna jump as he put his arm around her.

'Want a lift?'

'Yes, thanks. That's Irene's ex-husband and her parents,' she said, watching their car go past.

'I know,' he said, then burst out: 'Bastard got fifteen years, will probably serve even less; while that little girl will be twenty-seven years old when he gets out. *She's* the one with the life sentence.'

'Actually, Harry, I think I'm going to walk for a while, but thanks for the offer.'

'Up to you.' He started to walk away then stopped. 'Eh! I heard Langton's back – bloody unbelievable. We all thought he was a goner; tough bastard, isn't he?'

She nodded and walked away, not wanting to discuss

it or now to ask Harry to help her move the exercise equipment, after all.

'Been good working with you, Travis!' he called after her.

She turned and forced a smile. 'Thanks, Harry.'

Anna knew she would have a couple of days before she was assigned to another enquiry, so decided to put them to good use: maybe take a weekend at a spa and pamper herself. She tried not to think about Langton, but it was very difficult, with her hallway still occupied by his stuff. At home, her answerphone light was blinking; her heart thudded with the expectation of a message from him, but it was Brandon, saying he'd missed her after the trial. The second message was from Mike Lewis, congratulating Langton: he'd just heard the news – it was going round the Met like bushfire! She deleted the messages and then jumped as her doorbell rang.

It was a short square Indian, with a terrible striped sweater. He showed Anna his pick-up order and delivery drop.

She watched the poor man almost give himself a hernia as he carried out the bicycle and then took apart the rowing machine. He said he couldn't take the suitcase, as that was not on his list. Anna grabbed her purse and took out a ten-pound note.

'Just take it to the same address, would you?'

He agreed. After he'd left, she opened the kitchen windows for a through draught and lit a scented candle, to reclaim her space. She had to hand it to Langton. He didn't do things by halves – walking out and then hiring the van and driver, without even one call to her. Well, she could be just as cold. There was no way she would contact him now. She was just going to get on with her life and think back to that list she had made about how difficult it was living with him. Well, he was not living with her any more – and she hoped *that* went round the Met like bushfire!

Chapter Eight

Tom Adams, the landlord of the property in the New Forest rented by Gail Sickert, had done little with it since she had gone. The partly built henhouse that Sickert had been working on was left boarded up; stacks of planks leaned against it. The chickens had been sold, but Adams still made regular visits to feed the pigs and goat. Finding another tenant was not easy; the bungalow required extensive renovations.

Everything had been left half-attended to, from the manure heap to the broken fences. Children's toys still littered the bare lawn, and the drive had even more potholes due to the heavy rain. Driving his old jeep, as he arrived to feed the animals, Adams crashed the gears as it plunged into a small crater. Swearing, he continued round to the pigsties.

Tipping their food into the troughs, he was thankful that they at least had been left behind. The pigs had come as part of the deal; Gail had agreed to feed them and clear out the walled pens. When the time was right, they, too, would be sold. Adams sloshed through the mud to get the rakes for clearing up the sties, turned on a hose and began to swill down the pens as the pigs gobbled up their food.

Moments later, a patrol car hit the same mud-filled crater as it drove into the yard. Two uniformed local officers got out and approached the stinking pigpens, mindful of the mud and sewage that covered the old cobbled yard.

'You found my tenants then, have you?' Adams greeted them, switching off the hose. 'I was just thinking, at least they didn't take me effing pigs, but they left the place in about the same state. I don't think that woman cleaned the house once since they moved in.' He crossed to a small digger, and climbed up.

'Mr Adams? We've had an enquiry about your tenants; have you had any contact from them?'

'I'm not likely to, am I? They left owing me two months' rent.'

One of the officers put his hand over his mouth. 'The stench is terrible,' he said, gagging.

'It's worse than usual, 'cos they've not been cleaned out. I was just hosing down the pens before you came.' The man turned, pointing to the manure heap. 'I'm going to have to shift that over to the back field; they just bloody dumped it! You see the henhouse? They got me to pay for the wood to rebuild it – and look at it!' He started up the engine and headed for the manure heap.

The two officers stood around for a few more minutes and then took off, climbing back into the patrol car. They were almost at the end of the drive, when Adams came running after them, waving his arms and hollering at the top of his voice. They pulled up and the officer in the passenger seat rolled down his window.

'Jesus Christ, you'd better come back and see what I've found!' he said, then rested his hand against the side of the patrol car and threw up.

The partly decomposed body was minus limbs. But even in the appalling state of mutilation, the body half-caught in the shovel of the digger was obviously a female.

Anna was in bed reading, when the phone rang. It was Brandon. He didn't waste time apologizing for the late-night call.

'I thought you'd like to know: the local police sent to check on Gail Sickert reckon they have found her body.'

'What?'

'Yeah, and it gets worse. They think she may have been partly fed to the pigs; her limbs are missing. They can't be one hundred per cent sure it is her.'

'Dear God.'

'Yeah. So far, they've not found any remains of her kids. They asked for you to be contacted.'

'Why me?'

'You called them to check on her whereabouts, right?'

'Yes – yes, I did.'

'Well, they want to see you. They'll also need her mother to identify the remains. You've got her contact numbers, haven't you?'

'Yes.'

'No need to do anything tonight; call them in the morning. The murder enquiry will be out of our jurisdiction, so nothing more to do with us.'

'I'll do that, thanks.'

Anna replaced the phone, and then lay back on her pillow. There was no way she would call Beryl Dunn herself; she would give her details to the station and hopefully that would be all. At the same time, she could not help but feel guilty; it was hard to take in the full horror of what might have taken place. She couldn't get out of her mind the memory of the dirty little child in her play swing.

Unable to sleep, she got up, made herself a cup of tea and telephoned the station in the New Forest. She was told that there was no one she could speak to at that time of night, and that she should call the next morning and ask for a Detective Inspector Brian Mallory. She gave her name, and said that she had been an investigating officer on a murder enquiry dealing with Gail's brother, Arthur Murphy.

'I'll pass the message on.'

'Has the victim been identified yet?'

'I'm unable to give you any details, DI Travis.'

She was afraid he was going to cut her off. 'Just one moment – I also would like to give you a contact number, in case the victim needs to be identified. Mrs Beryl Dunn is Gail Sickert's mother.'

It seemed to take an interminable time for the duty Constable to take down the details. Anna ended up leaving her mobile number with him.

At seven-thirty the following morning, as Anna stepped out of the shower, her mobile phone rang. It was Mallory. He sounded very edgy.

'Detective Inspector Travis, I would really appreciate it if you would come to the station first thing this morning. You apparently called last night? I would really like to talk to you.'

'Have you managed to contact Beryl Dunn?'

'Not as yet.'

'Has anyone identified the victim?'

'No, and we have as yet not found any other remains.'

'Thank God.'

There was a pause. 'Detective Travis, the victim is still at the site. Could you meet me there?'

'Is it necessary?'

'Yes, it is. We have got a management team organized. How soon can you get here? It's just I would like as much information as possible, before an MIT team comes on board.'

Anna said she would meet him at ten, which gave her plenty of time to drive there. She wasn't stupid; she knew they were unable to say whether or not the body was Gail Sickert. That's what they needed her for; only then would they contact a relative for a formal ID.

Nowadays, the police system was run so differently from the way it had been in the past. Most local police stations dealt with traffic, burglary and any locally connected crime; murder was now only dealt with by a qualified and experienced team of specially trained detectives. An incident room would be set up at the local station and used as a base by the new team. Pathologists and forensic scientists would be brought in as quickly as possible. Anna hoped that by the time she did get to the bungalow, the murder team would be in motion and she could therefore get away as soon as possible.

The rain was lashing down and the drive to the bungalow awash; a number of patrol cars were parked up on the edges. She drove through the puddles and potholes as far as she could before a uniformed officer, wearing a cape, signalled for her to stop. She gave her name and said that she was here to meet Detective Inspector Brian Mallory. She was directed round to the back yard and asked to leave her car parked in the designated area.

Anna was glad she had put her Wellington boots and umbrella into the passenger seat-well. She wove her way round thick pools of mud and slime, and approached the yellow police crime scene cordons. She could see a lot of white-suited forensic officers moving in and around the area, their wagon parked up. The digger had been moved back and they were erecting a big white tent to cover the partly dug manure heap.

'Is Detective Inspector Mallory here?' she asked a female officer, who was standing with a big black umbrella.

'Far side of the piggery, under the tarpaulin,' she said.

Anna skirted around the crime scene ribbons towards the makeshift shelter. The officers were huddled together, as the rain was now even worse. Parked over to one side, away from the action, was the catering truck known as Teapot One.

Anna ducked beneath the tarpaulin and shook her umbrella outside.

'Hi, are you Detective Inspector Travis?'

Anna gave a tight smile. 'Yes, I'm DI Travis. Are you DI Mallory?'

'Yes.' Mallory was a thick-set man with iron-grey cropped hair and a red face with puffy cheeks. He reached out a big, thick-fingered hand to shake hers. 'Thanks for coming; you want a coffee or tea?'

'No, thank you.' She looked around. 'This is pretty grim.'

'We've got masks if you go into the forensic tent, but it's pretty well stinking all round. The pigs have been shut up, but they're going to be moved out this morning by the landlord.'

The stench was getting to her, and she wrinkled her nose with distaste. 'Wow, this is bad, isn't it?'

He nodded. 'We can talk in one of the patrol cars.'

'I'm fine here, but I would like a mask.'

'Right, I'll get one for you.'

The other men under the tarpaulin were all in uniform; she gave a small nod to them, as Mallory returned with a mask in a plastic bag.

'Have you found any other remains?' she asked.

'No, but then we didn't do much of a search until we had the forensic teams in. We didn't know what we should do. You know these murder teams like to get busy and not have their crime scene messed up, so I did it by the book. To be honest, we can't cope with a major incident like this.'

Ripping open her plastic bag, Anna took out the mask, hooking the strings round her neck and pushing it up over her nose and mouth.

'Who's handling the investigation?' she asked, her voice muffled.

'Not been informed; being here, I'm not up to speed about what's going on at the station.'

'Anyway, you wanted to talk to me?'

'Yes. You came here to interview Gail Sickert, or Summers, as she was called. I know you came back for a second visit.'

'Yes.'

'Well, we took your report seriously. I sent two men out here, but they didn't get into the place; then when you contacted us again, I sent them back and ...'

He nodded over to the white tent that was now almost fully erected and the forensic experts getting ready to check over the corpse. 'We will have to pull down the henhouse and check around the pigpen, but we can't really do that until the animals have been moved out.'

Anna nodded and then, without being asked, gave a detailed explanation of why she had been at the bungalow and her subsequent meeting with Gail Sickert's mother. 'I did explain to the station last night.'

'Yes, I know, but the phone number for Mrs Dunn has been cut off – bill unpaid – so we are getting someone from Newcastle on standby to visit her. We'll need to ID the victim if possible.'

'She had three children,' Anna said quietly.

'I know. Like I said, we've not done a thorough search so we won't know yet. I'm praying to God we don't find them, but they could be anywhere around this awful place.' He turned away, his red cheeks puffing out like a blowfish. 'Worst scenario is they might have been cut up and ...' He shook his head. 'Terrible to even think about it, but it's been done before. Pigs'll eat anything.'

Anna pressed her mask to her face and glanced over to the white tent. 'Well, let's do it. Have you asked the landlord to look at her?'

'Yes. He couldn't say either way. She's pretty decomposed, partly due to the manure eating away at her.'

Anna stepped out and put up her umbrella. Mallory followed and they headed towards the tent.

Inside the tent, the only good thing that could be said was that it was dry. The stench was overpowering and her mask didn't give much relief. She was guided towards the white plastic floor sheeting; lying exposed was the head and torso. Anna had by now been on a number of very gruesome murder cases but this was, if possible, one of the worst.

The dead woman was naked, apart from a pink brassière around her exposed breasts. Her arms and legs were missing, and her face and body were covered with manure and millions of maggots. Her thin blonde hair covered one side of what was left of her face. Anna could only see her profile.

'Can you move the hair away for me, please?' Anna asked one of the scientists. He knelt down and, using a thin wooden spatula, eased back the mud-clogged hair.

Anna had to lean in very close; she moved around to the other side, staring down at the remains. She straightened up.

'I can clean her face up a bit more if you like?' the scientist suggested; Anna nodded. With a tissue, he carefully wiped some mud and grime away and gently turned the dead woman's head to face upwards.

Again Anna bent down; this time when she straightened up, she was certain.

She looked towards Mallory. 'Yes, that's Gail Sickert.'

'Oh,' he said flatly, and gestured to the body. 'I was just hoping it wouldn't be her, because of the children.'

Anna thanked the forensic scientist who had cleaned Gail's face. He gave a rueful smile. 'This is going to be a very unpleasant job. We've got a lot of area to search for any other remains. I'm getting help shipped in; we are going to need it.'

Anna returned to the station with Mallory, who would now give the go-ahead for Beryl Dunn to be contacted and brought to the mortuary. At least she would not have to see the state in which her daughter had been discovered.

Anna followed Mallory into the local station's small

169

car park. He was talking on his mobile as he gestured for Anna to go in ahead of him. By the time he joined her, he was looking even redder in the face. Anna thought that perhaps he had been given more news about the children.

'Have they found more?' she asked.

'No no, that was from Scotland Yard homicide division; they're sending in some DCI to handle the case.'

'Did they give you a name?'

'No, they didn't. But it's unusual, isn't it? I mean, we're in the sticks out here. To be honest, I'm way out of my depth,' he continued as he ushered Anna towards his office. 'We've had a number of bodies over the years – you know, dumped in the forest – but not like this. I'll be glad to hand over the reins.'

He plumped his wide backside into a swivel chair, saying, 'I just need to take down all the information,' and searched in a desk drawer to take out a statement notepad.

Anna sat opposite him. 'Perhaps they are interested because of the victim's connection to Arthur Murphy?'

'Could be.' He was now looking for a pen.

'The SIO on the Murphy case was a DCI Sheldon.'

He shook his head and then patted his pockets. 'Got it. Right, let's go from the top. The first time you met Gail, she was using the surname Sickert; previous to that, Summers, and her maiden name was Dunn – that all correct?'

It was painfully slow; Mallory wrote everything down in full, constantly holding up his hand for her to pause. He would reread everything she had just said, before he continued.

'And on these two occasions you met her, did anything else happen?'

Anna described the interaction with Sickert, but did not mention the threat he had made to her. She just said he was very aggressive.

'Can you describe him? You say his Christian name was Joseph.'

Anna nodded and then tried to conjure up his face; she was only really able to give the details that he was black, wore his hair in dreadlocks and that he was very well-built and over six feet tall.

'Did she seem afraid of him?'

'Yes. She was worried by the presence of the police.'

'I see. So far, we have been unable to trace him. We've got prints from the house, but we've no previous on him.'

'Yes, I was told.' Anna looked at her wristwatch, impatient now to leave.

'Can you describe the children?'

'Well, the youngest child, Tina, is a toddler. There was a daughter Sharon, blonde and very skinny; I think she is seven. The boy, Keith, I only saw once. I am sure the local school will be able to give you more details, as will the social services.'

Anna stood up as his desk phone rang. He excused himself for taking the call.

'DI Mallory.' He listened, then put his hand over the phone. 'It's Newcastle; they've traced the victim's mother.'

'I can show myself out, all right?'

He nodded and returned to the phone call. By the way his cheeks puffed out, she knew it was someone important. She made her escape fast, closing the door quietly behind her. As she passed through the station, she saw an incident room being set up: the telltale desks being moved along a corridor and two officers carrying computers. She pressed her back against the wall as they squeezed past, then continued out to the car park, where she sat for a while in her car. She could still smell the stench on her clothes. She closed her eyes, not wanting anything more to do with the hideousness, but it lingered like the smell of death mixed with manure. She hoped to God they would not find the remains of the children.

The first thing Anna did when she got home was shower and wash her hair to get rid of the stench. As she stepped out of the shower, her landline rang. She wrapped a towel around herself to answer it.

'Anna?' Langton's voice sent shockwaves through her.

'Yes,' she said, almost inaudibly.

'I'm going to head up the murder enquiry.'

She remained silent.

'You were out there this morning.'

'Yes.' She was shaking.

'I asked to be put onto the case. You will obviously know why.'

She swallowed.

He continued. 'I don't want there to be any mention of Sickert's taped shouting match with you. Did you bring it up at all?'

'No.'

'Good. I'll mention it when it's the right time, but it's obvious that there would be grave concerns if there was a direct link to my attack. Hampshire police are setting up the incident room; I've got Mike Lewis on board, and—'

She interrupted him. 'Why are you calling me?'

'Because, like it or not, I have requested you join my team.'

'No!'

'What?'

'I said no. I'm sorry, I just don't think under the circumstances it would be—'

'Bullshit! Whatever our personal differences are, we leave them out of it. I want you with me.'

'I can't, I'm sorry.'

'Yes, you can.'

'No, I can't.'

'Listen to me! You don't have any option.'

'I will not work with you!'

'You are the only person who can recognize this Sickert bastard! You also have to feel some guilt about what has happened.'

'Well, I don't.'

'That's more bullshit! I know you, and I know you knew the victim; if they find her kids buried with her, you will want to be on the enquiry. The bastard chopped her to pieces, Anna.'

'You shit!'

He ignored this and went on. 'I'm on my way there now, so the sooner you can get yourself back to the murder site, the better. Also, I've brought in Harry Blunt, as Barolli wasn't available. Plus I've asked for some serious back-up on the forensic, as it's apparently a hell of a job and Hampshire police are a bit out of their depth. Anna?'

She took a deep breath. 'I really do not want to work with you, so I am asking you again: please, get someone else.'

'See you there as soon as you can make it.' He cut off the call and she stood there holding the receiver, still dripping from the shower.

Right, she thought. If this is the way he wants it, fine! He's not going to make me act unprofessionally, no way. I'm going to be there, DCI Bloody Langton, and I'll show you how I can act as if nothing had ever gone on between us!

It was after three when Anna returned to the bungalow. This time, she was dressed for the rain and filth. She didn't use her umbrella but wore her raincape and headed straight for the crime ribbons. The first person she saw, looking very green, was Harry Blunt.

'Afternoon, Harry,' she said.

He turned. 'Dear God, the stench in the forensic tent is overpowering. I've already puked up.'

'DCI Langton in there, is he?'

'Yeah, with his pal Mike Lewis. Have you got any spearmint?'

'No. Sorry.'

'So, back together sooner than you thought, eh?'

'What?' She thought he was referring to her and Langton.

'You and me.'

'Oh yes.' She pulled on her white paper suit and overshoes as Harry stripped off his.

'I'm going over to the incident room,' he said. 'They're taking her to the mortuary any time now, so I've made excuses – anything to get out of here.'

'Not found any other remains?'

'No, thank Christ, but they're not even in the piggery section yet. They've been carted off, the pigs; apparently

174

the landlord of the place swilled everywhere down and hosed their pens, so maybe we won't find anything. I hope to God we don't.'

Anna fixed her mask in place, and drew back the flap of the tent to go back in.

Langton was kneeling, leaning in very close to the body. As he straightened, he saw her and gestured for her to come to his side. Her heart felt as if it was going to explode in her chest; she felt the blood rush to her cheeks. She clenched her teeth to maintain control, thankful the mask hid part of her face.

It was as if the past eighteen months of living with him had never happened and the horror of his injuries had not taken place. He showed no sign of any kind of emotion on seeing her; on the contrary, he was cold and professional, even down to the tone of his voice.

'You've identified her, right?'

'Yes, sir.'

'Do you want to take another look, just to be certain?'

'They have contacted her mother.'

'I know, but it's going to take some time to bring her here from Newcastle, so I'd like to be sure.'

Anna bent down and again looked at the mottled, beaten face of Gail Sickert.

'Yes, it's her.'

'Good. Right, we might as well let her go to the mortuary now, so we can head back to the incident room.' Langton gestured to the forensic team. 'They're going to have to sift through that heap of bloody manure and then do a search of every inch of the place. He could have fed the kids to the pigs, but the landlord—'

She interrupted. 'I know – he swilled the pens down.'

'Right.' Langton walked ahead of her and lifted the flap to exit.

Anna followed and began to remove her paper suit. He was already rolling his into a tight ball and chucking it into the bin provided.

'You remember the Fred West case?' he grunted.

'Of course I do.'

'The only way the teams could sift through his stinking garden was to shovel everything through women's tights. We're a bit more advanced, but not that much, so these poor bastards have a filthy job on their hands. We're looking for bone fragments; anything that might indicate the children died here as well.'

Anna followed him as he strode across the muddy yard; the rain had stopped, but the puddles were still deep. He was wearing big black Wellington boots and his old brown Driza-Bone raincape. As he reached the area where the squad cars were parked, she saw him light a cigarette. So much for his health regime!

Langton turned and saw her Mini parked on the bank at the side of the potholed drive. 'See you there.'

He got into the patrol car and was driven away. He had shown not so much as a flicker of emotion, nor had he made any reference to the situation between them. It was hard for her to be able to maintain her cool, but Anna felt that so far, she'd done well. Question was, would she be able to keep it up?

The incident room in the Hampshire station was still pretty rough, but they had shipped in more computers and there now were eight desks. Anna placed her briefcase onto her allocated desk next to Harry Blunt's; he was sucking peppermints.

'Christ, the stench clings to you, doesn't it?'

'Yes,' she said, taking off her jacket and placing it onto the back of her chair.

'You think the fucker fed the kids to the pigs?'

'Harry, I don't know – but like you said, I hope to God he didn't.'

Langton walked in and signalled to Anna to join him.

'I want you to sit with the artist we've brought in from London and get an Identikit picture of this Sickert. We need it out as fast as possible. We've no trace on him or any kind of record, so he's using an assumed name, is an illegal immigrant, whatever. Wherever he is, if he's still got the kids with him, he's going to be easier to trace.'

Langton turned to Mike Lewis, who gave Anna a half-smile of acknowledgement as he handed over photographs. 'Local school had these taken at half-term, so they're up to date: a boy aged six, and a girl aged seven, both white . . .'

Anna interjected, 'The baby, the little girl I saw, was also white, about eighteen months old.'

'She's twenty-four months,' Langton said. They had reports on her from the local clinic. He gestured at the board: as yet, it was empty. 'We are hoping Gail's mother will bring some photographs of the victim, but we want these kids' faces up there and out to the press. So, Anna – get cracking on the drawing, and then work on an ident computer image. We want it out asap.'

The whole place was hopping. The local officers attached to the investigation were running around like scalded hens. Langton threw out instructions and orders at such a pace, you could see them virtually tripping over each other.

Anna sat for over an hour with the artist. By that time, he had a likeness, or as much of one as she was able to remember. They then worked together on the computerized images to see if she could better it.

Langton walked in and leaned against the back of her chair. 'How much longer?'

'I am going as fast as I can,' the artist said.

Anna remained silent and concentrated on the computer image. She could feel Langton close, almost touching her; she moved away slightly.

'Okay. As soon as you are through, Anna, I want you in the incident room for a briefing.'

She was about to say something when he walked away.

Anna was printing off the images of Joseph Sickert when she was called to Langton's office. This was connected to the incident room, but was very small and cramped.

'Is this about the briefing?' she asked.

'That tape recording of Sickert – you still have it?'

'Yes, I've brought it in.'

'Good. You can leave it with me.'

She nodded. 'I'll go and get it.'

She walked out and returned to her desk. She had just taken the tape out from her briefcase, when Langton appeared and bellowed that he wanted everyone gathered for a briefing. As he made his way to stand in front of everyone, she noticed that he limped slightly; maybe the damp and wet from the piggery had got to him. She thought how much she would have liked to tip that manure over his head.

'Okay, everyone, listen up.'

They gathered round, the locals standing at the back

of the room. By now, the incident-room board had been worked on. Photographs of the two children and the sketch of Sickert were now pinned up. There were also numerous other pictures and details that Anna was unable to check out at that moment, as everyone was focused on Langton.

'We have a pretty solid ID of the victim made by DI Travis, but we will still need her to be formally identified by her mother, who should be here around six o'clock. The mortuary by then will have cleaned up the victim; she will be covered so as to cause as little anguish as possible. We have the children's photographs, as you can see; as yet, no remains have been recovered. We also have an Identikit picture of our suspect, known as Joseph Sickert.'

Langton continued the briefing, covering the ground usual at this early stage of an enquiry. The post mortem and subsequent report would not be available to them for some time; all they knew was that the body had been mutilated; her arms and legs were still missing. He told everyone that it was imperative they get as much help from the locals, the social services and the local stores.

'They lived there for over a year, so they must have known plenty of people. So get out there and find out as much as you can. The focus is on Sickert: we have to find him. We need to track down anyone with any information.'

Langton went on, asking for the landlord, Tom Adams, to be pumped for more information. The pigs had been taken to another location; the police would perform tests and possibly even slaughter one or more to find out if they had human remains in their intestines. He made everyone laugh when he said that Adams was up in arms about them being slaughtered; he'd said, in a state of fury, that they were not ready. He planned on feeding them up before selling them onto the market and it would be down to the police to pay for them!

Langton then gave a brief rundown of what they had otherwise been able to get from Mr Adams: he did recall Joseph Sickert, and had had a few exchanges with him, as he had done with Gail's previous husband. Adams had agreed to pay Sickert some money, as the man had said he would clean the piggery and build a henhouse.

The only other person that Adams admitted to seeing at the bungalow apart from Gail's children was . . .' Langton smiled and lifted a statement.

'I'll quote his actual words, so no one's going to aim anti-racial slurs at me. Mr Adams says, "There was another darkie standing in the kitchen, but if it wasn't for his hair being shorter than Sickert's – he wasn't wearing that carpet thing on his head – I wouldn't have known if it was him or not, as they all look alike to me!"'

Anna had to hand it to him; Langton was a performer, able to mimic Adams to perfection. The team smiled.

Langton held a long pause before continuing. 'One last thing. I don't know how much you have been told about my recovery, but to assuage any gossip, I have been given the all clear – upstairs and down. I intend to give this case one hundred per cent and I want each and every one of you to do the same. I want this man Sickert caught. He is our prime suspect.'

He did another one of his famous pauses and tapped a desk with his pencil.

'Travis and Harry Blunt got a tip-off in their investigation of Irene Phelps's murder from a photograph of Gail Sickert's: Arthur Murphy was hiding out with a known criminal and child molester, Vernon Kramer. They were able to pick up Murphy because of his association with Kramer. Kramer may well have fathered Gail's youngest child. Our missing suspect would also have known Kramer, so I am making him a priority. I want to interview him as soon as possible—'

Langton was interrupted by Mike Lewis, who had taken a call at his desk.

'Sir, could you please take this call? It's from the murder site.'

The room fell silent as Langton picked up the phone. He said little, listening to the caller; it seemed to take an interminable time until he ended the call with a long sigh. He then faced the room.

'Ladies and gentlemen, I'm sorry – it's not good. They have just discovered the skull of a small child.'

Chapter Nine

Vernon Kramer was not a happy man. He was in Wandsworth prison for his part in harbouring Murphy and, as he had broken his parole in so doing, he was now forced to serve out, in addition, what remained of his previous sentence. He now faced three and a half years inside. He was brought before Langton and Anna with two guards, who remained outside the interview room. Vernon was already sweating, and after Langton introduced himself, he seemed even more agitated.

'Okay, Vernon. Tell me about the time you went to see Gail and Joseph Sickert. You went to see them at the piggery – the place we found Gail's body. Vernon?'

Vernon's mouth gaped open and he sat back in his chair.

Anna glanced at Langton. She knew that, in reality, he was just surmising that Vernon had to have met Joseph Sickert; they still could not be certain of this.

'No, I never saw them there. I swear before God, I didn't see them.'

Langton leaned over the table. 'Quit fucking around. You went to visit Gail and Joseph Sickert. When was this?'

'Oh, shit.'

'*When*?'

'Just before me trial. Listen, this Rashid almost broke me door down and he punched me around.'

'Rashid? Who's he, Vernon?'

'He was at the same hostel.'

'What's his surname?'

'I dunno, I swear to you.'

Langton glared at him.

'Maybe it's Burry, somethin' like that. I just know him as Rashid, nothin' else. He came and went at the hostel; I dunno if he was supposed to be there, but he was. When she,' he nodded towards Anna, 'when she turned up at the hostel, he got very jumpy.'

'Was this Rashid the man who slammed the door in my face?' Anna asked.

'I dunno, just he knew the cops were there, and he didn't like it.'

'Did he also know Arthur Murphy?'

'Yeah, yeah, I guess so.'

'Describe him,' snapped Langton.

Vernon twisted in his chair. 'He was a huge black guy; had some missing teeth in the front.'

'So, why did you go to see Sickert? Come on, Vernon – we know that you and Murphy were there together, so, this second time, why did you go?'

''Cos Rashid told me he was sick.'

Langton sighed. He began tapping the table with his fingers.

Vernon started to fidget even more in his seat. 'Look, this is the God's honest truth. Rashid was in a real bad mood, because the cops were crawling all over the hostel. When I come back, he starts on me – you know, wanting to know what was going on. I said to him it was

Murphy: he'd been done for murder and they done me for letting him kip on my floor.'

Vernon then told them about a phone conversation: Sickert had called Rashid to say the cops had been to the bungalow. Rashid was very edgy about what was going on. Apparently, some friend of his had 'cut up a cop', and he was paranoid that was the reason they'd been at the bungalow.

Anna gave a covert look at Langton. She could see that his whole body had tensed, and could feel her own nerves jangling. The interview was taking a very dangerous twist.

'He thought they was there because they'd sussed it out.' Vernon was now shaking.

'Sussed what out?' Langton asked.

'Rashid really put the frighteners on me, you know – asking if the Murphy thing was for real, or just a cover to get into the hostel and check who was there. I said to him that it was for real. I knew about this bloke that got cut: it was in the paper on the seat of the cop car. I then said to him that it might be, you know, a sort of double-up check as *she* was in the car.' Vernon pointed to Anna again.

'Just go over that again, Vernon. You are in a patrol car?'

'Yeah, I was carrying back fish and chips, right? Been down the chippy when I get busted. I get manhandled into a cop car – it was round the corner from the hostel, right? I get shoved in the car and there's a uniformed bloke at the wheel and another standing by the car, right? And I am sittin' there – I mean, I knew I was done for, right? So I wasn't gonna create, and there's this newspaper on the back seat. I pick it up and there's a big headline about the cop what got slashed. Now, I swear before God, I dunno the connections, I dunno nothing about it. Then *she* gets into the passenger seat.' Again Vernon gestured towards Anna.

'Go on,' Langton grated.

'Well, the driver leans over and takes the newspaper off me, and he says to her,' Vernon pointed at Anna, 'he says something about it was still making headlines. I mean, I can't remember the exact words, but it was something about did she know him, what a great bloke he was; and she says they was close, something like that.'

'Go on.' Langton wafted his hand with impatience.

'I told Rashid about what I'd heard, that was all, then he kicked me and went back to his room. He might have been doing business there, I honest to God don't know. I dunno if he was even supposed to be living there, but a day later he come and said to me that I needed to take some medication to Sickert. I didn't argue; he give me this box of pills and stuff and I went to see Gail. I never saw Sickert apart from for a few minutes when I give him the box. I swear before God that was the only time I was there, after when me and Murphy went to see her.'

'Did Sickert ask about me?' Anna interjected.

'Well, I repeated what I had told Rashid: that this policewoman's bloke had been cut up, and that I was certain she wasn't at the hostel because of it – it was just a coincidence.'

'What else did you say to him?' Langton asked.

'I said she had red hair, that was all. Then he took the stuff I'd brought and told me to get lost.' Vernon looked from Anna to Langton; sweat was glistening on his face. 'That's all, I swear before God, that was all that happened. I mean, I got nothin' to do with Gail's murder. I swear on my life.'

'So you took Sickert what, exactly? Drugs? Medication?'

'I dunno. Rashid said that Sickert needed it; he's got some blood disease, that's all I know.'

'Blood disease? You mean like sickle cell anaemia?'

'I dunno.'

'Are you the father of Gail's youngest daughter?' Anna asked.

Vernon turned towards her. '*Me?*'

'Yes, you.'

'No way! Listen, I mean I don't wanna speak ill of the dead, right, but she put it about. I mean, all her kids had different fathers, an' I'm not one of them.'

'What work did this Rashid do?'

'What?'

Langton sighed and tapped the table. 'What work did this guy Rashid do?'

'I dunno. Like I keep on saying, I didn't really know him. I swear before God I've told you all I know about him.'

'Describe him,' Langton snapped.

'Who?'

Langton shoved the table hard towards Vernon and he crunched back in his seat.

'I already did, for Chrissakes! He was a big black mother with muscles. That's it – I keep on telling you I didn't really know the guy.'

'Think – what else?'

'Shit, I dunno. I'm gettin' threats in here; they think I'm a grass.'

Langton stared at him, waiting.

187

'Like I said before: teeth missing, but one or two gold capped ones, in the front.'

And then Vernon smiled nervously, showing his own crooked, tobacco-stained teeth.

Anna felt drained when they drove away from Wandsworth. Langton was in a very dark mood.

He asked her over and over again to repeat the description of Rashid. They soon realized that it must have been Rashid whom the landlord had seen at the bungalow, when he had met Sickert in the kitchen there, to discuss the new henhouse.

When she had gone to the hostel on the day they had arrested Arthur Murphy, Anna had only had a quick glimpse of the man who slammed the front door in her face. He was wearing boxer shorts, was big and muscular and, as far as she could recall, had gold teeth in the front of his mouth.

'No coincidences,' Langton muttered.

This also raised the possibility that Rashid could have been involved in Gail's murder and, most importantly, that he could also have been one of the two men who had slashed Langton to pieces.

'Well, I said I'd get the bastards, and it's looking like I'm getting closer,' he said to himself.

'I'm sorry, what did you say?' asked Anna.

'Nothing.'

'Yes, you did.'

'I just said it feels like I am getting closer – the murder of Gail and her kids, okay?' He made no reference to what he really felt he was getting closer to. Before Anna could pursue it, Langton's phone rang. It was Mike

Lewis. Langton listened to the call, then covered the mouthpiece and turned to Anna.

'Forensic have just had confirmation that the child's skull found at the piggery was a relative of Gail Sickert, most likely that of the youngest girl, due to its size. They've not found any other remains yet, but they're still working there.'

Langton returned to the call. 'I want a trace on a black male: Rashid Burry.' He spelled it out. 'He was at the hostel, and now we are sure he was also at the piggery. Also, our suspect Sickert may be suffering from sickle cell disease as he was in need of medication, so get someone checking hospitals down there.'

Anna watched Langton and felt very uneasy when he laughed softly and said, 'Okay, Mike, keep at it. Shaping up, isn't it?'

Then he cut off the call and rested back, closing his eyes.

They were now armed with more information with which to press Murphy to assist them. Driven in a squad car, they had a long journey over to the Isle of Wight to Parkhurst prison, Langton remaining moody and silent throughout.

Anna felt humiliated that she hadn't realized how Vernon had discovered her connection to Langton. She had been so busy accusing everyone else, when it had been something as simple as a newspaper left on the seat of the patrol car.

'I just didn't realize,' she said out loud. 'About the newspaper, I mean.'

Langton murmured for her not to worry, but she did;

she was so angry with herself. She leaned forwards from the back seat and tapped his shoulder.

'I am really sorry. I wanted to tell you, but I kept on putting it off. At least now we know.'

'Know what?'

'That Sickert had a reason for frightening me. He is connected to your attack, or knows who did it.'

'Yeah, but I think it's got more to do with this Rashid Burry. We might want Sickert for the murders, but I want Rashid brought in under suspicion as well.' He turned towards her. 'Don't bring up my attack. It's too early to make any connection, and the last thing I need right now is to get the top brass worried that I might have an ulterior motive for wanting to be involved with the investigation. Anna? You hear what I'm saying?'

'Yes.'

'Good.'

Lewis called again when they were on the ferry, to say they had come up empty-handed on Rashid Burry, but were working with the probation departments, so might have more news later. Detective Constable Grace Ballagio, who was checking hospitals in the local area, also made contact: she had had no luck so far tracking down any local patient with sickle cell anaemia, so she was now going further afield, to hospitals within a twenty-mile radius of the piggery. Langton said she should also keep running with the name Rashid Burry and see if it paid off.

It was after four when they arrived at Parkhurst. The prison Governor had asked that they come directly to his office. He was a mild-mannered man, balding, with spectacles. He offered coffee or tea but they both refused.

'I am afraid I have some rather bad news,' he told them. 'You asked to interview Arthur Murphy; at the time, he was available to you.'

'But he isn't now?'

'No, he's not.'

Langton frowned irritably. 'He has refused?'

'No, he was knifed during his exercise period. He died last night.'

'Jesus Christ! Wasn't he on Rule 43?'

'Yes. The two men who were involved are child-molesters from the same wing.'

Langton put his hands over his face. 'The attack: was it made by white prisoners?'

'No, black. One shared a cell with Murphy. Right now, we are very overcrowded. I am not making excuses for what has happened to Arthur Murphy, and there will obviously be a full enquiry, but right now there are over ten thousand foreigners behind bars in Britain; they send to us, over here, some of the worst offenders. One of the men was waiting for a deportation order to come through. Nationals account for a mere one in eight inmates. It's costing the taxpayer a staggering amount, almost four million pounds per year, and we are in dire need of funds to extend the secure units.'

Langton listened, but hardly paid any attention to the figures. The man obviously did need to make excuses for what had happened.

'I would like to interview the two men involved in the murder of Arthur Murphy.'

'I'm afraid that won't be possible.'

'Why not?'

'For legal reasons.'

'But I need information. These two men may be connected to the brutal murder of a young woman and her two-year-old child. If you can't let me talk to them now, then when can I gain access to them?'

'When we have completed our investigation. They are held here in isolation, and until we have all the facts, we cannot allow anyone to interview them. We cannot afford any bad press—'

Langton interrupted, his voice harsh. 'I am not the bloody press, but let me tell you, if you do not give me access to both these men then I will make a public statement.' Anna could see the muscles in his neck twitching as he tried to control his rage. 'Arthur Murphy's sister has been brutally murdered and her child's body fed to the pigs. Now, if you are refusing to allow me to question these two men, you are—'

'I am sorry, Detective Chief Inspector Langton, but—'

'No buts!'

'I am aware of your investigation. I have your report in front of me as to why you wished to speak with Arthur Murphy, but I have to tell you that one of the men involved in his attack has been in prison for over three years and the other almost six months, so I cannot see how they could give you any details about your case. The local police have obviously been informed and these men will be held in police custody eventually.'

In all the time she had known Langton, Anna had never seen him so angry. He had his fists clenched and looked as if he might swing a punch at the Governor. He jabbed the air with his finger very close to the man's face.

'You have just sat there giving me a load of facts

and figures. Well, my facts are this: Arthur Murphy was scum, a rapist and a killer. I don't give a fuck about him; what I need to know is why these two men attacked him. If they are sex offenders, like Murphy, you know as well as I do that they protect each other; discuss their filthy antics with each other. Why knife *him*? They're sex offenders, child sex offenders! Right now, I have a suspect on the loose and two small children at risk, a suspect who has . . .'

Langton suddenly went chalk-white and had to sit back in his chair. His face glistened with sweat. He took out some pills and asked for a glass of water.

Anna leaned close to him. 'Are you all right?'

Langton nodded, taking pill after pill, gulping at the water. The prison Governor remained silent, then got up and excused himself, leaving them alone.

'Do you want to lie down?' Anna asked. He shook his head, then leaned forwards, bending his head down low. She watched him gasp for breath. It was some time before he slowly leaned back, his eyes closed.

When the Governor returned, he was sweating almost as much as Langton. 'I'm sorry. I am acting on orders from the Home Office. However, considering the seriousness of your enquiry, I will allow you access to each prisoner, for ten minutes.'

'Thank you,' Langton said quietly.

The Governor moved to sit back behind his desk. 'Prisoner 3457, D Wing, is called Courtney Ransford. He is here after escaping from Ford Open prison in 2001; he was picked up for murder two years later. This is his record sheet.'

Langton reached over for the papers. Anna stood up to read over his shoulder.

'The second man involved is an illegal immigrant waiting for a deportation order, Eamon Krasiniqe.'

Langton looked up in shock. 'What?' The man he had arrested for the murder of Carly Ann North was also called Krasiniqe. As Eamon Krasiniqe's file was passed over, he skimmed the pages. He turned to Anna, pointing to the name. There was no mention of siblings or family.

'Can you check if this man is related to Idris Krasiniqe, sent down for murder? There's no mention of family living here.' The connection was shattering to Langton; he simply could not believe it.

'We have no documentation on his background. He came into Britain on a forged passport, so even his name could be a fake; it's quite possible that others are using the same name and same papers. We were in the process of trying to discover exactly how he entered the UK and from where. He was charged with drug dealing and abduction of a fourteen-year-old girl.'

'Jesus Christ,' Langton muttered.

'We obviously stripped both their cells, and found nothing that gave us any indication of why it had happened. There is also something that I think I should tell you. One of the reasons we have been in discussions with the Home Office about this situation, and why we cannot allow it to be made public . . . I mentioned to you how many foreign inmates we have, and how many are of ethnic origin.'

'Yes, yes.' Langton was hoping he would not have to listen to another lengthy 'facts and figures' monologue.

'Two days ago, during his recreational period, Krasiniqe asked to make a phone call. He had only a few pence left on his phone card, so wanted to make a reverse charge call. This was denied. The following day, he had acquired enough money to make a call. He was waiting some time, as the phone on his wing was in use. Krasiniqe became very abusive about waiting, as he said it was a very important call. The officer on the wing gave instructions for the prisoners ahead of him to get a move on, or the recreational period would be up. This is the reason we are aware of the call. He finally got to make it; according to the duty officer, it was after the call that he started to act oddly.'

'Oddly?'

'Yes. He became very subdued, and when told to return to his cell, he appeared to be very disorientated. He was led to his cell, and lock-up went ahead. During the night, the officers reported that he was not in his bed, but standing up. He was told three times to go to his bed, but made no answer. The following morning, he was still subdued and didn't eat. During recreation—'

'The phone call: you record all outgoing calls, right?'

'Well yes, but you know we have hundreds per day. We did find on a cigarette packet a phone number; it could have been the one dialled by Krasiniqe. It's a mobile phone number; no name.' He passed over the report of the contents of both prisoners' cells, and Langton copied down the number that was listed.

Langton was then shown photographs of the body of Arthur Murphy. The knife had cut his throat in one slice.

The Governor gathered up the reports and photographs. 'Krasiniqe has not really spoken since the attack. He is vacant and submissive, and does not seem to recall anything of the incident.' Langton sipped a glass of water as the Governor continued. 'The other accused,

Courtney Ransford, has made a statement that he was coerced into holding Murphy down whilst Krasiniqe cut his throat.'

He licked his lips, stacking the reports on his desk, packing them neatly into the files. 'He claims that Krasiniqe was "zombied" and if he didn't help him, he would suffer the same fate. Do you know what zombied means?'

Langton looked to Anna and then back to the Governor.

'It's a voodoo term,' the man explained, 'the ability to make someone appear like a zombie. It sounds incredible, I know, but if somehow Krasiniqe was got at, and if his belief is strong enough, then God only knows what the mind will do. Surely now you can understand: if this was made public inside here, it would create havoc.'

Anna and Langton were shown into a small interview room. A uniformed officer waited outside. There were just two chairs and a table, so Anna would have to stand during the interview.

Courtney Ransford was led into the room handcuffed, wearing prison issue denims. He was a big, raw-boned man with stiff spiked hair, and his hands were like big flat shovels.

Langton spoke very quietly, forcing Courtney to lean forwards to hear clearly. He had never heard of Joseph Sickert, he said, he had never heard of Gail Sickert and he did not know Rashid Burry. His bulging, red-rimmed eyes were vacant; when asked to explain what had happened in the exercise yard, he hesitated, then, in a voice that was like a growling animal, said he couldn't remember anything.

'You held a man down whilst his throat was cut, and you claim not to remember anything about it?'

'Yeah, that's right.'

'This action will put ten years on your sentence. How does that make you feel?'

'Bad.'

'So why don't you help me? Because I can help you.'

'Oh yeah?'

'Yes.'

'What can you do for me?'

'Get you maybe a lighter sentence; depends on how much you are willing to—'

Courtney leaned even closer across the table. 'Man, you can't help me, and no way do I want it known that I even said two words to you, so fuck off and leave me alone.'

'That scared, are you?'

'Yeah, you could say that.'

'Scared so bad you are willing to get another life sentence?'

Courtney leaned back, looked up to the ceiling and started sucking his teeth.

'I could also get you moved to another prison.'

Courtney shook his head. 'Listen, man, there is no-where, no place they can't find me. That creep deserved what he got, so why bother me?'

'Who's they?'

Courtney glared.

'If you give me names, I'll see what I can—'

'You can do nothin', man, hear me straight? You can do nothin', not for me, just like I ain't doin' nothin' that can make me like that poor fucker. He's walkin' dead.'

'And you're not?'

'No. No! Officer! Officer, get me out of here!' Courtney screamed for the officer waiting outside; he showed
for the first time a real fear.

Langton tried to calm him. 'What are you so scared
of?'

It had no effect. Courtney wanted out, and eventually
Langton had no option but to let him leave.

They waited for almost fifteen minutes before they
heard footsteps outside the room. Eamon Krasiniqe was
twenty-two years old, yet he shuffled into the room like
a frail old man. He was glassy-eyed and his hands hung
limply at his side. He had to be helped to sit; he seemed
so vacant, as if he had no idea where he was.

Langton tried to question him, but Krasiniqe made
no reply. His lips were wet and he dribbled saliva down
his chin. His huge expressionless eyes were like dark
holes and he didn't look at either Langton or Anna but at
some fixed point ahead of him.

'Why did you kill Arthur Murphy?' Langton asked.

Krasiniqe slowly lifted his right hand and pointed
with his index finger to the space between Langton and
Anna. He then twirled his index finger in a slow circle.
They both turned to look behind them; there was a
clock on the wall. They had no idea what it meant,
unless he was indicating their ten minutes were up!
Having got nothing, not even one word out of him, they
watched as he was led back to his isolation cell.

When they left the room, a prison officer was waiting
to take them back to the main gates. He was a friendly,
broad-shouldered man in his thirties. Langton walked
ahead of Anna, asking the officer what he reckoned
had gone down. He said the attack had caught everyone

off-guard, as there had been no lead-up to it. Murphy appeared to get along with Courtney, and they were often seen playing table tennis together. Courtney also knew Krasiniqe well; as the latter was so young, Courtney had taken him under his wing. They had never seen the three men arguing. It had happened very quickly. Murphy was left lying on the ground, as Krasiniqe stood there with the shiv still in his hand; he made no attempt to palm it. Courtney had tried to extricate himself from the murder, but he had blood sprays over his denim shirt.

Langton mentioned that the only response Krasiniqe had made was to imitate the movement of the clock's hands in the interview room.

'Yeah, he does that all the time. Sort of points ahead of himself and twists his index finger. No idea what it means, but then we have no idea what's the matter with him. Doctors have checked him over and it's not drugs; there's whispers going round about voodoo. We've all been given instructions to sit on them – you know, not let it get into a rumour that starts a bush fire.'

As they were boarding the ferry to head back to London, Langton got the first good news of the day. DC Grace Ballagio had run the name Rashid Burry by numerous hospitals and learned that he had been attended to in the emergency section of a hospital twenty miles out of the New Forest area, suffering from a kidney infection, and had given his address as the hostel in Brixton. The date of his admission and treatment coincided with the days after Anna had been to see Gail, and matched the date that Vernon had admitted to being at the piggery. It also fitted with the time Gail went missing. However, the description of the patient did not fit Rashid Burry – but it did Joseph Sickert.

By the time they reached the Hampshire station, it was after eight o'clock. Langton was looking very tired, and said that he would give a briefing the following morning.

As the team packed up for the night, ready to return for an early start, Langton remained in his office. Anna walked out to the car park with Mike Lewis. He had had a frustrating day, moving from hostel to hostel between probation departments in an attempt to trace Rashid Burry and check out the other occupants; he could not believe their incompetence. The hostels in their target areas were inundated with prisoners on release, parolees and ex-prisoners waiting for deportation, and the number of the men who had simply disappeared was a disturbing factor for the services as well as for their enquiry.

Anna did not get home until after ten o'clock. With the station being so far out of London, she had a long drive back and forth. She was fast asleep as soon as her head hit the pillow.

Langton, on the other hand, remained at the station until very late; he had booked into a Bed and Breakfast close by. He sifted through all the new information, and, although some of it was hard to believe, he knew intuitively they were getting close to discovering the identity of the man who attacked him. He was certain that, in some way, it was linked to the murder of Arthur Murphy. Whatever Murphy knew had got him killed, and whoever owned the mobile phone that Krasiniqe called must have given that instruction. Langton made a note for his team to try and trace that person. He then sat staring at the incident-room board, one leg outstretched in front of him. He was in a great deal of pain and his knee was badly swollen. Grace had also been working at her desk, and went up to the canteen for some dinner. When she returned, Langton was still sitting on the chair in front of the board, slowly rubbing his right leg, so immersed in his own thoughts that he never even acknowledged her quiet goodnight.

Chapter Ten

Anna had stopped on her way into the station to buy a cappuccino, but was still one of the first to arrive. Mike Lewis followed her into the incident room, eating a bacon and egg roll with one hand, a takeaway coffee in the other. Harry Blunt came in and walked straight over to the trolley. He helped himself to the stack of doughnuts piled up on a paper plate, then stopped to stare at the board.

'Bloody hell! Local primary school been let in, have they?'

Lewis gave a half-smile at Harry's joke, but was actually taken aback by the mass of information written up. The board was covered with events and suspects, scrawled notes and diagrams.

'Boss been busy, hasn't he?' Lewis looked to Anna.

'I guess so. I left him here last night.'

'He's moved into a B and B just up the road,' Harry said, his mouth full of doughnut.

They gathered round, looking with some confusion at Langton's work in progress. There were lists of names, in some cases ringed or with big question marks above them, and thick red felt-tipped pen arrows linking one to the other. Standing out, in large green letters, was the word VOODOO in block capitals. Conversation was muted as they tried to fathom it all out.

Langton was the last to arrive. He was smartly dressed but looked very pale; he asked the room to give him five and then he'd join them. He went into his office.

Lewis turned to Anna. 'Popping more of his painkillers.'

'What?'

'Come on, haven't you noticed? He's taking them all day.'

'No, I haven't,' Anna said snappily.

'Well, he is. And something to keep his energy up – and it's not vitamins!'

Anna made no reply.

'Listen, I'm not telling tales. I worry about him, you know? The rate he's pushing himself, he's gonna break, and now you're not around to pick up the pieces . . .'

'Mike, leave it out, will you?'

He shrugged, and crossed to his desk.

Harry was talking to Grace when Langton came in from his office.

'Okay, everyone, quieten down. Let's get on with it.' He crossed to stand by the board, he picked up a ruler and pointed to a photograph of Carly Ann North. 'This was the victim in my last murder enquiry. The suspect, Idris Krasiniqe, was arrested and charged with her murder. Let's call this case number one.'

He then pointed to Krasiniqe's mug shot. 'He gave us the names and address of the two other men who were at the scene of the murder, but they did a runner.'

He indicated the two names, and then the address of the hostel in Brixton where he, Lewis and Barolli had followed up this lead. 'One of the men was a black

Jamaican; his pal was more like a Somali, but we have no ID for either, and both men got away.' Langton failed to mention the almost fatal injuries he sustained that night. 'Idris Krasiniqe subsequently said he made up the names, however, and refused at trial to admit to giving us false information.'

Langton moved along the board and jabbed with the ruler. 'Case number two: the murder of Irene Phelps. The man wanted for her murder was Arthur Murphy. DI Travis went to another hostel in Brixton, to try to find out whether a Vernon Kramer was harbouring Murphy. This second hostel was not only minutes from Irene Phelps's house, but also four streets away from the first hostel, where my attack took place. When DI Travis approached the house, using the old voting register enquiry scam, she was refused entry by a black Jamaican with two gold teeth to the right side of his mouth. We are now pretty sure that this man is Rashid Burry, and we now think he slammed the door in Travis's face because he was paranoid that she was there to arrest him in connection with case number one.'

Langton went on to explain that Arthur Murphy was subsequently arrested and charged with Irene's murder. Vernon Kramer was also arrested, and charged with perverting the course of justice and harbouring a wanted criminal; however, he was released on bail.

'During the time Vernon was on bail, Rashid Burry put him under pressure to find out how close we were to picking him up for case number one, not knowing that DI Travis was actually on case number two. What he did find out, however, was that DI Travis and I knew each other.'

'Case number three: the murder of Gail Sickert and

her youngest child. Gail was Arthur Murphy's sister. She was living with this man, Joseph Sickert.' Langton pointed to the ident picture that Anna had worked on. 'Sickert suffers from sickle cell anaemia and needs medication, which he usually obtains from Rashid Burry. Rashid – still, we think, paranoid that we are close to arresting him – gets Vernon Kramer to hand over the medication on his behalf. When Vernon hands it over, he mentions to Sickert that Travis was in on the arrest of Arthur Murphy, and that she knew the cop who got "cut up". We know that Sickert later panicked when Travis called on Gail again. Travis was not there for any reason other than to discuss the photograph of Murphy and Kramer that Gail had given her, but Sickert puts two and two together to make a lot more.'

A murmur ran round the team as they followed Langton's arrows.

Langton indicated the victims' photographs and descriptions. 'The piggery is still being searched for other remains. After extensive press coverage, we have no information as to the whereabouts of Sickert, Gail's other two children, or Rashid Burry.'

Langton then pointed to a second picture of Murphy. 'Call this case four. Arthur Murphy was killed in Parkhurst prison. His cellmate was young, possibly Somali, with no papers of any kind. They do not know where he's actually from, or if the name he was charged under is his real name, but the name he is known by is Eamon Krasiniqe. This links directly back to case one, my last murder case: the killer has the same surname as Idris Krasiniqe. We do not know if they were related, or both used the same assumed name, but it is a bloody coincidence.'

Langton sipped a glass of water before he continued. 'Travis and I interviewed both the prisoners involved in the murder of Arthur Murphy. The first, this guy Courtney, would give us nothing as to why Murphy was a marked man. The second, Eamon Krasiniqe, is in a stupor and unable to speak; the prison is in about the same state.'

Langton drew up a chair and sat down in front of his work. He rubbed his knee, and asked for a coffee. From the chair, he pointed to the board. 'We have to find out what Murphy knew that warranted his throat being cut. We have to trace Sickert and Rashid: either they, or someone close to them, have or has enough power to terrify someone inside a prison so much that they would kill.'

He sighed. 'It also emphasizes that Gail Sickert's two missing children, if not already dead, are in a very dangerous situation. We've had a lot of press coverage and television news, but nothing has come from either.'

He stood up as if sitting pained him more than standing. He now turned to the room and asked for any developments.

Grace gave a report on the hospital that had seen Joseph Sickert. He had walked into the emergency department and given his name as Rashid Burry. He said he had been staying with friends locally when he was taken sick, and gave as his address the hostel in Brixton.

'He had a very high temperature and was very obviously a sick man. The doctor advised him that he should have a Doppler echo-cardiography test, but Sickert did not want to remain there for any length of time. He was given medication for high blood pressure—'

Grace was interrupted by Langton. 'Grace, we don't need all this. Did you ask if there were any kids with him?'

'Yes. Apparently he walked in alone and was seen quite quickly, as he was very agitated. He was shouting and being abusive and at one time lay on the floor, saying he couldn't get his breath.'

'How long did he stay at the hospital?'

'Twelve hours. He was about to be transferred when he discharged himself and walked out.'

'The two older kids and Sickert have now been missing for nearly three weeks! Somebody, somewhere must have knowledge of their whereabouts, so we go with another round of press releases.'

'The doctor warned Sickert that he was heading for a crisis, as he was vomiting and, as I said before, had a very high temperature. In this state, he is very susceptible to infections. I would say, wherever he is, he will need further medical treatment.'

Mike Lewis was next up. 'We have been checking out hostels in the Harlesden, Hackney, Brixton and Tottenham areas. Some people who live there have been ordered to move in by the courts, as a condition of bail, or are on parole. Others become resident when they have been required to do community service, as the courts believe that they need supervision. We were repeatedly told that offenders living in hostel accommodation are not free to come and go as they please, but have a strict set of rules, including a curfew, usually from 11 p.m. to 7 a.m. Most hostels were manned around the clock, and staff were very keen to make it clear they were in contact with their local police and local community. If residents don't abide by the instructions of those staff, then they stand a chance of being returned to prison or having their parole withdrawn. They are not allowed to bring in intoxicating drinks, drugs that are not prescribed by a doctor or nurse, or any solvents and so on. Rooms are, I was told, checked out on a regular basis.'

Lewis looked up. Langton sat, head bowed – bored.

Nevertheless, Lewis continued. 'Okay, that's what is supposed to be what goes down in these hostels and half-way houses. In reality, those places are a shambolic mess, but to get anyone to admit it was like pulling teeth. They are all understaffed and under pressure. We have here a list of offenders who have simply cut off their electronic tags and walked out – and this, you won't believe: some of these bastards free early on release are being allowed to take foreign holidays while still on licence! Apparently, the bloody Government dropped a long-standing ban on overseas leisure travel for those under supervision. One probation officer was at his wits' end.'

Langton yawned. Lewis turned over a few pages in his notebook.

'He said thousands of offenders, including rapists and armed robbers, are out there, fucking enjoying them-selves abroad, while technically serving out their sentence on probation – even though there is no indication that foreign authorities are even being informed! One of the staff said it was getting harder to keep a check on the occupants, as many did not speak English. Did you know that in the press recently, there was a bloody illegal immigrant working as a security guard at the Old Bailey, despite having been jailed for crimes and deported twice! He'd got fake birth certificates, and he was often on duty guarding the main entrance to the Central Criminal Court, which has countless terrorism trials—'

'For Chrissakes, get on with your bloody report!' snapped Langton.

'Sorry, Gov. Okay, we know that Vernon Kramer had Arthur Murphy hiding out in his room at his hostel. We checked at the same hostel for Rashid Burry; they said he was a friend of one of the residents. We also have a Rashid Burry listed by a Hounslow hostel: one of Burry's friends there, another resident, is a real dangerous psychopath. Four weeks ago, he cut off his tag and has not been traced. To date, we have no previous prison record on Rashid Burry, so we can only presume he was visiting; he seems to have come and gone as he felt like it. It's possible he was dealing drugs.'

Mike Lewis sat down. Langton said nothing; he just watched as an officer marked up the board with even more names.

Harry Blunt was next up. 'I was with Mike at the Hounslow place, but got bogged down with the time it took to get anything out of these hostel officials, so I talked to a young kid on community service. I think this may be a very valuable link.'

Langton sat with his hand resting across his face. Anna watched him wince with pain and yet again rub his knee.

Harry pointed to the board. 'The kid told me about a resident who came for a short time to do community service. He said this bloke was a real freak and, whilst he was there, bragged about how he had access to hundreds of fake documents, from passports, to work permits, to visas. His name is Clinton Camorra and I reckon he is that psychopath – the same bloke that Mike Lewis was informed about.'

Langton looked up, listening intently now.

Harry continued. 'Clinton Camorra was detained in

2000, suspected of smuggling hundreds of illegal immigrants into the UK, many of them children, but because of the deportation fiasco he is still at large. He was jailed for four years for people-trafficking and was also quizzed over a ritual killing of a six-to-seven-year-old boy whose body was found in a bin-liner in Regent's Canal. On his early release, the authorities put him in the same hostel with Vernon Kramer where, as we know, Rashid Burry was also a visitor. The lad said that Camorra was living in or around the Peckham area. When I checked his record, he first came to the UK in 1997, using the name Rashid Camorra.'

Langton shook his head. 'This is bloody mind-blowing. How many Rashids do we have, for Chrissakes?'

'It was probably a fake name. When Camorra was on trial, the judge sent him down for four years, and ordered his deportation to Nigeria!'

Harry picked up the black felt-tipped pen and wrote in capital letters the name Clinton Camorra (in brackets, *also known as Rashid Camorra*), then he underlined the name.

'As Rashid Camorra, he claimed he had fled war-ravaged Sierra Leone. He was granted asylum. Now they have checked out that he was actually from Benin City, Nigeria.' He looked to Langton and apologized for being so long-winded, but felt that the details were important.

'I hope to Christ you get to the point soon,' Langton said.

Harry ignored him. 'If we lose the name Rashid,' he went on, 'and go back to what I think may be his real name, Clinton – well, it's widely known that Clinton Camorra is a voodoo enthusiast. It's a bit more than just playing around: he apparently terrified the prisoners, and at the hostel, he threatened anyone who got in his way.'

Now Langton was 100 per cent attentive. Harry passed over the mug shots taken of Camorra after his arrest, to be pinned up on the board. Camorra was quite light-skinned and rather handsome, his lips parted in a faint smile, and with dark, hooded, wide-apart eyes.

'When he was in jail, the team investigating the murder of the boy found in the bin-liner questioned him. They came away certain that he was involved somehow; they suspected that the kid had got into the country illegally and was used in some kind of voodoo ceremony. They got nothing from Camorra, but his reputation in the prison was pumped up. He lived like a prince, and if he didn't get what he wanted from any of the prisoners, he would threaten them.'

Langton looked at the board, and turned back to Harry. He was very tense. 'Good work. Do we have any idea where this Camorra bastard is now?'

'All I know from the boy at the hostel is that he was somewhere in Peckham, and with a lot of money.'

The murmuring team started to discuss the new developments as Langton, Harry, Lewis and Anna grouped together by the board. Langton stared at Camorra's face. Something in that smirk made the hairs on the back of his neck prickle.

He spoke softly, tapping the photograph. 'If we say that this Camorra guy smuggled Sickert into the country, he would have a hold over him. If he was also in the same hostel as Vernon Kramer, where Murphy was hiding out, we have the links. Maybe Murphy found out something and that's the reason he got his throat slit?'

Anna agreed, and interjected that it also meant the two

missing children were now in an even worse situation – if that was possible.

Langton underlined the importance of trying to trace the call made from Parkhurst prison if it was, as he now suspected, to Camorra. Langton also gave out the orders to track down Camorra and Rashid Burry, and to pump out the press on Sickert. He reckoned that, with Sickert being so ill, he would be the easiest to trace. Although if the wanted men had someone with access to fake documentation, they could be anywhere and using God knows how many different names.

But at least, and at last, the murder team were moving forwards again.

The duty manager was assigning details of the work to be done to each officer as Anna sat at her desk, waiting for her assignment for the day. Langton had returned to his office. He looked dreadful: in need of a shave and with sunken eyes. She wondered if Mike Lewis had been right about him popping painkillers to keep going. She could see how much discomfort he was in, and his limp was very pronounced.

She was not given a schedule so, confused, went and knocked on Langton's office door. She was in two minds whether or not to disturb him, so waited a while before she knocked again.

'Come in,' Langton said irritably.

'Sorry, but I've not had my schedule, and—'

'We go back to Vernon Kramer after the press interviews.'

'Okay. We doing them at Wandsworth?'

'Yes.'

'Okay. When you're ready.'

'Gimme fifteen minutes and I'll be out.'

She nodded and quietly closed the door. She was very concerned. He was taking something, it was obvious; his pupils were like pinholes and he was shaking – she could tell by the cigarette between his fingers.

As Anna returned to her desk, Harry was passing, and she said, 'Good work, Harry.'

'Thanks. I thought I'd just go and have a jar with the Gov.'

'I wouldn't. I think he's busy with the press reports.'

'Oh, okay.' He hesitated, and looked around. 'Mind if I ask you something?'

'Go ahead.'

'Is it my imagination, but isn't he kind of playing down the fact that this guy Camorra and this Rashid Burry might have been involved in his attack?'

Anna bit her lip and then shrugged. 'I think if they were, the Gov wouldn't play it down, Harry – on the contrary.'

'Yeah, right; it was just a thought. See you later – I'm off to Peckham! See if we can trace this bastard Camorra.'

Anna watched him head out, and sighed uneasily. She was certain Langton *was* playing down the importance of the Camorra connection, and she knew why, but it was nevertheless worrying.

Langton waited for the shakes to stop, smoking one cigarette after the other. His head was throbbing, his knee agony and he had pains across his chest. It had taken so much willpower to stand for so long in the incident room, but it had taken even more when the mug shot of Camorra was pinned up on the board. Langton had hardly been able to control his emotions. Camorra was, he was becoming sure, the man who had attacked him, the man who had almost sliced him in two – and the physical shock of that recognition had hit him like a terrible panic attack. It took him half an hour to calm down. He picked up his electric razor and shaved, then drank a bottle of water before he felt capable of leaving his office.

'Right Travis, let's go!'

Anna hurried after him; as always, he never ceased to amaze her. She had been taken aback at how ill he had looked earlier, but now he seemed refreshed and energized. If he was popping pills, then he must obviously need them: the question was, how many and how often? She had no idea how much he was relying on them, and what he was suppressing with their help. It had taken all his willpower to allow Harry and Mike Lewis to begin to trace Camorra rather than do it himself, but when they did, Langton would have him.

Chapter Eleven

Vernon Kramer was brought into the interview room in handcuffs. Langton said they could be removed. The officer asked if they needed him to stay in the room. Langton said that it would not be necessary; he was surprised that Kramer was even wearing handcuffs.

'You been acting up, have you, Vernon?' he asked.

'You got no right to keep comin' in to see me. I done nothing and you know it.'

Langton waited until the officer left the room; he would be outside in the corridor if required.

'You can have a solicitor present if you want,' Langton said.

'What for?'

'You might need one.'

'Listen, I'm not rocking my fucking boat. I got done in 'cos of breakin' my friggin' parole. I done nothin' but help you, an' being taken off the wing all the time gets me into trouble. I'm no fucking grass.'

'Was your pal Murphy one?'

Vernon swallowed and the sweat started forming beads on his forehead. 'I dunno what went on with him; I just want to serve my time and get out.'

'Well, Vernon, you might be in for a lot longer than your sentence.'

Vernon's jaw dropped. 'What the fuck for?'

'You heard about one of the prisoners that cut Murphy's throat?'

Vernon shook his head.

'You don't know?'

'All I know is, Arthur got sliced.'

'How did you find that out?'

'In the nick, there's a lot of guys who know what goes on. Just because they're banged up, don't mean that they don't make contact with the outside world. If you gimme two hundred quid, I can get me own mobile.'

'So tell me what you know about the murder of your friend Arthur.'

'Look, I was just told he got done in, that's all. To be honest, I don't wanna know any more. Maybe it's connected to the fact you come in here asking me questions and the next minute, he's had his throat cut.'

'Is that why you kicked up when you were told I was back?' Langton leaned forwards, resting his elbows on the Formica-topped table. 'You see, Vernon, I don't think that you've been straight with me.'

'Shit, do me a favour. I told you all I know.'

'No, Vernon. No, you haven't.' Langton got up and walked over to lean against the wall, his hands stuffed into his pockets. 'You seem well informed about how your pal died . . . what else do you know about it?'

Vernon swivelled his head round to look at Langton. 'That's enough, isn't it?'

'Not really. You know anything about the two guys that did it? One held him down and the other cut his throat.'

'No, I dunno nothin' about them.'

'Kid called Eamon Krasiniqe?'

'Never heard of him.'

Langton walked on around the room and came to stand directly behind Vernon. 'He's not in a good state.'

Vernon swivelled his head round again. 'Nothing to do with me. I never heard of him.'

'But you do know Rashid Burry?'

Vernon sighed. 'Yeah, I told you – he was in the same hostel as me, when Arthur was kippin' down on my floor, and I tell you, I wish to God I'd told him to piss off.'

'Tell me more about Rashid.'

'Jesus Christ, I told you: he just came and went in the place and I dunno where he is now.'

'I think you know a lot more about him.'

'I don't!'

Langton now moved to sit back at the table. 'How well did Arthur Murphy know him?'

'I dunno. Like I said, he was just lying low in my room. They don't do food, you know, so I used to go out and get fish and chips and takeaway stuff for him to eat.'

'I see. So when your room was checked out, where did he go?'

'Hid in the toilets.'

'So no one from the hostel knew he was there?'

'Obvious, yeah.'

'But Rashid Burry knew, didn't he?'

'I guess so. Yeah, he might.'

'So Murphy could also have had access to Rashid, maybe talked to him?'

'Yeah, it's possible, but that guy is not to be messed around with. He's a bit crazy.'

'So you didn't get along with him?'

'I never said that.'

'Did Murphy get along with him?'

'I don't fucking know!'

'Okay. What about Clinton Camorra?'

Vernon was visibly shaken.

'You do know him, don't you?'

'No.'

'Sometimes he called himself Rashid Camorra?'

Vernon swallowed. 'Never heard of him.'

Langton rocked back in his chair and then let it bang forwards. 'Don't fucking lie to me, Vernon, because I've had it right up to here!' He hit his forehead. 'I am sick and tired of your bullshit. I have given you every opportunity to come clean with me, isn't that right?'

He looked to Anna. 'I think maybe it is time we got in a solicitor for Mr Kramer, if he is withholding evidence about the murder of that little boy.'

Vernon started to panic. 'What? What are you talking about?'

Langton smiled. 'Reason I'm here, Vernon, is we believe that you had something to do with the murder of a small boy found in a bin bag in the canal at Islington.'

'No, no! This isn't right!'

'I'd hoped you would come straight with me, but as it's obvious you are still withholding evidence, I've lost my patience.'

'No, no – wait! You can't bring me into that. I don't know anything about it, I swear before God I don't!'

Anna looked as if she was starting to pack up her briefcase, placing her files into it.

'Listen to me, I—'

'You listen to me, Vernon! We are investigating a series of murders – Gail Sickert, her two-year-old daughter – and we think there is a connection between you, Murphy and—'

'No! No, there isn't!'

'What are you so afraid of, Vernon?'

'I'm not!'

'You think you'll get the same treatment as Murphy? Is that what scares you? Or what about the kid that knifed him – you heard about him?'

Vernon's eyes were like saucers.

'Walking dead – you scared that'll happen to you?'

Vernon covered his face with his hands. 'This isn't fair, it's not bloody fair.'

'What isn't?'

Vernon licked his lips and rubbed at his eyes. 'You don't understand,' he said, almost inaudibly.

'Didn't hear you? What did you say?'

Vernon sat back and sniffed, close to tears. 'I wish to God I had never let Arthur stay with me.'

'Well, we know one reason: you got banged up for harbouring him and two years from your old sentence tagged on, but there's other reasons, right?'

Vernon nodded.

It took two beakers of water and a lot of patience for Vernon at last to come clean, with a whole new story.

A while back, Arthur Murphy had paid a visit to his sister, Gail, to arrange for Joseph Sickert to stay with her as a favour to Rashid Burry. While Arthur was on the run for the murder of Irene Phelps, he discovered that Sickert and Gail had become lovers. Arthur had got very angry about it; he and Vernon had got drunk, paid them a visit and got into a big row. Frightened, Gail threw Murphy out and called the local police.

Vernon had, at first, refused to allow Murphy to hide out at his hostel, but was coerced by Murphy and Rashid Burry into letting him stay; they reckoned no one would look for him there, right under the noses of the authorities. Murphy knew Rashid Burry from a previous hostel; he also knew that Burry had a contact who would help him get out of the country. This contact was Clinton Camorra.

According to Vernon, Camorra had a big network of people who could supply passports, visas and work permits. Rashid Burry knew Camorra well because he himself had got into the country using Camorra's forged documents. Murphy had to get some money to pay for the documents and he gave Camorra his word that he would find two thousand pounds.

Rashid had the documents from Camorra ready for Murphy at the hostel, but he wanted the money to pass on to Camorra. This was the time that Anna and the team had gone to the hostel to arrest Murphy. Rashid got very nervous and, even though Vernon told him that it had nothing to do with him, he contacted Camorra. Camorra was furious. If Murphy informed on Camorra, his network would be exposed. Camorra took his anger out on Rashid, threatening him unless he got it straightened out – and fast.

Vernon licked his lips. 'This guy Camorra is rich; he's got heavies working for him, and by now, he was really pissed off.'

Langton held up his hand. 'Did Camorra arrange for Sickert to come to the UK?'

'Yeah, along with another few hundred; he's bringin''

illegal immigrants in by the shedload every few months. Newspapers say that there's one immigrant coming into Britain every minute. A lot are coming in via Camorra, that's why he's got so much dough.' Again, Vernon licked his lips.

Langton glanced at Anna and back to Vernon. He sighed. 'That's a lot of people, Vernon. I know some are just kids, but tell me: how does this Camorra manage to keep afloat without someone grassing him up?'

'They're too scared to ever finger him – well, they would be. One, they're on forged papers, right? And then . . .' He shrugged.

'Then what?'

'Depends if you believe it or not, but the darkies do, so I guess he's got them both ways, know what I mean?'

'No, I don't.'

Vernon bowed his head. There was a long pause. He then looked up and faced the wall, not looking at either Anna or Langton.

'Voodoo.'

'Voodoo,' repeated Langton flatly.

'Yeah. I mean, I think it's a load of tosh, but they don't, so he's got them, like I said, by the short and curlies. That's how he survives; lives like a fucking prince.'

'So you've met him?'

Vernon's eyes flickered.

'Come on, Vernon. You've been straight with us so far – give it up.'

'I want to get out of here, into Ford, somewhere like that – an open prison. I mean, the inmates here have ears that can pick up anything, and they know I've been brought to be interviewed.'

'Do you think that Murphy talked?' Langton wanted to change the subject to calm Vernon down; he was twisting and turning in his chair.

'Yeah, I think he opened his mouth about Camorra, and maybe he said it to the wrong guy, I dunno.' Vernon leaned forwards. 'I heard that the kid that knifed him is in a voodoo trance – so it's obvious, isn't it? Camorra even got strong arms in the nick over there, see what I mean? You got to protect me.'

Langton nodded. 'Okay, listen to me, Vernon, this is the deal, and I give you my word. I am being dead straight with you. I'll talk to the prison Governor and I'll get you moved to Ford, but there is one condition.'

Vernon sighed. 'There's nothing else. I swear I have told you everything – I swear it on my mother's life.'

'Very well, it's a deal – *if* you give us the whereabouts of Camorra.'

Vernon swore he did not know. Langton said, in that case, there was no deal. Vernon was shaking with nerves, but eventually told them that he did not know the address, he only knew Camorra lived somewhere in Peckham.

'So, did you go to his house?'

Vernon admitted that he had met Camorra at his home. Rashid had taken him there in a car with blacked-out windows. He was blindfolded, and he had his hands tied with electric wire. Not until he was inside the house was the blindfold removed. He described the house as a big double-fronted one, but had no idea which street; he knew the house was big, because there was a double garage, and they had walked from there into the house down a long hallway. He had never seen Camorra's face, as he wore a white hood with eyeholes cut out. Camorra had questioned him about the arrest of Arthur Murphy, trying to find out if there was any connection to himself. Vernon had explained that Murphy was charged with the murder of Irene Phelps and needed to get out of the country fast.

'He made these threats to me: said if there was so much as a whisper about his connections, I would pay for it. He said that I should also get word to Arthur to keep his mouth shut, and warn Sickert to do the same thing.'

'Did you warn Sickert?'

'Yeah. I think Rashid also give him a warning.'

'Do you think that Camorra was involved with the murder of Gail and her child?'

'I don't know.'

Vernon then began to cry, blubbering that now he'd told them everything, he was scared to go back on the wing. Langton opened the interview-room door and asked the officer to take him out. He then returned to the table and picked up his notes and briefcase. Anna stood up as the very frightened Vernon was led into the corridor by the officer.

'You'll keep the deal?' Vernon said.

Langton didn't answer, but checked his watch. They heard Vernon swearing and calling him a lying bastard as he was taken back to the wing.

'You going to ask about moving him?' Anna enquired.

Langton shrugged. 'I'll think about it.' He then took a bottle of water from his briefcase, and a bottle of pills.

'You monitoring how many you take a day?' she asked.

Langton looked up, stared at her, then turned away.

Sometimes he sent chills up her spine with that look: cold, dismissive, hurt.

She had hardly said two words during the long interrogation of Vernon; she had never really been given the incentive. Langton had controlled it from the moment Vernon walked in; he now said nothing as they were led back to the prison reception to sign out.

'What about Vernon?' she asked again, tentatively.

'What about him?'

'Well, he's spilled the beans. He could get hurt.'

'Break my heart. He's a snivelling, lying piece of garbage; he's preyed on little kids all his life. A few years, he'll be free to keep up his sick fantasies. That's more of a worry to me than what happens to him in there. I hope he gets his dick sliced off.'

Langton eased himself into the passenger seat of the patrol car, Anna taking up her usual position in the back. He suddenly turned and grinned at her.

'Did good in there; opened that little prick up. This Camorra is looking like a prime target.' He turned back to stare out of the window as he gave their driver instructions to head back to the incident room. 'Let's hope the boys have some luck tracing him. It shouldn't be too difficult.'

Anna sat back in the car, her mind churning over the interview with Vernon Kramer. Their investigation centred on the murder of Gail Sickert and her child, yet Langton had hardly even referred to it as his main priority.

She leaned forwards. 'Have they completed the forensic search at the Sickert place?'

'Yes, no further evidence.'

'You mean no other bodies.'

'Correct.'

'So the two children and Sickert—'

She was interrupted as he turned to face her. 'They are somewhere; just God knows where.'

'I realize that, but it's just I feel the investigation is sort of . . .' She trailed off as she tried to find the right words.

'Sort of what?' he demanded.

'Well, we are now focusing on this Camorra character, so you must think there is more than just a connection, but we're going in so many different directions.'

He sighed. 'Yes.'

'Maybe Camorra did bring Sickert in; we know he's possibly involved in Murphy's murder. This Rashid Burry character seems to be some kind of go-between: he links to Murphy and Vernon and Sickert, but we still have two missing children, and we still have no sighting of Sickert.'

'So what do you suggest?' he asked quietly.

'I'm not suggesting anything. All I am saying is, we seem to have lost focus, and the hours spent attempting to trace Rashid Burry and Camorra should be spent on a bigger manhunt for the kids.'

'Why don't *you* try to piece the jigsaw together, Anna?'

'What jigsaw? The facts are, we have two young children with Sickert; we have Gail and her baby dead! It stands to reason that we have to step up the search.'

'What do you think I'm doing?' Langton asked. 'Ignoring the missing kids? Is that what you think?'

'No, I never said that. I just said that maybe all this added search for Rashid and Camorra is taking the focus off—' She should have known that she'd be interrupted again.

'Really? Well, think about it: sit back and think how it all links together. Camorra is at the top of the pile: he instigated bringing in Sickert to the UK. Rashid fixes up medication and false papers for him.'

'Do you think Sickert's taken the kids out of the country?'

'You tell me. Where would he go, on the run, with no money?'

'What if he was given money by Rashid, as well as his papers?'

'So Sickert wanders off to the airport with two white kids; you think Camorra also got passports for them? Think! No way. The biggest lead to the children and to Sickert has to be Camorra; if Sickert was going anywhere, it would be to him. Camorra trades in bringing in children, Anna; if they are anywhere, they will be in his claws.' At that moment, Langton broke off, leaned forwards and had a coughing fit. His whole body shook; he seemed unable to get his breath. The driver asked if he wanted him to pull over and Langton shook his head, but his face was red and he was sweating as he gasped for air.

'Pull over, up by that row of shops on the right,' Anna ordered. The driver slowed down and then indicated to park on the street. Anna told him to go into the small newsagent's and get some water while she got out of the back seat and opened Langton's car door. He was hunched forwards in his seat; the coughing had stopped, but he was gasping and still hardly able to breathe.

Anna told him to try to straighten up, but he remained crouched forwards, panting. The driver hurried over with a bottle of water, undid the cap and passed it to Anna.

'James, here: take some water. Sit back if you can.'

Langton slowly uncurled his body and sat back against the headrest. She passed him the bottle and he gulped at the water, drinking almost half the bottle before he gave it back to her.

'Do you think you should get out and walk for a minute?' she asked concerned.

'No.' It was hardly audible. He patted his pockets for his pills, and she leaned over him to take them out.

'Not those,' he said hoarsely. 'Try the briefcase.'

Anna reached for his briefcase and opened it: there were four bottles of pills stuffed into the flap. She took one out and showed it to him, but he shook his head. She showed him a second bottle.

'Yes, two.'

Anna took out two pills and passed them to him with the water. He took them and his chest slowly stopped heaving.

'What are these for?'

'Chest pains; be okay in a minute.'

Anna screwed on the cap and put the bottle back into his briefcase. She then felt his forehead. 'You've got a temperature.'

'No, it's just the sweats. I'll straighten out in a minute. Shut the door; go and sit back in the car.'

The driver was outside, leaning on the roof, unsure what he should do. Anna closed Langton's door, and nodded for him to return to the driving seat. They sat for a few more moments, then Langton said he was fine and they should keep going. They drove on, Langton leaning back on the headrest, eyes closed. Anna remained silent, watching him, deeply concerned; then she saw that he was sleeping and she started to relax. She caught the driver's eyes in the rearview mirror looking at her.

'He's overworked,' she said quietly.

He nodded and continued to drive. Anna, like Langton, closed her eyes, but she didn't sleep. Instead, she tried to piece together the jigsaw and how the links all led to Camorra, as Langton had suggested. Had this nightmare man got hold of Gail's two young innocent children? If Vernon was the father of Gail Sickert's little girl, even though he had denied it, he didn't even react when he was told that both mother and baby were dead. These people, Anna thought: these sick, perverted men.

She also thought about the unidentified little boy whose body was found in the canal. The investigation into his death had concluded that the child could well have been used in some kind of voodoo ritual. He had quite possibly been brought into the country illegally; she wondered if he had any link to Camorra and decided that, on her return to the incident room, she would contact the officers involved in that enquiry.

When they arrived at the station, Langton was still sleeping. In a low voice, Anna told the driver to go and get himself something to eat, and not to close the car door.

She crept into the driving seat and sat beside him. His breathing was now calm, and she was loath to wake him. She checked her watch. It was after four, and she wondered if the team had any results; she could see by the line-up of unmarked patrol cars that they were back in the station, probably waiting for Langton. She eased open the car door, not wanting to wake him, but he stirred.

He sat up and looked out of the window. He said sleepily, 'We back?'

'Yes.'

He turned in surprise to see her sitting in the driving seat beside him. 'What you doing?'

'I sent the driver to get something to eat. It's after four. I was just going to wake you.'

'Oh.' He took a deep breath and opened his door. He then hesitated, and turned to her. 'Might need a bit of help getting out; my knee's frozen up.'

She walked round and he held out his hand to clasp her arm as he slowly and painfully winched himself out, almost making her topple over as he stood up.

'Sorry about this,' he said softly.

'It's okay.'

He could not let her go, he was that unsteady.

'Why don't you take off to that B and B you're staying at and get some rest?' she suggested.

'I'll be okay in a second; my knees just got cramped from sitting in the car for so long.'

Being so close to him, literally holding him up, she felt such overwhelming emotion. If she had released her hold, he would have fallen.

'Like old times,' he whispered.

She looked up at him. His five o'clock shadow made his face even more gaunt, and his eyes had deep dark circles beneath them.

'I'm worried about you,' she said.

'Don't be — and give that driver a quiet word: tell him not to put this about. You know what gossips these stations are. See? I'm okay now.' He let go of her and bent into the car for his briefcase; he grinned, swinging it. 'Better get to work,' he said, as he slammed the car door shut.

She dangled the car keys. 'I'll give these to reception and see you up there.'

'Okay,' he said, and moved past her; the strength of will it took for him to walk unaided and with no sign of pain touched her. She turned away to get her own briefcase out and lock the car, so she didn't see him lean against the wall, gasping, as he pressed in the entry code to gain access to the station; nor did she see him haul himself up the stairs, one at a time.

She also missed his entry, as he banged into the incident room and said cheerfully, 'We all gathered? Gimme a few minutes and we'll have a briefing.'

He sauntered into his office, everyone oblivious to how ill he felt and how much pain he was in, he slammed the door closed and shut the blinds, then opened his briefcase and took out a bottle of pills. He downed them using a cup of cold coffee left on his desk.

Anna went into the canteen and got a sandwich and coffee to take into the incident room. She had that quiet word with their driver, who was halfway through his eggs and chips, and had just reached her desk, when Langton's office door opened and he strode into the incident room. He was energized and showed no sign of fatigue or pain. He clapped his hands.

'Okay, everyone, let's get cracking. I had a very interesting conversation with Vernon Kramer.'

As Anna ate her sandwich, Langton made large notes on the board, drawing more arrows linking the named suspects and pinpointing Camorra as the prime target. At the end, he tossed the pen aside and, hands on hips, looked to Harry Blunt and Mike Lewis.

'Right – let's hear about your day!'

Blunt and Lewis detailed their search for Camorra's residence. They had trawled the streets and the electoral roll, to no avail. They had questioned estate agents in the Peckham area, and done street searches of any property possibly owned by Camorra, but at the end of the day, had come up with zilch. They had no result from the press articles asking for information and no result from the television news coverage, apart from crank calls.

Langton was edgy and impatient; everyone was coming up blank. Even the update on Murphy's murder was negative. Both men involved were still held at Parkhurst, and there had been no change in the zombie state of Krasiniqe, apart from him now being incapable of feeding himself.

By now, it was almost six o'clock; everyone was tired and ready to quit for the night. It was Grace who stirred up their energy. She had read in the *Evening Standard* that a refuse company had called in the police after the discovery of a limb, found in a skip.

Langton covered his eyes, shaking his head. 'For Chrissakes, Grace, what is this to do with our case?'

'It was in a skip close to Peckham; so far, the forensic scientists have been able to ascertain that the limb, a right leg with the foot attached, a sock and trainer—'

Langton moved closer to Grace. 'Yes – and? Come on, Grace, it's bloody six o'clock; what's this got to do with our investigation?'

'The leg, sir, is of a black adult male, around twenty-five years of age.'

'Yes – *and*?'

'We have been trying to track down Camorra; we know he's supposed to live in Peckham and you have already stated in your briefing that it is possible that Joseph Sickert on the run would turn to Camorra. DI Travis's ident picture of him is in every newspaper . . .'

'Jesus Christ,' Langton muttered, as he rubbed his face. 'I'm with you. I'm with you.'

'They are still testing the dismembered limb and they will have results by tomorrow, but I just thought I would bring it to your attention. From the tests, they should be able to ascertain if the limb belonged to someone suffering from sickle cell disease.'

'Well, if it is connected to our case, then it's a step forwards!' Langton joked, and it eased the tension.

The team then broke up for the night with instructions for an early start the following morning.

Anna drove home, feeling tense and irritable. She made some hot chocolate and toasted cheese, and took it to bed, where she read the evening papers, including the article about the discovery of the man's limb. Sighing, she put the paper aside and decided that, first thing in the morning, she would do something that she had never done before: she would call in sick.

She felt she needed to sit back from the enquiry – and from Langton. She had not been able to add anything to the briefing; Langton had given all the details from their interview. She had felt under-used, and she didn't like it. She knew Langton was covering the fact that he was sick and in constant need of painkillers. If anyone should take time out, he should, but she knew he'd be first into the incident room in the morning. She was certain he would also be taking more of whatever had given him the energy for their briefing.

Anna sipped the chocolate. It was cold and she'd eaten only a few bites out of her toasted cheese. Tomorrow, she would take a long slow look at the entire enquiry to date. She would also instigate a couple of interviews and judge for herself whether or not the case should be reviewed and Langton brought to task. It felt strange to dissociate her personal feelings towards him from the way he was running the case, but she no longer had any hope of them getting back together. She did not look on this as any kind of betrayal; if he was moving out of control, he needed to be replaced, for his own protection.

Chapter Twelve

Anna left a message with Grace to say that overnight she had come down with some kind of flu. If she didn't feel any better later in the morning, she would go to her doctor.

That done, she called the incident room who were investigating the discovery of the limb found in the skip, in her capacity as one of the DIs on the enquiry into the murders of Gail Sickert and her small daughter. She then spoke to the administration department at Wakefield prison to arrange an interview with Idris Krasiniqe, the man convicted of the murder of Carly Ann North. With the two appointments organized for the morning and the afternoon respectively, Anna sat down and, as Langton had done in the incident room, listed cases one, two, three and four.

Gail Sickert's murder was number one. Gail Sickert was, at first, known to them by her maiden name, Gail Dunn, but when she took over the lease of the bungalow, she had actually been married to someone called Donald Summers. They appeared to have no record of who he was, where he was, or if he even existed. All they did know was that, when they first interviewed Gail, she referred to Joseph Sickert as her partner and, by that time, she was using his surname. According to the dates that Vernon Kramer had given for Sickert's arrival at the bungalow, it seemed that there was only a matter of weeks before Gail and Joseph Sickert became involved with each other.

Anna checked her notebook for the date she had gone back there to confront Gail over the photograph. This was the time she had been confronted by an irate Joseph Sickert, who had threatened that she would get the same treatment 'as her bloke'.

Anna worked on through her copious notes. Just before Arthur Murphy's trial, she had been contacted by Beryl Dunn, worrying about her daughter. Nothing more was heard of Gail until her mutilated body was discovered at the bungalow (or, as Langton described it, the piggery). The murder team had also unearthed the body of Gail's little girl; or her skull, at least. They were now searching for Sickert and Gail's two other children.

Case two: the murder of Carly Ann North. Idris Krasiniqe had tried to bargain by giving the names of his two accomplices. Langton was then attacked in a halfway house. After that attack, Idris had withdrawn the names, denying he had ever given them to the police. Langton was hospitalized and almost died, and as yet no one had been charged with the attack. Idris was sent to trial and attempted to plead diminished responsibility, but the judge gave him fifteen years. He subsequently refused to discuss either the attack or his two accomplices, saying he had made their names up; he also maintained that he was scared of voodoo being used on him if it was discovered that he had given up information. Anna underlined this section, as Langton had not brought it up as a major factor in his enquiry.

Whilst Anna was working on the murder of Irene Phelps, using Gail Sickert's photograph of Arthur Murphy and Vernon Kramer, she had come face to face with the man later identified as Rashid Burry. This same Rashid Burry was connected to Sickert because he had helped him out with medical treatment for his sickle cell anaemia. Burry was also connected to Camorra, a known people transporter, who had at one time also lived at the same hostel. Camorra was also linked to Sickert, as it was likely that he had arranged his illegal entry into the UK.

Case three: the murder of Arthur Murphy. Killed in prison, his assailant was Eamon Krasiniqe, apparently no relation to Idris, though Eamon was also an illegal immigrant. Eamon was now in prison, in a zombie-like stupor caused by a so-called voodoo hex.

Anna underlined the two voodoo links. It was only ten-fifteen, yet she already felt tired out by trying to fathom how the cases all linked together. The unpalatable but obvious explanation that kept presenting itself was that Langton *wanted* them to be linked: this way he could, whilst ostensibly working on the Gail Sickert murder, make enquiries into his own attack.

At half past ten, she had to stop working and drive to Hounslow police station, where she would meet the DCI running the enquiry into the dismembered limb found in the skip. When she went into the reception, she was disappointed to be told he was not available; however, she knew it wasn't a wasted journey when Barolli walked in.

'Eh, I heard you were coming in,' he greeted her.

'I don't believe it, are you on this one?'

'For my sins.'

'I'd like you to tell me as much as you can,' she said affably, quite pleased to see him.

Barolli took her into an empty interview room and placed down a beaker of coffee. 'Listen, I don't mind who knows it, but when I was brought in on this – it's a step down, ha ha. Actually, we're all sick of footloose jokes – but I was surprised that Jimmy never asked for me to join his team.'

'I heard it was because you were on a case.'

'I was, but winding down – I could have moved over. Mind you, schlepping out to the New Forest every day must be a pain.'

'It is.'

Barolli munched on a sausage roll. She saw that he had indeed put on a considerable amount of weight, as Langton had jotted down in his notebook.

'You got any further in ID-ing the owner of the leg?' she asked.

'Yeah. We also know he was heavily into drugs – crack cocaine. We reckon he may have been a dealer, but why he was bumped off, we're no closer to finding out. DNA gave us nothing from records. Young kid was tipping in bottles when he saw it; that was at eight-thirty. The skip gets emptied at eight forty-five, so it was a stroke of luck we found it. We've found no other body parts, so we were making enquiries with known drug dealers, then we got a call in from a woman reporting her bloke missing. Poor cow had to come into the morgue to see if she recognized his sock!' he chortled. 'What she did okay was a scar on his knee, as her boyfriend had recently had keyhole surgery.'

'So do you have a name?'

'Yeah, Murray White. We're still checking, but

nobody has seen him for a couple of days; I reckon they'd spot him if they saw him, hopping along minus his right leg.'

'What about his drug contacts?'

'What about them? We're not going to get much out of any of them. As for the rest of him, he could have been sliced up and chucked in God knows how many skips around the area, been crushed and on the tips by now.' Barolli suddenly went quiet. 'How's Langton doing?'

Anna hesitated. 'Well, he's still in a lot of pain.'

Barolli shook his head. 'I honestly thought he'd never pull through. I had a couple of weeks' leave afterwards, you know. I just sort of folded. It all happened so fast, and seeing him covered in blood . . .' He sniffed. 'Keep on thinking, could I have done more? But I was behind him; when he got cut he fell against me, almost knocking me down the stairs.'

'I know Mike Lewis feels the same way,' she said.

'Yeah, but I sort of felt that maybe he reckoned I should have done more, you know? Reason why he didn't want me working alongside him again.'

'I doubt that.'

'When I talked to him, he sounded . . . Well, not like himself.'

'When was this?'

'Last night. I gave him all the details we'd got to date.' He cocked his head to one side. 'That why you're here?'

'Yes, just checking it all out.'

'Well, I don't see how it's connected to your case.'

'Did Langton think it was?'

'I guess so – reason he called.'

'But you don't think it has any connection to the attack on him?'

Barolli shook his head. 'Nah – well, apart from the guy being black – but he's not, as far as we know, connected to the murder of Carly Ann North.'

Anna sipped her coffee, aware she had to play the interview carefully. The last thing she wanted was for Barolli to be suspicious and contact Langton.

'This guy you sent down for Carly Ann's murder?' she began.

'Idris Krasiniqe? Is he connected to our dismembered limb? I can't see it; we've not come up with any links to illegal immigrants. Our bloke – if it is him, and we think it's pretty positive – was born in Bradford.'

'What was he like?'

'Who?'

'Krasiniqe.'

Barolli took a deep breath. 'Crazy son of a bitch. We don't know if that's his real name, since all his documents were fake – but he admitted the murder; couldn't not, as he was found with the fucking meat cleaver in his hand trying to hack off her head. I tell you, this world is getting sickening.'

'He's in Wakefield, isn't he?'

'Yeah, down for fifteen, then they'll probably want him deported, but if you read the papers, that's a joke. All we really knew about him was that he was probably Somali – but even that could be a lie. He took all the blame, but there were two other blokes with him; after he gave us their names, he withdrew the statement and said it was a lie, but we acted on his information, and you obviously know the fucking result. We reckoned that even though the names were fake, the address wasn't, because of what happened to Jimmy, so someone had to have got to Krasiniqe whilst he was held at the nick. Suddenly he knew nothing? Bastard.'

'You know there was a murder of a prisoner?'

'Yeah, I know, and by another Krasiniqe; maybe they just take someone's legitimate name and keep on using it.'

'What about Camorra – you know anything about him?'

Barolli shook his head. 'No. Jimmy asked me, but I've never come across him.' He sighed. 'I know it must really tear him up. He almost dies, and it's like these bastards just run into the sewers like rats and disappear. I tried to track them down, but just hit a dead end.'

Anna looked at his fat round face, sweat already standing out on his forehead. 'You feel bad about it, don't you?'

'Not as much as he must do, but like I said, I had to take two weeks off, it affected me so badly. He's a great guy, a one-off. I really did feel bad about him not using me.' He took another deep breath then changed the subject. 'Those two kids – you found the missing boyfriend yet?'

'No.'

'Been enough press, but like I said, there must be some kind of network that lets them scurry into the sewers.'

'Hard with two kids though.'

Barolli nodded. 'They still looking for other body parts at the piggery?'

'I believe so; the pens have all been torn apart, but there were a lot of outhouses, so I don't know if they have given it the all-clear yet.'

'Pigs eat anything.'

She picked up her briefcase; things were depressing enough, without Barolli adding to it. 'Thanks for your time.'

'My pleasure, and do me a favour? Put in a good word for me, would you? 'Cos this'll be wound up soon, and if . . . Well, I leave it to you.'

She patted his arm. 'I'll do that, and don't say anything about my being here − you know the way he is. I'd hate him to think I was double-checking.'

He cocked his head to one side. 'Are you?'

'Just keeping the records straight.'

His dark eyes bore into her. 'Is he okay?'

'Yes. Like I said, he's doing really well − just has some pain.'

'Don't we all,' he said softly.

Anna's next port of call was Wakefield prison, to visit Idris Krasiniqe. Instead of driving, to save time, she took the train. Sitting at an empty table, she made a call to the incident room to say she had taken herself off to a doctor for some antibiotics. Harry Blunt took the message. She asked if there had been any developments and he said that there had been no result on the search for Sickert and the children. They had also as yet not discovered the whereabouts of Camorra, but were working on it. He suddenly paused. 'Hang on.'

Anna waited for some time before he came back to her.

'Jesus Christ, you won't believe it; just as the forensic team were packing up, they've found more remains.'

'The children?' Anna asked immediately.

Harry was having a muffled conversation with someone and had obviously covered the phone with his hand.

'Hello?' Anna waited.

'Anna?' It was Langton.

'Yes, I was just calling in.'

'You sick?'

'It's just a sore throat. I should be back tomorrow.'

'Well, take as much time as you need,' he said.

'What's happened?'

Langton said they had unearthed part of a skeleton buried beneath the henhouse. 'The area had already been searched, but it was in a pretty shambolic state. That pest of a landlord was hovering around, making sure everything was back to better than it was before – he was virtually asking the blokes to rebuild the bloody thing! Anyway, they removed some planks from the floor and there it was, under a thick layer of manure. It looks as if it's a grown man, not a child, thank Christ.'

'Sickert?' she asked.

'I dunno. We'll know more when they've taken it to the lab, but it's a bloody nightmare.'

'I'll get back as soon as I can.'

'Good.' He put the phone down.

Anna sat back and stared out of the window as a waiter appeared.

'Are you having lunch?' he asked, removing the stained paper mat left on the table.

'No, but I'd like a coffee.'

'This is the first-class dining section. There's a buffet bar further up the train,' he said, whipping another mat off the table opposite.

Anna went to the buffet car and stood in line for a beaker of terrible coffee and a sandwich. She then made her way to a second-class compartment and had to sit opposite two women who were, thankfully, asleep. She put her briefcase on the table between them and began to search through her old notes; then after a while, she too sank back into her seat, closing her eyes.

Langton stood by the trestle table as the skeleton was pieced together. The body was totally decomposed, and had been buried naked. The skull still had some blond frizzy hair attached, so it was obviously not Sickert.

Langton sighed. 'This is bloody unbelievable. Who the fuck is this? I mean, how many do you think have been buried in the outer fields, never mind the piggery?'

It would take a considerable amount of time before they would get any kind of a result from the skeleton: DNA would be extracted from the bones and hair, and dental records checked. Judging by the look of the teeth, the skeleton was not that of a young man but someone in his mid-thirties or forties, as there were some missing, and numerous fillings.

Langton returned with Harry Blunt to the patrol car. He was in a foul mood as they drove back to the incident room. 'This was all we bloody needed.'

Harry's phone went.

'It's me again,' Anna said.

'How you feeling?'

'Lot better. I had a look over my old notes on the investigation into Arthur Murphy, when we were searching for him.'

'Yeah – and?'

'We know Gail used the name Sickert, but before he came onto the scene, she was actually married to a man called Summers. They took out the lease on the bungalow together – the piggery as you now call it. We never even questioned him, because by the time we went to interview Gail, Sickert was living with her. I think you should get on to her mother, Beryl Dunn, and find out about the husband and his whereabouts. How old would you say the skeleton was?'

'We can't be sure; around thirty or forty, judging by his teeth. He had sort of sandy hair.'

'Well, maybe get a description from Mrs Dunn. It's just a thought, but if we have Sickert as prime suspect for her murder, he might have also killed her husband. I've got his name down as Donald Summers.'

'Okay, thanks – we'll look into it.'

Anna went to the taxi rank and asked to be taken to Wakefield prison. The driver looked her up and down, and then nodded. 'Visiting, are you?'

'Yes.'

'Your old man, is it?'

'No – I am a police officer,' she snapped.

Langton listened as Harry repeated Anna's telephone message. He didn't want any further interaction with Beryl, as he had disliked her intensely when he had met her. If these were the remains of this man Summers, it was even more of a headache. With the body count mounting, the pressure was on; Langton was getting very urgent calls from Scotland Yard for an update on the case.

It took Harry Blunt over half an hour to call all the various phone numbers they had for Beryl Dunn. Her phone had been cut off and her mobile was dead. He had ended up phoning her local police station in Newcastle, and they agreed to call on her and get her to speak to him on the phone.

Anna waited in the Governor's office to interview Idris Krasiniqe. She had said it was in connection with the death of a prisoner in Parkhurst: Idris had the same surname and they were attempting to discover if the two men were related. She was told that she would probably not get much out of him, as he remained sullen and uncooperative. When he had first arrived at the prison, they had put him on suicide watch, as he was very disorientated and kept banging his head on the wall. He had rarely spoken to anyone and had made no so-called friends inside. He refused to partake in any prison activities and had no visitors. He had subsequently been segregated from the main wing for throwing food at officers and wrecking his cell. As soon as it was lock-down for the afternoon, they would bring him out.

Beryl Dunn had refused to get into the patrol car, scream-ing that she had done nothing. It took some time before she understood that the police were not there for any of her criminal offences, but as part of the investigation into the murder of her daughter. Eventually, she quietened down and agreed to accompany them to the station, where they would call the New Forest incident room.

The moment Harry Blunt was called to the phone, Beryl started badmouthing their incompetence; it was a while before she answered coherently anything Harry asked her.

'Mrs Dunn, could you give me any information about your daughter's husband?'

'Which one? She was always saying she was married to

some down and out, but it was all in her head. She just hitched herself to one loser after another. I never met this black guy. I said all this before. I never met him and I wouldn't know what the bugger looked like!'

'We are asking about the man your daughter was involved with before Joseph Sickert.'

'Christ, I dunno. As I told that WPC, my daughter had three kids by three different blokes.' Beryl then burst out: 'You know, I blame it all on my son! Arthur wouldn't leave her alone when she was a kid, and he tormented her all her life. Now he's dead, she's dead — and my grandkids . . .'

Beryl started crying down the phone. Harry rolled his eyes while he waited. She made loud sniffing noises before she spoke again.

'There was a bloke drove her up here once, to get her money.'

'Could you describe him?'

'He was a window cleaner, from two streets down; she took off with him, I think. Well, he's not been cleaning windows round here for months.'

'Do you know his name?'

'Ken? I think it was Ken something or other.'

'Could you describe him?'

'How do you mean?'

'Was he tall? Short? Dark-haired? Red-haired?'

'Oh, sandy-haired, yeah. Big bloke, about six feet — come to think of it, he had no front teeth, the two in the front were missing. He used to clean the windows in these baggy shorts and checked shirt; had a van with a ladder.'

Harry continued pressing Beryl for more and more details until at last she came up with his surname.

'Summers – that's it! I just remembered what his name was – Donald Summers!'

'Not Ken?' Harry interjected.

'No, I was wrong about that. It was Donald Summers and I tell you why I remember, 'cos his mother plays bingo and she's a right tart.'

Beryl continued to make derogatory remarks about Mrs Summers as Harry jotted down the details for the team to check out. As soon as he was able to get her off the phone, he asked the local police to help them out again and see if they could contact Donald Summers's family and, if possible, obtain the name of his dentist.

Anna waited in the small interview room for over half an hour. She spent the time looking back over the reports of Idris Krasiniqe's arrest and trial. Carly Ann North had been missing for four days before her body was discovered. She had a string of previous prostitution charges and arrests. No matter what a wretched life she had, to have been raped and butchered was sickening. Idris had admitted to the crimes, he also admitted to trying to dismember her. He pleaded guilty to all charges, but denied that he had ever given the names of the two other men at the scene; he swore that they were just passing and that he didn't know them. However, the police had two samples of semen from the victim. One was matched to Idris; DNA from the other remained on file. When questioned about her rape, he said that Carly Ann was a tart and had probably been with a number of men before him. According to a friend of hers, however, she had been trying to clean up her act: she was off drugs and had started going to a rehab centre of her own free will. There had been a sighting of a white Range Rover close to where Idris was arrested, which had driven off when the uniformed officer approached. It had never been traced. Anna underlined this: she could not recall if this had ever been brought up.

Anna looked up as she heard footsteps, then keys turning in the door. She shut her briefcase and put it down beside her chair.

The uniformed officer looked in and smiled. 'We've got him for you, but we've had to cuff him. Shall we bring him in?'

'Yes, please.'

'Do you want someone in here with you?'

'Just outside the door, please.'

'Have to keep his cuffs on then.'

'Of course.'

He held the door open and a second officer gestured for Idris to be brought into the room

Anna was taken aback at how young he was. He was astonishingly handsome. His skin was a golden olive shade and he had piercing blue eyes. He was about five feet ten and very slender. He was wearing a prison jumpsuit zipped up to his chest.

'Sit down, Idris,' she said politely.

He remained standing rigidly. The officer took him by his shoulders and rammed him into the seat. It took a few moments before he bent his knees and sat. He held his hands in the cuffs in front of him.

'Can we have some coffee?' she asked, and then looked at Idris. 'Or do you want tea?'

He shook his head and looked at the floor.

Anna said in that case, she wouldn't either; the officers hovered until she gave them the nod to leave. Idris swivelled round to look at the door closing behind them. He then turned back to stare at Anna.

'My name is Anna Travis,' she said.

He bowed his head.

'I wanted to see you, as I am taking care of a prisoner held in Parkhurst prison. His name is Eamon Krasiniqe.'

No reaction.

'We are very concerned about him.'

No reaction.

'He is very sick.'

No reaction.

'He also committed a crime inside the prison. Do you know, or have you ever met, an Arthur Murphy?'

No reaction.

Harry Blunt hung up and went over to Langton's office. He knocked and entered.

Langton was sleeping at his desk, his head resting on his folded arms. He jerked awake when Harry tapped on the desk.

'It's looking like Travis could be right,' Harry said. 'We just had the dental records sent over to the lab. This Donald Summers had three teeth missing from his top layer. He left Newcastle, presumably with Gail Dunn and, according to his mother, moved into some place out in the New Forest. She hasn't seen him for the last eight to ten months. She said she'd had one phone call to say that he was working on a farm. He's got sandy hair and is six feet one, aged forty-two.'

Langton yawned. 'The lab come back with anything on how he died?'

'Well, there's a crack in his skull the size of a meat cleaver, but nothing's firmed up yet. The manure on top of him did a good job at fermenting his remains.'

'Okay, start asking around all the locals again, and get that bloody landlord back in; see if he ever met him.'

'Will do.'

Langton sat back in his chair. 'Still nothing on Camorra?'

'Nope. Could be he moved out of Peckham. He could be Christ knows where.'

'The leg wasn't his,' Langton said.

'Yeah, they got an ID on a drug dealer it belongs to. Bloody terrifying, isn't it? I mean, that case you were on, Carly Ann North – the bastards were hacking her body up.' Harry gave a gesture of despair. 'Bloody animals out there on the loose. I got two kids and I keep on thinking about those two little souls. I mean, I don't know what else we can do. They've had their pictures in every paper for weeks now, and not so much as a whisper. Gov?'

Langton's head was back down on his folded arms. Harry hovered for a few moments and then walked out. He went into the incident room to find Mike Lewis.

'Is he okay?' Harry asked, jerking a thumb at Langton's office.

'Why do you ask?'

'Well, he was sleeping when I went in, and just sort of went back to sleep whilst I was talking to him.'

'Maybe he's tired of your voice.'

'Very funny. It's not as if we're dormant in here, is it? Bloody body count's mounting every five minutes.'

They were interrupted by Grace, who had just received confirmation that the skeleton *was* that of Donald Summers.

'Oh, that's terrific!' Harry grunted and threw up his

hands. 'Just got to find the bastard that put the meat cleaver through his skull!'

Anna had kept talking. She explained how she had arrested Murphy, she discussed the death of Gail and she mentioned Sickert – and she had not had one single response from Idris. He either stared at the floor or directly at her with his ice-blue eyes. She was beginning to think she had had a wasted journey.

'Idris, I have been trying to explain to you the reason I am here. If you are not related to Eamon Krasiniqe, then you can't help me, but it's so sad: he's such a young man.'

She had saved this until the end.

'I have been given a lot of help from Doctor Black; I don't know if you are aware of who he is, but he has a clinic in the East End.'

Anna was really playing off the cuff: she had read about this Dr Black, but had never met him.

'But he needs to have some background detail, or he can't help Eamon. So I was just hoping you might have information, otherwise he will die from whatever voodoo hex was put on him.'

At last there was a reaction: the blue eyes widened and the perfect full lips were sucked in.

'I am aware of how terrifying voodoo threats can be, how much they can harm an individual, but Doctor Black—'

'Voodoo,' Idris whispered.

Anna shrugged her shoulders but her heartbeat quickened; she'd got to him and she knew it. 'Maybe you don't believe in it, but Eamon does. Unless we can understand more about why he should be so affected . . .

Poor boy is like a zombie, have you ever heard that expression? I think it's called the walking dead.'

Idris was now attentive. He sat bolt upright, his cuffed hands clasped together. She waited a moment but he said nothing. She was trying to think what to do next; then she remembered.

Lifting her right hand, Anna pointed her index finger just above Idris's head and made the slow circular movement, just as Eamon had done. His blue eyes flickered from side to side; he turned to stare at the wall, then looked back to her.

'Time.' He whispered so softly, she could only just catch it.

Anna leaned forwards and lowered her voice. 'Idris, he doesn't have it – he's dying. Please tell me anything you can that might help him.'

Idris lowered his head to look over to the door. Anna followed his gaze. Through the glass window, they could both see the outline of the waiting officers and, in the pause, could even hear their whispered conversation. As if suddenly aware that they could not hear Anna's voice from the room, one of the officers peered in through the glass, shading his eyes to see clearer.

Anna lifted her voice slightly. 'Obviously anything you say will not go any further.' She then leaned closer, whispering, 'They can't hear us, Idris.'

He slowly lifted his cuffed hands to point to her notepad.

She picked it up. 'You want this?'

He nodded. She passed it over, together with her pencil. He spent a few moments staring at the empty page then, like a child, wrote very slowly; then sat back and turned the notebook towards her.

He had written in childish looped writing. '*He is my brother.*'

'Then you have to talk to me,' she said urgently. Again, he took the notepad; this time, he wrote faster, but with the same intense look on his face.

Again, he passed the notebook back. *Save him, I talk, I tell you things.*

'But Idris, I need to know more. I can't use this – it means nothing. If you are his brother, then for God's sake, tell me what you know.'

He shook his head, a stubborn expression on his face.

'All right, listen to me. I am going to repeat the names of people I need information about. If you know anything, then nod your head; you don't even have to say a word.'

He chewed his lips.

'You don't even have to write it down.'

He gave a short nod of his head. Anna started to list all the names of suspects they wanted to question: she started again with Sickert and, this time, Idris nodded. She said a few more and got nothing; then, at the mention of Rashid Burry, again he nodded his head. He stared blankly when she asked about Gail and her children. He gave no reaction to DCI Langton's name. The only major reaction was to Camorra: when she said his name, his face twisted and he licked his lips, his blue eyes darting back and forth. She then asked if he had lied about the men who were with him on the night he had killed Carly Ann North and he gave a small shake of his head.

Anna could feel him closing off. She reached over to take the pencil back, knowing never to leave a prisoner anything he could take back to his cell.

'You have to help me a bit more,' she said.

He shook his head and gestured again at the officers. He then bent forwards, his hands clasped together in his lap, and spoke softly. 'Help my brother. I talk then.'

As soon as she got home, Anna sat down and wrote up all the new information she had acquired. It did not look much. The relationship between Idris and Eamon Krasiniqe might turn out to be important as a connection to Camorra; however, none of it looked like it was leading towards to the killer of Gail Sickert and her little daughter, nor did it connect to the death of Gail's husband, Donald Summers – unless Camorra was the link between all the murders. If this was true, then Langton was not, as she had suspected, re-routing the murder enquiry for his own ends. Just as she accepted this, her doorbell rang.

Langton leaned against the doorframe.

'I was going to bring you some chicken soup, but then I found out you were fucking lying. You'd better have a very good explanation.'

She led him into the lounge, her cheeks flushed. 'Sit down,' she said.

'Thank you.' He sat on the sofa and looked at the coffee-table loaded with her notes and files.

She sat opposite him. 'How did you know?'

He looked up: he had planned to visit Krasiniqe himself, so had called the prison – only to be told that a DI Travis was already interviewing him. Langton stared at her.

'What the fuck do you think you are doing?'

Anna hesitated. 'I just felt I wasn't doing enough.'

He shook his head. 'Really.'

'Yes, and I'm sorry – it was unethical of me.'

'You can say that again.' Langton rubbed his knee, and then leaned back, closing his eyes. 'I could throw the book at you, Anna.'

'I know.'

'Any reason why you think I shouldn't?'

Anna paused. 'I have been very concerned about you.'

He opened his eyes.

'You are taking on too much. It was obvious the other day and so, I just thought if I could do some legwork—'

'If I had wanted you to do that, I would have asked! This was a bloody stupid and, as you said, unethical way of you so-called helping me. You simply took off, making enquiries without supervision, without permission and whilst lying about being ill; constantly calling into the incident room to see if there were any developments, while you were busy working on your own. You want to take over the investigation, is that it? You think I'm incapable or something? What is it with you, Anna? This has happened before. You got off lightly then, but I don't know if I am going to accept the excuse that you were acting because of—'

'You are sick,' she interrupted him.

'Not sick enough to allow anyone to take over my case without permission!'

There was a pause. Anna sat, head bowed.

'I will think about what I am going to do with you, but you could be taken off the case.'

'I was hoping no one would find out.'

He sighed. 'Sometimes, Anna, your crass naivety stuns me. You think that because of your connections with me, you can do what you bloody well feel like doing.'

'That isn't true.'

'Then what is the truth?'

Anna stood up. 'I was afraid you were allowing the case to run out of control because of personal reasons. I was concerned that you were widening the case to include your attack. Then, when you collapsed, I had serious concerns as to whether or not you should still be working.'

He shook his head, smiling, as if stunned by what she had said; then he wiped the smile off fast and gritted his teeth. 'So, DI Travis, what were you going to do about it?'

She could hardly get her breath. She had to swallow over and over, then excused herself to go into the kitchen. She fetched a glass of water and returned to the lounge to find him sifting through her notes.

'I said, what were you going to do about it?'

Anna sat down. 'I would do anything for your well-being.'

He gave a short bark of a laugh.

'It's the truth.'

'It's bullshit; you were going to have to make a report, right? Get me removed from the case. Why can't you tell the truth?'

'Because I . . . that is not the truth.'

Langton sighed and rubbed his knee again. 'Well, I don't want to waste time bickering. Did you come up with anything worth breaking the rules for?'

She passed him her notebook. 'They are brothers, Eamon and Idris; the only way I got Idris to open up and to write this was because I brought up the voodoo hex on Eamon. It was the only time he showed any sort of reaction. I gave him a story about visiting a voodoo doctor who thought he might be able to help Eamon. Idris bought it, and then wrote this.'

Langton read the scrawled writing and put the book down.

'Idris is afraid of voodoo himself; he speaks to no one in prison and is terrified of anyone knowing he even talked to me. He's had no visitors and remains in his cell during recreation. I asked him to give me a signal if any names I mentioned meant anything to him; the only ones were Sickert, Rashid and Camorra. I think if we can get some help for his brother, he will keep his bargain and he will talk.'

Langton nodded. 'Just how do you think we can do that?'

'There are numerous voodoo specialists; we contact them, see if they can get to Eamon. If he's still alive, then we should try and do what we can – possibly even arrange some kind of meeting, so we get Idris out of the prison.'

Langton pinched the bridge of his nose.

'If that would be possible,' she added lamely.

'He is still alive – just,' Langton said. 'They are trying to feed him intravenously, but he won't let them. He even tried to bite off his own tongue.'

She looked at him. 'What are you going to do?'

'About you?' he said softly, without moving.

'No – Idris. I am certain he has information, and if this is a way to get it then we should move fast.'

Langton gripped the side of the sofa and rose, gritting his teeth; he was very obviously in pain. 'I'll organize something.'

'Great! Do you want something to eat?'

'No. I need sleep. I'm going back to my place.'

Anna walked with him to the front door. 'What about me?' she asked.

He turned, resting his hand on her shoulder. 'Ah, Travis, you will have to wait and see. I've not decided, but it's going to have to be put on report – you know that, don't you?'

She stepped back. 'Do I also put on a report that you are still suffering—'

He gripped her shoulder tightly. 'Don't try making a fucking deal with me. You are so out of line, and lucky I haven't already kicked you off the case. I haven't, let's say because of past relationships, but from now on, you tread the line or I'll bloody get you demoted – do you understand?'

She felt his fingers digging into her, and it hurt. 'Yes, sir.'

He released his hold on her and she opened the front door. 'First thing, I want you to go over to Clerkenwell station; a pal of yours is part of the enquiry into the body of the boy found in the canal – DI Frank Brandon. Have a talk to him and see what they have come up with. Then get back to the incident room for a briefing at two.'

He walked out, not looking back at her as he headed for the lift. He never used to take it, but she knew that he was unable to walk down the stairs without pain these days.

'Goodnight,' she said quietly.

He turned to look at her; he had such a strange look on his face. 'You are a clever girl, Anna. I care about you. Don't blow your career. You have just come very close to it.'

The lift opened and he stepped in before she could

say anything. She shut her front door and went into the kitchen. From the window, she watched him limping across the road. There was an unmarked patrol car waiting; she hadn't seen him drive since his attack. She saw how much difficulty he had getting into the front seat; eventually the driver came round to help him.

Anna returned to the lounge and stacked all her notes and reports into her briefcase ready for the morning. She felt as if she was on automatic pilot. Even getting ready for bed, cleaning her teeth, putting on her night-shirt, she couldn't kick her brain into action. Unable to sleep, she got up and brought her briefcase to bed. She sat, propped up by pillows, and forced herself to read up on the case of the unidentified boy whose dismembered body had been found in the canal.

It was now many weeks after the wretched discovery. To date, they had no report of any missing child of his age and race. He was estimated to be six or seven years old; his head was missing, as were both hands. He had marks to his small torso that were possibly linked to some sadistic ritual. It had been estimated that hundreds of children had been brought into the UK illegally and then disappeared without trace. Gail Sickert's children – about the same age – were still missing. She doubted that they could have been taken out of the country, but this was a possibility; another was that somewhere in the UK, they were being used for sexual perversions or sadistic rituals, possibly voodoo ceremonies.

She shut the file. If Camorra was involved in their case, either directly or indirectly, she was certain they would eventually trace him. However, if Camorra had instigated illegal entry for Sickert, Rashid Burry and God knows how many others, he could have a virtual army to make sure he was protected. He must also have a lot of money; these desperate people were paying thousands for fake documents to get into the UK. It would also mean Camorra had a hold over them for the rest of their lives.

Anna glanced at the clock: it was coming up to 2 a.m. She put all her files back into the briefcase and turned off her bedside light, then lay staring at the ceiling in the darkness. Langton was right – she was more and more sure of it. As he often said, there were never any coincidences, just facts.

Back in his own flat, Langton had taken a double dose of sleeping tablets to try and obliterate the pain in his leg. It had got no better; in fact, it seemed to feel worse. He topped the pills off with half a bottle of whisky before he crashed into a deep, troubled sleep. The mounting case file and lack of results tore at him. He knew he had to watch his back from now on: the one person he had cared for deeply was also the one ready to stab him in the back, and the revelation had shocked and pained him.

Old Jack Travis had spawned a detective as wayward and as obsessive as he had been. As a young, wet-behind-the-ears detective, Langton had wanted to prove himself better than anyone else on Jack's team. The old man had taken him out to a pub and ordered a pint for each of them.

'You are the best that's come out of training school in a long while, Jimmy, and you've got a big future ahead of you. But unless you become a team player, and play on my team, I am kicking you off my investigation.'

Langton had almost swallowed his beer backwards; he had thought Jack was taking him out to congratulate him on his work.

'Every man and woman working on this enquiry answers to me, and I protect them. You will need for the future to build friends, not make enemies inside your own camp.' The big man had put his arm round the chastised young Langton's shoulders. 'You earn loyalty, Jimmy; you earn it.'

After the case had been filed, Langton was promoted as a result of a report made by Jack Travis. In part, that was the reason why Langton had brought Anna onto his team for her first murder case. It was also the reason he had saved her career in the Red Dahlia investigation: he was loyal to Jack Travis. He would now have to give Jack's daughter the same lecture Jack had given to him. It was not going to be easy.

Chapter Thirteen

Anna and Frank Brandon sat opposite each other in his station's canteen. He was back to using that same cologne that made her eyes water, but he was still very friendly and greeted her warmly.

He stirred his milky coffee, shaking his head. 'My God. From what I hear, you are up to your eyes in a nightmare case.'

'You can say that again. It's the reason I'm here.'

'Yes, I know. Your boss had words with my SO. I can take you down to the incident room, if you can call it that; we're about to close the file. We've come up with zilch – no identification. We've tried every avenue. I guess we'll get what's left of him buried.'

'So you've still got his corpse?'

'Yes.'

'I'd like to see it.'

'Sure, I can run you over there, but you won't get much, bar a bad night's sleep; poor little sod.'

'Doesn't he have markings on his body, as if he's been subjected to some kind of ritual?'

Brandon nodded. 'Yeah, but we're not sure what kind. We've even been to see a voodoo expert at London University. He seemed pretty clued up – spent a lot of

time in Louisiana and New Orleans. We also went to
see some quacks in the East End.'

'Can I have all these contact numbers?'

'Of course. He also suggested that they could be
tribal markings, but we've not got any confirmation.
All we know for sure is he was around six or seven years
of age, and died from asphyxiation, but even the autopsy
was hedgy. His last meal was rice and fish, but he was
quite undernourished.' He sighed. 'He was somebody's
son and yet no one has come forward, which underlines
the fact that he could have been brought into the
country illegally.'

Brandon then changed the subject to ask about Arthur
Murphy. Anna gave him all the details that she knew
about his murder, and Brandon gave a soft laugh. 'Well,
he got what he deserved; and it saves the Government a
lot of money – fifteen years of three meals a day. I bet
old Harry was well pleased. He'd have strung him up but
then, if he had his way, he'd give lethal injections to
every paedophile and killer clogging up the prisons.'

Anna drained her coffee and said that she was due back
at her own station by two, so if they could get cracking,
she'd be grateful.

The incident room was as Brandon had described,
with only a few officers present. She was given access to
all the case reports and statements and was surprised at
how much paperwork had been done without any result.
The black bin-liner had been traced to a factory and
matched with a bulk load made six months prior to the
discovery. The interviews had focused on the area where
the body had been found, but it seemed that every
possible clue as to how the child had ended up in the
canal had resulted in a blank. He was naked, so they

could get nothing from any clothes and, without his hands or skull, they obviously had no dental records to check and no fingerprints to file. His DNA would be kept on record, along with a thick dossier of forensic photographs and autopsy reports. As Brandon had said, all they could do now was bury him.

Brandon did not accompany Anna into the cold storage; he'd already viewed the body too many times to want to see it again. She understood why. Seeing the tiny child's headless body, his hands severed, was not something she would ever forget. His torso had deep welts across the chest and, between them, a cross had been cut into the skin. The tissue had had time to scar, which led them to deduce that the cuts had been inflicted some weeks before he had died. This was further horror, to think the child had been subjected to this torture whilst still alive.

Professor John Starling agreed to see her at eleven; she did not contact the other voodoo doctors, as she knew she would not have enough time before the briefing back at her own station.

When Anna was shown into his office at the London University campus on the edge of Bloomsbury, she was surprised by the Professor's appearance. He was very tall and slender and wore a loose-fitting tracksuit. His greying-blond hair was long and tied in a tight ponytail. He had a rather handsome, long face with pale blue eyes. Incense had been used in the room and hung lightly in the air, a musky sweet smell.

'Please come in, sit down,' he said courteously, gesturing towards a low sofa.

He offered her water, not tea or coffee. The walls of

the office were lined with rows of framed credentials. His qualifications ranged from Egyptology to Hieroglyphic analysis, Anthropology and Criminology. He saw her looking at them, and laughed.

'I switch interests; I have a drawer full of even more certificates. I also collect Persian carpets but, as you can see,' he tapped the floor with his foot, 'this is not one of them.'

He apologized for his tracksuit, but said he was due to give a yoga session to some of his students. He then crossed his legs to sit in front of her on a woven Japanese mat. She found him fascinating – quite unlike any professor she had ever come across at Oxford. She was amused at the thought of Frank Brandon interacting with him; his cologne would compete with the smell of joss sticks that hung in the air.

Starling remained silent as she opened her briefcase and took out the details of the young boy's body.

'I've been shown these before,' he said, as she passed them to him, then reached up for a large magnifying glass from a desk with stacks of files on every inch of it.

'I was wondering if the markings could be made by some kind of voodoo ritual,' Anna said.

'No – well, not in any ceremony that I have come across, though it could be some amateur, professing knowledge of voodoo. Voodoo was originally used only for healing; it was very positive. Practitioners were kindly and knowledgeable people and probably came into the US via the slave trade. They had herbs for medical treatments. The slaves were snatched from their own environment, and many suffered severe mental disorientation; they would look to anyone who could ease that agony of separation. Voodoo priests and priestesses therefore became like present-day therapists, giving their patients mental and physical comfort. To dance into exhaustion was healing, to wail was a release, and it was not until many years later that the powers wielded by these priests led them to pervert the original concept.'

He continued to use the magnifying glass, carefully scrutinizing each photograph of the unidentified headless boy.

'Haiti and many other offshoot countries began to elaborate the ceremonies, because they realized it would generate money. They discovered the power to manipulate their patients using drugs and mind games: the threat of voodoo is a very simple device used to exert control, but only those who believe in its powers will succumb to them.'

He suddenly looked up, and cocked his head to one side.

'I remember when I was about sixteen years old, a group of us were messing around with a Ouija board. We sat holding hands in a darkened room. One of the kids placed a glass in the centre of the board and started asking questions in a weird high-pitched voice. There was a girl there, Christina, the same age, but from a pretty dysfunctional family. Anyway, we messed around and started pushing the glass backwards and forwards, when it suddenly shot towards her. I didn't touch it, but I presumed the other kids were moving it.'

He frowned, turning away. 'I am trying to recall exactly what she asked. I think it was, "Will I be married?" You know, nothing freaky. The glass spelled out NO and there was a lot of whispering and giggling as she asked, "Why not?" And the glass moved to the letter D, then E, then A, and T, H.'

He closed his eyes. 'How the mind can play tricks. I don't know which one of us pushed the glass towards her, but six weeks later she was found hanging from the banisters in her parents' home.'

'Was that why you have made a study of . . .' Anna looked around the room at his many credentials.

'Good God, no! I am first and foremost an Egypt-ologist; everything else is more or less simply down to interest and fascination.'

There was a long pause as Professor Starling returned to studying the photographs. Anna wondered if he had told the truth; perhaps it was he who had spelled out DEATH to the young teenage girl.

'They have found no sexual abuse to the child, correct?' the man asked.

'Yes.'

He slowly gathered the photographs and stacked them neatly before passing them back to her. 'His head and hands were removed, and the body dumped in a black plastic bin-liner in the canal, as if it was no longer of any use. Yes?'

'Yes.'

He somehow managed to get from the cross-legged position to standing upright in one fluid movement. 'I would say that the poor child was used by some perverted group of people; if they did not use the child for sex, they used him for some kind of ceremony. I cannot say categorically whether it was voodoo or Satanic.'

He went to a bookshelf and looked along it, trailing his fingers, then removed a book. Anna looked at the open page he offered her: there was a shrunken skull, hanging by its hair from a cross, and around the neck of a man wearing a white robe and carrying the burning cross was a necklace. Attached to the necklace were what looked like blackened birds' claws.

'This is a picture taken in around 1940 of a priest in Haiti. As you can see, he has the skull hanging from the cross, and around his neck the shrunken hands.'

Anna looked up from the book. 'My God, do you believe that is why the child was mutilated?'

'It's possible. I would say the markings on his body were done for a sort of show. Whatever madman is behind this, he will be controlling and terrifying people for his own ends.'

Anna thought of Camorra. She explained the murder of Arthur Murphy and how Eamon Krasiniqe was in a stupor, starving himself to death. Could someone, with a single phone call, make a another person believe he was the walking dead?

Professor Starling shrugged. 'Well, the prisoner would have to believe that whoever made the call could have that power. As I said, it's all in the mind. I have witnessed cases where this zombie ailment had taken over certain people.'

He closed his eyes again, and quoted softly, '"The mind is its own place, and in itself can make a heaven of hell, a hell of heaven."'

Anna hesitated. 'Milton?'

'Indeed. *Paradise Lost.*'

'May I borrow this book?' She could see that he didn't want her to, but he gave a small nod. 'Is there any cure for the person suffering from the so-called zombie curse?'

'Yes, but you have to tap into the brain.' Again Starling returned to the bookcase. 'I know they found no trace of drugs in the young boy, but there have been various cases in the US; there is a veterinary drug used to demobilize horses if they require treatment. It acts as a total freeze of all muscles in the body, but does not affect the heart. It would, if injected, bring on the exact symptoms of a zombie-like state.'

Anna made a note of the drug, as the Professor began discussing how, in Ancient Egypt, dead royalty often had their living servants buried alongside them, and how the latter were sedated with various herbs before the tombs were sealed. Anna took a look at her watch, but she remained listening for another ten minutes before she could make her exit. She had to interrupt him, and he was taken aback.

'I really have to leave, Professor Starling. I can't thank you enough for your time.'

'Oh yes – well, my pleasure.' He did not shake her hand but gave a small bow, and held his office door open. 'You know where I am if you need to talk to me again.'

The entire team was gathered, some still eating their lunch. Anna tried to slide in unnoticed, but Langton turned towards her.

'Cold better, is it, DI Travis?'

'Yes, sir – thank you.'

Langton turned to everyone. 'DI Travis did not have a cold; she took the day off to visit Wakefield prison and interview Idris Krasiniqe. Anyone else on my team who decides to take off on their own enquiries will be off the case. Is that understood? We work as a team and our loyalty is to each other; any findings, we pool together. I will not have any officer working with me who thinks they have the right to make any decisions without my approval.'

Anna flushed as everyone glanced towards her. She felt humiliated, which was obviously his intention, but then it got worse.

'Firstly, DI Travis, would you please inform the team why you decided that you would, without permission from me, or bothering to tell the duty manager, make the journey to Wakefield prison?'

Anna licked her lips.

'We're waiting,' Langton said, staring at her.

'I . . . erm . . . felt that the enquiry into the murder of Gail Sickert and her child was becoming bogged down with other cases. We are accumulating so many suspects, and I just felt that I needed time out to really get my head around all the different possibilities. I apologize to you, the duty manager and everyone else if I acted out of line. I will obviously not do so again.'

'Really,' he said, then stuffed both hands into his pockets. 'The truth is that DI Travis was concerned about my health. So, I would now like to assure everyone that, contrary to Travis's concerns, I am, as you can see, perfectly fit – mentally and physically – to head up this enquiry and do not in any way feel that we are becoming bogged down with irrelevant issues. I am certain we are on the right track, just as I am certain that, unbelievable as it may seem, the tentacles that are embracing so many other crimes do link directly back to the death of Gail Sickert and her child.'

Langton picked up his marker pen.

'I think this man Summers's murder fits into our investigation as follows. As we know, Joseph Sickert needed a safe place to stay and, with the help of Rashid Burry, Gail was persuaded to take him in. This would have been very shortly after she moved in with Donald

Summers. The older children were enrolled in a local school and Summers began work at the bungalow. A relationship then developed between Gail and Joseph Sickert, resulting in the death of Summers. Okay, let's bring it all up to date. Sickert then cohabits with Gail. DI Travis visits Gail, trying to track down Arthur Murphy for the murder of Irene Phelps.'

Langton began to link everyone he named with thick red lines.

'In the same halfway house where Murphy is hiding is Rashid Burry, the very man who arranged for Sickert to stay at Gail's bungalow stroke piggery. In the process of arresting Murphy, DI Travis is seen by Rashid Burry.' He turned to the team. 'All still with me?'

There was a low murmur of assent; some of this, they already knew.

'Okay. Burry visits Sickert to help him out with treatment for his sickle cell, tips off Sickert and goes to ground. Sickert starts to panic. Travis then visits Gail again, to sort out the issue of whether Gail had given her the photo of Murphy and Kramer willingly or not.'

Langton looked at Anna. 'Travis is, it seems, constantly acting without back-up! An irate Sickert threatens her. Murphy gets sent down for murder, and is put into Parkhurst prison. Gail Sickert disappears, along with her children.'

They were now focused on the case they had all been brought in for.

'Now we come back to the mounting coincidences. As we know, Idris Krasiniqe was arrested for the murder of Carly Ann North, the case I was investigating. During the interrogation, Idris gave the names of two accomplices. Lewis, Barolli and I tried to track these two guys down: guess where? A hostel in Brixton, a few streets away from the halfway house where Vernon and Murphy and Burry were living. You all know what happened to me; you all know, too, that Idris Krasiniqe then withdrew his statement and insisted he was acting alone. However, a white Range Rover was seen at the murder site. We have been unable to trace it, but whoever was driving it may have brought Carly Ann's body to the wasteground and even driven Idris there, although he denied ever seeing the car. Remember, Idris Krasiniqe is an illegal immigrant.'

Langton was using his marker pen again, as he now drew a line to back to Murphy.

'Arthur Murphy is murdered in Parkhurst by another prisoner, Eamon Krasiniqe. Eamon is also an illegal immigrant: so is Sickert, and so is Rashid Burry, which brings us to our main target. All we can be sure of is his surname: Camorra. He is a known people trafficker and a known voodoo dabbler, who's already spent time in prison. This man links to all the others involved in the various murders.'

He turned to Anna, who walked from her desk to stand in front of the incident board. She opened her notebook, feeling very nervous after her dressing-down, but determined not to show just how humiliated she felt.

'Idris Krasiniqe had stated that he had no known relatives in the UK when he was arrested for the murder of Carly Ann North. He had forged papers and passport. We now have confirmation from him that it was his brother, Eamon Krasiniqe, who killed Arthur Murphy in Parkhurst. After the murder, Eamon went into a catatonic state. He seems unable to speak or move and is refusing food. He is terror-stricken and believes that he has a voodoo hex on him, making him what they call the walking dead. Idris himself is afraid to come out of his cell at Wakefield prison, scared that a hex will be put on him too. I gained some reaction from Idris when I mentioned Rashid Burry and Joseph Sickert, but the biggest reaction came from Camorra's name.'

Langton watched her closely as Anna talked the team through the rest of her interview with Idris and then her meeting with Professor Starling. She repeated much of what he'd explained about voodoo and the way drugs could be used to immobilize the victim's muscles. She showed the photograph of the voodoo priest with the skull and dried hands used as a necklace.

Anna now had the team's total attention.

'If the body of the small boy in the canal was used by Camorra to put fear and terror into the men around him, I think if it's in any way possible to remove Eamon Krasiniqe from Parkhurst and get treatment to save him, then I believe we will get the information we need from his brother Idris.'

Anna sipped some water before she continued. 'It is hard to believe that after three weeks we still have no sighting of Sickert or the two children. This means either he is dead and the children, God help them, are also dead; or, they are being used by Camorra.'

Anna paused and checked her notes again. Langton was about to end the briefing, when she raised her hand.

'I think we are missing a link – something we might have overlooked in the murder of Carly Ann North.'

Langton frowned.

'It still doesn't add up that her body wasn't just

dumped. Why was Idris attempting to sever her head and hands? Because she could have been identified by her prints from her previous arrests? She was a known prostitute and heroin addict; however, weeks before her death, she was attempting to straighten out her life. Did she know something? Had she seen something? I think we need to go back into that murder enquiry to see if there is any connection.'

'You think we need to go back into the enquiry and see?' Langton was angry, slapping his desk with the flat of his hand.

'I can't see why you are so furious.'

'Can't you? What are you insinuating – that I didn't oversee that case properly? Not satisfied with trying to make me look like a prick on this one, you are now attacking my previous—'

She interrupted, going right back at him with as much anger. 'You were in hospital for the latter part of the enquiry, and you were never able to go to the trial. Did you know that after your attack, Barolli had to take two weeks off because of the trauma of seeing you injured? Mike Lewis was left overseeing the trial and, like Barolli, he must have been traumatized; all I am saying is *perhaps* something was overlooked. Krasiniqe pleaded guilty, so the murder charges were virtually cut and dried before even going to trial.'

Langton took deep breaths, calming down.

'I just want to look into her background a bit,' Anna went on, also calming down. 'We know she was a prostitute, we know she was brought up in various foster homes. But we also know that before her death she was off drugs and no longer working the streets. What was her relationship with Krasiniqe? Who else did she know, or *what* else did she know that we've never uncovered because the case was closed?'

Langton sat down behind his desk. 'Get Mike Lewis in, let me talk to him.'

Anna nodded and walked out.

About half an hour later, Mike Lewis came up to her desk.

'What the fuck is going on? I've just had him tear a strip off me! Suddenly you want to open up the Carly Ann murder? You put me right in it. I did my job, Anna, and I don't like any implication that I skipped anything, all right?'

'I am not implying that you did, Mike.'

'Well, bloody Langton is.'

'Then I'm sorry. Barolli was unable to work; that left you carrying the can for the trial.'

'Krasiniqe bloody admitted it, for Chrissakes.'

'Yes, I know — but why chop off her hands, try to decapitate her? It doesn't make sense.'

'No? Listen to me. These fucking illegal immigrants come out of war-torn areas, they cut up anything and anybody that stands in their way. If she refused his advances, if she did anything—'

'But you don't know why he killed her. He's twenty-five years old, his brother's just twenty-two—'

'She was raped,' Lewis snapped.

'I know that, but what do you know about where she was and who she was seeing before she was killed?'

Mike Lewis sighed. 'She'd been on the game since she was a kid, she'd left her foster home years before, she'd lived rough — what more do you need to know about her?'

'Well, did she come into contact with Camorra? Do we know that?'

'No, I don't bloody know that. Until recently, I'd never even heard of him.'

'Right. The Krasiniqe brothers may have been working for him; maybe Carly Ann also knew him, and when she stopped selling her tricks, stopped pumping herself full of heroin, maybe, just maybe . . .'

Lewis turned away. 'I'll check into what we have on record for her.'

It was obvious that Mike Lewis really had it in for her. Anna could see by the covert looks of the rest of the team that they were all ganging up against her too.

She felt slightly better when Langton called her into his office.

'I've got Mike pulling out everything we have on Carly Ann, but I want you to cover for him as well. If you re-interview anyone connected to the case, then you go with him.'

'He won't like it.'

'Tough shit. Get on with it.'

'Right. We also need to double-check these two guys that Krasiniqe put into the frame before he withdrew his statement. We all know what happened when you went to interview them; what we don't know is if the names were for real or if there is any connection to Camorra.'

'Both names proved to be bullshit,' Langton said. 'They could have been shipped out of the country or Christ knows what, but we could find no record of them from immigration. Krasiniqe may not even have known their real names. Those guys disappeared into thin air.'

'But they were staying close to Rashid Burry.'

'Yes, but we can't find that bastard either; he's gone to ground.' Langton gave a mirthless laugh, raising his hands. 'It's bloody mind-blowing. We can't trace Sickert, the two missing children, we can't find the guy that ripped me to shreds . . .' He opened a file and flipped it round to face her. 'Here's the descriptions: one of them had two gold teeth — I see them in my nightmares. Maybe it was Rashid Burry. But how many of these guys have gold-capped teeth? The other, the one with the machete, is a blur. I couldn't tell you what age, how tall; it happened so fast. One minute I was moving up the stairs, the next . . .'

Langton made a gesture of defeat, and Anna asked if she could take the file and work on it. 'Yeah, take it.'

She flipped through it there and then. Attached was a picture of Carly Ann that Anna had never seen before; she had only ever seen the brutal photographs taken at the murder site and on the pathologist's slab.

Langton's desk phone rang and he snatched it up, listened for a few moments and then replaced the receiver.

'Mike Lewis is waiting; he's contacted the woman Carly Ann was staying with.'

Anna looked up from the file. 'She was beautiful,' she murmured.

'What?'

'I said, she was beautiful.' Anna stared down at the photograph. Carly Ann had tawny skin, perfect features and wide, slanting blue eyes. She was tall and slender, at least five feet eight, and in the photograph, her lips were parted in a seductive, almost secret smile. Around her neck was a thick gold chain and a cross.

★

Mike Lewis was driving, Anna beside him in the unmarked patrol car.

'I didn't know how beautiful she was,' Anna said, staring out of the window.

'Didn't look that way on the table,' he grunted. 'Her eyes were bulging and her throat had deep lacerations. I think she'd put up quite a fight to stay alive.'

'When she was found, did she have a thick gold necklace round her neck?'

'No, like I said, it was almost severed. There was a lot of blood.'

'So Krasiniqe made an attempt to run?'

'Yeah, he tried, but the cop held him down; he got some back-up, and they took him into the local nick. We got called in the following morning.'

'Did he confess straight away?'

'Well, he didn't need to, did he? He had her blood all over his clothes and the blade dripping with it in his hand.'

'Did he appear to be drugged?'

'Dunno. By the time we saw him, he was cowering in his cell at the station. If he was drugged, he didn't appear that way – unless whatever he'd taken had worn off.'

Anna removed from the file Krasiniqe's statement. It was short and stated that he had killed Carly Ann after he had raped her. Anna asked where the rape had taken place.

'He had no known address, and said he had been living rough, which is where he said he knew the victim from.'

'But you don't know where?'

Mike Lewis sighed with irritation. 'Two days later,

Langton got cut to shreds, Anna. We had a suspect in custody who admitted the murder.'

'Yes, yes, I know. Please, Mike, don't be so defensive. I am just trying to piece it together myself. If one of these men was Camorra, it's odd that when Langton was attacked, he didn't recognize him.'

'It happened so fucking fast none of us had a clear recollection of either of the bastards.'

Anna nodded, deciding to change the subject. If Langton now recognized Camorra, he was not admitting it to anyone.

'What about this white Range Rover the police officer said he saw at the murder site?'

'Sorry?'

Anna turned over another page and read on. A witness had seen the vehicle parked close to the murder site: black tinted windows, engine running. 'When these two other guys with Krasiniqe ran off, did they go to the Range Rover? Drive off in it?'

'No, it moved off as soon as the uniformed cop walked up. We have tried to trace it, with no luck.'

Anna shrugged, and said that it seemed all along the line they had not had much luck.

They did not really make any further conversation until they reached the estate in Chalk Farm. Graffiti was everywhere and, although it looked as if the council had made an attempt to clear the place up, it was nevertheless a very rough and tough area. On the walkways outside the flats hung strings of washing; Anna and Mike bent beneath them, as they made their way to number forty-one.

'Okay, the place is rented by a Dora Rhodes. Well,

she's listed as the occupant, but Christ only knows how many times it may have changed hands.'

'You interviewed her, didn't you?'

'Yeah, she came into the station and identified Carly Ann, as she had no family. She runs a community centre.'

'Doesn't sound like the usual flatmate for a prostitute.'

'She's not usual, believe you me. Carly Ann had only just started living here, and this Dora was helping her get clean.'

They ducked under more washing to stand outside a blue painted door, rang the bell and waited. Anna noticed that the letterbox was hammered down, but the brass had been polished. The door was opened by a young over-weight black woman, with a floral scarf wrapped around her head.

'Hi, come on in, I've been waiting for you.'

Dora wore a multi-coloured African wrap over a bright red T-shirt, and rubber flip-flops on her plump little feet.

'Okay, sit yourselves in here and I'll bring in some coffee.'

Anna sat on a bright orange sofa which had many stains, as did the carpet, but the room was clean and bright, with children's paintings on the walls. Dora returned with a tray of mugs of coffee and cookies. She placed it down on a white hand-painted coffee-table.

'Help yourselves,' she said, as she plumped herself down in a sort of bean-bag chair. She was at least eighteen stone, with big muscular arms and a wobbly belly, but her hands, like her feet, were small. She wore a row of silver bangles, which she twisted round with her free hand. 'So, you come about my little darlin' Carly Ann?'

'Yes.' Anna picked up her coffee; Mike was already munching a cookie and seemed content to sit back and let the women get on with it. 'I was not on the original enquiry, so I would like to ask if you could tell me as much about Carly Ann as possible.'

Dora nodded. 'Well, be about nine months before she died that she moved in here with me. I don't often take kids in, you know; if you start, next minute you got a houseful, then the council will kick you out. Anyways, when I met her, there was just something about her; she came into the centre and said she needed help. She was on heroin and had been for a number of years, and she was selling herself to get the money to pay for it. I think she'd lived rough, you know; she was just a kid that ran away from one foster home after another. They all try to head to London, reckon the streets here are paved with gold, but then it's too late to turn back, and with Carly Ann being such a looker, the pimps were fast to get a hold of her.'

Dora took a deep breath. 'My Carly Ann was one of the most perfect creatures I have ever set eyes on. She was part-Jamaican, part-white, and her skin was a flawless soft tawny shade; she had this curly black hair, like silk. When you think of her living rough and pumping that shit into her veins, and still looking gorgeous . . .' She shook her head.

Anna nodded, and said that she had only seen one photograph apart from the mortuary shots. Dora got up, opened a drawer and took out a number of snapshots.

'Here she is. She was trying her best to get clean, and I would give her a few quid to help me out at the centre.

I mostly deal with young kids, so I put her in touch with a drug rehab, and she'd go there in the mornings and work for me afternoons. You know, she wasn't using when they found her, that's what makes it all the worse – she wasn't drugged. I don't believe that she was back on the game, no way. She swore blind to me that she would never turn another trick; she hated it, and the more she was around me and the kids, the more she realized what she had been doing to herself. I held that girl in my arms when she sobbed and told me that I was her only angel, she'd never had no love, no parents; until we met, my Carly Ann had never known a decent home, and you should have seen how she flowered. I mean, she wasn't all perfect and she could have troubled times and dark times, but when she laughed, it was sunny.'

Anna looked over the snapshots of the dead girl: bending over a few kids with a birthday cake, blowing out candles; at a theme park, her on a slide roaring with laughter.

'On the photograph we have at the station, Carly Ann is wearing a very thick gold chain,' she said. 'Do you know where she got it from?'

Dora shook her head.

'After she died, were any of her belongings still here?'

'Yes, still here – no one else to claim them, I suppose. 'Cos I been so distraught, I just never got round to sorting them and passing them onto some needy girl. I'll do it eventually.'

'What about boyfriends?'

'All the while she was here with me, she was only out late a few times. She went off once or twice for a weekend, disappeared without a word, and when she come back, I give her a dressing-down and a warning.

I said after the last time, if she ever did it again, she was out. She cried and said she was sorry, then it all blew over and she settled down; be about a month later, she didn't come home again, but this time it was a couple of months. I got worried 'cos she was away for so long. I even went out on the streets looking for her, then I read about the murder.' Dora wiped her eyes with a tissue.

'So you never met anyone she was friendly with?'

'No.'

'Did you ever see anyone in a white Range Rover?'

Dora nodded. 'I never saw the driver, seein' as the windows was blacked out, but I saw that car a few times, waiting down below. Carly Ann never went out when it was there. I think it might have been a pimp, or someone she'd known. I even said to her that if she wanted me to call the police on him, I would – but she wouldn't let me. Then it just stopped coming round, so we never contacted the cops.'

'Did she ever mention to you her killer, Idris Krasiniqe?'

'No.'

Anna stood up. 'May I see her things, please?'

Dora nodded, and plodded in her flip-flops to the door. 'It won't take a minute. I got them all in a suitcase.'

Anna followed Dora along the narrow hallway, Mike just behind her. The box room was very small, with just a single bed and a narrow wardrobe.

'Like I said, it wasn't much I could offer her, but she loved this room; said it was her home.' Dora picked up a cheap brocade suitcase. 'This was hers, and I just put everything in it. Well, I got my friend to, as I was too upset, but there's all her things in here. I also got Esther to list everything, so if you take it away, I know what's in it.'

Anna smiled. 'I won't need to take it, Dora, but I would like to look through it, if you don't mind.'

'You go ahead.'

Anna opened the suitcase and started to sift through the neatly folded clothes. Some were cheap market purchases, but others surprised her: they were designer labels. She took out her notebook and began to list everything, including the sexy underwear. The case had a musty, musky smell, perhaps from her old perfume. There was a pink satin bag filled with toiletries, and a square carved box. Anna eased off the lid, and started looking at the jumble of necklaces, rings and bracelets. Like her clothes, some were cheap baubles, but then Anna picked up the heavy gold necklace. It was eighteen carat and weighed a lot; there was a matching bracelet and two diamond rings. There was also a clatter of gold bangles, all heavy African gold.

'What you got?' Mike Lewis leaned on the doorframe.

'There's a lot of very good jewellery here, solid gold and two big diamonds; I'd say this was worth about ten, fifteen grand.'

He whistled. 'If she was just a cheap tart hooked on heroin, she had to have some heavy clients; all this is worth money.'

'Like Dora said, she was a beauty. Maybe she walked away from being a good earner for her pimp? You know what these creeps are like.'

As Anna put the clothes back into the case, she felt around the edges for anything she'd not seen, and patted the lining. There were no handbags or purses, or any sign of anything like letters or address books.

Mike and Anna rejoined Dora, who had made fresh coffee, even though they didn't want it.

'No handbag or letters?' Anna queried.

'No, that's what she came with. I don't even know where she was living before, but I think wherever it was, she got out fast – you know, did a runner.'

'Maybe from a pimp?'

'Maybe. She wouldn't tell me, said she was ashamed of her past life. I dunno, only sixteen and with a past life; makes me sad.'

'She has some very valuable jewellery.'

Dora looked up, surprised.

'There are gold bangles and necklaces, diamond rings.'

Dora shook her head. 'Maybe that's what they were after.'

Anna leaned forwards, suddenly alert. 'What was that?'

'I was broken into just after she died; they made a mess of the place, but nothing was taken. All her things was packed and locked in the case – I had it under my bed. My next-door neighbour disturbed them and called the cops. They'd gone by the time they got here.'

'Did you also speak to the police?'

'Yes, ma'am, I did, an' I also give them the registration number of the car, just in case the guy came back.'

'I'm sorry, which car?'

'That white one; the one you asked me about before – the Range Rover. I took his number-plate down when he was hovering around Carly Ann.'

Anna glanced at Mike Lewis, then back to Dora.

'I think we just got lucky,' she murmured.

Chapter Fourteen

Anna was just entering the incident room back at the Hampshire station to type up her report, when she stopped. Harry Blunt was in full throttle.

'I don't effing believe it! How come you get just a bloody limb of a guy and, within weeks, you got an ID and a suspect banged up? We've been running around like blue-arsed flies, trying to track down this bloke Sickert plus his two kids, and we've got sweet FA!'

Frank Brandon was sitting with his back to Anna, perched on a desk. 'Well, you can call it exceptional, dedicated policework, pal.'

'Hello Frank,' Anna said.

He turned and grinned. 'Eh, how you doing? I was just telling Harry here we got lucky; seems your team are a bit out on a limb.' He laughed.

'Well, we did get a break today,' she said, crossing to her desk. 'So, what brings you out here?'

'Joining your team, of course. From what I've gathered, you need all the help you can get.'

Across the room, Harry raised his eyebrow at Anna. 'What's the break you've got?'

Anna told him they had a registration number for the white Range Rover seen at the site of the murder of

289

Carly Ann; Mike Lewis was running it through the DVLA computers to discover the owner/driver. Starting to type up her report, she asked where Langton was.

'Gone down the East End to see some voodoo doctor; Grace is with him.' Harry came and leaned over the back of her chair. 'What else did you get this morning?'

'Well, for one, Carly Ann was a stunner; she was clean, off heroin, off the game and living with a community carer called Dora. The white Range Rover seen at the murder site was often parked by her flats; Dora said she thought the driver might have been Carly Ann's pimp.' Anna stopped typing. 'She also had some very good quality jewellery. If it was her pimp, he was paying well, or keeping her in bling.'

'Did this Dora know anything about who Carly Ann was working for?'

'No, she never discussed it. My feelings are, whoever was pimping for her would not have wanted her to quit. With her looks, she must have been a gold mine.'

'You reckon the guy in the Range Rover was her pimp?'

'If he was, he was also watching them try to hack her head off.'

At that moment, Mike Lewis walked in and flung his hands up in the air. 'Okay, we got the registered owner of the Range Rover; he lives in Kensington. I spoke to his wife – they sold it a year ago.' He sat glumly on the edge of Anna's desk. 'The geezer bought it for cash; looks like he gave a fake name and address.'

'Any description of the buyer?'

Lewis took out his notebook. 'Tall, black guy, well

dressed in a suit, spoke good English, appeared very charming, et cetera, et cetera. Because he paid cash, they did a deal on the price.'

'Well, we've got the licence plates so we can put that out – see if we get anything.'

'Already done.'

Harry ruffled his hair. 'Not the usual vehicle wheeled around by pimps, is it? Too noticeable. I mean, white Range Rover, black tinted windows.'

'By the amount of gear Carly Ann had, I'd say he was a bit more than a cheap pimp.'

'If she worked for him, maybe he didn't like the fact she was getting cleaned up?'

Anna frowned. 'Unless.'

Mike and Harry looked at her.

'What if she was more than just his whore? What if he really cared about her? What we need to do is try and trace anyone who knew her before she went to live with Dora; see if they can give us a clue as to who this guy was.' She turned to Mike. 'You have anything on record from your case?'

'I'll go and check; I think we did question a couple of girls.'

As Mike walked back to his desk, Harry said heavily, 'Clutching at straws again. I mean, this is a new line of enquiry. Meanwhile we're hovering around, looking up our own bumholes, waiting for a break.'

'You never know, Harry, this might just be it. Do we have any trace on Camorra yet? If he's living in Peckham, somebody must know where he is.'

'Maybe they do, but we've had no tip-off. We got the locals there still doing a search.' He turned to look back at Frank Brandon. 'What's *he* been brought in for?'

'I'd say it was pretty obvious, wouldn't you?' Anna joked. 'Clutching at straws!'

'Making the place stink like a whore's bedroom.'

'You'd know about that, would you?' Anna teased.

'No, but he's still wearing enough cologne to knock you dead at six feet.'

Mike Lewis returned with a report sheet. 'I got two names. We questioned both the girls; neither had seen Carly Ann for months, but before that, they hung out together.'

'Did she live with them?'

'Well, she used their address the second time she was picked up for ducking and diving around Shaftesbury Avenue.'

When Anna asked for their address and said she'd like to interview them, Mike shrugged and said he doubted they would still be there. It was a valid registered squat in Kilburn.

As Langton was not in the station, Anna made sure she did nothing out of order. She told the duty manager that she was trying to contact the girls and that she would take Brandon along with her. She handed in her report of the interaction with Dora about Carly Ann and, after a quick sandwich and coffee, she and Brandon left the station.

They drove in silence for a while, then Brandon asked if she could fill him in on a few areas he had not had time to catch up on.

She told him about the Krasiniqe brothers, and the fact that they hoped to find something to help Eamon in Parkhurst; if they did, they might get some information from his brother Idris at Wakefield.

'Bloody makes me sick,' Frank said. 'I mean, if this bastard is holding out . . .'

'He's terrified of voodoo,' Anna told him.

'That's bullshit.'

'Maybe it is, but if you'd seen him, then you'd think differently; he was totally freaked, like a zombie. They have been trying to force-feed him to keep him alive.'

'For what? He killed Murphy, didn't he?'

'Yes, but if we can get any information out of his brother, it's worthwhile at least trying.'

'Both illegal immigrants?'

'Yep.'

'Bloody insane, isn't it? You read the papers today: never mind the flood of illegal immigrants we've already got, we've got a new wave coming in from Eastern Europe. Under some ridiculous fucking law, so-called human rights, we could get more than six hundred thousand Poles and others coming in. I tell you, I'm thinking of fucking emigrating to Australia. They got the right idea – shut the gates. You know how many this bloody Government estimated would be coming in? Thirteen thousand. Well, they miscalculated, didn't they? I tell you, the Government are guilty of blatant duplicity in trying to hide the truth: they have totally and utterly failed to control immigration and we are having to bear the brunt of it all. You know what it means: schools, hospitals, housing, welfare and wages are all going to be swamped. Fucking freeloaders! My brother lives in Peterborough and they've got two thousand Poles coming there. Unemployment is already high, so what the hell are they all going to be doing?'

Anna stopped the car outside a large rundown house, one side covered in graffiti. 'This is it.'

Brandon looked out of the window. 'Pigsty. Fucking legal squat! Would you want to buy a place in this street?'

Anna got out of the car. Brandon was starting to annoy her; he sounded more and more like the bigoted Harry Blunt.

The front door was off its hinges. A couple of guys were sitting on the steps and when Anna asked if Barbara Early lived there, they just looked at her and shrugged.

'Do you speak English?' Brandon snapped.

They shrugged again. He pushed his way past them and Anna followed.

The dingy hallway was full of black bin bags, a stray dog sniffing at one of them. Anna knocked on one door and got no answer, while Brandon had the same result from two more. Heading down the stairs was a skinny black girl, with a leather bomber jacket two sizes too big, a pair of tight satin shorts and stacked high heels.

'I'm looking for Barbara Early,' Anna said pleasantly, blocking the end of the stairs.

'She's not here no more,' the girl said.

'Okay, how about Jinny Moorcroft?'

The girl hesitated. 'What for?'

'Nothing to worry about; we just need to have a chat to her about someone.'

'Two floors up at the end of the corridor.'

'Thank you.'

Anna stepped back to allow the girl to pass, just as a scruffy white boy with his hair in dreads yelled down, 'Hey, Jinny! Will you get some milk?'

Brandon moved fast; he gripped her arms. 'Now that wasn't nice, was it, Jinny?'

She wriggled and tried to get away from him.

'Okay, Jinny, we can have a chat here, or I can take you into the police station. You are not under arrest, nothing like that; we just need to know a few things about a friend of yours.'

'If it's Barbara, we dunno where she is. She OD'd weeks ago and they took her away.'

'This is not about Barbara; it's about Carly Ann North.'

Jinny seemed to deflate; she almost toppled off her shoes.

'Is there somewhere we can talk in private?' Anna kept her voice calm and steady.

Jinny hesitated, and then looked back up the stairs. 'Here's good enough.'

Anna sat beside Jinny on the filthy stairs as Brandon hovered. 'You knew Carly Ann, didn't you?'

'Yeah.'

'She lived here for a while. She gave this address when she was arrested.'

'Yeah, top room with me and Barbara, but Barbara's gone now.'

'How long did Carly Ann live here?'

'Dunno. She was here when I got my room; that was over a year ago.'

'Did you share a room with her?'

'Yeah.' Jinny scratched at her hands and rubbed at her arms beneath the jacket. Her eyes were glazed and her nose had a red crust around it. Her fingernails were bitten down to the quick. She was probably on heroin, Anna thought.

'Did you work with Carly Ann?'

'Sometimes.'

'Did she have anyone special? A special client?'

'No – well, not at first. She was just one of us, you know.'

'So you worked the streets together, right?'

'Sometimes.' Jinny looked up the stairs and then bent her head. 'He takes care of us, Mark upstairs.'

'So Mark also took care of Carly Ann?'

'Yeah, for a while, but she got into a row with him.'

'About money?'

'Yeah.'

'Did he kick her out?'

'No, *he* got kicked in the head.'

'Who – Mark upstairs?'

'Yeah. This bloke come round and said he wanted to take Carly Ann. Mark said he could go fuck himself and then this bastard beat up on him.'

'Can you describe him?'

'No, I wasn't here.'

'So did Carly Ann leave?'

'Yeah. Well, after what happened, Mark didn't want to get into any more aggro from them.'

'Them?'

'Yeah, there was a few of them come round. I dunno who they were, but they drove up and one man come in to get her.'

'But you weren't here?'

'No, Mark was. They went up to our room and took her stuff. She was outside; she didn't even come in.'

'Do you know what kind of car they were in?'

'Yeah, a white one. Big thing with black windows; it had been outside before, couple of times. Carly Ann came back home in it a few times.'

'Did you ever see anyone in the car?'

'No, the windows was black.'

'Did you see anyone at all that came in with Carly Ann?'

'No. She got very secretive, 'cos he was paying her a lot of dough; then she said she wasn't gonna do any drugs nor nothing, and was gonna live with this guy. We reckoned it was bullshit, 'cos she could tell big lies. She said he was gonna look after her.'

Brandon asked quietly, 'Was this the white car you saw outside?' He showed her a photograph of a white Range Rover.

'Yeah, it was like that.'

Anna looked to Brandon, then eased her body closer to Jinny.

'We will need to speak to Mark,' she said in a low voice.

'Oh Christ, don't have a go at him 'cos he'll take it out on me.'

'We just want to talk to him.' Brandon headed up the stairs and Jinny watched him go, fearfully.

'Did Carly Ann get some jewellery from this man she was seeing?' Anna asked.

'I dunno. If she had anything of value, she'd hide it. Mark would have it off her otherwise. He takes care of us, you see.'

Anna looked at the young drug-fuelled girl, no more than seventeen, and ripped a page from her notebook.

'Jinny, if you decided to get away from this, call this lady. Her name is Dora. You can get help to get you off drugs – you know, to get yourself straightened out.'

Jinny looked at the piece of paper, and folded it over and over into a small square. 'She's dead, ain't she?'

'Carly Ann?'

'Yeah. I read about it. They come here asking about

her, but we didn't know nothing. I suppose Barbara's dead an' all; she was shooting up meths mixed with Christ knows what. She was a nice kid.' Jinny shut her eyes.

'Carly Ann was brutally murdered, Jinny, so if there is anything you can think of that could help us, anything at all . . .'

'They got the one that done it, didn't they?'

'Yes, but we think there are more people involved, and they got away.'

Jinny pointed with her foot in the stack-heeled shoe. 'She left these, and some other gear; said she wouldn't need it any more as she was gonna be looked after. Well, she was lying again, wasn't she? Nobody looked after her. They done her in.'

'So you liked her?'

Jinny nodded; her eyes filled with tears. 'I know she told lies and stuff, but she was sort of different from us all – you know, clean, always washing herself, afraid she'd pick up something.'

There was a lot of banging coming from the floor above. Jinny looked up fearfully.

'I gotta go an' get some milk.'

'Thank you for talking to me, Jinny. Please, if you want to get out of this, call that number. Dora seems a really nice woman and I'm sure she'd want to help you.'

Jinny teetered to her feet. 'Yeah, I'll call. Can I go now?'

Anna stood up, watching the fragile figure wearing the dead girl's shoes totter out of the front door. The two guys sitting on the steps laughed; one put his hand up her skirt but she swiped it away.

Brandon came down the stairs; he was sucking his right hand.

'Fucking piece of shit. He threw a punch at me, so I got one back at him and he tried to kick me in the nuts! He missed – but I didn't.'

Anna walked out of the door, passing the two lounging boys; she looked at them, almost daring them to touch her, but they cowered away.

Back in the patrol car, they headed out of the rundown street, Anna at the wheel.

'Okay, Mark identified the bloke from the white Range Rover: six feet four, black, two gold teeth, missing tooth in the front.'

'Sounds like Rashid Burry,' she said.

'He told Mark to put Carly Ann's gear into a bag, said she wouldn't be coming round any more, and that if he tried to find her, he would wind up with his throat slit. This, I reckon, was about a year before she ended up dead. Mark was scared rigid, he said. After the bloke had gone, he looked out of the window. He said there were maybe two other men in the car, but he didn't see clearly; she wasn't there with them though. There was someone dressed in maybe a white tracksuit, 'cos the car door was left open, and then clothes and stuff got thrown onto the pavement, like they weren't worth keeping. He seemed to think that Carly Ann had found some rich punter, 'cos the bloke gave him two hundred quid after kicking him around; threw it at him, and warned him not to try to look for her.'

'So he never saw her again?'

'Nope.'

Anna sighed, trying to calculate how long Carly Ann had to have been with the so-called rich punter before moving to Dora's; it could only have been a matter of months. In that time, she was given a lot of jewellery and fine clothes, too much for someone just using her as a whore — unless the clients he was able to pass her on to paid big money. It made sense that if Carly Ann walked away from this person, they wouldn't like it.

Langton had not only shipped in Frank Brandon to swell the murder team, but they now also had a mass of clerical workers and uniformed officers attached to the station. The manpower was costing a fortune. Langton's budget was severely depleted; he had put in numerous requests for further finances. When he eventually joined the team, he looked exhausted.

He stood staring at the board, his eyes roaming over the mass of information, as everyone quietly gathered. Drawing up chairs to sit in a semicircle around him, they waited.

He gave a long sigh.

'Okay, I tried to contact your Professor Starling about the voodoo connection, Anna, but he's gone to Luxor on some dig or other, so Grace and I have been to various quacks, trying to get something that might help us. It seems to me that our only possible hope is to break this Idris Krasiniqe and see if he does have some information that can assist us. As you can all see, we need it. It beggars belief that, after this length of time, we are still at square one. I am not aiming fault at any one of us; we've all been working our butts off, but it seems we just can't get a break. The last report in we have about the medical condition of Eamon Krasiniqe is he's fading fast, so time is against us.'

He was about to continue when Harry Blunt raced in. Langton turned, irritated.

'Call's just come in from a crusher's yard: they've got the Range Rover. They've not touched it more than to sit behind the steering wheel.' Harry had to heave to get his breath. 'I've had the squad at Scotland Yard send it over to their guys; I said to start on it straight away.'

Langton gestured to Harry for him to calm down. 'How did it get there?'

'Guy walked in, paid over the money, said someone had put sand in the ignition and it was screwed. He said he wanted to watch it going up the ramp to make sure they didn't fuck around with it. They agreed and went through the deal, then had one of 'em remove the plates – got to have everything recorded. The bloke was getting real uptight, but when he sees it heading up to the crusher, he pisses off, leaving the plates behind. The boss smells something isn't kosher, stops the machine and calls in the locals. Gov, it's the missing Range Rover! White body, black-tinted windows and the licence plates tally!'

The buzz went round the incident room: just as they felt they were going nowhere, at last they had a break. Harry gave the description of the driver as a tall, black guy, well-dressed. He had someone waiting for him outside the yard in a red four-door Mercedes, but they didn't see who.

No sooner had the buzz died down, when a second call came in. This time, it was Brandon who took it.

'Scotland Yard: they've opened the Range Rover. There's something in the back of it.'

The naked body was wrapped in black bin-liners. It was that of a black male, around six feet four, with cropped hair, minus a front tooth but with two gold teeth. The body had been virtually folded in half to make it fit inside the boot.

The patrol car with Langton and Anna sped up to London, followed by Harry Blunt and Brandon. The crusher's yard was already awash with spotlights when they arrived and a team of experts was preparing to strip the car down. The boot remained open; the body had not as yet been removed.

Langton took Anna's elbow and led her to the back of the Range Rover. The black plastic had been slit to enable them to see the dead man's face. A scientist wearing gloves and a mask gently eased the head round for Anna to get a better view. She moved closer and, from behind her mask, asked if they could use a spatula to lift his lips, so she could clearly see his teeth.

'Yes, it's Rashid Burry,' she said.

Langton nodded for them to continue working; the police would be able to confirm the man's identity from fingerprints on record. There was little else for them to do until the scientists and pathologist were ready for them. The mortuary van pulled in, ready to transfer Rashid to the mortuary, as Langton spoke briefly to the head forensic officer. He confided quietly that they were desperate: they needed anything they could get from the car that would help their investigation. He was reassured that forensics would remove the seats and the wheels to check the vehicle inch by inch, inside and out.

Mike and Brandon remained at the yard, but Langton wanted to get back to the incident room. Returning to the car, he seemed very subdued.

Anna gave him a small smile. 'We just got lucky. I'm sure this is a major step forwards.'

Langton wasn't that confident. He sat in the front seat, eyes closed, as Anna contacted the station to tell everyone that Langton wanted a press blanket on the new development.

By now it was after nine. Anna was tired, but needed to collect her own car from the Hampshire station. She couldn't think of anything more to say to him, as he remained with his eyes closed, so she gently reached out and touched his shoulder.

'You okay?'

'Yes.' He rubbed his eyes.

'You want some water? I have a bottle with me.'

'No.'

She looked out of the window, and watched as the night traffic passed. She wanted to ask Langton about his sessions with the voodoo doctors, or cranks as he called them, but he seemed not to want any interruption. The driver drove in silence, never glancing back to her in the rear seat. She closed her eyes, then opened them quickly when she heard a soft low moan; she leaned forwards to look at Langton, but he appeared to be asleep.

Langton could feel the blade cutting into his flesh, the flash of agony erupting through his entire body. He fell forwards as the blood spurted; the slash to his thigh cut it wide open, slicing through his clothes as if they were made of butter. Then he fell backwards down the stairs. His heart pumped so ferociously he truly felt it had been hacked apart. His brain was splitting in two with the searing pain.

He wasn't sleeping: he was wide awake.

The man grinning, as Langton's blood sprayed over him, was the man whose face he had just seen through the slit in the black bin-liner – a face he had been unable to recall in any detail until now. But Rashid was not the man who had slashed him; he was the man standing behind his attacker. Rashid Burry had been there. Rashid Burry had witnessed the attack – and he had laughed.

Langton kept his eyes closed; he would keep this to himself. It was imperative that no one knew. If it was made public, he would be replaced – and the case was what was keeping him going through the persistent pain he had to deal with every day and night. Langton knew he was getting closer to tracking down the man who had wielded the machete. He didn't want to find Camorra dead; he wanted him very much alive.

Chapter Fifteen

Rashid Burry's photograph, pinned on the board, now had a red cross over his face. He had been garrotted, the thin cord still left around his neck, and had been dead for around forty-eight hours. They would have to wait for further information until the post mortem and the forensic examination of the Range Rover were complete but, as everyone gathered for an update, there was a much more positive feel.

Langton appeared, refreshed and energized, as he gave the details of the discovery. He then discussed his inter-action with the voodoo doctors; he made them laugh, with some funny stories about the cranks and timewasters he'd had to interview. He then moved on to the one meeting he felt might have been beneficial.

'Okay, we have a doctor calling himself Elmore Salaam – whether that's his real name or not, who knows? He has a pretty substantial practice in the East End, with certifi-cates plastered all over the waiting room. He has worked in Haiti and Jamaica, and is originally from New Orleans. He's married to a woman called Esme, who acts as his receptionist and nurse; she is the one who shepherds his patients in to see him. He works on what appears to be a mostly cash basis, but it looked legit; he assured me that he pays his taxes, and I believe him. He looks the business: long white robe, heavy crucifix and a lot of gold rings, but I noticed he had pretty expensive loafers on underneath! He was very eloquent and gave me a long diatribe about his work as a healer. His patients are often suffering from anxiety and simple afflictions, for which he prescribes herbal remedies.'

Langton paused to sip his coffee before he continued. 'To get him on to voodoo took some time, as he was at pains to explain that it was not his practice; that said, he is an authority on its rituals and has written a number of paperbacks.'

Langton held up a few thin volumes that looked as if they had been printed off his own computer.

'He was very serious, explaining that some of his patients have been scared rigid. Many of the people who come to him are illiterate, and it takes many sessions using his knowledge of psychology – in which he has a degree – to calm them into understanding that whatever curses or hexes have been put on them can be eradicated.'

Harry Blunt stifled a yawn. Anna knew that he didn't believe in any of that crap and would be impatient to know where it was all leading, but just then, Grace Ballagio joined Langton.

'Okay, whilst the Gov was getting the info from the doctor, I spent some time with Esme. She was not very forthcoming to start with, but opened up when I did a bit of Pinocchio, saying my aunt lived in New Orleans and that, unlike my boss,' she grinned at Langton, 'I was a believer.'

Grace continued, explaining that they were interrupted every so often by patients with their so-called prescriptions, so Esme was kept busy, measuring out powders and counting out pills by hand in a small anteroom, which gave Grace the opportunity to have a quiet look around. There was a desk with a diary and a chart, with a list of names. When Esme returned, Grace asked her about this, as she would be very interested in learning about her husband's work. Esme told her that she would have to talk to the doctor himself, as this was a private practice.

'I tried to get her to open up and explain what the private practice was. She was very edgy and said that she didn't approve, but running the practice cost money, and some of the patients didn't have any, so they did what they had to do.'

Langton placed his hand on Grace's shoulder. 'Doctor Salaam is a voodoo practitioner: he teaches it to specially chosen students and does not – and he took great care to emphasize this – does not go into the "darkness". That's his word, by the way.'

Grace continued. 'The students obviously pay a lot of money. I asked if Esme could give me names, but she refused. I then changed the subject and asked her if she had something for a migraine. She went into the anteroom, so I nipped back to the diary – but she caught me and snatched it back.'

Langton took over again. 'This was the moment I came out of Elmore's office. His wife said something to him, in I dunno what language, and the friendly priest-cum-doctor-cum-psychiatrist got very nasty. He accused us of being there on false pretences. I had to show my ID again, calm him down, but he was very unpleasant. I got a bit heavy about how he was running his business, but said I didn't want to cause trouble: I was there because I needed his help.'

At this point, Harry Blunt got up and walked across the incident room. Langton glared at him. 'Where you going?'

'I need to take a leak. To be honest, Gov, I dunno where all this is leading, but you've taken a hell of a long time to get to the point.'

'Sit the fuck down!' Langton snapped. He stared around the room. 'Anyone else think this is a load of shite? I am going into the details of what went on for a fucking reason. You want to hear it or not? Right now, we're still flailing around like arseholes. You want to carry on taking a piss, Harry, go do it – and don't come back.'

'For Chrissakes, Gov, it's eleven o'clock. I'm up to my ears in coffee.'

Langton ignored him, then crossed to the board and slapped the name Camorra with the flat of his hand. 'This bastard has been paying Elmore for years. He's obsessed, to such an extent that the doctor started to get uneasy. The only thing the fucker was interested in was the "darkness", for want of a better word.'

Anna sat straight-backed; she couldn't believe it. Langton had not even mentioned this to her. Brandon and Lewis shot covert glances at each other; they, too, had been left in the 'darkness'!

The incident room fell silent.

'Camorra gave them a false address and numerous mobile phone numbers; he changes them frequently, almost weekly. He had sessions with Elmore until his wife said he should not continue: the bastard scared the shit out them, culminating when he brought in a shrunken head and two claws. A child's hands! You want to take a piss now, Harry?'

Harry sat down, sheepishly.

'We need Doctor Salaam, because the one lead we might have is the Krasiniqe kid in Parkhurst who believes he's got a hex on him and is dying. Okay, Harry, if I continue?'

'I'm sorry, Gov.'

Langton outlined the arrangements for Dr Salaam to come in and discuss what he could or could not do to help Eamon Krasiniqe. Time was running out; the boy was dying, so it had been arranged for Elmore to come in and talk to them that same afternoon. They would then make the journey to Parkhurst.

It was after twelve when the briefing ended. Langton had slammed into his office, leaving everyone taken aback. There was quite a lot of ill-feeling from the team, especially Anna, who felt that she should have been informed. She was also somewhat jealous that Grace appeared to have taken her place beside Langton: it was obvious that he no longer wanted her as his sidekick.

At one o'clock, Rashid Burry's post-mortem results came in. He had been injected with a horse tranquillizer, so when he was garrotted he had been unable to move a single one of his massive muscles to save himself. The forensic reports from the search of the Range Rover were also coming, but in dribs and drabs. So far, they had discovered a great number of dog hairs in the rear of the Range Rover, possibly from a longhaired breed, like a German shepherd. The hairs had been sent to a different lab to be tested by an expert in canine DNA. They had found saliva and blood inside the black plastic bags that covered Rashid's body, which were being matched with his DNA. The bags were also being matched to the bag containing the dead boy in the canal, since each roll of bags would have distinctive markings.

They had also found blood and hair in the right-hand rear seat. This was being tested as a match for Carly Ann North. The steering wheel and dashboard had been wiped clean, but fingerprints were being recovered from the rear door and the passenger door. More hair and fibres were found in the front passenger seat, plus mud on the carpet. They were also testing mud from the wheels and the chassis. The teams were working flat out and they hadn't even removed the seats or carpet yet.

Langton read down the list from the forensic report. At long last, the case felt as if it was moving, albeit in many directions. These developments renewed his energy and he hoped that Dr Salaam could move them on a stage further; the Camorra connection had spurred him on and he was getting to feel like his old self, adrenalin buzzing. They still had not been able to trace the property in Peckham linked to Camorra; Langton surmised he had long gone and taken up residence elsewhere.

Early that afternoon, there were further press conferences and interviews, at which the police asked if anyone had seen the Range Rover parked up and, yet again, requested information from the public in connection with Joseph Sickert and Gail's missing children.

The team had been given various tasks, but the main focus of the day was the arrival of Elmore Salaam, to discuss how they would approach Eamon Krasiniqe. They were getting regular bulletins in from the prison authorities: the young man was fading fast. He had been transferred to the hospital wing and was in isolation. The usual medical staff had been overseeing his progress and had called in various different specialists, in an attempt to keep him alive. Sick as he was, he was still able to rip out any attempt to feed him intravenously. They had put him in an oxygen tent, as his breathing had become laboured. According to the prison doctor, he still lifted his right hand to point to the opposite wall and make a slow circular movement, but even these gestures had become less frequent, as he was so weak. Krasiniqe just lay with his expressionless eyes wide open, staring at the ceiling.

Anna had been given the assignment of contacting Missing Persons, in case they had any information regarding the children. It was a time-consuming and depressing job; the number of young children missing was heartbreaking. Many of them had been kidnapped by one parent or the other and taken abroad; others had simply disappeared. Seventy per cent of the children were of ethnic origin and aged between two and eight years old. She was also in contact with immigration, getting lists of children who had been brought into the country under new legislation that allowed family members residing in the UK to act as guardians. There had already been a shocking case of a little girl shipped to a so-called aunt and uncle, and subsequently found brutally abused by both. The child was dead and the adults were now in prison. Anna skimmed the reports to see if any of the social workers had come into contact with Camorra. He was known to be a trafficker, so there was a glimmer of grim hope that perhaps one of these missing children had been part of his vicious trade.

Langton walked out of his office; he motioned to Anna and Grace. 'The doctor and his wife are on their way. I don't want them brought through the incident room; we'll use an interview room. I will need the photographs of the Krasiniqe brothers, medical reports from the prison and so on.'

Grace moved off; he remained by Anna's desk and looked at the mound of paperwork she was dealing with.

'Anything?'

'No, not yet. It makes very depressing reading.'

He nodded and went over to Harry Blunt, who had returned from trying to gather information on Rashid Burry.

Harry wafted his sandwich towards Langton. 'The fucker was only claiming benefits. Gave the same address we had for him at the halfway hostel – bloody unbelievable. We have this bastard's face plastered over the newspapers, in every police station, and he just walks in and picks up his fucking benefits!'

Langton sighed; sometimes Harry's tirades irritated him, but he had to agree with him on this one. 'What you got?'

Harry opened his notebook. 'Last seen Wednesday at the hostel. Social worker – and she was fucking brain dead not to contact us – says he gave her this bullshit about starting work on a building site. She gave him the benefit slips, and asked for a forwarding address; by rights, he was no longer under a probation order, but somewhere ticking in her brain was the fact that we had been there half a dozen times asking about him. Anyway, he gives her a load of bullshit and walks out. She called the local cops to say he had been there; according to them, they were in the process of contacting us! She also said – and this I could believe – that he scared her; one of the reasons she didn't want to get into a confrontation with him was that he was built like a brick shithouse.'

Harry thumbed through his notebook and bit into his sandwich. 'There was a kid there with probation order and tag – probably have that cut off in a few days – anyway, I'm asking around if anyone saw the hulk Rashid, and this boy—'

'How old is he?' Langton interrupted.

'Sixteen: done for aggravated burglary and threatening a police officer – got two years and out on probation for six months.'

Langton gestured for Harry to continue.

'Rashid asks the boy if he wants some extra cash; kid said he was up for anything and Rashid gives him this mobile number.' Harry passed over a Post-it note. 'We've been trying to track it down, but it's another pay-as-you-go bugger, so we might not get much luck; it was over two weeks ago.'

Langton asked whether, when Rashid's body was found, they had also found a mobile.

'Nope, pockets stripped, nothing on him; surprised they left his gold teeth.'

Langton sighed. 'Okay, keep on pushing.' As he turned away, Grace informed him that the doctor and his wife had arrived.

'I'd like to sit in on that one,' Harry said, his mouth full of the last of his sandwich.

Langton smiled and walked out of the incident room, gesturing to Anna to join him.

She was on the telephone and signalled for Langton to wait. 'I've got something,' she mouthed.

'Can't it wait?' he snapped.

'No, it can't.' She had to take a deep breath. 'Two children have just been dumped at a playground in Tooting. Teacher said a black guy was seen at the gates, holding the kids by the hand; then he walked off. They're white – and their ages match those of Gail Sickert's missing children.'

'Jesus Christ, get over there!' He then stopped, frowning. 'No, I need you in with me.' He nodded over to Harry. 'Give him the details, then come into the interview room.'

Anna returned to the caller. 'Have they been able to give their names?' She listened, then said, 'Someone is coming over there straight away.'

It took a while longer for Anna to take further details, before she was able to send Harry to pick up a Family Liaison Officer to accompany him to the Tooting nursery school.

'Fingers crossed, Harry, we might have found Gail Sickert's kids, but neither is talking and both seem traumatized. Pick them up and arrange for a counsellor. You know what to do.'

Harry nodded and sat down to make sure he had all the details as Anna hurried to join Langton, Dr Elmore and his wife Esme.

Anna was taken aback by the stature and appearance of the doctor. He was way over six feet tall and wore an immaculate charcoal grey-suit. His wife Esme was in traditional African wraparound skirt and flowing loose top, with a matching cotton turban. They were a quiet and unassuming couple, with excellent manners. The doctor waited for Anna to sit down, helping her move the chair closer to the table, before he sat down opposite her. Esme did not meet her eyes, but kept her head bowed and her hands folded in her lap.

Langton had already described in detail the murder of Arthur Murphy and the resulting condition of Eamon Krasiniqe. He said that the boy had refused food and was now in isolation, with an oxygen tent helping him breathe.

Anna said nothing as she opened her notebook, listening to Langton.

He explained how Anna had subsequently interviewed Idris Krasiniqe, the sick boy's brother. Dr Salaam asked her to give as much detail about Idris as possible — how he had behaved towards her, and whether she had any more information about the boys' backgrounds. Both were illegal immigrants, she told him; the police were not even sure if their names were real, as they had come into the UK on fake passports.

'Are they twins?' was his next question.

Anna looked to Langton, and they both shrugged; not according to their passports.

Langton continued, moving on to the murder of Carly Ann North. Dr Salaam made no further interruptions. He occasionally glanced at his wife, but she never raised her eyes. Langton went on to outline the death of Gail Sickert and her small child; even though there was now a possibility the other two children might have been found, he implied that they were dead, or being used as sex objects. Esme looked up at the details of the children, then turned away, shaking her head. Langton kept his voice low; in the bare room, the silences when he paused hung in the air. Anna watched him draw on the emotion and aim it especially at Esme.

Langton showed the children's photographs, placing

each one down slowly. Elmore Salaam took out a case and put on a pair of gold-rimmed glasses. Next Langton brought out the hideous mortuary shots of Gail Sickert's body and the skull of her dead child, followed by the photographs of Carly Ann. Lastly, he opened the envelope containing pictures of the torso of the dead boy found in the canal.

'We believe that all these murders have a link to Camorra. We have also just discovered this man, Rashid Burry. His body was found in the rear of a white Range Rover. He had been garrotted and stuffed into black plastic bin-liners; the vehicle was to be crushed.'

Elmore peered very closely at Rashid Burry's photograph; his wife, by now, was sitting well back in her chair, her head averted from the appalling array of death laid out on the table.

Langton gave a small nod to Anna.

'Doctor Salaam, Mrs Salaam,' she began, 'we are very much in need of someone to help with the boy Eamon Krasiniqe. If we are able to save him, his brother Idris has promised me that he will give us information. We believe that both the brothers were involved with Camorra, but Idris is too afraid to speak to us. He is in prison for the murder of Carly Ann North. He admitted the murder, and when first arrested he—'

Langton interrupted her. 'He gave us two names – men he said were part of the murder – but we were unable to trace them.'

Anna looked at him. He made no mention of his attack and, by interrupting her, made sure she did not bring it up either.

'Idris pleaded guilty to the murder, but retracted his statement,' she went on. 'He said no one else was involved, and that he alone committed the rape and attempted mutilation of her body. We have two samples of DNA taken from her body, so we know Idris was not the only man who raped her or had sex with her before she died.' Anna looked nervously at Langton, wondering if he wanted her to give even these details.

Amongst the array of mortuary shots and pictures of Gail Sickert's children was the computer e-fit of Joseph Sickert. Dr Salaam, who, unlike his wife, had shown no emotion, pointed to it, and Langton passed it to him. He stared at it, then turned to his wife. Side by side, the couple gave the picture their full attention, then placed it down on the table in front of them.

'Do you recognize this man?' Langton asked.

The doctor gave a slow nod of his head, and his wife seemed to agree.

'I think it is the same man,' he said. 'He came to see us about ten months ago. He was very sick, suffering from a blood disease. It was advanced: his eyes were yellow with kidney infection. Esme said she was certain he had sickle cell anaemia, but we would require blood tests. We arranged for another appointment and gave him some herbal remedies to help his condition.'

Esme spoke up. 'We do not have the facilities to carry out blood tests; that would have had to be done at the local hospital, as with any medical practice. With advanced sickle disease, if not given the correct medication, the organs begin to fail. This man was very sick.'

'So what happened?'

Esme looked to her husband. 'He never kept his appointment. He was also unable to pay for the treatment. We never saw him again.'

Dr Salaam placed the e-fit picture of Joseph Sickert to

one side, almost on the edge of the table away from all the other photographs. He then drew forwards Rashid Burry's picture. 'This man brought him to my surgery – the man found in the car; he was very unpleasant and threatened my wife. He said that he would pay for the treatment. Correct?' He turned to Esme and she nodded.

'Was he a regular patient? I mean, did he bring other people to your surgery?' Langton asked, hardly able to contain himself. Rashid Burry's photograph had been plastered all over the newspapers and on television crime shows, along with Joseph Sickert's, and yet here were this couple, calmly identifying them.

'No, he did not. As I said, he was very unpleasant and threatened my wife. I told him he was not welcome to come to my place of work again and that if he did, I would call the police.'

'So you were never paid?' Anna asked Esme.

The woman glanced at her husband, her eyes half-closed; she had the faintest of smiles on her full lips. 'Yes – yes, he did pay. Some patients we do not even ask for money; others, especially men like that one, do eventually pay – sometimes a lot more than we have asked.'

Dr Salaam reached out to gently cover his wife's hand, as if warning her to keep silent. He then picked up Gail Sickert's photograph.

'I do not know this sad woman.'

He left that photograph in front of him; next, he took the picture of the headless corpse of the little boy and placed it on top of Rashid Burry. The child's skull he moved aside, as if not interested. He collected Idris and Eamon's mug shots and stacked them on top of the Rashid Burry picture. Lastly, he passed the picture of Carly Ann North to Esme, who looked at it very carefully and nodded as he added it to the pile.

Langton and Anna watched in fascination, no idea what he was doing or why, as Dr Salaam then placed his hands gently on top of the stack and bent his head. His deep voice was even lower.

'They are connected,' he said.

Langton waited and glanced at Anna, who sat staring at the massive man's beautiful hands spread over the pictures. Grace, who had not said one word throughout, but sat silently listening to everything, was as nonplussed. The three of them were unsure what to say next.

'We will need protection,' Elmore Salaam murmured. He then sat bolt upright, picked up the mug shot of Clinton Camorra and placed it to one side.

'The link between these souls is this man. His real name, I believe, is Emmerick Camorra. He uses many aliases, but the name by which he is known to me is Emmerick Camorra. If I help you with this tortured boy Krasiniqe, if it is known that my wife and I are involved, we will be targeted by Camorra. He has an army of crazed, dependent soldiers. They will do anything he asks, and if it is to cut my throat, rape and murder my beloved wife, they will do it. If we agree to see this Krasiniqe boy, it must be kept secret; if it isn't, then we cannot help you. Remove him from the prison, remove his brother to somewhere safe, and we will attempt to help you; if this cannot be done, then we cannot place ourselves at risk.'

Langton was speechless. He half-rose out of his seat and then sat down again. 'Doctor Salaam, I assure you that I will arrange round-the-clock protection for you and your wife. We have been unable to track down Camorra, but if you could help us and assist—'

Elmore Salaam leaned over the table. His voice boomed. 'I do not think you have any understanding of how dangerous this man is. I do, because he learned from me; but then he became obsessed, and not with the good. Camorra has embraced the devil and worships Satan; he uses terror and threats to naive innocent souls who believe that he is a high priest.'

Salaam eased himself away from the table and walked to the far wall. He pointed, just as they had seen Krasiniqe do. 'This is someone controlling time; when they stop, you die. This boy is trying to keep the hours to live. If he can no longer lift his hand, the finger of death has stopped his heart.'

Esme quietly rose from her chair and went to her husband's side. For the first time, they could see that he was close to weeping. She held his hand, and it seemed to soothe him.

'We have to go now,' she said.

Langton remained sitting, staring over the table covered in photographs, while Grace took the doctor and his wife out. They refused to leave in an unmarked patrol car, but had chosen a circuitous route of trains, buses and taxis, afraid lest anyone should find out about the police interview.

Anna began to gather up the photographs. She felt really shaken. 'What do you think?' she asked Langton.

He yawned and stretched his arms above his head. 'What I think is, why the fuck didn't they come forward before? We're months into an enquiry. Don't they read the fucking newspapers?' He mimicked the doctor. 'Oh, this is Joseph Sickert, he came as a patient.' He banged the table. 'We've been hunting that bastard for fucking weeks: he's been on the front page of all the papers, on the TV news, on TV crime shows. Oh, and yes, we've got the wrong name for the bastard. They call him Emmerick not Clinton.' Langton held up the mug shot of the man they knew as Clinton Camorra. 'And they fucking know him! Taught him his sicko voodoo shit! Yet God forbid they know where he is now. It makes me wanna strangle the pair of them. This bastard Camorra's gonna do my fucking head in. *That's* what I think.'

'Well, maybe they were scared.'

Langton picked up the dead boy's photograph. 'Tell that to this little child, his head and hands cut off; don't give me that shit about them being scared. That bastard has been shipping in Christ knows how many kids, and they've been doing their crap stuff out of their make-believe surgery with all those bullshit credentials.'

'What about giving them protection?' Anna asked.

'Oh, they'll get it; it'll look like we've got Bin Laden under fucking wraps! My budget's already through the bloody roof.'

The door opened midway through his tirade. It was Grace.

'Harry just called in. We have found Gail Sickert's children.'

Langton's reaction surprised Anna: he put his hand over his face and almost wept. 'Oh, thank Christ!'

Chapter Sixteen

Harry Blunt was sitting at his desk; he had the telephone cupped to his ear.

'Kiss them goodnight for me and tell them I love them. I'll be late, sweetheart, so don't wait up.'

Anna put down a cup of coffee as he replaced the receiver. She gave him a kindly pat on his shoulder. 'Maybe we won't be that late tonight.'

'Thank you, sorry to be ... At least they'd been fed and they were quite clean – well, the little girl was, but the boy had soiled his pants.'

'You think it was Sickert who dropped them at the nursery school?'

'I guess, I dunno. It was a pretty poor description, but it could have been him.'

Anna sighed. 'Well, they're in good hands now, and the counsellors will help. They'll stay with them at the unit.'

'Good hands? Their mother's dead, *and* their little sister – and Christ only knows what's been done to them. Those units are pretty sterile. You know what, Anna? I wanted to pick them both up and take them home. Tore my heart out, the little girl especially. She clung onto her brother ...' He turned to Anna. 'I bent down to talk to her, you know, trying to get on her level, and she shrank away from me with such a look of terror on her face, and the boy, Christ, as young as he is, he put his fists up as if he wanted to protect her.'

'Well, don't think about it,' she said gently.

He shook his head. 'One day, you might have kids, and let me tell you, your whole perspective changes. They become the most important part of you. If anything happened to mine, I'd bloody kill for them.'

'Have they contacted their grandmother – Beryl Dunn?'

Harry shrugged. 'I wouldn't leave a stray cat with that woman, but yes, I guess they will speak to her. In the meantime, they're just gonna try and see if they can get the kids to talk; neither one's said a word. They're like mutes.'

Mike Lewis joined them, looking depressed. Like everyone else in the incident room, he'd been told about the children. With one toddler and a new baby, he had also been upset.

Langton decided they should call it quits for the night. Tomorrow, they would have more details from the forensic department and, by then, he would also have a safe house and round-the-clock protection arranged for the doctor and his wife.

Negotiations with the prison service were proving tough. Langton wanted both brothers removed from their prisons. They would require a secure room at a hospital, with officers guarding both of them. Eamon Krasiniqe would be lifted by emergency helicopter from Parkhurst. This would also require medical staff on board, and staff waiting to take him into the allocated hospital wing. The planned removal of Idris Krasiniqe from

Wakefield also entailed numerous officers and vehicles. The prison authorities had kicked up about removing Idris, but Langton had talked himself hoarse in explaining the importance of his presence at the hospital. After much discussion, it had been decided the safest place would be the Contagious Disease Unit at Farmworth. The cost was breaking the back of his already depleted budget, and the hours of calls and discussions had taken its toll. He looked exhausted; they all did.

Langton gave a look around the incident room and clapped his hands. 'Tomorrow is going to be a big day, so get a good night's sleep and let's hope to Christ it'll all be worth it.'

Anna was packing up her desk when Langton passed; he gave her a small half-smile. 'You think this is all going to play out?'

'I don't know.'

'Terrific,' he muttered. 'You don't know, I don't fucking know, but I'm pulling out all the stops. Those two voodoo experts could be quacks, but they're all we've got. You instigated the Krasiniqe situation.'

'Well, I just reported what Idris said to me. He could be bullshitting,' she said defensively.

'Now you tell me!'

'I am not telling you anything! I just reported back to you what he said to me, but if you want me to take the responsibility for the set-up tomorrow, then fine.'

He snapped back at her, 'That's my job. No way would I want you or anyone else to take responsibility for my decisions; it's just taken me bloody hours to arrange.' He gave a hands-up gesture. 'Maybe I just needed some assurance, I obviously came to the wrong person.'

'Please don't. You know that I − in fact, everyone on the team − we're behind you one hundred per cent. You don't need any of our assurance, because whatever you are doing is for one reason, to get this case closed.'

He cocked his head to one side and leaned close. 'No. It's to get Camorra. That's who I want.' He walked away before she could answer.

She watched as he invited everyone to the pub for a drink. His mood changed so fast; he laughed and bellowed as he shrugged into his overcoat. 'I dunno about anyone else but I need a drink; I'm in the chair.' She watched Grace hurry to his side, saw him rest his arm around her shoulders. Lewis, Brandon and Harry all trooped around him as they left the incident room.

Anna continued clearing her desk. She felt paranoid, certain that Langton had deliberately not included her. She was sometimes at a loss how to even talk to him. At least she no longer felt like having a good cry over his behaviour; she was, if anything, becoming more adroit in dealing with him. Picking up her coat, she looked around the depleted incident room and hesitated: should she go to the pub? Langton had told her in no uncertain terms about being a team player; and here she was, dithering about whether or not she should join the team for a drink. Getting into her Mini, Anna drove to the local pub that they had commandeered as their drinking hole.

The Anchor was a large, modern, rather tacky place, with a lot of bingo machines and piped music, but the landlord was a very open and friendly man who joked that having the cops in every night had lost him some of his customers, but not the ones he missed!

Anna felt very self-conscious as she joined everyone at the bar.

Langton turned, a surprised expression on his face. 'Ah, Travis! Well, come and sit down. This is a first. What'll you have?'

'White wine, please.'

Langton ordered, as Brandon drew up one of the high stools. She perched next to him as a rather sweet and tepid white wine was placed in front of her. She lifted the glass to Langton to thank him, but he was listening to one of Harry's shaggy dog stories. It felt as if he was pointedly ignoring her; she drew a bowl of peanuts closer.

'I was thinking of grabbing some fish and chips,' Brandon said, as he dug into the bowl. 'You fancy coming along?'

'No, I'll just have this one and then hit the road.'

'There's an Italian joint, if you'd prefer it,' Brandon continued. 'They do a reasonable spaghetti meatballs.'

Anna smiled. 'Thanks, but I'm not that hungry.'

Harry finished his shaggy dog story; Langton laughed and launched into one himself, at the same time gesturing to the landlord for another round. Anna noticed he was drinking beer with whisky chasers; empty packets of crisps were crumpled in front of him.

She had to apologize to Brandon, as she realized that he'd been talking to her and she hadn't heard. 'Sorry, what was that?'

'I said, there's also a Chinese takeaway.'

'Frank, I'm not hungry, really.'

'I suppose a fuck's out of the question?'

'What?!'

'Joke! Just a joke. By the look of the Gov he'll be here all night. He is here most nights, but then he's only a few yards down the road; the rest of us have to schlep back to London.'

Anna sipped the tepid wine, another glass already placed down beside it.

'What about going out one evening in Town? I know some really good restaurants.'

'Yes, maybe – that would be nice.'

'When?'

'What?'

'I said, when do you want to come out?'

She suddenly realized Brandon was asking for a dinner date, and she flushed. 'Well, it depends on when I'm free. Right now, it doesn't look as if any of us will get time off.'

He put his arm around her waist, leaning in too close for comfort.

'Let's take a rain check,' she said, uneasy at his hand pressing into her back.

At least he'd cut down on his cologne. She didn't touch the second glass but excused herself, saying she had a long drive. It was a cue for everyone to go. She left, with Brandon and Lewis, as Harry went to the gents. Waving goodbye, she headed for her Mini. She dug in her pockets for her keys, then in her handbag. She swore: she was sure she'd had them in her hand when she went into the pub. Certain now that she must have left them on the counter, she went back in as everyone drove off.

Langton was still sitting at the bar, resting his head in his hands. She looked around the stool she'd been sitting on, then saw the keys on the floor. She picked them up and glanced over to him; he didn't seem to notice she had returned. She was about to walk away, when something made her change her mind. Going up to him, she touched him lightly on his back.

'Dropped my keys,' she said.

He raised his head and turned to face her. He looked terrible.

'You all right?'

'No. My leg's stiffened up.' He sighed. 'I can't get off the bloody stool.'

'Well, let me help you. Lean on me.'

He placed one arm around her shoulders as she bent forwards, grimacing in agony as he tried to ease himself into a standing position. She could hardly take the weight of him, and almost toppled over.

She looked to the landlord and gasped, 'Could you give me a hand?'

With his help, they got Langton standing and, with one either side of him, he walked very slowly to the door.

'This is getting to be a nightly ritual,' the landlord joked, as he helped Langton and Anna out into the car park.

Together, they got him into the passenger seat of her Mini, pushing it as far back as it would go, with a lot of moans and groans from Langton. He directed her a short distance across the car park and into a road of terraced houses. The end house was the small Bed and Breakfast.

Anna had a hard time helping him out to stand upright; again, he needed to lean heavily on her shoulders to walk up the path. He fumbled for his keys and passed them to her. Anna opened the front door as he leaned against the doorframe.

'Okay, I can make it from here. I'm on the ground floor.'

Anna ignored him and continued to prop him up until they reached his bedroom door.

He grinned and made shushing sounds. 'Don't let the old biddy hear; we're not allowed company!'

The room was old-fashioned, with a large dressing table, heavy oak wardrobe and awful flowered carpet. The bed was a single, with a candlewick bedspread. His clothes and shoes were strewn around the room, and beside the bed were files and old newspapers.

She got him to sit on the bed and removed his shoes and socks; he took off his own jacket, chucking it across the bed to land on a wicker chair. He loosened his tie. His face became red with exertion as he tried to undo his shirt buttons.

Anna looked around for some pyjamas, but couldn't see any. He flopped back onto the pillows. On the bedside table were a couple of empty whisky bottles and an array of pill bottles and containers.

'Do you need to take any of these?' she asked, looking over them.

'No, I'll sleep now.' He offered his hand, and she clasped it. 'Sorry about this; no need to mention it to anyone, okay?'

'As if I would,' she said.

Still he clasped her hand. 'You okay to drive home?' he asked.

She shook her head, smiling. She found it farcical that he was concerned about her. 'One glass of wine!'

Eventually, he released his hold of her hand.

She suggested he take a shower and get into bed but he laughed, saying there was only the shared bathroom and no way was he going to get up.

'Just leave me, let me sleep it off.'

She bent forwards, wanting to kiss him. She still cared deeply about him, and it hurt to see him so crumpled. 'I'll see you in the morning.'

He gave a half-smile. 'I'll be okay, just need to crash out.'

By the time she had folded his clothes and tidied up the room, he was asleep. She switched on the small lamp by his bed and took a long look at him. In the half-light, the face she had loved so much seemed grey. Even in sleep, it was etched with pain. It was distressing: she felt as if she was looking at a shell of what he had been, thinner and more gaunt than ever. She suspected he wasn't eating properly, and the overflowing ashtrays she'd tipped in the bin were proof that he had not given up smoking as he had been warned to.

It was late by the time Anna got home. She hadn't eaten, but she was now too tired. She crawled into her clean fresh sheets, but sleep didn't come easily: she was unable to stop thinking about Langton.

In theory, she knew that his health issue should be made known, but no way could she make out a report, detailing that DCI Langton should be given leave of absence because he was dependent on alcohol and painkillers to get through the day.

She was surprised when her alarm rang; she'd fallen into a deep, dreamless sleep, leaving the bedside light on.

Operation Eagle was to swing into action mid-afternoon. This would give the team time to co-ordinate all the different cases. Anna arrived at half-past eight; the incident room was already a hive of activity. Just as she reached her desk, Langton's office door banged open. She could hardly believe her eyes.

He strode in, wearing a smart suit and fresh shirt, his energy level at top notch. He clapped his hands.

'Joseph Sickert has been traced. He's in Westminster Hospital. He walked into Casualty and collapsed; he's on a life-support machine.'

He gestured for Anna and Mike Lewis to accompany him. It was doubtful Sickert was going to last long; his blood disease had reached crisis level and his organs were failing.

As they drove out, with sirens blasting, Langton turned to face Anna and Mike in the rear seat. 'Bloody unbelievable. We've got one dying prisoner being flown in, now we've got another bugger at death's door.'

'How bad is he?' Lewis asked.

'Dying; liver and kidney failure. He's on a dialysis machine but they have said it's only a matter of time. His heart's giving out as well, bastard!'

If Langton had pains in his leg, it didn't show as he marched along the hospital corridor. They were met by a battery of doctors and nurses, who did not feel the patient could be interviewed.

Langton let rip. In no uncertain terms, he set out the reasons why it was imperative. He brought up the dead child, the skull at the bungalow; they wanted to question him and they should be given access, whether he was dying or not.

'Just keep him alive long enough for me to talk to him, that's all I ask.' Langton faced down the doctor, almost daring him to argue.

The young doctor was shaking; he said that his

responsibility was to his patient. Langton almost pinned him against the wall.

'That animal you are so intent on saving butchered a two-year-old toddler – cut off her head, all right? Now, ultimately, I don't give a fuck if he lives or dies – all I want is ten minutes with him.' He didn't shout; it was more unnerving as he kept his voice low, but he was so angry, he was frightening.

Langton insisted on speaking to anyone with the authority to allow him access to Sickert. Lewis raised his eyebrows at Anna, but she turned away, refusing to be drawn into approving or disapproving of Langton's actions.

After fifteen minutes, they were given permission to be taken to the Intensive Care Unit.

As they followed two nurses, Langton turned to Lewis. 'Fucking brilliant, isn't it? Illegal immigrant, murderer – and look at the way they are treating him – like he was royalty! This is where our taxes go. How much do you think it's costing to keep this son of a bitch alive?'

The Intensive Care Unit was manned by specially trained nurses, who moved around his bedside. There was so much equipment, Sickert could barely be seen. The oxygen pumped away, making loud hissing noises. Anna looked through the window into the room, Langton by her side.

'Can you see him?' Langton demanded.

'Not really.'

'For Chrissakes, is it him?'

'I don't know – I can't see him,' she said tetchily.

Langton signalled to a nurse for Anna to be gowned up and taken into the room. He was still waiting for the moment when they could question Sickert and, judging by the amount of concerned activity in the room, it was not looking likely to be any time soon.

Anna was led to the bedside. She shook her head; it was impossible for her to say if this was the man she had met for that brief moment at Gail's bungalow. He had been muscular, with dreadlocks. Now all she saw was this wizened creature, whose frame was like a skeleton and whose face was obscured by an oxygen mask.

Anna rejoined Langton. 'I can't say if it's him.'

'Shit! Well, whoever it is has sickle cell blood disease, and it's killing him. He gave his name as Joseph Sickert. He must have been walking around without medication, deteriorating until he crawled into Casualty. You want to take another look?'

'I've told you, that man is rake thin and shaven-headed. The man I saw was huge and muscular, with dreadlocks.'

'This disease wastes muscles. It can affect the heart, lungs and kidneys; his blood count is almost zero and his heart is only just holding out, so whether you can ID him or not, I'm going in. If he's been living rough for all the bloody weeks we've been searching for him, then he might have lost some fucking weight.' Langton took off to talk to the same, very nervous doctor.

Lewis and Anna were handed a plastic bag containing the patient's clothes. Sitting on hard-backed chairs, they checked for anything that could help identify him. There was a small blue teddy bear, chewed and worn, almost bald, stuffed into the pocket of an old denim jacket. They also found a screwed-up five-pound note, some loose change, bus tickets, a broken pencil and, folded over and over until the cracks in the photograph almost made it fall apart as it was opened, a picture of two small black children and a woman wearing a wraparound cotton dress. Nothing was written on the back; neither Lewis nor Anna recognized the people in the photograph.

'Not a lot, if this was all he had,' said Lewis, placing the items into a plastic evidence bag. Anna continued to search through his clothing: she patted the filthy jeans, turning the pockets inside out. Lewis did the same with a flowered shirt; it stank of body odour and was torn almost to shreds. There were socks, equally stinking, and a pair of filthy trainers. They smelt disgusting but Anna felt inside them, almost pulling them apart. They were a big size, at least twelve; she frowned and then looked again at the denim jacket.

'It's huge, so are the trousers; do we know how tall the patient is? Sickert was at least six foot three. I mean, if he's been sick for weeks . . .'

At that point, Langton approached to say he was being allowed to go in.

Anna showed him the photograph. 'We don't recognize them though.'

Lewis felt his mobile jangle in his pocket; all around the corridor were notices forbidding their use. He got up and walked a short distance away. Langton took the photograph in its plastic bag and went over to a nurse, who was waiting with a gown and mask.

Lewis huddled in a corner, listening to Harry Blunt. Forensic had unearthed some more information from the white Range Rover. Tests on the wheels of the vehicle were proving very positive: there were small traces of manure and mud. Each sample had been sent to a special laboratory for analysis; they had confirmed that, at some stage, the vehicle had been at the bungalow. They were still carrying out further tests on hairs and fibres, and would have more results that afternoon.

Anna had remained sitting on the hard-backed chair outside the ICU; Lewis updated her, then looked through the window.

'He talking yet?'

'Not that I can tell; Langton's only been in there five minutes.'

'Christ. What if, after all this, it isn't him?'

The patient's clothes had all been packed into plastic containers and put on the seat next to Anna. She picked them up, so Mike could sit next to her. On the top, in a plastic bag, was the small, moth-eaten teddy bear.

Anna stared at it and tried to recall the child in the swing at the bungalow. It had all been so long ago, but she concentrated.

'You okay?' Mike asked, as she sat very still, her eyes shut.

She sat up. 'I am not one hundred per cent certain, but I think this was at the bungalow; the little girl Tina had it in her mouth. I think it's the same toy, but I just can't be sure.'

'Well, they'll get DNA off it.'

Inside the unit, Langton stared into the face of the dying man, trying to recall if he had been at the halfway house. Spittle had formed in globules around the patient's thick pallid lips. His eyes were like dead purple flowers; his fingers were swollen, the nails a strange milky white.

The more Langton stared, the more he was certain it was not the man who had cut him down.

He carefully unfolded the photograph and held it close. 'You need to let them know where you are.'

No response.

'I can contact them for you – get them to come and see you,' he whispered.

No response.

'Two little children – are they yours? And this lovely woman – is she your wife?'

No response.

As Langton folded the picture back up, one of the bulbous fingers lifted, as if to stop him putting it away.

'Do you want it?'

No response.

Langton began to unfold the photograph; he saw tears filling the washed-out eyes.

'I need to talk to you. Are you Joseph Sickert?'

He nodded. It was such a small movement, but at last Langton had the confirmation that the dying man was Joseph Sickert.

'Gail's kids are safe now,' Langton whispered, saying that he knew Sickert had helped them.

This also elicited a response, another small nod of his head.

'Did you have them with you? Did you take the children from Gail?'

No response.

The heart monitor was jumping; Langton could almost hear the dying man's lungs filling with fluid. The staff were getting agitated; Langton knew that any moment now, they would kick him out.

Langton stood up and leaned over him, his voice like the hiss of the machines. 'Gail was found in the yard, mutilated, her body fed to the pigs; is that what you want to die with? It'll haunt you; you'll lie with the devil, you bastard! Talk to me, talk to me!'

The doctor entered the room; the nurses looked to

him in a panic. He was about to ask Langton to leave, but Sickert lifted his thick, bulbous hand and tried to reach out to Langton. The word, 'No ...' sounded out loud. Langton leaned over him, trying to catch the words that Sickert spewed out between terrible guttural gasps, as the phlegm in his lungs moved up into his throat.

Anna and Lewis were astonished to see that Sickert was talking; they could not tell what he was saying, as Langton's arched body hid him from their sight. It felt like a long time, but it was no more than two minutes at the most before Langton was ushered out. He didn't seem in any way emotionally moved by what had taken place; he merely ripped off his mask and gown, tossing them aside.

'Let's go,' he grunted, heading down the corridor, and they hurried after him, carrying the evidence bags.

As they left the building, Mike informed Langton that the Range Rover had been at the piggery. He just nodded his head and looked at his wristwatch; time was against them, and they had one hell of an afternoon ahead.

Anna reported that she was certain the teddy bear had belonged to Gail's dead toddler. He slammed the door of the patrol car, turned and glared at her; then faced front.

'I think Sickert's belongings should be dropped off at the lab,' she added.

Langton snapped that they should call in a squad car to take them; they didn't want to lose time.

Mike Lewis put in the call and Anna sat chewing her lip, waiting. Lewis finished the call, glanced at Anna and gave a shrug. Langton had still not said one word about the interaction with Sickert.

'So, did you get anything, Gov?' Mike asked finally.

Langton nodded and again looked at his wristwatch. 'We'll have a working lunch, then get over to do the interviews with the Krasiniqe pricks and the voodoo nutters.'

By the time they reached the New Forest, they had confirmation that Operation Eagle was on course. There were now fifty more officers brought in; Langton knew he could not put on pressure for any more.

He strode into the incident room, his positive energy and physical appearance still confusing Anna. He appeared to have no ill-effects from the previous evening; on the contrary. He paused only to tell Grace to order in sandwiches and coffee, as there would be a lunchtime briefing. Just as he reached his office, Grace received a call from Westminster Hospital; she asked if he wished to take it. He shook his head.

Joseph Sickert had died fifteen minutes after they had left the hospital. Langton didn't even react; he simply nodded his head and then instructed her to arrange for the body to be taken to the mortuary, as he wanted a post mortem. Then he strode into his office and shut the door.

The room erupted, everyone wanting to know what had taken place. Anna and Lewis filled them in as much as they could, but they did not know if Sickert had said anything of any consequence; Langton had not discussed it with them.

'Well – one down. Still a few more bastards to get,' Harry Blunt said.

Langton closed the blinds in his office, took out three painkillers and uncapped a flask to gulp them down with vodka. Then he opened his notebook and began to write copious notes. As he returned the flask to his desk drawer, he glanced down at Camorra's details. He touched them lightly with his index finger.

'Getting closer,' he whispered.

Removing his tie, he neatly folded his jacket into a pillow and lay down on the floor, closing his eyes. He would need all his strength for the afternoon. He just hoped to God that he would still be able to stand upright, let alone cope; he knew better than anyone else that this was killing him.

By three o'clock, Operation Eagle would be rolling; the vast number of officers required was costly and he would have to prove it worthwhile. If he didn't, there would be major repercussions: first and foremost, the Met would bring in another team. Langton had, at no time, even hinted to the incident room just what was on the line. However, if he got Camorra – and he fully intended to physically get to him before anyone else – the man who had, to his mind, almost destroyed him, then nothing else would matter.

Resting flat out on the floor, his head on his folded jacket, the constant ringing of the phones and the murmur of voices in the incident room lulled him into a deep sleep.

Harry was sitting on the edge of Anna's desk; he had just got a call from his brother-in-law. He squeezed a small rubber ball in his right hand.

'It's fucking unbelievable. He goes to start work on a big building project, only to be told that he and his crew won't be required – they've fucking hired a mound of Polish workmen at half the price. He's got three kids, what's he supposed to do? Agree to work for a pittance?

He said that Westminster Council's homeless teams are warning the Government about them; they've started on substance abuse, criminal activity and prostitution. It's bad enough with the bloody Romanians—'

'Harry! Please give it a rest, will you?'

'Sorry, sorry. It's just seeing those two little kids – it really got to me, you know? I couldn't sleep last night. It's just all kind of crazy, I mean, what's happening? If you think what it costs to keep Ian Brady alive . . .'

'What?' Anna couldn't follow his train of thought.

'He was a fucking child killer, right? Been banged up for over thirty years – how much has that cost? Thousands, bloody thousands. Meanwhile, they got killers escaping from fucking open prisons, no idea where they are. Have you any idea what dangerous men are on the loose?' The constant squeezing of the rubber ball showed how much Harry was on edge.

'Harry, please – go and get a cup of tea.'

'Hang the bastards, that's what I think – get rid of them for good. Catch them and then let them rot.'

Anna was relieved when he moved off, with his rubber ball, to bend someone else's ear. She checked the time. Everyone in the incident room was visibly tense; like Anna, they were all waiting for Langton to appear. The clock was ticking, and if Operation Eagle was on schedule, both the Krasiniqe brothers would be heading towards their destination. She gave a silent prayer that it would be worthwhile; for she was certain that, if the vast cost to arrange it culminated in no gain, she would be in trouble.

She looked over to the closed blinds of Langton's office, unaware that, despite all the mounting pressure, he was fast asleep.

Chapter Seventeen

Langton had still not made an appearance. Harry Blunt, who had been trying to track down information about Sickert's background, was still in his usual state of belligerence.

'The bloody Government is in paralysis! They were supposed to have made the criminal system a top priority, and after four Home Secretaries, forty-three pieces of legislation, and nine years, it's still a total effing shambles.'

Frank Brandon raised his eyes to the ceiling. 'Give us a break, Harry.'

'I'd like someone to fucking give us one. Sickert isn't on any single scrap of paper! He comes into this country, slices up kids, runs off with two others; Christ only knows what he was doing to them.' He turned to Grace. 'We got anything more from the Child Protection Unit as to how those two little ones are doing?'

Grace shook her head.

Harry paced around, still squeezing his rubber ball in his fat hand. 'Damaged for life, poor little sods. I'd like to have got my hands round his throat.' He sat back in his chair with a thud.

The tension of waiting for the briefing was getting to

all of them. Coffee and sandwiches were wheeled in on a trolley; they gathered around it.

Anna took her lunch to her desk, and then went to Langton's office. Just as she was about to tap on the door, it swung open.

'Right, everyone gathered?' he asked, as he passed her. He paused at Harry's desk and leaned in to talk to him. 'Listen, Harry, you got to start keeping that yapping mouth shut, whatever your private feelings are. You want to go up the ranks, you won't stand a hope in hell if you carry on like that. Maybe we all feel the same way – just don't broadcast it, okay?'

'Yeah, sorry, Gov.'

Langton patted his shoulder, walked along to the incident board and then turned to the room. 'Okay, Operation Eagle is set to roll. Doctor Salaam is in a segregated unit at the hospital, with his wife and both prisoners.'

Anna and Lewis would accompany Langton to the hospital; he then listed priorities for the rest of the team.

When told by Harry that they still had no information about Sickert, Langton shrugged; he had been expecting as much.

'Did you get anything from him?' Harry asked.

Anna glanced at Mike Lewis; both had been waiting to hear what had been said in the ICU.

'Not a lot. When shown the picture we found in his clothes, there was a reaction, but who the two children and the woman are, we probably will never know. Travis is pretty sure the small teddy bear found in his jacket pocket belonged to Gail's dead child, so we are testing it for DNA.' Langton dug into his pocket and brought out his notebook. 'I didn't have long to question him, and most of his answers were physical reactions.'

Langton reported that when he had asked Sickert about Gail, the sick man had said what sounded like, 'She was good to me.'

'I asked him how she had died, and he became agitated. When I told him how we had discovered the death of her young daughter, he gave a guttural moan. When I asked if he had killed Gail and the toddler, he shook his head.'

Langton continued to go through all his questions. Sickert's responses were often unintelligible. He did, however, manage one whole sentence. This was connected to Gail's two children.

Langton read from his notebook. '"I took care of them; I took them. I knew they had come for me."'

Langton sighed. He had pressed for clarification – like, who had come for him? – but got no response. He did get a reaction, however, when he asked if the people who came to the piggery drove a white Range Rover: Sickert had nodded his head.

Brandon put his hand up to say that forensic had verified the vehicle had been there from soil tests. They were still waiting for results from tests on the inside of the vehicle. Prints had been taken and run through the database; so far, that had come up blank.

'One step forwards, two back,' Langton muttered, and shut his notebook. He then turned to the board. 'There was one name that made the dying man almost lift off the bed: I asked if Clinton Camorra had arranged for him to enter the UK.'

Sickert had gasped, and tried to get hold of Langton's clothing. 'Bad man, bad man – him powerful. He want me dead.'

Langton picked up a red marker and crossed out Sickert's face on the board. 'Well, he is now.' He paused. 'This is yet another link to this bastard Camorra. I tried to get out of Sickert his whereabouts but, by this time, he was fading fast. We found a couple of bus tickets in his jacket: I want the areas checked out as they are not in Peckham, where we've concentrated on trying to find Camorra. He could have moved to Christ knows where, but one ticket is Tooting, another Clapham. It's a bit of a wild-goose chase but, Harry, it's worth getting onto the transport people to find out which stops the tickets are from.'

Langton looked at his watch: time was moving fast. He next concentrated on Grace and the Child Protection Unit. He needed to find out if either of the children had been able to give any details of where they had been. Grace could only state that, after numerous calls, the Unit had said neither child was fit enough to be questioned; they were still very traumatized.

'Cut out the phone calls, Grace, and get over there. Talk to them yourself, if you can. Traumatized or not, we need some answers. They were bloody missing for weeks.'

Grace was very uneasy about having to put pressure on the two children. The boy had been sexually assaulted, but the little girl had not. They had both been well fed and, although they had headlice, they were not in poor physical shape. Mentally, however, they were still terrorized.

'Sometimes, we all have to do things we don't feel are appropriate,' Langton said tiredly, reading her expression. 'We might get some detail of where they were held, and if they had been kept at Camorra's place. So, do what you have to do.'

'Yes, sir. Are we still calling him Clinton Camorra, or are we using the other name given by Doctor Salaam – Emmerik?'

'Listen, call him both. With so many false names, who in Christ knows what he's really called. See if the kids react to either.'

Langton sighed. 'Okay, that's it. We move out in half an hour. Frank, put pressure on forensics to see if they can give us anything more from the Range Rover. We're still running pretty much on empty; let's hope to God, after this afternoon, that changes.'

The convoy of unmarked patrol cars left the station at two o'clock and arrived at the hospital shortly before three. It was a modern building, set well back from the road, with a high wall and wrought-iron gates. The Contagious Disease Units were listed as A, B, C and D; they were to use D gate, and D building. This was used for highly contagious diseases and was set apart from the rest of the hospital. Two armed guards stood at the entrance.

Parked outside was a prison van and a back-up car of uniformed officers; they had brought Idris Krasiniqe from Wakefield. There was also a police ambulance; this had picked up Eamon Krasiniqe from the local airport, where the emergency medical helicopter had brought him from Parkhurst.

An unmarked patrol car, which had been used to bring Dr Salaam and his wife Esme to the hospital, was also parked nearby. They couple had been installed in a safe house, and would remain there until the doctor agreed that it was safe to return to his surgery. This added cost had made Langton tear at his hair, but the Salaams had insisted and refused to take part in the session with Eamon Krasiniqe unless he agreed.

Langton, Lewis and Anna were led through a maze of white-walled corridors. There were no notices, no advertising, no signs directing anyone anywhere. They reached a thick glass sliding door. Waiting for them was a white-coated doctor, who said he would lead them to the first anteroom, where the Salaams were waiting. He had travelled with the patient from Parkhurst prison. They were led through yet more white-walled corridors; only the odd fire extinguisher was visible and, high up on the ceiling, cameras and speakers.

The room was glass-walled, with a vast amount of equipment including oxygen cylinders, heart monitors and breathing apparatus. In the centre of the room was a trolley, with a white sheet over it. The window to the next consulting room was covered by a green blind.

Dr Salaam was standing at a steel table, a medical case open, various bottles and rows of folded packets of herbs inside. His wife was beside him, carefully checking the contents; both were wearing white coats. They turned as Langton and his team entered. The silence was palpable.

Salaam did not waste time. He spoke so softly that it was, at times, hard to hear what he was saying. 'The medical team that brought Krasiniqe here are very concerned. His blood pressure is very low and he is suffering from malnutrition.'

Langton nodded; this was all he wanted to hear. It wasn't going to do much for them if he died. 'But he is alive?'

'Yes, he is alive, but I have not been allowed to examine him yet.'

'Well, we'd better get on with it fast,' Langton muttered.

Salaam held up his hand. 'One moment. I first need to ask you some questions.'

'Very well.'

'I have the patient's medical history. I have asked if the man who assisted him in the assault—'

'Bit more than that, Doctor; he slit a man's throat.'

Salaam nodded. 'Did anyone physically check out the man who helped in this murder?'

Langton shrugged, and said if it was not on any medical report, then he wouldn't know.

'Specifically for puncture marks.'

'Like injections?'

'Yes.'

Langton sighed. He looked to Mike Lewis and mimed picking up a phone. Lewis nodded and walked out.

Esme placed onto the table a large square leather box. She opened it, and Anna saw that it contained electrodes, old-fashioned ones, and a rubber mouth-guard. She wondered if they were going to give Krasiniqe ECT treatment.

'Right,' Salaam said, as he shook out a pair of rubber gloves. 'Let me have a look at him.'

Eamon Krasiniqe lay on a narrow bed. The room was otherwise empty, apart from a small steel chair. There was, above the bed, a large domed light that could be drawn down. Langton, Travis and Esme were led into a small viewing room. They gathered by the window and looked in, as Dr Salaam switched on the overhead light and aimed it at the sick man. He lay completely still. Only his breathing showed that he was still alive. His body seemed stiff; the hands at his sides were straight, his fingers outstretched.

The doctor took a wooden spatula and brought the lamp down over the sick man's head. He was painstakingly slow, examining every inch of the thick black tight curly hair. He then checked each ear, behind and inside, and then around his eyes and nose. It was eerie: as Krasiniqe's eyes were opened, he just seemed to stare into the light. The doctor placed the spatula inside his mouth and focused the light to get a clearer view.

Langton glanced at Anna. Salaam was certainly taking his time. He went over the sick man's body literally inch by inch: chest, arms, fingers, belly. Then he drew the light very close; opening the legs a fraction, he bent down and searched over the genitals. He then took out a small silver pen-light and bent even closer.

Langton whispered to Anna, 'Well, he's very thorough . . .'

After a while, he straightened to examine the legs. As he turned the man over, Mike Lewis joined them and quietly said that the other prisoner involved in the murder, the one who had held Murphy down, had not been physically examined, but he had been drug tested. They had found traces of marijuana, but nothing else; no heroin or cocaine.

Langton gestured for him to be quiet: Salaam was turning off the overhead light.

They all reconvened in the anteroom. Salaam sipped a glass of water.

'There is a drug that can create a zombie-like effect.

It's actually nicknamed Zombie's cucumber or Jimson weed; the Latin name for it is *Datura stramonium*. This is a poisonous plant, similar to deadly nightshade, and is often used in voodoo practices by quack witch doctors. In those who have been injected over a period of time, it produces an inability to talk or move. They get delirious and often have hallucinations. The effects can last for days or weeks, depending on the dosage. It can also cause seizures and comas, and will eventually kill you. There is no antidote.'

Langton looked at the doctor and waited, but he remained silent. 'Is that what he's got?'

Dr Salaam gestured for him to stay quiet. 'You have to understand, if someone believes in voodoo and is threatened that a hex will be placed on him, it is the strength of the belief that is of most importance. If that person has been, shall we say, unwilling to do whatever is wanted, and that person then ingests even a little *Datura stramonium*, he would feel frightening symptoms. All parts of the plant are toxic. The poison causes a dry mouth, dilated pupils and a high temperature. The early psychological effects are confusion, euphoria and delirium. According to Eamon's medical report, he showed signs of all of these; even, I believe, during his trial. At times, he was incoherent, babbling and confused, is that correct?'

Langton was getting impatient. 'Is that what he's got? Is that why he is the way he is?'

Salaam took out a large white notepad with the outline of a male body. Using a pen, he indicated with tiny dots. 'Eamon Krasiniqe has several small puncture marks: on the top of his head, right earlobe, and four more around his genitalia; he also has another near his anus. These puncture marks are still visible, but they can be very easily overlooked. I will obviously require blood and urine to test, but I would say from all his symptoms that he has been fed a considerable amount of this poison over a considerable length of time.'

'Can you cure him?'

'No. Medical intervention should have been sought earlier. We may have some time, but he will eventually have a cardiac arrest. He is dying, both from the poison and from his own conviction that he is under a voodoo hex, making him one of the walking dead.'

Anna coughed. Everyone turned towards her. 'Would ECT help? Maybe give him more time?'

'Possibly. His mind is controlling him. He has been punished for something; we do not know what. He does not understand that he has been poisoned, not controlled by voodoo witchcraft.'

Langton looked at his watch. He asked if they could get some refreshments brought in for the doctor and his wife. He would need time to discuss the doctor's prognosis with his team.

Langton slumped down in a leather chair; Mike Lewis rested on the arm of another.

Anna sat down opposite them. 'We need to get permission from his brother to give him ECT. If he knows everything we've just been told, he might agree; unless he does, I doubt if we will be able to give the go ahead.'

Langton said brusquely, 'Listen, if it could help, fuck getting any permission – we do it. The kid is dying.'

Anna sighed. 'I know, but we need Idris Krasiniqe to help us. He will only do so if his brother is seen to recover. If he's not – and, judging by what we've been told, he won't recover – then this is all a waste of time and money.'

'You think I don't know that?' Langton snapped.

'I am sure you do; all I am asking is, can I have time with Idris? If necessary, we bring in the doctor to talk to him. Maybe we hedge round the fact that it's unlikely that Eamon can be saved, but if we give him hope ... What did that boy do, to deserve to be poisoned like this? It had to be something big; maybe something connected to Camorra.'

Langton turned to Mike Lewis. 'I want the names of everyone who visited Eamon Krasiniqe in the cells, at the police station, at his trial; anyone who could have got to him there, and in the prison.'

'He had no visitors at the prison,' Anna said.

'Maybe he didn't, but what about the bloke who held down Arthur Murphy? See who visited *him*. There has to be a link somewhere. If some bastard was controlling his mind through this poison, it had to have been fed to him. You heard what the doctor said: he's got Christ knows many fucking needle pricks all over his body, so somebody was still doing it to him, right?'

Anna nodded. Langton was working himself up into such a temper. She tried to calm him down. 'In the meantime, can I talk to Idris? Bring in the doctor if need be, yes?'

Langton nodded.

'How long will we have him for?' she wanted to know.

'The doctor?' Langton asked.

'Yes.'

'As long as we bloody need him. We can take him

back to the safe house and bring him back here again if necessary.'

Anna nodded and then gave a small smile. 'I'll go and talk to him.'

'Fine by me. I just want a few words with Mike; you go ahead.'

Anna left the room.

There was a long pause. Finally, Langton sighed. 'This is gonna cost me and I'm not just talking about the budget that's gone through the roof.' He leaned back in his chair. 'Sometimes I feel as if I've lost my way. I think I have let this get out of hand.'

'Not if we do get something.'

'Come on, you saw the kid; he's on his way out, and we're pinning our hopes on the bastard who murdered that little hooker Carly Ann North. It doesn't make any sense. I'd like to go in and beat the shit out of him – maybe that would get him to talk.'

'Maybe it wouldn't. He's got fifteen years for murder; that's not much incentive to give us any help.'

'*She* seems to think he knows something.'

'Anna?'

'Yeah, Anna. A lot of this is down to her interview with him.'

'I wondered about that. She just took off, did she?'

'You could say that.'

'So you never told her to talk to Idris Krasiniqe?'

'Don't go there, Mike.'

Lewis paused for a moment. 'You mind me asking what happened between you two?'

Langton closed his eyes.

Mike hesitated, but continued. 'One time, you seemed pretty close; you were living at her place, and she was certainly taking good care of you. I used to see her either coming or going to the hospital, long schlep out there every day and night.'

Langton nodded.

'So what happened?'

Langton shrugged his shoulders. 'I'm not easy to live with.'

'I would guess that. I'm sorry – she's a good girl.'

Langton took a deep breath. 'Look, we'd better get on to the station and see if they've come up with anything for us; might as well do something constructive. I also need some coffee – can you see if you can find the right corridor that'll take you back to reception? They must have a canteen or something somewhere.'

'Okay. You going to stay in here, or go back to the voodoo doc?'

'I'll stay here; make some calls.'

Mike nodded and walked out, leaving Langton sitting, dejected, in the chair.

Mike felt very concerned about his boss; in all the years he had worked with him, he had never seen him so lacklustre, and to hear him say he had lost his way really hit home. Langton had always driven each case they had worked on with total control. Sometimes, he had appeared to be too controlling, but now . . .

Mike looked up and down the empty corridor. He had no idea which way to go; he'd just been walking and not paying attention. He turned this way and that, then swore, deciding to retrace his steps. As he turned into yet another corridor, he saw Anna heading towards him.

'I'm totally lost,' he said, waving his arms.

'Where are you going?'

'To get some coffee for the boss; he's sort of deflated.'

'Where is he?'

'Same room you left us in.'

'I've asked the doctor to see Idris.'

'Did you talk to him?'

'Idris? I had a few words. I said I wanted him to know exactly what we knew and then I would talk to him later.'

Mike nodded and walked off, leaving Anna standing in the corridor. She looked around until she had her bearings, then headed back towards the anteroom. As she approached, she could hear Langton talking on his mobile. She quietly opened the door.

'I'm not holding out much hope re this voodoo quack, but we do need to get every single visitor to both brothers checked out, plus the guy sharing Eamon's cell, just to cover our tracks. It could have been in a hypodermic needle or powder, so check any food parcels, anything handed to our zombie whatsoever. Also, check out who had access to him during his trial, because somebody pumped this stuff into him; his body is like a pin cushion.'

Langton turned and gestured towards her, before continuing his call. 'If Grace gets anything, call me; ditto forensics.' He carried on firing off instructions, asking if Harry Blunt had come up with anything from the bus tickets, or whether Brandon had anything. By his long sigh, she could tell that there was obviously no new information. He cut off the call and turned towards her.

'I talked to Idris and now the doctor's with him,' she said. 'I told him to go through everything he spoke to us about.'

'Well, that'll take for ever, if the doc takes as long as he did to tell us. In the meantime, the kid is fading fast.'

'There's a one-way glass, if you want to sit in and listen.'

He nodded and then sat down, rubbing his knee. 'I need some coffee.'

'Mike's sorting it,' she said.

After a few minutes, he gripped the arms of the chair and stood up with a grimace, then had to sit down again, swearing.

'Do you want me to ask if Esme has anything that might help the pain?'

'Terrific, yeah. Gimme some of the poison, finish me off.'

'What do you want me to do?'

'Just give me a fucking few minutes,' he shouted. Then he looked at her. 'Sorry. I'm sorry – for a lot of things, Anna. It's just I get so frustrated with this bloody knee. It freezes up and hurts like hell.'

'I know. I wouldn't dare suggest we ask for a walking frame – they may have one here.'

He glared at her.

'I was joking! I know you'd never use one.'

'I guess you do. Sorry again.' He paused. 'I know I have behaved like a real shit at times with you, and I want you to know, I don't . . . I don't ever mean half of it. I suppose I reckon that, knowing me so well, you can take it.'

'Well, I try, but sometimes it hasn't been easy.'

'Come here.'

He lifted his hand towards her. She walked over and he held her tightly.

'You are very special. I appreciate all you have done for me.'

'Thank you.'

'Okay, now give me a haul up, and let's get cracking.'

She saw the pain etched across his face as she helped him stand. She was doubtful he would make it down all the corridors but as soon as they walked outside the room he moved ahead of her. He was limping but, as always, looked like he was in the lead.

Dr Salaam was indicating where the puncture marks had been discovered on his brother. Idris sat, expressionless, but listening intently. Anna switched on a speaker, so that they could hear what was being said.

'They were also around his anal and genital area,' the doctor said.

Idris shook his head. 'So, is he going to live?' His voice was very low and hardly audible.

Dr Salaam hesitated.

Idris leaned towards him. 'I need to know: *is he going to live?*'

Langton pursed his lips, swearing under his breath; the last thing they wanted was for the doctor to say that there was no hope.

Anna reached over and touched his arm. 'He knows not to say anything.'

Dr Salaam drew up a chair to be closer to Idris. 'His heart is very weak.'

'Can't you operate?' Idris interrupted; he was now speaking clearly.

'It's too late for that, but we are hopeful that if we give him ECT, it may jolt him back into consciousness.'

'Shit, that's those electrode things. I know about them: you plug them into fucking electricity.'

'I would need your permission to do any kind of resuscitation.'

'Listen, I'll agree; but tell me what can happen if that don't work?'

'Idris, your brother is in a critical condition,' the doctor said gravely. 'He has refused all medical treatment that might have helped him. You have to understand that he is very sick. There is no antidote for this poison.'

'So why do you want to put those electrode things on him?'

'It might jolt him out of the terror inside his brain and give him some peace. He is a believer, isn't he?'

'You mean Christian?'

'No, voodoo.'

Idris turned away.

'Has he ever been involved with voodoo, or someone whom he believes has voodoo powers?'

Idris nodded slowly.

'Do you need some time alone to think about what I have told you?'

Idris nodded again. Langton swore: the last thing he wanted was to give Idris any more time. The doctor tapped on the door and it was unlocked. Langton immediately walked out, leaving Anna alone in the viewing room.

Outside in the corridor, Langton conferred with Dr Salaam. He was not taking any crap from Idris. If there was any hope that Eamon could be jolted out of his coma, then the doctor had to do it; they were wasting time. The doctor insisted he confer with his wife, so they both headed back to the anteroom.

Anna watched Idris. He remained seated, staring ahead at the white wall, then he bowed his head and began to weep. Anna switched off the intercom and left the room. She went up to the officer guarding Idris and asked to be allowed inside. When she walked in, he looked up, wiping his eyes with his cuff.

'How you doing?' she asked softly.

Idris gulped, trying to control his weeping.

'We could have lied to you, but we felt it was imperative to be totally honest with you. Surely now you can see that someone has been slowly killing your brother? He has been suffering and must be in terrible pain, mentally and physically. So, if you have any idea who may have done this to him, tell us! Surely you'd want us to punish him?'

Idris wiped his eyes and whispered, 'I'm scared.'

Anna reached out to hold his hand. 'Talk to me, Idris – trust me.'

Anna hurried along the corridor and into the anteroom to find Dr Salaam passing Langton some tablets.

'We're going to do the ECT, permission or not,' Langton said, swallowing the pills. He then turned with a smile to Esme. 'You sure these aren't the deadly nightshade?'

She smiled back and shook her head. 'I am also going to make up a list of tablets and powders that'll help you.'

Anna was impatient. 'Listen, I think Idris is going to talk, but first he wants to be examined by Doctor Salaam. He's terrified that someone could be feeding him the same poison. He has been segregated for weeks, he's never gone on the recreational ward and he's been paying for one of the kitchen staff to make his meals – those he eats in his cell – but he's scared.'

Langton raised his eyes to the ceiling.

'He called it Jimson weed,' she said.

Dr Salaam said this nickname for *Datura stramonium* came from when it was used against the British soldiers in Jamestown, USA. It was sprinkled on their salads and a tincture of it was put into their drinks.

'Well, thanks for the history lesson, Doc. Now please, go and have a look at him, and make it as fast as possible.' Langton opened the door for the doctor; then checked his watch and followed him out.

Making sure they were out of earshot of the room, he lowered his voice. 'Hold it one second: I want you to "find" some small trace of this Jimson weed in his system that you say can be cured. Feed him pills, if you have to; do anything you can to make it authentic, okay? We need something to scare the pants off him.'

Dr Salaam nodded and walked away, as Lewis arrived with coffee and some curling sandwiches.

Langton updated him as they both walked back into the room. 'This is getting to be a farce. Every minute we lose, that kid could snuff it; now all his brother is worried about is that he's got it as well.'

Lewis had obtained the list of visitors. The first to visit Eamon Krasiniqe after his arrest was Rashid Burry, now dead himself. The others they had not yet begun to question; Frank Brandon was checking out the addresses left with the prison's visitor officers to see if any were authentic. They were also questioning Eamon's legal team from his trial.

Langton fretted inwardly. This meant yet another run-around for the team; it was making their case spread, and look even more out of control.

Lewis smiled. 'Got some positive news from forensic though, Gov. Hairs and a partial fingerprint have been matched to Carly Ann North. There were also some fibres that could be from wherever her body was kept before it was taken to the dismemberment site.'

The interior of the Range Rover had been given a thorough clean but, beneath the glove compartment, they had also found two clear prints belonging to Rashid Burry; a third print was being tested but was, as yet, unidentified.

Langton seemed to relax, perhaps because they were moving forwards, or perhaps because the herbal pills were working, if not on his leg, then his mood. He munched on one of the stale sandwiches and helped himself to tepid coffee from a pot.

Esme was quietly unpacking her box of equipment: the rubber guard for Eamon's mouth, the electrode plungers and suction caps. She laid them all out very neatly on a piece of white cotton and used a disinfectant cloth to wipe them all down.

She looked up at the clock on the wall and gestured with her forefinger, moving it round in a circle. 'Time is ticking. We should check on Eamon Krasiniqe.'

Anna recalled seeing the same gesture made by the dying boy in the prison cell. 'You know, that was the only gesture that Eamon made.'

Esme gave a small shrug. 'You mentioned it before; it's just a habit, you know, to indicate time. Some of the patients we have are illiterate and cannot tell the time, so I often use this as a sort of indication.' She pointed again to demonstrate. 'When the large hand is back to twelve, you come in to see me.' She gave a soft smile. 'When we put the clocks forwards or backwards, that causes confusion: they believe they have lost an hour as punishment!'

'Did Camorra see you do this?'

'Possibly.'

'Did you ever see the Krasiniqe brothers?'

'I would have to check my books, but you know many use assumed names and give false addresses.'

'Come and have a look at him,' Anna said, then hesitated, looking at Langton. He gave a small nod of his head.

He watched them both leave the anteroom. 'Should have thought of that myself,' he said, reaching for another sandwich.

Whilst Dr Salaam examined Idris Krasiniqe, Anna led Esme into his brother Eamon's room.

He lay completely still, eyes open and staring at the ceiling, his body rigid, his breathing very shallow.

Anna stood by the door as Esme moved to the sick boy's bedside. She leaned over him and, with one hand, she gently soothed his head with soft strokes. He showed no reaction; she rested the back of her hand against his cheek.

'Poor boy; my poor boy.' She held onto his hand, all the time making soft hushing sounds, as if to a baby.

'Do you recognize him?'

'No, I don't – but you know, we have so many patients, and over so many years. He might have been to see us, but I don't honestly know. I'm sorry.'

They left the room and went back to where they had left Langton.

Esme seemed upset; she asked Anna why, with all the equipment here, they didn't use any of it. Anna was surprised; with all her herbal remedies, she wouldn't have thought that Esme would approve of intravenously feeding him or attaching him to a heart monitor.

'When he was first taken to the prison hospital, they tried to help him, but he refused to have any treatment. He even signed the documents.'

Esme shook her head. 'He wouldn't have known what he was doing.'

'But we have to take it as that being what he wants. When they had IRA prisoners who went on hunger strike, the prison officers were not allowed to feed them or give any form of resuscitation if they collapsed.'

Esme rested her hand on Anna's arm. 'Those people were using their bodies as weapons against authority; that poor boy probably didn't even know what he was signing.'

Anna felt irritated; Esme seemed to be accusing her. 'Well, if that is the case, you won't have any reason not to give him ECT.'

Esme pursed her lips. 'That will not be my decision.'

No, Anna thought to herself, it will not be. The person who would be making the decision was Langton and he, as they saw when they re-entered the room, was fast asleep, lying on a trolley.

Chapter Eighteen

Idris Krasiniqe was zipping up his prison jeans. He had lowered them to his knees so that Dr Salaam could check his genitals for possible puncture-marks. There were none. He asked Idris whether he often felt that his mouth was dry; he replied always – the officers in the prison got pissed off with him forever asking for water.

When asked if he also felt that his face was red, Idris had managed to smile, shaking his head. 'I'm partly black – so I dunno if my face goes red or not! It feels hot sometimes, but I dunno about it being red.'

Dr Salaam bent down. There was a small tattoo on Idris's right wrist.

'Wait one moment; how long have you had this, Idris?'

The young man looked down and shrugged. 'When I first got to Wakefield, months ago. Bloke in the cell I shared, he used to tat all the prisoners. Since Eamon got sick I been in solitary, I don't mix with nobody.'

Dr Salaam peered closely at the tattoo. 'When did your dry mouth start?'

Idris hesitated, trying to recall the exact date. 'Maybe a few months back?'

Dr Salaam used his small pen torch to examine the rather crude small star: it was not even filled in but was just a dotted outline.

'I was gonna have a bigger one done, but this hurt like hell. It's like Eamon's, but he got a moon – well, that's what he told me.'

'Your brother does not have a tattoo, Idris. I would know, as I have examined him – but this is how you might have been injected.'

Idris gaped. 'Shit, man! Oh fuck, man – you gotta help me! *Can* you help me?'

Langton clapped his hands. 'Brilliant! The more he's shitting himself, the better.'

'I think it would now be beneficial for him to know the condition his brother is in before I give him something that will help,' said Salaam.

'You going to give the electric shock treatment?' Lewis asked.

They all waited. Esme took her husband aside and whispered to him.

He nodded his head. 'My wife is doubtful it will have any effect at this late stage.'

'Fuck that. Let his brother watch: now he's given us permission, we can get Eamon on a heart monitor, put him under an oxygen tent – anything to show us in a good light. If he dies, he dies; it'll be even more of an incentive for Idris to talk. If he won't talk, we withhold his own medication.'

Langton was so aggressive that no one argued. His energy levels back to normal, he then set the wheels in motion for Idris to be brought to see Eamon. Anna suggested they allow Esme to be with him, saying that she had a very calming influence; she knew that if Langton took Idris anywhere, he would scare the living daylights out of him.

The monitor was bleeping, indicating Eamon's erratic and slow heartbeat. He also had an oxygen mask on; the respirator pumped on behalf of his weakened lungs. A doctor from the hospital had been brought in and was quietly sitting to one side, talking in hushed tones with Dr Salaam.

Anna, Langton and Lewis watched from behind the one-way glass.

'How did you swing this?' Anna asked Langton.

'He's in private practice – just does the odd visit here, so we got lucky. About time, but he'll cost. And he's African, so that also helped.'

They fell silent as the door was opened and Idris, accompanied by Esme, walked in. The uniformed officers who had led them down there locked the door behind them.

Idris was obviously shaken; seeing his brother in such a state, and after so long, made him weep. Esme did her gentle whispering to him, taking his hand and drawing him closer to the bedside. He moved to stand beside his brother and then, like Esme, he began to stroke Eamon's head, as he wept.

'Eh, bro, it's me, just come to see you. Can you hear me?'

There was no reaction. Idris leaned closer and repeated that he was there, then he kissed his brother's forehead. The heart monitor bleeped and Idris turned to look at it, then back at his brother, who remained motionless.

'I love you, bro – I love you.'

The monitor then bleeped louder and the red zigzag flatlined.

'Fuck, he's gone,' Langton said.

'Do something, man! Do something to help him!' Idris shouted.

Electrodes were connected and a tube placed into the dead boy's mouth, as rubber pads were put on his chest.

Anna had to look away. It was the panic in Idris she hated to see; he was flailing his hands and weeping. Esme tried her best to control him as the first jolt of electricity went through his brother.

The dead boy's body jerked and then lay still; three more times, they watched his body being moved by the electricity. Then there was an almost unanimous sigh of disbelief: the heart monitor reconnected, like a miracle. The beat was strong, though erratic.

'He's alive, he's alive!' Idris shrieked, trying to get closer to his brother.

'I want you to leave now,' said Salaam. His voice was firm and loud.

Idris looked at him like a helpless child. 'Is he gonna be okay now?'

'Let's pray, brother, let's just pray.'

Esme almost had to drag Idris from the room, banging on the door for it to be unlocked.

Dr Salaam came to the window. He could not see them through the one-way mirror, so just stood there, not sure where to look. 'The reaction you are seeing is a false hope. It is the electricity that has started the machine and maybe allowed his heart to beat for a fraction, but he's gone. I thought it best that your prisoner had some hope, but there is none. He's dead.'

Langton got up and closed the blind. Both Anna and Mike remained silent, not sure how to react.

'Doctor Salaam is something else, isn't he?' Langton said.

He turned as Esme walked in. She seemed very tired. 'Idris wants to see DI Travis, no one else. I think you should go to him as quickly as possible.'

Anna looked to Langton.

'Go do it.'

If he had felt any degree of irritation that Anna was the one to talk to Idris, he didn't show it; instead, he shook the coffee pot and handed it to Mike Lewis.

'Get us a refill, will you?'

Lewis took the pot and walked out.

Langton waited until the door closed before he spoke. 'Your husband ... Whatever my own feelings are about his practice, about what the pair of you do, I think your husband is a very special man.'

'He is,' she said quietly. 'He has very special powers and works only towards the good. If he wished, he could unleash a darkness, but he would never even contemplate doing so.'

'Like I said, he has my admiration. He's worked hand in glove with us and I am very grateful.'

'Thank you. I hope you get a successful result.' She hesitated. 'May I talk to you on a personal level?'

Langton was slightly taken aback. 'Sure. In fact, I was going to ask if you had any more of those herbal painkillers.'

'You need so much more,' she said softly. 'You carry a big open wound.'

'Yeah, I do. I got cut through the abdomen, chest and was almost sliced through my heart.'

Esme counted out four more painkillers. 'Well, I didn't know about that. My reference is more esoteric. We all carry scars.'

'Really?' He was not interested.

'Yes. Mine is the child I lost.'

He nodded, not wanting to get into any of her so-called esoteric mumbo jumbo or, even worse, her private life.

'Someone left you with such pain,' she murmured now.

'Ma'am, I was almost sliced in two. There's nothing esoteric about it, just a brutal bastard who almost killed me.'

Esme placed her hand on his heart. 'In here,' she stated.

He could feel incredible heat from her hand. He gasped, not wanting her to take her hand away. He didn't understand. Her hand remained on his chest and he felt an overwhelming need to weep, but he tensed up. 'It's my knee joint,' he said lamely.

'You never released the pain.'

'I don't know what you are talking about. I'm taking every pill I can lay my hands on to release the pain. I want you to stop this.'

When she withdrew her hand, he felt a terrible emptiness; it was indescribable.

'My wife died.' His voice sounded distant. 'She was young, she was beautiful, she was clever, and I loved her. We wanted to have a family; our children would have been the light of our lives, because we wanted more of each other. She died of a brain tumour. One moment, she was laughing, so full of life and energy, then it had all gone; *she* had gone. I could never believe it could be over; that she wouldn't walk back into my life.'

'But you have buried it; you have never released her light.'

'There was no light after she died.'

Esme touched his hand. 'You have to let her go. You need the light now. You need it, because you are moving downwards.'

'Well, maybe I'll be with her. You think I'm going to die?'

'No, no. She is the light – she is forever a light. I feel her and know she is a vibrant force that you must embrace. There is no guilt, there should be no remorse, and you could have done nothing to save her. Let her go, or you will never get well.'

'I'm doing okay,' he muttered, angry with himself. No one knew what anguish he had lived with when he lost his beloved, and he didn't understand why this tragic part of his life was being opened up now.

'I can't deal with this now,' he said quietly.

'I understand, but you must one day. Don't leave it too late.'

She gave him some water to take the painkillers. He joked again that she was feeding him Jimson weed. She gave a soft laugh, but neither was amused.

'Come and see me when this case is over,' she said, packing up her packets and bottles.

'Right, will do.' He had no intention of keeping in contact and wished he'd kept his mouth shut. He stood beside her as she checked her medical case.

'What does this Jimson weed look like?' he asked curiously.

Esme touched a bottle with a red cross on the label.

'This is the tincture, and these are the tablets; they can be crushed into a powder. My husband brought them to show you. Usually both are kept in a locked cabinet; it's obvious why.' She turned as Mike Lewis walked in with the fresh pot of coffee.

'Just to let you know, the firearm section guys outside are getting impatient and want to know when we'll be through.'

'When I say so,' Langton rapped out. He gestured to Mike that they should go and see how Anna was doing. He was keen now to get out and away from Esme.

Esme opened the viewing blind. Her husband had removed all the equipment from Eamon and packed it away. He was now washing the body down.

Esme closed her eyes in prayer. She then locked her medical case and placed it on the floor beside her chair. She sat with her hands folded in her lap, watching Elmore finish washing Eamon and then reverently place a sheet over the dead boy's body.

Anna had taken it very slowly with Idris. He was in a state of shock and grief. While he believed that his brother was still alive and that there was some hope, he was also terrified that he, too, had been poisoned. He constantly drank water, his mouth dry, and repeatedly asked Anna if the doctor could help him and Eamon. Anna had repeated just as often that she was certain he could. Calming him had taken over ten minutes; now she knew she would have to put the pressure on.

'I am going to tape our interview,' she said.

'Okay, okay, but what about me being returned to Wakefield? I mean, if this gets out that I've been talking – I mean, this bastard that did the tattoo, will he be taken care of?'

'Yes, and we will arrange for you to serve out your sentence in another prison.' She could not be sure they would get permission, but it was now imperative they get some answers.

She had only just switched on the tape when Idris blurted out, 'He loved her.'

Anna looked up, unsure that she had heard correctly. 'I'm sorry – what did you say?'

'My brother – he loved her. He was crazy about her. I mean, he was supposed to just be sort of looking out for her – you know, like a bodyguard.'

'Can you just explain to me who—'

He interrupted her. 'Carly Ann – my brother and her. He loved her.'

Anna sat back. This didn't make sense. 'I don't understand. If you knew that, then why were you found with her body?'

'It was set up.'

'What was set up?'

Idris sighed. He slumped, clenching his hands tightly. '*He* found out – found out they were going to run off together – so he punished Eamon. He said anyone who ever crossed him would live to regret it. He was acting crazy, all dressed up in this white robe with crosses and shit, and they held Eamon down while he ranted and raved at him. That's when he must have injected him.'

'Who was this?'

Idris looked at her as if she was stupid. 'Camorra – who the fuck do you think I'm talking about?'

Anna swallowed. She then said that she did know but,

for the benefit of the tape, she had to hear him say the name.

'Carly Ann was Camorra's meat. He'd seen her on the street, liked the look of her and got two of his guys to pick her up and bring her to him. He had her washed – and I'm not kiddin' – in milk. He then got all this gear for her, clothes and shit, and said she was his woman. She had these blue eyes, man, like clear sea; yet she was black. It was a sign to him that she was special. He then got my brother to be her sort of keeper, to make sure she didn't get back on the junk. It was Eamon's job to take her out, when she went shopping and stuff. She was buying gold bracelets and necklaces, 'cos Camorra gave her all this money. Eamon was with her round the clock. Camorra had to go do his business, so they was alone a lot together.'

Idris lowered his head. 'He fucked her.' Idris wiped his eyes. He said his kid brother was dumb; he didn't know the place had hidden cameras. It was all on film, so it wasn't difficult for Camorra to find out.

'Where was this?'

'He had a big house in Peckham, but he's got places all over London. The guy has so much money, all cash.'

'Did he own a white Range Rover?'

'Yeah, he's got a lot of cars. He's got BMWs, Mercedes – you name it – even a Ferrari.'

'Where does he keep these cars?'

'I dunno, different places.'

'Do you know any other addresses?'

Idris sighed impatiently. 'No, but what happened with Carly Ann went down in the Peckham house.'

'What did go down?'

'She had run off with Eamon; Camorra had all his henchmen searching for them. She got to some woman in a care place, who was looking after her. I dunno if she really cared that much about my brother, but he was on the loose. I was scared to help him, you know, even though he was my brother, but I met up with him once and gave him some money. He said they were gonna go maybe to Manchester. He didn't have no passport, so he couldn't leave the country.'

Idris opened a bottle of water, gulping it down. He said that a couple of Camorra's henchmen had found Carly Ann and taken her back to the house. She told Camorra where his brother was and they got him too.

'He tied her up, like on this altar thing he had, and he brought in Eamon.' He started to cry.

Anna waited. He drank more water and then managed to go on.

'He raped her. Then he made me do the same. All the while, my brother was forced to watch. Camorra said no one ever crossed him and, as he'd got us both into the UK, he would have us arrested or deported, but I knew that was a lie. I knew he'd kill us if we didn't do what he wanted.'

'What did you do?'

Idris began to shake his head from side to side. 'I didn't kill her, he did. I didn't kill her. I carried her body out into the car.'

'The Range Rover?'

'Yeah. Rashid Burry helped, and there was another guy. Camorra said he wanted us to bring back her head. We had to cut off her hands so no one would know who she was.'

Idris broke down, weeping uncontrollably, incapable

of talking. He just sat, his elbows resting on his knees, his head bent forwards, sobbing.

Dr Salaam was sent for and gave Idris some calming tablets, nothing else, but Idris was convinced they would cure the poison that he believed he had been given via the tattoo. His mind was playing tricks on him: his dry mouth was due to nerves, not Jimson weed.

Having talked to Anna for over an hour and a half, he was exhausted, mentally and physically. He was returned to Wakefield prison, to be kept in solitary confinement until the authorities decided whether he could be transferred to another prison. He was told that Eamon was also being taken back to prison. He was not informed that his brother was dead.

It took a long time for all the papers to be signed so that Eamon Krasiniqe could be released to the mortuary. A post-mortem was required, to confirm the cause of death. Afterwards, he would remain there until it was determined what should be done with his remains.

It was after seven in the evening when a tired Dr Salaam and Esme were taken back to the safe house. With the new information the team had from Idris, it was agreed, without any question, that they should both be protected, just in case word got out that Idris had been talking.

Langton and Lewis were driven out of the hospital at eight; Anna followed in the second patrol car. She was glad to be able to rest back and close her eyes. The nightmarish jigsaw was coming together piece by piece, but the last and most important section was still missing: the whereabouts of Camorra. The manhunt to find him would now be stepped up. Armed with the new information, Langton would be able to bring in as many officers as he needed. Their main concern was that, if Camorra found out that Idris Krasiniqe had talked, he would skip the country.

It was after nine when they reached the Hampshire station. Some of the team were still hard at it. Harry Blunt was trying to get any further information from the bus tickets used by Joseph Sickert, but to no avail. Frank Brandon had been tracing the visitors to Parkhurst prison to find anyone who could have passed the poison to Eamon Krasiniqe. The dead boy had had no visitors; but his cellmate Courtney Ransford had. The visitor had used fake ID and an assumed name. Frank was preparing to travel to Parkhurst the following day to interview Ransford.

Langton sent them home and, tired as he was, began to update the incident board ready for a team briefing first thing in the morning. Anna began to transcribe her tape-recorded interview with Idris, while Lewis plotted out the team's work for tomorrow.

Langton stared at the incident board. Eamon Krasiniqe's face now had a red cross over it, as did Rashid Burry, Gail Sickert, her toddler, Joseph Sickert and Arthur Murphy; however, it was as if parts of the edges of their massive jigsaw were still missing, as well as the central piece. Why had Eamon Krasiniqe murdered Arthur Murphy?

Langton tapped the photograph of Vernon Kramer. Could this no-good piece of shit, now serving his time at an open prison, hold any answers? Kramer was connected to them all. He sighed, too tired to think straight.

He looked at Mike Lewis – his tie undone, dark circles

beneath his eyes – and said, 'Call it quits for tonight, Mike. Go get some sleep.'

Mike was relieved; he didn't argue. He'd only eaten two stale sandwiches since lunch and his head ached.

Langton looked over to Anna. Headphones on, she was still working on her report. She jumped when he put his hand on her shoulder.

'That's enough for tonight,' he told her.

She eased off the headphones and leaned back in her chair.

'Good day,' he said softly.

'Yeah, long one though.'

Langton stuffed his hands into his pockets. 'You did good work. A lot of this new development is down to you.'

'Thank you.'

He hovered, hands still in his pockets. 'You found it difficult working alongside me?'

'Not really. I'm pretty used to you by now,' she said, closing down her computer.

'I have. Sometimes.'

'You have?'

'Yes. Mike was asking me earlier, you know, about you and me. You can never keep anything private in an incident room. He said how much you'd done for me when I was at the rehabilitation house. I mean, I know you did, of course I do, but I've never really thanked you enough. I don't know how I would have coped without, you know, you being there for me.'

'I wanted you to be well, and you have thanked me, so you really don't owe me any more thank-yous,' she smiled.

'Well, if you say so . . .'

She looked at him, still hovering. His eyes were sunken with tiredness and the five o'clock shadow under his prominent cheekbones made him look haggard.

'What?' she asked gently.

'I, er . . . I had a talk with Esme, the doctor's wife.'

'You did?'

'Yes.'

She waited. He turned and walked into his office. She picked her jacket off the back of her chair and stood up, stretching; as she lowered her arms, he walked out again. He had his wallet in his hand. He opened it and held it out for her to see a photograph.

'This was my wife.'

She looked at the photograph and then back to him, unsure why he was showing it to her. She was taken aback: his eyes were brimming with tears.

'I loved her.' He could hardly get the words out.

Anna didn't know what to say.

He closed the wallet, he turned to the incident board and gestured with his hand. 'Deal with death every day, every case; you learn early on not to get involved on a personal level – can't do your job otherwise.'

'Yes,' she said, unable to look at him. She knew he was trying to explain something to her.

It proved too difficult. 'Goodnight, Anna. See you in the morning.'

'Yes, see you in the morning.'

He returned to his office. She picked up her brief-case and walked out of the incident room. From the car park, she could see his office light was still on, his shadow across the blinds, as if he was watching her.

Anna had successfully suppressed her feelings for him, but at times like this evening, they rose to the surface.

She couldn't help thinking that if he had put his arms around her, she would have had no idea how to deal with it. All she wanted to do was hold him close; she wished he could be the same man who used to draw her into the curve of his body as they lay in bed together. She felt the ache in the pit of her stomach; it was impossible to simply stop loving someone. She knew it would be a long time before she was truly able to say it was over.

Chapter Nineteen

You could feel the adrenalin pumping as Langton gave the briefing. Both Krasiniqe brothers were illegal immigrants, shipped into the UK as very young teenagers. Both had been drawn into Camorra's world, used and abused by him, and totally dominated by his perversions, his threats and his so-called voodoo powers. They now knew how Carly Ann North's death linked to the brothers, and to Camorra. Along with his illegal traffic of immigrants, they now wanted him for her murder.

They were pulling back on press releases and television coverage, as it was imperative they did not tip off Camorra to leave the country. They now had another team of extra officers to push up the hunt for him; they also had, from Idris Krasiniqe, a good description of the house in Peckham where he was known to reside.

The stunned team listened as Langton listed the pieces of the jigsaw that were still missing. They needed to interview Eamon Krasiniqe's cellmate, who was believed to have fed the poison to him. Who was the visitor listed with the assumed name and fake ID? Who wanted Arthur Murphy dead? Langton was also going to get

Vernon Kramer brought in for questioning again, this time at the station.

Langton suggested that what they were looking at was a massive clean-up by Camorra: all the dead were connected to him, and he had simply got rid of them. Rashid Burry had been found in the same white Range Rover that had been used to transport Carly Ann's body. They knew Joseph Sickert had needed a safe house and, assisted by Arthur Murphy, he had ended up at the piggery. The Range Rover had been to the same location.

Langton was at full speed. 'Did Camorra want Gail's children? He's a sick perverted bastard. I reckon Sickert saw Rashid and co. turning up at the farm and knew something bad would happen. They took Sickert and the two older children; he presumed Gail and the toddler would follow. The biggest reaction I got from him was over the murder of Gail and Tina. He must have known about it – it was all over the news – so, Sickert takes the kids and goes on the run. Right now, our priority is to find out where he and the children were first taken.'

Langton ran his fingers through his hair. Holding the reins on this case was a nightmare.

'We know the immigration service is totally screwed, but we do not know how many bodies this man has shipped illegally into the UK. We keep on hearing about his wealth and that it's cash; we hear he has a fleet of vehicles and houses. He must have money stashed somewhere. He couldn't bank it, unless he also uses the poor souls he ships in to open up strings of accounts. We are talking about them paying up to five thousand for transportation and God knows how much on top for visas and passports. Maybe these bank accounts are well hidden, but that is another area we need to start digging into.'

Anna felt that this was one of the keys to the whole case, but it was like a loose end dangling, with no one quite catching hold of it.

At this point, a call came in to say that they had found the house in Peckham. It was empty and, according to neighbours, had not been used for some weeks. A team of SOCO officers were ready to break in and begin searching for evidence. Frank Brandon and Harry Blunt left the station to join them.

Grace had little to add to the briefing; she had not been able to gain any further details from the two children held at the Child Protection Unit. Langton asked Anna to take over and, if she got anything, to join them at the Peckham property; he would go over there after interviewing Vernon Kramer.

There was a lot of movement with officers and squad cars moving out; after the initial high, the incident room fell silent. Langton waited for Vernon to be brought in and taken to the holding cells. They had had a bit of an argy bargy with the open prison Governor, who said they could conduct the interview there, but Langton refused. He wanted no prison authorities breathing over his shoulder, no prison officer privy to the interview. Mike Lewis had instructions to cut up rough: to use, not a squad car, but a white prison van. Langton wanted Vernon cuffed.

Vernon Kramer's photograph had been almost the first up on the incident board, with Arthur Murphy's beside him. It had a few red arrows linking him to Gail and to Joseph Sickert; he was also linked to Rashid Burry, but a question mark was over his relationship with Camorra.

He had given them only a very vague description of Camorra's house but, even so, he had a red line linking him to the prime target.

Harry Blunt and Frank Brandon had got into a heated argument. The house was, as Harry said, hard to fucking miss, but they *had* missed it. Now there was a team of SOCO officers, plus two forensic scientists and three assistants, ready to enter the premises. The usual police warning was given, in case there were occupants, then they burst open the front door. It took some hammering, as there were so many bolts and locks; although it looked like wood, it was, in actual fact, a steel security door. There was a similar door at the rear; whoever had been there had obviously left via this back door, as the bolts were not thrown across.

Brandon gave instructions for the SOCO team to be wary, just in case the place was booby-trapped. After the house was deemed safe to enter, Brandon and Harry went inside.

From the outside, it appeared to be an ordinary property – a three-storey house with a double garage and an overgrown front garden – but the inside was something else.

Harry whistled. 'It's like one huge brothel, from the old days! Look at the mirrors, and the drapes.'

'I'm looking, I'm looking,' Frank muttered. Everywhere hung massive gilt mirrors, reflecting ornate reproduction furniture.

'So when were you last in a whorehouse this size?' Harry dug his toe into a once-white carpet, now stained and dirty.

Frank took in the heavy chandelier and the matching

wall lights with crystal drops. The wide staircase had a black boy figure at the bottom, holding a glass-flame torch. 'You buy this gear in a place in Marble Arch. The Arabs love it.'

'Lotta marble – that's not cheap,' Harry said, running his hand over a hall table; it was thick with dust.

'Well, he flashed his money around, didn't he?'

Frank looked through a set of double doors into a dining room. A large oval table with gilt legs and fourteen fabric-covered chairs dominated the room, which was hung with yet more elaborate mirrors, above cabinets full of Capo di Monte figures. The lounge was next, with dirty white leather sofas and a massive plasma-screen TV. The kitchen was filled with every possible kind of culinary equipment, all filthy. The once black-and-white tiled floor was greasy and the cooker looked as if it had never been cleaned. The smell was pungent. There were baskets of rotting vegetables; food had been put in the waste disposal unit, but no one had bothered to turn it on. The fridges and deep freezes bulged with yet more food. There was an industrial roll of black bin-liners left on the floor; a few bags had been filled, as if someone was trying to clear up, but had just abandoned the rubbish instead of removing it.

The first-floor bedrooms were equally over-dressed, with drapes and mirrors, and equally filthy. The wardrobes were empty, but grimy sheets were still on the unmade beds. These were removed for tests. They had, thus far, found no indication that anything untoward had been happening. It was, to all intents and purposes, merely the home of someone with pots of money and no taste, who hadn't been able to hire decent cleaners! Not until they moved up to the next floor, did an all-pervading feeling of something wrong hit everyone.

This floor was also carpeted, but in a deep burgundy; it was threadbare, in some places worn down to the floorboards. The three bedrooms had locks and chains on the outside. The one bathroom for that floor was old-fashioned and filthy. Each room was bare, apart from single beds with dirty sheets. The top floor had another two rooms, again with locks and chains on the doors. Inside were children's toys and cots, again stained, and an overpowering stench of urine; faeces were growing mould on the floor. There was no bathroom at this level, just washbasins; in one, they found dirty nappies and some children's nightclothes.

Brandon and Harry returned to the ground floor to check if any papers or documents had been left behind. In a small anteroom by the kitchen was a printing press; acid had been poured over it and the two boxes of papers alongside, which contained stacks of hard-backed passport covers.

Brandon poked around as Harry looked over the printing press. 'So this is where he forged the documents.'

They found some charred papers in a fireplace, and more in the bins outside.

'Shit!' Harry turned over a piece of paper. It was handwritten and burned almost black, with some of the words crossed out, but what was left of it described the availability of a white eight-year-old boy.

They turned when a SOCO officer appeared in the doorway. 'We've opened the cellar.'

They stood at the cellar doors and looked down a flight of stone steps. The cellar was much larger than one would have thought; it ran the entire length and width of the house. There were wrought-iron candleholders spaced three feet apart, leading down; by now, forensic had brought in some lamps. The white-suited scientists were already at work; there were markers on the steps to indicate where they shouldn't tread.

'Jesus Christ,' Harry muttered.

On one wall was a massive cross; in front of it was a stone altar. Grotesque masks, skulls and hideous shrunken heads hung on the walls, and robes in various shades of red hung on hooks.

'Oh my God,' Brandon breathed.

There were deep red stains over the stone altar. The forensic team was gathered around it, taking scrapings. There was a hideous smell that made their nostrils flare. Both men knew it was the stench of rotting flesh.

Anna was led into the Child Protection Unit's 'home' section by the carer working that morning, Alison Dutton. This was an area dressed like a warm, friendly house. The nursery was decorated with paintings and big colourful posters. A doll's house and boxes of toys were placed neatly against one wall. The room was bright and cheerful, with coloured bean bags and small children's tables and chairs. Nothing gave any hint of the torment that brought these children into this environment; everything was designed to help the children adjust to normality, yet the entire place was somehow fake to Anna. The women she met were kindly and helpful but, at the same time, protected their charges with a set of rules and regulations made by the Government. The children were waiting for the social services to find them a foster home; until a satisfactory one had been found, they would remain at the protection house.

Anna was told that the little girl, Sharon, was making

great progress; she had not started to talk yet, but had formed a strong bond with one of their team. At first, she had refused to eat and never slept; it had taken time and patience for them to get her to the point that she could now be spoon fed and had begun to play with the toys. She had not, after examination, been sexually abused, but she was deeply distressed. She could not control her bladder and would easily become hysterical, screaming continuously.

'What about the little boy?'

They were having problems with him; unlike his sister, he was not responding. Although he did sometimes talk, he was quite violent if anyone touched him. His medical examination had been very difficult, as he was so traumatized. They ended up tranquillizing him. When examined, it became obvious that he had been sexually abused. His anus was ulcerated; he also had wounds to his genitals and marks on his wrists as if he had been tied up. They were concerned that the infection in his bladder was not responding to the antibiotics.

Anna felt tears stinging her eyes. But she was there for a reason. She spent considerable time explaining the need for her to at least attempt to talk to Keith.

When she got a cold, flat refusal, she went on the defensive. 'Alison, do you think I want to do this? That little boy's mother was found mutilated and his other sister decapitated; all I want is to find out what he might know.'

'Detective Travis, all I have trained for, all I do, is to try to help these wretched children in any way I know how. Yesterday he held my hand – only for a second – but that was my first breakthrough. You want to try to talk to him about his dead mother, his dead sister? Don't you understand? I am trying to heal what has been done to him.'

'Please, let me just have a few moments with him. I am not asking to be alone with him; you can be in the room and monitor whatever occurs between us. If you want me to stop at any time, I give you my word that I will. It's just possible too, that what I need to know might help him.'

Mike Lewis tapped on Langton's door, then popped his head round. 'Kramer's in the holding cell, and not a happy man.'

'Right.'

'You want him brought up here?'

'No, he can stay down in the cell, and Mike – keep the uniforms off my back, will you?'

Lewis hesitated, then gave a nod and closed the door.

Langton flipped a pencil over while he looked at his watch. Five minutes passed before he got up and walked out.

The Hampshire station had only four holding cells; these were situated at basement level. Used mostly for drunks and smalltime burglary suspects, they were cold and bare. They smelt of mildew, stale vomit, urine and disinfectant. The cell doors were the old heavy steel studded ones, with a central flap that opened for officers to monitor the prisoner. At ankle level was a second flap, used for pushing in meal trays. The walls were a dim green, and the stone floor a dark red. Each cell was as unwelcoming as it could be.

Langton carried a clipboard, holding all the statements that had been taken in the previous sessions with Vernon.

Printed by the side of Vernon's cell door, in chalk, was his name and time of arrival. Langton noisily opened the flap, purposely banging back the bolt. He looked into the cell, just half his face showing.

'We need to talk,' he said.

'Too bloody right we do. What the fuck is going on? I want a lawyer, because this isn't fucking right. You got no right to bring me here and bang me up!'

'Have you been offered a cup of tea?'

'I don't want a bloody cup of tea, I want to know what the hell is going on. What you got me here for?'

'To talk.'

'I'm all talked out with you. I am not saying a fucking word until I got legal representation.'

'I need some answers.'

'To what? What the fuck are you up to?'

Langton clanged the flap back into place and shot back the bolt. He turned to Lewis. 'Leave him here to stew,' he said loudly. 'I'll come back in the morning.'

'You can't leave me in this Victorian shithole!'

Langton kept his voice raised so Vernon could hear. 'See if we can get a lawyer in; this time of day, one probably won't be available until tomorrow. Maybe we can contact the guy he used before.'

Vernon screeched, banging on the door, 'You can't do this to me! You listen to me! You can't leave me in here! I know my rights!'

Langton looked at Mike and smiled; they both remained silent.

'Eh, you still out there? You bastard!'

Vernon could be heard kicking and banging; there was a thump as his mattress hit the door. It then sounded as if he was trying to haul his bunk bed across, only to discover that it was bolted to the floor. In a rage, he then threw himself at the door: there was a thud, thud, then another kick.

Then there was a pause, as if he was trying to hear what was going on outside the cell. 'You still there?' he called out.

Langton let a few minutes pass before he shot the bolt again and opened the flap. Vernon was calmer now, having exhausted himself.

He looked up at Langton. 'Why are you doing this to me?' he said, near to tears.

'I just want to talk to you, Vernon, and get some answers.'

'To what, for Chrissakes? We've been through it all before, ain't we?'

Bang. The flap closed and the bolt went back across: Langton was starting to get impatient. He checked his watch and sighed.

Lewis wasn't exactly sure what was going on. It was a game that could get them both into trouble. Obviously, Langton wanted to unnerve Vernon and get him to talk, but about what, Lewis didn't know. Vernon had given a statement that Rashid Burry had been at the bungalow with Gail. He had also given details of being taken to Camorra's property; sketchy they might have been, but Lewis didn't understand what more they could get from him.

Langton obviously had a different opinion. The charade of opening and shutting the flap in the cell door continued, as did Vernon's accusations. He veered from threatening legal action, to abusive screaming, to throwing himself against the cell door, kicking and punching at it. Eventually, he huddled on the mattress on the floor, crying. Langton gestured that the cell door could be opened.

'I can leave you in here for the night, or we can talk and you can be taken back to prison. Up to you, Vernon.'

'Can I have a cup of tea?' The man gave them a strange look, all fight gone, and then got slowly to his feet. His next words were hardly audible. 'I knew it wasn't over.'

Anna built a garage from wooden bricks and drove a few toy cars inside. Keith, Gail's son, had not said one word for over an hour. He stood with his back pressed against the wall while Anna built a fire station and then a house with the toys available for the children. All the while, she was watched by Alison, the Child Protection Officer, whose patience was running out.

Anna knocked down the garage and built a square pen. She went over to the farmyard filled with plastic animals and brought back two pigs. She crawled on the floor, making snorting noises, and put the pigs inside the pen.

Keith moved away from the wall; he came and sat beside Anna. It was an electrifying moment. He had been so silent, so unapproachable. Without a word, he picked up the wooden bricks and began to assemble square pens of his own. He then pointed to the two plastic pigs. She handed them to him and he placed them inside the pens.

'Oink oink,' Anna said.

She would never forget the way he looked up at her, his tiny freckled hand holding a pig. His head had been shaved to a crew cut because of the head lice. It made him appear older and tougher than he really was. The expression in his clear eyes was so painful.

'Mummy,' he said.

'Do you remember this place? Did you help feed the animals at the bungalow? There were hens too, and a henhouse.'

He nodded, and began building something else. He was very focused, looking around to find the right bricks, all the while remaining totally silent. Another carer, younger and more junior than Alison, came in and handed her some notes. They sat whispering together as Anna watched the boy select toy cars from all the various types littering the play area. He was very careful, discarding one after another, then choosing a red and white car to place at the side of the house he had built. It took a long time.

'Is this your house?' Anna asked.

He stared at her and then went to pick up a red bus; he stood with it in his hands.

'Oh, that's a bus. Did you go on a bus?'

'Yes.'

'Do you know where this house is?'

He stared at the house he had built and then angrily kicked it apart, stamping on the bricks. He put the bus down and started to crawl around, running it up and down the worn carpet.

'Did you go with Joseph? Leave the house with Joseph?'

It was so frustrating and, at the same time, so emotionally draining; the child was so tense, so far out of reach, and yet so close to answering. His lips moved as if he was saying something, then he went and sat in a corner, holding the bus and refusing to even look at Anna. She stood up and stared at the carers.

'Thank you,' she said. Then: 'I think I should go.'

Alison joined her; she could tell that Anna was upset. 'It takes a long time. If we do have any breakthrough with him, we'll contact you. You did actually get him to interact with you, which is more than we have been able to do.'

'It's heartbreaking,' Anna said, turning to look at the boy huddled in the corner with the bus.

'Yes. We have tried to get his grandmother here; she has promised twice and not turned up, which is even worse. I don't think she wants any involvement, to be honest. We obviously didn't tell the children she was due to come. We've learned never to make promises.'

'What will eventually happen to him and his sister?'

'We are waiting on suitable foster carers, but they will have to be very special.'

'Will they be able to stay together?'

'I can't say. It will be a big decision for whoever takes him on; his little sister is doing very well, but she is still mute.'

They walked to the door, speaking softly so that he wouldn't hear. 'But she was not sexually abused?'

'She was not penetrated, but she was used for oral sex. We use dolls and play games; well, you must know how we work.'

'Dear God ...' Anna closed her eyes, near to tears. Everything in her wanted to say, 'Let me take them, let me care for them!' In practical terms, it was ridiculous to even contemplate, but she felt so angry and emotional; she felt she needed to help these two defenceless children. She knew that numerous foster families felt the same way, but few were trained to deal with such traumatized children; even sadder was the fact that siblings sometimes had to be separated.

Anna was shaking Alison's hand when the younger carer who had been in the nursery room with them hurried out.

'Alison, can you come in quickly?' she said.

'What's happened?'

'He was using the crayons and began scrawling all over the wall. I told him to give me the crayon and then he started to urinate in the corner of the room. I went over to him, not to admonish him, but to take him into the toilets, and—'

Alison turned and hurried away. Anna hesitated, but then followed. The door was ajar. The little boy was screaming, kicking and fighting; then suddenly, as if all the fight had been sucked out of him, he ran into Alison's arms, weeping. She sat rocking him back and forth.

'It's all right, no one is going to hurt you. You're safe, shush now, there's a good boy.'

Anna jumped; the young girl had come to stand behind her.

'Thank God – at last.' She shut the door.

'I don't understand. What do you mean?'

'He's crying, letting Alison hold him; it means we've broken through.'

'You mean you'll be able to talk to him?'

'Maybe.'

The door opened again. Alison asked for some orange juice and biscuits, and a clean pair of pants. She looked almost with irritation at Anna.

'No, you *can't* see him,' she said. 'Please don't even ask.'

Vernon sat with his head in his hands, his elbows resting on the table. He looked in bad shape. Langton sat opposite him, Lewis to his right. Vernon had been talking for over an hour, and he was shaking. Langton checked his watch. It was almost four. He picked up his clipboard and jotted down a note.

Lewis glanced down. Langton had scrawled: *He's still holding back.*

'What's going to happen to me?'

Langton said they would get a duty solicitor in but, until they had pressed further charges, he would remain at the station.

'But I done nothing.'

'You withheld vital information, Vernon. If you had disclosed what you knew—'

'But I had nothin' to do with it, I swear before God. All I was doing was protecting myself. This isn't right. I could have told you where the house was, but you know I'd be dead meat.'

'You declined to have a solicitor present at the start of this interview: that is correct, isn't it?'

Vernon looked at the tape recorder and then at Langton. 'But we was gonna make a deal, you said to me.'

'I know what I said, Vernon, and the deal is you will continue this interview and make a formal statement.'

'I don't want a fucking lawyer.'

'That's your decision.' Langton stood up. 'If there is anything else you want to talk to me about, now is the time, because if you think you have a hope in hell of staying in a cushy open prison, you've got another big think coming.'

'You can't do this to me.'

Langton smiled, and said softly, 'You want to bet?' Then he turned to Mike Lewis. 'Arrange for him to be taken down to the holding cell.'

'Ah, don't put me back down there,' Vernon bleated.

'It'll be a lot cushier than where you'll end up.'

'In a box, you bastard! That's what'll happen to me!'

Lewis hesitated, then got up. He was confused as to whether Langton meant what he had said, and watched for a signal, but Langton had his back to him, looking down at his clipboard. Lewis walked out.

Langton looked at the tape. 'For the benefit of the tape, DI Mike Lewis has just left the interview room; time is four-fifteen p.m.'

He switched it off and suddenly picked up the clipboard; he swiped it fast across Vernon's face. Vernon gasped and sat back. Langton placed it back down in front of him as if nothing had happened.

'You have two minutes, Vernon.'

As Vernon gawped at him, Langton brought up the toc of his shoe and kicked him in the groin so hard that the man reeled back in his chair, clutching at his balls in agony.

'One minute,' Langton said, never taking his eyes off the sweating, frightened man. 'Talk, Vernon, fucking start talking to me. Tell me about Clinton Camorra.'

Vernon squeezed his eyes closed. 'It was all that prick Murphy's fault; he tried to blackmail him.'

Langton walked into the incident room, taut with anger. Anna had just returned to the station and was at her desk.

'We leave for the house in Peckham in five minutes,' he snapped, and slammed his office door.

Lewis came in; she asked what was happening.

'Vernon's down in the holding cell; bastard has been lying from the get go. It's taken bloody hours, but—'

Before he could finish, Langton bellowed for him to join him in his office.

Lewis had never seen him quite so angry.

'It's been staring at us in the face, but we concentrated so hard on the bloody illegal immigrants. Camorra used the poor bastards to bring in drugs as well as themselves! The women and kids too, all of them were mules; they not only paid the son of a bitch to get them into the country, they also swallowed condoms full of heroin. He's been concentrating on the poor – thousands of homeless in North Uganda, Somalia and Jamaica – making promises to care for their families. Joseph Sickert was one of the mules, brought in five years ago. He worked for Camorra and was sent to Gail's to look for Arthur Murphy because Murphy, on the run for Irene Phelps's murder, had threatened to talk unless Camorra got him out of the country.'

In the patrol car, Langton continued to fit the jigsaw pieces together.

'Camorra has a virtual army tied to him, afraid of him. He has used mules to open bank accounts in Christ knows how many names, but his bulk fortune is in cash. A control freak, he lost it when he murdered Carly Ann North; we know how he manipulated his henchmen, the Krasiniqe brothers and Rashid Burry. But now comes the twist: Sickert. Sent to track down Murphy via Gail, he starts to have a relationship with her, and when Murphy is arrested, he refuses to go back. Rashid Burry is sent to warn him and sees all her kids; he mentions that they would be useful to Camorra and that Sickert would get paid for bringing them to him.'

Langton rubbed his knee, grimacing with the pain. 'White kids, worth a lot of money; but by now, Sickert is involved with Gail and even cares for them. He's also sick. Whether or not he killed Gail's husband, we don't know, but he makes the big mistake of asking for Rashid Burry to help him get medication.'

Langton shook his head. 'This is now supposition, but maybe Sickert wanted out – who knows. But whatever went on at the piggery, I don't think he was involved in the murders. What he did do was take off with the two kids.' He turned to Anna. 'You get anything from them?'

'No. The little boy is still very traumatized, and the little girl hasn't spoken yet. Both have been sexually abused.'

Langton sighed. 'Maybe I'm wrong; maybe he did take them to Camorra. We know the white Range Rover was at the piggery.'

The car drew up outside the Peckham house. Patrol cars, forensic vans and SOCO teams were all still there.

'That scum Vernon, he knew this place. We could have got here sooner.' Langton slammed the car door shut and headed into the house. Anna and Lewis followed.

Brandon led them through the house, pointing out what had been taken for evidence; then they went into the cellar.

Langton stood looking around. No one spoke. After spending half an hour there, they left and drove back to the station in silence. The horrors that had taken place in the house sickened them all.

'It was well cleaned out,' Lewis said, when they were back in the incident room.

Langton sighed, closing his eyes. 'Camorra's had enough time – he could be anywhere, using Christ knows how many different names and passports. He's got rid of anyone that could finger him, and with the amount of money he's got stashed, we might have lost him for good.'

Chapter Twenty

The forensic lab had been hard at work for over a week. They had more than six different DNA samples from the bloodied altar; there could have been many more, but the stone had been scrubbed with disinfectant. They had also succeeded in matching the roll of black bin-bags, not only to those wrapped around Rashid Burry's body, but also the dead child in the canal: yet another murder linked to Camorra. They tested semen stains on the sheets taken from the bedrooms for DNA. Two matched the samples taken from Carly Ann after her rape and murder: one belonged to Idris Krasiniqe, the other was not on any records, nor was the third fingerprint taken from the Range Rover.

The team had all this incriminating evidence against Camorra, but still no clue as to his whereabouts. The charred documents revealed hundreds of figures, but there were no bank accounts in Camorra's name and the local bank in Peckham had no customers who answered to his description. The drug squad had been given his details: every day, mules and possible illegal immigrants were being arrested at the airports, so they were to work with the murder team on anyone who could be connected to the case. The fact that airports were so hot on security could also mean that Camorra might have gone to ground somewhere in the UK.

Staring down into the room from the packed incident board were the photos of the dead, red lines linking one to the other. It felt as if the jigsaw would never be completed.

Langton was in a permanent cold anger. His frustration often boiled over and he was edgy and aggressive with the team. Sickert's post-mortem results arrived, confirming that he died of organ failure and chronic heart disease. The sickle cell disease had destroyed him. Anna looked up at Sickert's picture on the board. Her eyes were drawn to the photo of the child found in the canal. As a thought, she fetched the Sickert file. The small square photograph of the woman and two children, cracked through being folded and refolded, was kept in a plastic cover.

She picked it up and went in to see Langton. 'I don't know if this will do anything for us, but the children in the photograph – one is a boy, the same age as the child found in the canal.'

Langton looked up.

'Now we have the DNA of Sickert,' Anna went on, 'I just wondered if, you know, we were looking for a reason for Sickert to protect the two children.'

'He didn't, did he though?'

'He did take them to that nursery. What if Camorra had brought Sickert's children over too? It would be a motive for him to—'

'Go ahead, test it, but it won't give us much; just another sickening fucking link!'

Anna walked out to set the wheels in motion for the tests even though, as Langton had said, if the child proved to be related to Joseph Sickert, it brought them no closer to finding Camorra.

Just as Anna put the phone down, it rang again. It was Alison from the Child Protection Unit.

'I just wanted to tell you that we have made a lot of progress with Keith,' she said. 'We have also found a foster carer who is prepared to take both children. She's been spending time with them here, getting to know them, and will be taking the children at the end of the week.'

'Could I come in and talk to Keith?'

'Yes, that is why I am calling. However, I don't have to remind you how precarious his recovery is. I can't allow him to be questioned too long and, if it is too emotional for him to deal with, then you will have to wait.'

Anna felt the hairs on the back of her arms standing up as she replaced the receiver. She then returned to Langton's office and gave him the update.

He sighed. 'Okay, do you want anyone with you?'

'I think I should go it alone; he has met me before.'

'Good luck then.' And he went back to his reports.

Langton was going over the statements of Eamon Krasiniqc's cellmate, Courtney Ransford. They still did not have the identity of the person who had visited Ransford. He had steadfastly refused to give any information, bar the fact he did not know the man who came to visit, and the death of Eamon had made no difference. Langton called in Harry; he told him to take Brandon and have another try.

'He has maintained that he did not know the bloke and was surprised that he had a visitor. He has also denied that he was passed any of this poison. Can we put some more pressure on him? He's awaiting trial as a category A prisoner for helping Krasiniqe kill Murphy: let's call that a twelve- to twenty-year sentence. Add to that a few more years when we charge him with fucking poisoning him, he could be a very long time behind bars.'

Harry shook his head. 'I dunno, these bastards – he doesn't seem to give a shit. But why should he? He's got three meals a day, gym, TV, bloody computer train—'

'Just go, Harry,' Langton snapped.

Alison met Anna in the reception, and said that Keith was in the play area. This was a larger room than the one she had first seen him in. A big open space, it had lots of toys and, in one corner, a games console. She couldn't believe the change. Keith was standing by the machine, playing with another small boy; they were shrieking and shouting.

'Keith, do you want to come and sit and talk to Anna?'

Keith continued to play, then jumped up and down, clapping his hands; he had obviously won! He turned to look at Anna, his eyes bright and his cheeks pink with all the excitement.

'This lady is a police officer,' Alison said. 'She's brought you something very special.'

'What?' he asked, like any normal inquisitive child.

Anna sat a small low table. Alison drew up a chair for Keith to sit on, but he hovered.

'What have you got?' he repeated.

Anna took out a very authentic-looking black plastic wallet. 'It's a detective's badge, Keith, like a real police-man's. A plain clothes one though, not a policeman in uniform. I have a proper notebook and a pencil as well, for you to write down notes.'

Keith sat down. He fingered the badge and then opened the notebook.

'That's for when you question a suspect. You have to always make notes, so you don't forget anything.'

'Have you got handcuffs?'

'Well, I can get you some, but we have to sort of test you, you know, to be a detective. I need to know if you could make an arrest.'

He nodded.

'Do you know what that means – to arrest someone?'

'Yes, put bad men away.'

'Correct – that is exactly what I meant. You question them, and it's called evidence, and you write it down in your book. Then you arrest them if they are bad.'

'Put handcuffs on them?'

'Yes, that's right! Do you think you would make a good detective?'

'Yes, I got a badge!'

'Yes, that is yours.'

'Can I go in a police car?'

'Oh, that depends. I will have to ask you some questions and then, if you can answer them, you'll get your handcuffs and a ride in the car.'

'Can I have a gun?'

'No, detectives don't have guns, they're only for the special squad.' Anna was on tenterhooks; it was going so well. She told him to open his notebook, ready to write down information. 'Do you know any bad men?' she asked.

He gave her a strange look, and she wondered if she had gone in too quickly.

'Or, can you tell me about the last house you were in? Or a house you think may have bad people inside?'

He became a little agitated, then twisted the pencil. 'How do you spell "detective"?'

'Oh, don't worry about spellings. It'll be your secret code. We often write words in a funny way.'

He began to write, the tip of his tongue poking out of his mouth as he concentrated, taking great pains over each word.

Harry and Frank Brandon waited in the visitors' section, in a room used for solicitors to interview their clients. It was a small room with three chairs and a table. The door was part glass, so the prison officers could monitor the interactions, but they could not hear conversations. A speaker was high up in one corner; the small window was also high up, and barred.

'How do we work it?' Brandon said quietly.

'Just like we discussed: give it to him straight. You got a problem with it now?'

'No, just checking we're playing the right roles.'

'Don't fucking start,' Harry said, as they heard footsteps.

Courtney Ransford was huge, with square shoulders and a body builder's torso. He sat down and his handcuffs were removed by the uniformed officers who had brought him in.

'Thank you for agreeing to talk to us,' Brandon said politely.

Ransford shrugged as the officers left. 'Anything for a bit of relief from the boredom. What's this about?'

Then, as Brandon opened a notebook: 'If it's anything to do with Arthur fucking Murphy, I'm not answering.

I've been questioned and shit so many times, I'm losing count. Why don't you just say that it was a job well done? The bastard was into rape; he was a sicko.'

'Couldn't agree with you more,' Harry said, and he meant it.

'I gotta stand trial for it. Arseholes.' Courtney flexed his muscles.

'You know Eamon Krasiniqe is dead?'

'Yeah. He was a crazy anyway.'

Brandon coughed and leaned forwards. 'You got a possible twelve to twenty for helping hold down Arthur Murphy. I am here to question you on another charge that could get you a lot longer.'

'*What?*'

'Murdering Eamon Krasiniqe.'

'Wait! When did this fucking go down?'

'I'm just here to discuss—' Brandon began.

'Discuss what, for fuck's sake?'

'– that you fed poison to Eamon Krasiniqe.'

Harry tapped the table. 'I was with him when he died. He said you'd given him something called Jimson weed. It's a poison – very potent.'

'Like fuck he did! He couldn't do nothin' but stare at the fucking wall, so what is this?'

'We have his statement and his post-mortem report. He was fed this poison in prison and we have you as his cellmate; we also have you being visited by someone who we believe passed you the—'

'I am not fucking believing this, man.'

Harry wagged his finger. 'Well, you'd better, because you got a lot coming your way for Arthur Murphy – you could be looking at another ten on top of that! Now, I am just here to help you. All I need is the truth. Who was this visitor and what did he pass you?'

'Jesus Christ, I didn't even know the bloke! I get the nod from the officers I got a visitor. They don't say who it is. I think, maybe he's a solicitor and, like I done today, I reckon anything to get out from the wing, right?'

'That is all very well, Courtney, but Eamon Krasiniqe died, and you are going to be charged with his murder.'

'The fuck I am!'

'I'm afraid you *are* fucked.'

Courtney sat shaking his head. He flexed his arm muscles so much, they looked like ebony; then he cracked his knuckles. They were obviously getting to him: the sweat was now standing out on his forehead.

'I think you were offered money, or something else worth your while, to give the dose to Krasiniqe. Now, they are about to arrest a guy called Camorra – you ever heard of him?'

Courtney stared.

Harry continued, lying through his teeth: they had no idea where Camorra was, let alone were on the verge of arresting him. 'He's a drug trafficker, also brings in illegal immigrants. He's got a lot of money and a lot of contacts. He wanted Murphy dead, because Murphy was going to inform on him.'

Courtney swallowed and shook his head. 'I don't know about this, man; I dunno about this.'

'Do you know this man Camorra? Clinton Camorra.'

Courtney suddenly put his hands over his face. 'Oh shit, shit!'

'You got relatives back in Uganda?'

Courtney pinched the bridge of his nose; his eyes were brimming with tears. He nodded.

'I hope to Christ they aren't kids,' Harry said, 'because you know what Camorra does to kids. Did you read about that little boy's body? Decapitated, found in a black bin-liner in Regent's Canal? He supplies boys like that to sickos. So, I certainly hope, Courtney, you have not got kids being brought in by this piece of filth. Now, can you give us anything?'

Courtney slammed his hand flat onto the table.

'Yes. Yes, I got something!'

Langton listened to Anna's call, almost with disbelief.

'Sweetheart, you can have a fleet of squad cars if that's what the lad wants.' He listened, and then rubbed his face. 'Whatever you need. Take it slow; this is the first lucky break we've had.'

Langton returned to the incident room in a really up tempo mood, just as Brandon and Harry walked in. Harry wafted a piece of paper in the air.

'What you get?' Langton asked eagerly.

Harry and Brandon, like two grinning kids, passed over the statement.

Courtney had been telling the truth when he said he did not know his prison visitor. What he had never divulged, however, was that the visitor had come with a deal. He said that he worked for someone with very high connections: someone who could bring his wife and two children to England – at a price.

Harry held up two fingers. 'He had to give two coconut rock cakes to Eamon Krasiniqe.'

'What? Fucking rock cakes?'

'Coconut rock cakes,' Brandon interjected.

'He was told they would make Krasiniqe dopey. Courtney was to say they had come from his brother. He was then to help Krasiniqe with Arthur Murphy, make it look like a prison fight. As it turned out, the poor kid had already been fed so much of the Jimson whatever, he went crazy and cut Murphy's throat in the exercise yard!'

Langton looked at the grinning pair and shrugged. 'Terrific – but what does this give us, apart from the rock cakes? We knew the bastard must have had something to do with it; this just confirms it.'

Brandon held up his hand again. 'We have more. You see, Courtney is still waiting to hear about his kids – like, when do they arrive. We gave him the lowdown on Camorra, and said he should pray that they don't get brought into the UK.'

'Laid it on with a trowel, we did,' Harry said. 'We were gonna make an arrest of Camorra, all that – then he gave this up. It's a mobile phone number. He said he'd called twice and spoken to the contact who said the deal was going down – which is why he agreed to help Krasiniqe kill Murphy, and why he's refused to talk before. For the sake of his wife and kids.'

'Jesus Christ, is it still active?'

'Gotta be, because Courtney was still keeping quiet about the rock cakes. We told him not to make another call to it until we got hold of the guy.'

'Did he give a description?'

'Yeah. A well-dressed black guy, over six feet, real smart. Wore a grey suit, white shirt; said he started off thinking he might be a solicitor, 'cos he looked like one.'

Langton clapped his hands; at long last, it looked as if the case was turning around.

The mobile phone was still active, but they could not trace who it belonged to, as it was a pay-as-you-go account. They got in touch with the auxiliary team at Scotland Yard, who had to get a trace on the phone; they would try to keep the owner on line to get the location where it was being used.

Anna felt drained; she had been with Keith for an hour and a half. Painstakingly slowly, she had gained details from him. She did not bring up his mother or Sickert, just 'bad men' that he could arrest and whom they could only go and get if he could recall where they were. She had tried testing out locations from Sickert's bus tickets – Tooting and Clapham – but these had brought no reaction. She did not say Peckham, since she was afraid that would traumatize him. Instead, she asked simple questions about the size of the house, the cars and garden. Keith said there was a big dog on a chain, but he didn't know what kind; they had talked about dogs for a while, until she could draw him back to more detailed descriptions of the house. It did not match the Peckham property. This meant Keith had been taken somewhere else.

Regent's Park, Hampstead, Croydon, Maida Vale, Kilburn and Chalk Farm all got no response, so she started to move on to locations further out of London. A clue came when he asked if he could go to the theme park in the patrol car. He described a water ride and a shooting range where you fired a gun and water spurted in your face.

Anna asked if he had been taken to the house on a train or bus.

'Motorway,' he said. He was starting to get frustrated and asked when he would get his handcuffs.

It was the young care worker who approached Anna;

she had been listening. 'Chessington? They have a theme park.'

'And a zoo,' Keith said. He began to talk about feeding the penguins. He described the monkeys and the chimps, and the two tigers.

Langton listened. Anna was certain that the second Camorra property was near Chessington. Langton asked if she had ever said the name Camorra to the boy: she said she hadn't. She was worried that anything that touched on the abuse he had been subjected to might stop him from talking freely.

Langton filled her in, in turn, on how they were about to put a trace on a mobile phone that might be connected to Camorra. They were using an officer with about as strong an accent as Courtney's, and were standing by for him to make the call as if he was Courtney talking from Parkhurst prison pay phone.

Anna felt very emotional: the little boy's face lit up when he was taken to the patrol car. The uniformed officer took off his cap and saluted him.

'Afternoon, sir.'

Keith sat in the front seat, as he was a detective. Anna and Alison sat in the back. He was allowed to hold the police radio and they made constant calls to him, addressing him as Detective Keith. Anna watched in the rearview mirror as the unmarked patrol car moved into position behind them.

The phone seemed to ring for a long time before it clicked on.

'Yes?'

The officer went for it, playing his role as Courtney Ransford to perfection, his voice low and harsh.

'I'm on the wing, man. I only got about ten minutes left on my phone card. You got some answers for me? I need to know, man, because something went down today that's freaking me out. I gotta stand trial for this Murphy business, right? These two motherfuckers came and started laying it on me about passing the gear, the rock cakes to Eamon, you hearin' me?'

'I said it would all be fine. You know these arrangements take time; with all the extra security at the airports, we have to be very careful. So, what's your problem?' The voice was soft, quite well-spoken, with only a slight burr of an accent.

'They wanna know about the weed; they said Krasiniqe put me in the frame.'

'He couldn't do that.'

'I am just telling you what went down.'

The mobile phone was being used by someone on the move, probably travelling in a car. They got the location as Epsom. As the officer talked on, they were able to pinpoint it as being close to the racetrack. Epsom was close to Chessington, but it was a massive area. There were many houses in both locations that were set well back from the road; many also had hidden access and tight security. Keith's description had not been very clear, but five minutes later they were dependent on it, as the call was cut off.

Langton now pulled in the locals, as well as all his teams, to give him even more bodies. Covering the area was going to be a nightmare. The child's description of the house was radioed in to stations at Chessington, Epsom and Leatherhead. Langton orchestrated the search.

He asked for no sirens, plain patrol cars only, and to watch radio contact: Camorra was likely to have a lot of toys that could tune into police frequency. Estate agents in the area were also being contacted and given the description of the house. Langton was back in his stride.

Keith continued to chatter; he recognized the signs for Chessington on the A3, but he couldn't recall when they left the motorway or on which route. They headed towards the theme park as the other cars covered the areas that fitted the description he had given.

Langton had now joined the search. He was with Mike Lewis; they were covering a section of properties past the racecourse.

'He might not even be there,' Langton said, lighting one cigarette from the butt of another.

'We're due some luck,' Lewis replied. The reality was they were looking for a needle in a giant haystack.

Anna was beginning to get concerned. Keith was tired; he no longer seemed interested in looking out of the window, but fiddled with the radio. Alison asked if he wanted to go back; he said he wanted a Coca-Cola. They pulled over to a small row of shops and Alison went into an off-licence. It only took a few minutes, but Anna was on edge: they were in a marked patrol car. She stepped away from the car to call Langton and say they were going to head back.

'We shall keep going,' he replied.

'You know, he's described two cars: one he said was a big four-door, the other was a red low sports car, maybe a Ferrari.'

'Yeah, yeah, gatepost, dog kennel, big fences, big hedges.' He was beginning to think he should have waited.

Anna got back in the car and asked the driver to do a U-turn and head back to the motorway.

Alison leaned forwards. 'Keith, hold the can up, love, you're spilling it.'

'Bad man. I want my handcuffs,' the boy said fiercely.

By now, the patrol car had turned round. They saw a man come out of the off-licence with a carrier bag. He took an *Evening Standard* from under his arm and flipped it open.

'Bad man!' screeched Keith.

'Let me check him out for you,' Anna said, opening her door as the car slowed down for her. She instructed Alison to calm Keith and for the driver to keep going.

Anna kept control: she opened her mobile phone and starting talking as she waited to be put through to Langton. 'But you said you'd pick her up from school, James! I'm at the shops ... well, I can, but she's waiting at the gates.'

The man continued to read the newspaper and turned left at the end of the row of shops. He had glanced at Anna, but dismissed her as some frantic housewife.

'Hello, what's this?' came Langton's voice.

'Maybe have target: the kid got very distressed. He's about ten feet in front of me now, turning into a cul-de-sac: Edge Lane. He's short, dark-skinned, suit, rimless glasses.'

Anna gesticulated wildly as if she was still having an argument on the phone as the target drove out of the cul-de-sac; he paused to let a cyclist pass, then turned left and drove off. Anna passed on a description of the car: a black Mitsubishi, registration number 345-A.

She crossed the road, as the patrol car reversed back to pick her up, and got in. Keith was very distressed, holding up his handcuffs, saying he wanted to get the bad man, he wanted to arrest the bad man. Anna picked up the radio and held it out, this time for real. 'You are going to be able to listen now: this is going to be really exciting.'

In came the radio call. 'We have target, heading past Chessington Garden Centre. Over.'

Langton looked at Mike as he studied the map; the vehicle had been picked up on the A23 heading towards Redhill. It was then a game of follow the target, as one car after another moved into position. The driver went round the big roundabout and turned down towards Redhill Lane. Unaware of the tail both back and front, he continued for a few miles before indicating and turning into the drive of a large gated property. The electric gates opened, and there was a sound of a dog barking.

Langton radioed to Anna: she, Keith and Alison were to swap into an unmarked patrol car. They were then to drive past the target property and not stop until they saw an open gateway, where he would be waiting.

Keith had perked up: he liked switching cars and, as Anna said, going undercover. Alison sat next to him in the back.

Anna turned to him. 'We are going to drive past the house that we think you've been telling us about. We will have to drive past and not stop, as the bad man might try to escape. Do you understand?'

'Yes.' The small boy was clutching his handcuffs.

It was only ten minutes before they, too, were heading down Redhill Lane. They passed the electric gates and the big posts that the child had described. The car slowed down; they could not stop in case they gave the game away, but they didn't need to. Keith began to cry, his small chest heaving, as he sobbed and garbled barely intelligible words: 'Bad men, bad men hurt me in there.'

Langton was waiting by the gateway as promised; as their car drew up, he opened the door. Alison had Keith in her arms.

'You the detective heading up this arrest?' he asked.

Keith looked at him: the fear had come back and he couldn't play the game.

Langton bent down to his level. 'Keith, listen to me: you are going to be okay. I am very proud of you and I am going to recommend you get a bravery award for helping us.'

It broke Langton's heart the way the child turned away, his eyes brimming with tears, his voice croaky from crying. 'Thank you.'

Alison and Keith were taken back into London by an officer in an unmarked patrol car. Alison had been very impressed by the way everyone had handled the situation. The small silent boy, who now had tears trickling down his cheeks, stared ahead; clasped in his hand were the handcuffs he had wanted to put on the bad man.

The same question was in all the officers' minds: *was this the right bad man?*

The house now under surveillance, Langton regrouped at the nearest police station to determine how many people occupied the premises and to work out the best strategy for entering. It would be getting dark soon. He ordered a helicopter to move over the house with an infra-red camera to determine what they would be faced with.

The property had extensive land, both in front and behind, with about an acre of dense woodland and a small manmade lake. They knew there were dogs at the front of the house, but didn't know if they would be loose or chained. There was a red Ferrari parked outside a double garage and, behind it, the Mitsubishi.

Langton was standing in a corridor, lighting a cigarette when Anna walked towards him.

'Only place you can smoke in here without the alarms going off,' he grumbled.

'We're ordering some food for everyone,' she said. 'You want anything?'

He shook his head, and took a deep drag on the cigarette; then rested his head against the windowpane. 'We've got the authority to deploy firearms officers. As soon as the armed response guys get here, we go in. I've waited long enough.'

She put her hand on the small of his back, but said nothing. She then returned to the waiting teams of officers, and gave a silent prayer that Camorra would be at the house.

Chapter Twenty-one

Leatherhead police station had never seen so much action. Boxes of pizza and beakers of coffee were handed round. Langton's team had taken over a large room on the first floor, used as an incident room when necessary. They now had a map of the area, plus a detailed layout of the property from a prominent estate agency, which had sold it about two years ago, for over three million pounds, to someone called Emmerick Orso. The previous owners, a Mr and Mrs Powell, had remained on the estate, retaining as their home what would once have been the staff cottage. The estate agency had recently been approached by Mr Orso, with the particulars of the property, to query the boundary line that crossed the lake. They had not as yet contacted Mr and Mrs Powell to discuss it, but were intending to do so.

Everyone was poised, adrenalin pumping, waiting for Langton's decision on how to orchestrate the raid. Langton joined them, and did actually have a slice of pepperoni pizza, but he was strangely distant and didn't interact with anyone. Eventually, he called Mike Lewis over and asked him to get the key team together. He needed a talk, and fast. In a small anteroom off the main incident room, allocated for Langton's personal use, his team gathered.

Langton sat on the edge of a table. 'I've put a hold on the armed response team.' He said it very quietly.

Anna glanced at Mike: he seemed as surprised as she was.

Langton continued. 'From the copter's aerial take, we have maybe four adults; the heat sensors said there could also be another two that might be children. Orso's married with one child, according to the electoral register. He's got a legitimate import/export company, shipping in artefacts from Africa, and a string of properties, including a warehouse close to Heathrow. He has no police record and he doesn't fit the profile of our prime suspect, Camorra, but we do know that Camorra, at one time, used the Christian name Emmerick. That's about all we know until we start pushing some more buttons.'

'You saying we got the wrong bloke?' Frank slurped his coffee.

'Something doesn't fit. What we have here doesn't match with that hellhole in Peckham. This guy, Orso: his kid goes to the local school, he's lived here for two years.'

'Was he the bloke the little kid saw?' This was Harry.

'The estate agent described Orso as tall, elegant, well-educated and very charming, which doesn't sound like that bloke, or Camorra. Camorra's a crazy voodoo freak, surrounded with sickos and heavies, whereas we've got a respectable business guy in Orso. We've so far got nothing on him, or the bloke at the off-licence.'

Anna sipped her coffee. They had already been to the off-licence and interviewed the staff, who knew the bloke only as a semi-regular customer. They did not know his name, just that he lived close by. He always bought good wines and spirits, and paid in cash. They had also checked, and the house did not have milk or newspapers delivered. They had not yet had time to question other local shops, like the butcher's; nor had they spoken to any neighbours.

Langton lit a cigarette, then put it out when he noticed the fire alarm sensor was above his head; he swore.

'My gut feeling is that this Emmerick has to be properly checked out. Up until now, we've been going along the lines that Camorra is the big cheese but, the more you think about it, the more it doesn't gel. We're saying that he's getting literally hundreds of thousands of pounds, from illegal immigrants to drug-trafficking, but we have found no trace of how he's been moving the money or where it is stashed: that would need very sophisticated accounting brains! I am not saying that Camorra isn't wily, because he is; but he's also crazy. My gut feeling is, he could not have engineered this trafficking solo. So, now we are switching tactics: not going in wham-bam-thank-you. We want to get more information. Yes?'

Brandon said that he was sorry to interrupt, but wasn't the key objective time? The longer they left it, the more chance Camorra had to skip the country, if he hadn't already. Harry agreed.

Langton shook his head. 'You think I haven't thought about that? If he is in the house, then we will pick him up. If he leaves, we'll pick him up. I think he could have gone to ground at Orso's, if he is the main man. We have hanging loose the last days of Joseph Sickert: did he go to the house in Peckham, with Gail's two children, and did something happen there that made him take the kids to Orso's place?'

'But what about the bastards we've been after?' Brandon asked, chucking his empty coffee beaker into a bin.

Langton was getting tired of their interruptions. 'We do a full-scale surveillance of the property day and night: we find out exactly how many people are in there and what they are doing. We get phone intercepts set up; we get every possible toy to find out what is going down inside. Anyone moves out, we tail them. In the meantime, we check out the warehouse and we check out Emmerick Orso. I want to know what this guy eats for breakfast.'

They broke up and joined the rest of the waiting officers. Langton would oversee the surveillance operation. His team was to return home, get a case packed, and book into local hotels, so they would be on site. In the meantime, the wheels were set in motion. The four officers already staking out the house reported that there had been no movement so far, other than someone putting some rubbish out at eleven o'clock. The house, apart from the security lights, was in darkness.

Anna packed a small overnight bag and was returning to her car, when she received a call from Grace. The DNA of the dead child found in Regent's Canal matched the DNA of Joseph Sickert: they were the same blood group. The dead child also had the sickle cell trait.

From her hotel room, Anna relayed the information to Langton who, at eleven-fifteen, was still at the Leatherhead station. She also said that she would contact

Alison first thing in the morning, to try and get further details from Keith. She had called earlier and been told that he was not showing any severely adverse reactions to the afternoon, but had been withdrawn and quiet. Alison said she would try to talk to him if he was still making progress, rather than regressing.

Anna asked that Alison specifically try to find out what the bad man did, and to now talk to the boy about Joseph Sickert. Someone took him to the zoo and to the Chessington theme park, and they needed to know who that was.

There were a few hours' delay, as Langton had to get clearance to allow Brandon and Harry to go into Orso's warehouse. He wanted a covert operation and photographs which, without prior authority, would be a breach of the Human Rights Act. He also organized for an actual customs officer to accompany them.

They were taken to a massive new storage warehouse, ten miles from the airport. There were over 40,000 square feet of cages, containing shipments from West Africa, already labelled as cleared by customs. Many of the wire containers were stacked with hand-woven baskets of various shapes and sizes, from laundry baskets to flat fruit bowls.

Harry peered at them. They had labels saying that all were handmade and took many weeks to complete; they had the maker's name for authenticity.

'Fucking brilliant. You ever think what China left – the dynasties, the artwork – and what did Africans do? Ignored their own diamond and mineral mines for centuries to make baskets.'

'You're a racist bigot,' Brandon said.

'It's the truth, though. Go to the museums and see: baskets and a few masks a kid could hack out of a tree trunk!'

'Just shut the fuck up and look at that mask: where have you seen that before?'

Harry looked. Stacked, with Bubblewrap between them, were big masks carved from dark wood. The one on top had been unwrapped: it was identical to the one in the cellar in the Peckham house. Just as they were about to take a closer look, the customs official joined them.

'This is Job Franklin,' he said, introducing a tall African in a brown overall. 'He is the manager here. This is customs official Frank Brandon and—'

Harry put out his hand. 'Harry Blunt. Nice to meet you, and thanks for helping us out. You've been told, have you, the reason we're here?'

'We had customs check these cargoes out last week,' the man said sullenly. 'They're all cleared and ready to be sent out.'

'I know, and we won't hold you up any longer than necessary, but I'm afraid we're gonna need to check the papers.'

'Why?' Franklin asked.

Brandon lowered his voice. 'They just picked up the guy that okayed this lot for taking bribes.'

'Not from us!'

'I'm sure they are all legit, but we have to just check.'

'Come into the office then.' Franklin led them round the back of the cages to a small office. He lifted down a massive file and placed it on the desk. 'These are all the particulars of the last shipment.'

'Mr Emmerick Orso is the boss, right?'

Franklin gave a small nod.

'He comes here on a regular basis?'

'No.'

'But you know him?' Harry said, drawing up a chair.

'Of course.'

'What kind of bloke is he?'

'I work for him.' Job Franklin was very obviously not about to get into a conversation with them about his boss, but he didn't appear to be nervous: more irritated at the intrusion.

'How many workmen do you have?'

'Fifteen, and five drivers.'

'You got their details?' Brandon asked.

'Naturally.' Franklin went to the filing cabinet and withdrew a file.

'Thank you very much,' Brandon said, sitting down himself.

'Do you need me to stay?'

'No, no, you carry on. We shouldn't be long.'

Brandon watched Franklin walk out. 'Well, he seems legit.'

Harry nudged him. 'Any money he's on to his boss now: take a look.'

Through the glass panel in the door, they saw Franklin dialling on his mobile as he walked away.

Harry took out a small camera and began to photo each page of employees, while Brandon did the same with the cargoes. They worked very fast, and didn't speak.

At eight-forty, the black Mitsubishi drove out, with the same driver as before at the wheel. Beside him was a well-dressed woman, in Western clothes, with heavy gold earrings. Seated in the back, safety belt on, was a small girl in a school uniform: a grey coat with a grey felt hat. They drove to the local private school where the woman got out to drop the girl off, leading her inside by the hand. After five minutes, the woman came back and the couple drove to a large Sainsbury's. Both went in. She did quite a grocery shop: steaks and chops with vegetables, fresh milk and ice cream. He carried the shopping back to the car and they returned to the house. At twelve-fifteen the driver and the woman, who they presumed was the mother of the child, collected her from school and returned to the house.

Langton had been through all the hoops to gain phone interceptions, but there had been no calls. They knew there was a gas Aga, and a gas hob and oven; the Aga heated water for one section of the house. At twelve-forty, the main gas link to the house was cut off.

At twelve-fifty, they had the first call from the house. A woman, calling herself Mrs Orso, phoned the Gas Board, asking someone to come out: their Aga had gone out and she didn't know if it was a problem with the stove or the gas. She was told that they would try to get someone out to her that day, but could not give a time. She complained, and said they needed it, as it also heated their hot water. She was told, again in typical jobsworth fashion, that they would try to send an engineer as soon as possible.

Mr and Mrs Powell sat with Langton and Anna. They had been very nervous to begin with, but Langton had told them they were investigating a tax fraud and it was nothing to be concerned about. It seemed to satisfy them. Mr Powell, ex-Army, said that he'd always wondered where the chap got all his money from. He was able to give a very detailed description of the man he knew as Emmerick Orso. It matched the one given by the estate agents.

The couple were unable to give details of anyone coming and going to the house, however, as it was so secluded, with the wood in front and the lake.

'We heard voices sometimes.' This was Mrs Powell.

'Yes, sound travels across the water,' Mr Powell agreed.

'Did you ever see anyone suspicious?'

'Not really. We did complain about the dogs being loose. They barked all night when they first arrived.'

'When was that?'

'Quite recently. I saw a tall man, out by the boat hut, and I said to him that we were concerned about the dogs. He was quite pleasant and said he would keep them to the front of the house.'

'Was this Mr Orso?'

'No, I think it was his chauffeur. Anyway, we had no real problems again; they do still bark, but it's not so intrusive.'

'Was there anything else? We are really interested in the people that Mr Orso has staying with him.'

'There was only the one time; it was very strange,' said Mrs Powell.

Mr Powell looked at his wife. 'Yes, that was very strange. When was it?'

'A few weeks ago, maybe even more.'

Langton waited: they were both wrapped up in trying to pinpoint the exact date.

Finally, Mr Powell said gravely, 'We wondered if someone had broken in.'

'It's amazing: the echo is so loud, even with the wood in between,' mused Mrs Powell.

'You said it was possible someone had broken in – to the main house, do you mean?'

'I don't know. They were searching around the water's edge with flashlights, and looking into the boathouse.'

'Before that, we heard children. They have a child, don't they?' said her husband.

Langton was losing patience, so Anna took over. What she was able to piece together was that the couple had heard children's voices and then some kind of argument. It had been so loud that Mr Powell had got up, as it was very late – well, to the elderly couple it was – they thought it was about ten in the evening. He had taken a flashlight and walked through the woods and to the edge of the lake; then it had gone silent.

Mrs Powell then interjected to say that they had found the small rowing boat on their side of the lake. There was an old rope attached to the small jetty; you could, she said, literally pull yourself across from one side to the other.

Langton coughed. 'So what, you think someone got into the boat and pulled themselves across?'

'Well, that's what we thought, but they weren't in the woods.' Mr Powell puffed himself up. 'I know that because I did a good search around. I had my flashlight with me, and my cosh, so if anyone was trying to break into our cottage . . .'

Langton sighed. The interview had really tried his patience, but at least now they had the Powells' permission for officers to camp out on their land. He was just worried that 'the General', as he nicknamed Mr Powell, might give the game away with his flashlight and cosh!

Anna called Alison to say that, when she spoke to Keith, could she ask him if he was ever in a rowing boat with Sickert.

'It all adds up, you know,' she told Langton. 'Dogs arriving: could be the ones from Peckham. Then to hear kids' voices by the lake and some kind of argument – maybe that's how Sickert got the kids out of there. It would also make sense of why Orso wants that boundary line: he could fence in the property.'

Langton leaned over and ruffled her hair. 'Little brain never stops ticking!'

She hated people who ruffled her hair!

He didn't notice her response, however, as he checked his watch. 'Mike must be in there by now.'

Mike Lewis, wearing a Gas Board boilersuit and accompanied by a real Gas Board official, was being shown to the back kitchen entrance by the tall man they knew as the driver. The kitchen door was opened by a good-looking black woman in her thirties. She was nervous, but gestured for them to come in.

The kitchen was massive, with a marble floor and a square central marble-topped chopping area; above it were rows of copper pans and utensils. There was a large round pine table in the bay window, which overlooked the lake. The table was set for lunch: four places.

'The Aga no work,' she said, pointing.

They kneeled down in front of it, as she hovered.

Mike then got up and turned to the woman. 'This might be a mains gas problem; does this also heat the water?'

She looked confused.

'Only I'll need to check the water tanks.'

'Excuse me.' She walked out. Mike had the tiny microphone in place beneath the table within seconds.

'What is the problem?' This was the elegant woman seen driving in and out.

'We think you have a gas block but, as this Aga also heats your water, I will need to look into your boiler room. Have you turned off the main gas taps?' He showed her his fake ID. 'Are you the owner?'

'I am Mrs Orso. Ella, stay in the kitchen please,' she snapped, then gestured for Mike to follow her.

According to Mike, compared to the house in Peckham, this place was like Buckingham Palace. It was very classy: full of antiques and clean as a new pin. He had not been able to get any microphones in the main dining room, lounge, or guest bedrooms, but he had one in the kitchen, one on the staircase close to the front door, another on the first-floor landing and one in the master bedroom.

'It's a huge place, bloody massive; from the plans, you can't really tell just how big it is. There are two Alsatians chained up in a kennel at the front by the garage. The rear is clear – access would be easy from across the lake, with good coverage from the woods – but the front is like Fort Knox. You've got the gates, that high fence, and a wall with a dense hedge all the way round. They also have a lot of automatic security lights; these are positioned right the way round the house and gardens. There's a wine cellar, but we couldn't get down there.'

Harry and Brandon arrived, and gave their report.

They had checked out the delivery lorries that belonged to the warehouse and would now process all the known employees. They had also discovered that Orso had shipped the same cargo into the USA.

'Who buys all these bloody baskets?' Harry said disgustedly.

'Same masks as the ones in Peckham house,' Brandon noted, then looked to Mike Lewis. 'How did the gas fitting go?'

'Okay. They're planted, but sadly not in the main rooms. We saw no one apart from a very nervous servant girl and Mrs Orso, who's a piece of work.'

Langton sighed. 'We've also no sighting of this guy Emmerick, or the other men in the house, apart from the driver.'

'Big place though; there was a whole floor I couldn't get to,' Mike said.

Langton sighed again, then looked up as the sound engineer opened the door and gestured for him to come into the van parked outside. There was a four-man team closeted in the van, working round the clock for as long as it took to get a result. Langton entered, and one of them passed him a set of headphones.

'Phone?' he asked.

'No – kitchen microphone.'

It was Mrs Orso and she was screaming. 'How can you ruin a steak, how can you ruin a steak? This is fillet steak, do you know how much this cost? What each of these steaks cost? Just get out of my way, get out!'

There was a clatter and rattle of what sounded like pans.

'She has been trouble from day one. I want you to get rid of her – she is driving me crazy! She still has no idea how to use the iron. I had to show her how to work the dishwasher, never mind the tumble-dryer. I want you to get me someone else.'

The voice was male, soft and cultured. 'Make do with her until we leave.'

'How long is that going to be? We can't keep taking Rose in and out of school; it's very unproductive for her. Will you have this one? It's the only one not spoilt. You know what I caught her doing? Boiling it! She was boiling fillet steak!'

'Yeah, well, they eat dogs where she came from.' This was another male; a cruder voice, lower-pitched.

Langton listened attentively. There was the sound of crockery and cutlery, and then Mrs Orso again.

'There's some salad, but God only knows what she would have put on that. She can't even mix a simple olive oil and vinegar dressing.'

'Gimme some Hellmann's,' said the crude voice.

'Sweetheart, go and see Rose, and get David in; maybe he likes shoe leather.'

There was a laugh, again from the crude voice. 'He'd eat it if it was pussy.'

'That's enough; keep your mouth clean round my wife!'

Langton felt the sweat run down from his armpits. 'That's got to be Emmerick; so if she's gone to get David, who's the big mouth?'

They listened as cutlery hit crockery; then in came footsteps and voice three.

'I've had Franklin on the phone. He says there's been customs officers crawling all over the warehouse, saying some bloke's been picked up for taking bribes.'

'Wasn't our man,' said Emmerick.

'They were there for a hell of a long time and he got into a panic.'

'Too late. The cargo was checked and clean, so just stay calm.'

'I am calm – I just thought you'd want to be informed. You know I didn't like that prick from Parkhurst coming on to me.'

'Then lose the phone!' Emmerick again.

'Christ, this is tough. I can't eat this shit,' said the crude voice.

There was a crash, as what sounded like a plate hit the floor and broke.

'You are beginning to get on my nerves. If you can't eat it, give it to the dogs, but you chuck one of my dinner plates around again and I'll—'

'Sorry, sorry, but it was disgusting. Gimme the Hell-mann's; I'll have some salad. I've not had anything to eat since breakfast and I'm starving. Being stuck up there is starting to drive me nuts. Maybe send the bitch Ella up to make my bed.'

'You know, sometimes your audacity makes my skin crawl. You didn't even consider what problems you caused by handing her over to me, did you?'

'I didn't know the prick was gonna turn up here.'

'No, but he did.'

'My steak's okay,' David interjected.

There was a pause as the crockery and cutlery clanked; then there was the sound of a cork being popped open, wine being poured and glasses clinking.

'How long will it take for Milton to get the gear ready? I've been printing them off for fucking years with no problem; now he's dicking us around. When is he coming?' asked the crude voice.

'When he's ready. If you hadn't fucked up at the house, none of this would have been a problem. In fact, you started going off the wall with that girl. Ever since then, you have been screwing up and we have been trying to clean up after you, so don't push me. I don't like it.' Emmerick sounded tense.

'Yeah, well, we all know why you put up with me: take a look around you! And it's not just this place – you need me. You need to treat me right and with respect, man.'

'I got some new videos for you,' said David.

'I fucking need something; I'm going stir crazy stuck up there.'

'They're on the hall table,' said David.

There was the sound of a scraping chair, more wine being poured and then receding footsteps.

'You got a real problem with him,' said David.

'I know,' responded Emmerick.

'How deep is that lake?'

There was a soft laugh; then footsteps as Mrs Orso walked back in.

'You want coffee? I've also got some plum tart.'

A second officer put his hand up. Langton watched as he switched to a different wire transmitter, then listened. They were picking up the microphone hidden in the hall.

'Hello, sweetheart, how was school today?' It was the crude voice again.

There were giggles and childish laughter, then footsteps.

'Rose, go into the lounge – now.' Mrs Orso.

More footsteps; then Mrs Orso back in the kitchen.

·'I told you not to let him even eat with us, let alone move in here. I don't want that animal anywhere near her.'

No one had said anything yet, but Langton was certain that the crude-voiced animal in question had to be Camorra.

Coming in now were the checks on the employees of Orso's company. Brandon and Harry had taken details, not just of the men working there at the present time, but all employees from the past two years. The list of names and addresses on Orso's payroll was endless, and they kept coming up as not registered.

Mike Lewis was nonplussed and contacted the Serious Fraud Squad: hundreds of thousands of pounds were being moved around in pay cheques.

They ascertained that the employees were illegal immigrants. The company opened bank accounts using their names. The cash was later transferred back into Orso's company, as sales.

Still no movement outside the house; no phone calls in or out; no visitors. The surveillance teams switched over and the night officers took up position, hidden in the woods, the boating shed and at another property across the street.

They knew that Emmerick Orso planned to leave with his family, as did the crude-voiced man that Langton was sure was Camorra. The question was, when? They surmised that it had to be imminent.

They had taken fingerprints from the nervous maid Ella and Mrs Orso, from the documents that the men from the Gas Board asked them to sign. They ran them through the database, but found no match.

They checked the local refuse collections and got lucky: the following day was pick-up.

Early the next morning, the dustcart was buzzed in

through the gates. Langton had earmarked for retrieval the pieces of a broken plate. The crude-voiced man had smashed it. It would have his prints.

Anna got a phone call from Alison, and a result from Keith. The little boy had said that he and his sister went in a boat, and the bad man had hit Joseph and made him bleed. He was also able to recall that, before he went to the big house with the bad man, Joseph had taken them to the zoo. Only when he had been asked about the house in Peckham did he pull back: this was obviously where the abuse had taken place.

Anna was now building a timeframe for when the children were taken from their mother at the piggery and on to the house in Peckham. At some point whilst there, Joseph Sickert had discovered something – perhaps that his own son had been murdered – that made him decide to take the children to Emmerick's house. From there, he then escaped with them via the boat. She could not as yet piece together how long they had been on the run. All she knew was the date that Sickert had left them at the nursery. That was, until they got a call from Mr Powell.

Langton had been wary about using the Powells' house for the undercover officers to take a leak or have a cup of tea, and was edgy when told Mr Powell had called to speak to him. He had therefore waved the call over to Anna.

Mr Powell was, in actual fact, enjoying the undercover operation and taking it very seriously. He had been thinking about the night of the possible break-in. The more he thought about it, the more determined he had become to pinpoint the exact date.

The date, he said – and he was certain that this was the

exact date, because his grandchild had got chickenpox, so had not come to see them as planned – was a Friday, eight weeks ago.

Anna worked out when Sickert left the bungalow with the children, arrived in Peckham and then turned up at the big house. He and the children must have lived rough for a week. She took her calculations to Langton.

He looked down at them, then up at her. 'Great. What does that give us?'

'Whatever happened must have tipped off Camorra to close down; other than that, I don't really know.'

Langton's mobile phone rang: at long last, they had some unusual movement at the house. A BMW saloon had just drawn up. They had the registration number: the car was owned by a Milton Andrews, who had an address in Coventry, but no record on file.

Officers tapping the house were having trouble with the bug in the hallway: it seemed that someone had put a coat over it! There was no conversation in the kitchen, bar Mrs Orso screaming at the maid.

Meanwhile, forensic came through: the fingerprints taken from the broken dinner plate matched the hitherto unidentified prints taken from the white Range Rover.

The BMW remained parked at the house until eleven-thirty. It was tailed to the end of Redhill Lane and then blocked off by two patrol cars.

Milton Andrews was taken to the station in a white-hot rage. When they searched the car, they found twenty thousand pounds in cash in a briefcase. At the same time, the police in Coventry broke into his house. They found printing equipment, passport stamps and numerous passport covers with no documents inside.

Milton at first refused to speak, but Langton didn't

waste time: he planted in front of him the mortuary photos of Gail Sickert and her dead child, and said they had found his printing equipment. Milton folded, pleading innocence for any other crime than providing a passport and driving licence for a black male, Stanley Monkton. When shown the surveillance photograph of the driver, Milton said it was the man who had provided him with Stanley Monkton's photograph.

Concerned that he could tip off their prime suspect, as well as the man who they believed would actually be using the passport, Milton was held at the station pending charges.

Things were moving, and fast. They had incriminating evidence on every member of the household, bar the maid and Mrs Orso. They even had confirmation from Parkhurst prison: Courtney Ransford, when shown the photograph of David, Orso's driver, said it was the man who had passed him the rock cakes during the prison visit!

The wiretap brought another result: the man they believed to be Camorra walked into the kitchen.

'Stanley Monkton! Fucking hell! Couldn't he have come up with a better bleedin' name for me to use than Stanley fucking Monkton? Jesus Christ!'

'Take a look at it though,' said David.

'It's perfect — beautiful job, worth every cent,' said Orso.

'I'm not saying it's crap, just I hate the name, and I'm gonna have to live with it, right? I gotta live with this Monkton shit.'

'Go and pack and shut your mouth. I'll arrange your flight.'

'Sooner the better.' Footsteps moving away.

There was a pause. 'You know, the longer I think about it, the more attractive that lake looks for that piece of pondlife to end up in,' said Orso.

David laughed.

They traced no calls to any airlines or travel agents. Langton, faced with the possibility that the man they had hunted for so long might be dumped in the lake with a weight round his neck, decided that they would go in.

The timing was almost a joke. Mrs Orso did the school run and brought her daughter back home. She said that she was going to eat her lunch with Rose in the playroom. No way was she going to sit and eat with that crude animal.

'Last one he'll have here, that's a promise,' said Orso.

As soon as they got the signal that all three men were sitting down to lunch, they would go in.

The Specialist Firearms Officers, SFOs, were now standing by. Two would come in from the woods; behind them, the four surveillance officers. From the front entrance, two Armed Response teams would climb over the high fence; another armed vehicle would ram through the front gates. They would burst open the front door and signal to their partners to enter the rear kitchen entrance at the same time.

Four more officers were standing by for the signal that the house and occupants were secure; only then would they enter and serve the warrants. They were Langton, Lewis, Blunt and Anna.

Langton chain-smoked. The months of waiting were now to be paid off. He would, at last, come face to face with Camorra.

'Going in,' came the quiet, steady-voiced command from the number one SFO.

There was no countdown; just a pause and then, 'Go.'

It was so well orchestrated that Langton could hardly believe his ears how quickly they got the radio contact to say all bodies were secured. By the time he walked into the kitchen, the three men were pinned against the wall, handcuffed and legs apart.

The screaming came from upstairs: Mrs Orso, her daughter and Ella were held in the child's playroom. Mrs Orso had become hysterical, and had been cuffed to keep her quiet; the little girl clung onto her, and the terrified maid Ella was on her knees with her hands over her head. They were led out to the waiting police van. Mrs Orso continued to scream her head off, but the maid had grown mute with terror. Anna tried to calm Mrs Orso, but she wouldn't shut up. She was having more effect on her daughter than any of the police. Anna drew the scared girl away from her mother to sit on a side seat, and fixed her safety belt. Mrs Orso began sobbing as she was pushed into her own seat; Ella sat without any persuasion, and wept.

Emmerick Orso was about six feet three and wore a well-cut grey suit and white shirt, his tie hanging loose. As the warrant was shoved into his face, and Lewis read him his rights before charging him with conspiracy to murder and defraud and accessory to murder, he said nothing. His handsome face was taut with rage, but he gave no other sign of aggression, and looked disdainful as he was roughly manhandled out to the waiting police van. Harry Blunt and Mike Lewis accompanied him.

Next, the driver was read his rights and told that he

was being arrested for accessory to murder. He snarled and spat at the SFO as he was dragged out; they held his cuffed hands high up behind his back, so he had to bend forwards to walk.

Lastly, Langton stood behind the man he had hunted for so long: Camorra. His face pressed against the wall, he wore a blue tracksuit and trainers. He gave no reaction as he was read the charges and his rights. The SFO officer hauled him round to face Langton. Blood trickled from his nose; he had been the only one of the three to resist arrest. He was smaller than Langton, but his mug shots didn't do him justice: he was very good-looking, with a chiselled face and deep-set, black eyes. He was quite slender but very fit.

Langton was finally face to face with the man who had cut him to shreds, a face that had been a blur of pain and blood. Now, in a flash of total recall, Langton was without any doubt that it was Camorra who had brought the machete down into his chest.

'Get him out,' Langton said harshly. As they dragged him past, the prisoner turned back to glare at Langton, but if Camorra recognized him, he didn't show it.

The vans took the prisoners to the New Forest police station, where Langton began orchestrating the interrogation of the suspects. They would only be allowed to hold the suspects for up to thirty-six hours, and he didn't want to lose a second.

Mrs Orso had by now quietened down; her daughter had been taken to her sister's. Ella was still in a state of shock and had not spoken. Emmerick Orso was demanding his lawyer. It would be a long night.

They would question Mrs Orso first, then Ella, then go for the driver, whose name was now known to be

David Johnson. Next up would be Emmerick Orso. Camorra would be kept until last.

Mrs Orso sobbed that she knew nothing. She kept saying she came from a very respectable family, that her parents were doctors who ran a hospital in Uganda, and that she was innocent: she had no idea who this man Camorra was or what he had done. She insisted that she knew nothing of her husband's business: she was just his wife and mother to his child. She did nothing but cry.

It was time-consuming and irritating but, as they got no information, she was possibly telling the truth. Via her solicitor, it was agreed that she could be released to stay at her sister's with her daughter, pending further enquiries. She would not be allowed to have any contact with her husband whilst he was detained, as she was co-accused in the same case. Anna had been wary about releasing Mrs Orso, as she felt that her being held in custody might be a strong lever on her husband. Langton dismissed her worries, saying that he felt Mr Orso would not care.

As the interrogations continued, the Orso house was being stripped and searched by SOCO teams. Bags of papers and files were taken away. The room occupied by Camorra was being carefully checked for fingerprints; his packed suitcase was opened, and items removed. The two Alsatian dogs were driven to police kennels and fur samples were taken to see if they would match the hairs discovered in the back of the Range Rover.

Emmerick Orso sat in his stinking cold cell, his shoelaces, belt and tie removed. Allowed to make one call, he had arranged for legal representation for himself and his wife. He was returned to his cell to wait.

Orso's driver, banged up next to him, was pacing with nerves. David Johnson was scared stiff: he had been charged with the attempted murder of Eamon Krasiniqe. He couldn't believe it and was trying to shout to Orso that he needed to talk to a lawyer. Orso asked the officer outside his cell to tell Mr Johnson that his legal representation was already organized.

Camorra sat in sullen fury. He would not give any of those bastards the pleasure of seeing him show any emotion. He had been taken aback when the murder charges were read: her name obliterated anything else. Carly Ann had been the only woman in his life he had ever cared about. All the others were just meat, and the one woman he had chosen had betrayed him; it still stung him and it was all he could think about. He had loved her; the bitch could have lived like a princess, but she had betrayed him and fucked one of his flunkies. It was all her fault; if it hadn't been for her, he would still be living the life of a prince in Peckham. Carly Ann's death had begun a spiral of murders to which Camorra gave not a single thought.

Anna called in Langton to sit with her as Ella put pieces of the jigsaw together, although some Anna had already determined. When asked her name, she had said it was Ella Orso, and when this was questioned, she shook with nerves. She wept throughout and crumpled the tissues provided in her hands. She had a terrible air of defeat; her body sagged, her voice was scarcely audible. After being given some tea and treated kindly, she stuttered that her name was Ella Sickert.

She admitted that Joseph Sickert was her husband. He had come to England five years before her. When shown the photograph found in his clothes, she sobbed heartbrokenly. She had seen neither child since they had been brought to England; she had been told that her sons were with a good family and being educated. Joseph had promised to send money from his wages. She waited for years, but none ever came.

'Did you see your husband?'

Ella looked to the floor. Anna persisted, asking if Joseph Sickert had made contact with her. They did not think she was going to be able to continue, but she straightened up and pushed herself back in the chair.

'Mrs Orso took me in when I arrived in England. I was told that Joseph would come to see me, but he was working. They said I had to give it time. I was always worried about my boys, but Mrs Orso said I was not to keep asking: I was in the UK illegally and I should be grateful to have a roof over my head.'

'So she knew you were an illegal immigrant?' Langton asked.

'Yes, sir – and Joseph and my sons.'

'So you never saw him?'

The woman began to cry. She explained that one night, two months ago, she had been told to stay in her room; from the window, she had seen her husband with two white children. Mr Orso had been very angry and there was an argument in the hall. Ella left her room and ran down the stairs. Joseph had tried to get to her, but she had been taken back. She said he had looked sick, hardly recognizable. She had not seen him or the children again, but knew the others were searching the woods for them. She said that Mr Johnson had punched her husband, and made the children cry.

She remained silent for a moment and then looked up. 'I heard Joseph asking for Mr Camorra: he made threats and he was very angry. He was asking him about our boys, they were only seven and nine years old. He kept on saying, over and over, "Where are my boys?"'

Anna asked for a blood test. There were tears in her eyes; it was so pitiful. She found it hard to produce the photograph of the child's torso.

'We think your son was murdered,' Langton said gently.

Ella gasped. If she had been defeated before, she now sat in mute grief.

'We do not know the whereabouts of your other son, but we hope we will be able to trace him.'

Ella nodded, but she was staring at the wall. A steady stream of tears ran down her cheeks and one hand rested on the photograph in the plastic evidence bag.

An officer came and took a swab from Ella for DNA testing. She was left in the interview room while one of the clerical staff tried to find a hostel where she could remain in protective custody until the trial. Once Ella had given her evidence, she would be handed over to the Immigration Services for a decision.

The Desk Sergeant had never in his entire career known so much action. The car park was filling up with an array of expensive vehicles, as Emmerick Orso's legal representatives arrived. They were each allowed to speak to their clients in private before the murder team interrogated them. All three would then be taken before magistrates, as Langton was not prepared to let them go after the obligatory thirty-six hours: he wanted a three-day extension, as the preparation for the interviews would be lengthy.

At ten o'clock that night, the team was released. They all needed to recharge their batteries: it had been an exhausting day and evening. The lawyers could sit with their clients through the night, if they wished: the team all needed time to recuperate. None had expected to sleep, but even Langton had crashed out without his usual handful of sleeping tablets.

The next morning, each prisoner was led out, handcuffed to an officer, and driven to court to go before the local magistrate. The amount of work to organize this had been a major headache, but it gained Langton three days for further questioning, due to the severity of the charges laid against them.

Harry Blunt and Frank Brandon were set to prepare the list of charges that would be brought against Camorra. Mike Lewis, with assistance from a Fraud Squad officer, began to plough through the mass of paperwork they had accumulated against Emmerick Orso. The paper trails were so complicated that even to pin down the ownership of the house in Peckham took half an hour. They wanted to know just how much he was involved with Camorra; if he did own the house, then he would have been privy to the flesh trade and barbaric murders that had taken place there.

Camorra refused to eat the food offered, insisting it was his right to send out for a proper breakfast. He appeared not to care about the charges mounting up against him; quite the reverse. He was cocky and kept on calling out to Orso, who remained silent, determined to distance himself from Camorra as much as possible.

Langton had decided they would go for the weakest link first, the one who appeared to be most agitated: Johnson.

He sat sweating and twisting his hands. His solicitor

tried to calm him, as Langton told Johnson that he had been identified as the man who had visited Courtney Ransford in Parkhurst prison and had passed poison to him to be given to Eamon Krasiniqe. Johnson would therefore be implicated in Krasiniqe's murder.

He interrupted. 'Listen, I just work for Orso, right? I do what he tells me to do. I was told to take the stuff in; it was nothing to do with me, I just carried out orders. If I didn't do what he wanted . . .'

'So are you saying that Emmerick Orso handed you these rock cakes?'

'No, he didn't give them to me. I had to go to Peckham and collect them from Camorra. I didn't know what shit was in them; I swear before God, I didn't know. I am not going down for this. I just did what I was told to do.'

Langton sighed. 'Yes, but who told you to do it?'

'Camorra – well, my boss sent me over there. He said Camorra needed to sort something out. It was connected to this guy Arthur Murphy, that was all I knew. I swear before God I didn't know it would send the kid crazy.'

'Did you know Arthur Murphy?'

'No.'

'How often did you go to the house in Peckham?'

Johnson gasped, taking short sharp breaths; his eyes bulged.

Langton tapped his pencil on the table with impatience. 'Did you go on a regular basis?'

'No, no, I didn't. It belonged to Eugene Camorra.'

Langton turned to Anna. 'Eugene Camorra? You sure about that?'

'Yeah. He uses a lot of other names, but that's the one I know him by. Eugene, that's his real name.'

'Do you know what the house was used for?'

'No.'

'So how often did you go there?'

'Not recently – I didn't go there recently.'

'Well, if you didn't go there recently, when did you go?'

'Few years back.'

'One? Two? How many years back?'

'Listen, Eugene was doing stuff there. He's a freak. I mean, sometimes I'd go, you know, for sex – but not recently.'

'Sex?'

'Yeah, he had girls working for him.'

'What girls?'

Johnson was now sweating; he used the same box of tissues that poor Ella had plucked at to wipe her face. 'Oh shit, every time I open my mouth I feel like I'm digging myself into a hole, but I done nothing.'

'These girls, were some of them underage?'

'What?'

'I said, were some of the girls underage?' Langton snapped.

'I never went with them, but yeah, some of them were.'

'Do you know this girl, Carly Ann North?' Langton slapped down the photograph that Dora had given them.

Johnson stared for a moment, then shook his head. 'No, I don't know her. I had nothing to do with her.'

'What do you mean by that?'

'Ah, shit man. I'm getting all wound up. This isn't right. I didn't know her.'

Langton now placed the mortuary shots of Carly Ann in front of him. Johnson recoiled. This was followed by the horrific photo of the mutilated boy found in the canal. Now Johnson was really caving in: the sweat stained his jacket and dripped down his face.

Langton placed more photographs down as if he was dealing a game of poker: Arthur Murphy, Eamon Krasiniqe, Rashid Burry, Gail Sickert, her little girl. The more he was forced to look, the more agitated Johnson became. Lastly, he was shown the e-fit of Joseph Sickert.

'No, no, I didn't know him,' he said, gasping for breath.

'Let's start again from the top, Mr Johnson. Tell me what you know about Carly Ann North.'

Johnson stood up. He was shaking. 'No, you can't. I got nothing to do with these people, I swear before God.'

'Sit down!'

The man slumped into his seat. His lawyer leaned close, whispering; he sat listening, his head bowed. He repeated that all he had done was take the food into Courtney, that's all he had ever done, and he was not connected to any of the other crimes.

'But you do know about them, don't you?' Anna said. 'You must know about Rashid Burry. You said you went to the house in Peckham.'

Johnson's lawyer held out his hand. 'Could I please have a few moments alone with my client?'

Langton spoke into the tape recorder that they were leaving the room and turned it off.

Anna followed Langton into the corridor. 'He's sweating like a pig and we haven't even got to his boss yet.'

Mike Lewis walked towards them. 'Thought you might like to know: we have been on a paper-chase that was mind-blowing. Emmerick Orso bought the house in

Peckham eight years ago. It was buried as a company pur-
chase, for use by his employees. Water bills, electricity
and gas bills are sent to a box number in Clapham. So
far, we've got over a hundred and fifty different post
office boxes! Household bills also appear to be paid out
from another property in Clapham and another one in
Tooting. We reckon he also owns numerous others, but
I thought you'd want to know about the Peckham house
and the other properties as they link to the bus tickets
found on Joseph Sickert.'

Langton nodded and turned, as Johnson's lawyer
came out and said quietly that his client wished to give
a statement. In return for assisting their enquiries, he
wanted a deal on the charge of being an accessory to the
murder of Eamon Krasiniqe. 'I truthfully believe that my
client is only directly linked to that case; perhaps he has
information regarding the other.'

'I can't offer any deal until I know what he's got in
exchange,' Langton told him.

'I think a deal will really be beneficial, Detective Chief
Inspector Langton.'

'For him or for us?'

'For you, obviously: he's going to give information on
Eugene Camorra.'

Anna and the rest of team were unaware that Langton
already knew that Camorra was the man who had
attacked and almost killed him.

'Let's see what he's got then, shall we?'

Chapter Twenty-two

The case that had felt as if it was running away from them was now back on track. David Johnson's work as bodyguard and driver to Emmerick Orso had been lucrative. He had kept his mouth shut, and it had paid off: he and his family owned a house in Esher. He had been a trusted employee, working first at the warehouse, but said he knew little of the actual running of the business; he had been orchestrating the deliveries and the lorry drivers. He had, however, been fully aware that the cargo was often not African artefacts, but illegal immigrants.

He said that he had first met Joseph Sickert at the warehouse; he was an illegal immigrant, one of the loaders, and had been a big strong man, with no signs of his sickle cell disease obvious at that time. As Sickert couldn't drive, he was moved out to work at the house in Peckham, as one of Camorra's henchmen. It was here that Sickert met Arthur Murphy and Vernon Kramer; this was before Murphy murdered Irene Phelps. Rashid Burry was dealing drugs and often used the women at the house. Camorra ran the house, selling children and women, who often were addicted to drugs by this time.

'Sickert was a big guy and knew how to handle his

fists; he could be a real mad bastard. Nothing phased him – he was always ready for a fight.'

Johnson was unclear about what had caused the rift between Camorra and Sickert; all he knew was that Sickert was being kept short of money. Sickert's earnings were being siphoned off to pay for his wife and two children to be brought into the UK, and he constantly asked when this would happen.

Johnson became a little confused about the exact time it had all started running out of control. Sickert had begun to be disgusted by the scene at the Peckham house and tried to get to see Orso, turning up at the factory and causing trouble.

Camorra was heavily into voodoo and drugs, and had orchestrated a sickening ceremony with a young boy who had just been brought to the UK. Carly Ann North, his girlfriend at the time, was terrified and tried to run away. She had started to have sex with one of the Camorra gang, Eamon Krasiniqe; when Camorra found out, he went berserk. He caught up with Carly Ann and brought her back to the house, where he raped her and then forced Idris, Eamon's brother, to also have sex with her. Then he killed her.

Rashid Burry ordered Idris Krasiniqe to dump her body and cut off her head and hands. When Langton asked Johnson if he was one of the men in the white Range Rover, he denied it, but said he was certain that Camorra was sitting in the car, watching, with Rashid Burry. He said that Burry had told him what a close shave it had been when the street cop had turned up.

When Idris Krasiniqe was arrested and charged with Carly Ann's murder, he named two other men who were with him: both had been, at some point, working for Camorra. Camorra and Rashid Burry went to a halfway house to track them down. This was, coincidentally, the same time that Arthur Murphy killed Irene Phelps and went into hiding at Vernon Kramer's hostel – the time when Camorra had, wrongly, surmised that the police were closing in on his operation.

According to Johnson, this was also around the same time that Orso became concerned by Sickert. Orso wanted him taken care of. Orso knew that Sickert's two sons were in the UK: he was even employing his wife, Ella, as his maid! Orso had given Johnson orders to get rid of Sickert. The latter was sent to stay at Murphy's sister's bungalow.

Then Murphy turned up, threatening Camorra. He had killed Irene Phelps and he wanted a passport and money to get out of the country; if Camorra didn't supply them, he said he would tip off the police about the Peckham house.

Murphy was caught and sent to Parkhurst prison, where Eamon Krasiniqe was already an inmate. Krasiniqe had been forced to work for Camorra like a pack mule, due to his relationship with Carly Ann; he had also been pumped full of drugs, and was out of his skull when he was arrested.

The mess that Camorra had created was threatening to come too close to Orso's business empire. When Orso was informed about Arthur Murphy's threats, he gave the orders for Camorra to get rid of Murphy; he didn't care how he did it.

All Orso needed was for Johnson to deliver something to Krasiniqe, who would deal with Murphy; that would end all the problems.

Johnson said he wasn't feeling good about it, but Orso

insisted he should go along with it. 'I swear before God, on my children's lives, that was all I did. Orso told me to pick up this package and go to visit a bloke called Courtney Ransford. I was to hand it over. That was all I did.'

Langton pressed on, asking about Gail and her children.

Johnson closed his eyes. 'No sooner did Camorra sort out the Carly Ann thing, than another problem surfaced. Sickert was getting uptight: the police had been round looking for Murphy and he got his wires crossed – he thought they was coming for him. He was sick and he was screwing Murphy's sister. I dunno what went on there; all I know is Mr Orso was furious and went round to Camorra in Peckham. I drove him there. I dunno what happened, as I was parked outside; he was there no more than fifteen minutes. Next thing, it all spirals out of control: the press is full of pictures of Sickert and these two kids, and the bodies found at Murphy's sister's place. Mr Orso said to me he was shutting down the Peckham house, as Camorra was too much of a liability; but his main worry was that Camorra knew his entire business. He said he would bring Camorra to his place and keep him holed up there until he could get him out of the country. He said he had to clear up the Sickert problem first.'

Johnson continued, explaining that Orso and his wife and daughter went abroad for a holiday, while his men went to the bungalow. Camorra and Rashid Burry brought Sickert, and Murphy's sister's two kids, back to Peckham.

Langton leaned over the table. 'So, are you saying that Camorra and Burry went to pick up Sickert?'

'Yeah, I guess so.'

'Gail Sickert was found murdered; so was her small daughter.'

'I swear before God I dunno what they did. I was just looking after the house in Redhill.'

Johnson said that when Orso and his family returned from their holiday, he expected it all to have been finished with. However, Camorra was at the house when Sickert turned up with the two kids. He saw his wife, Ella, and started screaming about where his own boys were. Orso tried to calm him down.

Johnson was tired out. His head drooped, and he sucked in his breath. 'Sickert did a runner out the back door with the kids. I couldn't find him. I dunno where he went.'

'Did you have a fight with him?'

'I tried to get him to calm down, but he was real crazy; we had this fist-fight. One of the kids – the little boy – was trying to pull me off him.'

'And Camorra was also at Mr Orso's residence?'

'Yeah, I'd picked him up while they was on holiday. By this time, he'd shut up shop in Peckham and Mr Orso was making arrangements for him to leave the country.'

It took another hour for them to read back David Johnson's lengthy statement to him, and for him to sign it. When the trials were mounted, he would become a vital prosecution witness. The statement would have to be checked out; until Langton was satisfied, Johnson would be held at the station.

Armed with the information from Johnson, Langton waded into the interrogation of Emmerick Orso. On the advice of his solicitor, Orso refused to answer any questions and said only, 'No comment.' His arrogant, handsome face showed not a flicker of remorse when the charges were read out; he just stared straight ahead. Langton decided not to waste any more time on him and had him taken back to his cell.

The team were gathered in the incident room, taking a break, when Langton was asked by one of the uniformed officers if it was still permissible for Camorra to have food brought in. Langton joked that he wanted to personally check it out: with what Camorra had got away with so far, he wouldn't be surprised if he had the key to his cell in the steak tartare! As they ate sandwiches and coffee, Camorra ate a three-course meal. Harry Blunt went on a tirade about allowing the bastard to eat special meals: his lawyer had requested the permission, as his client had an eating disorder! Langton seemed in no hurry to begin the main interrogation. Time was on their side.

Camorra was brought to the interview room with his solicitor. He was cocky, and said that he should be allowed to have a change of clothes; he indicated his scruffy tracksuit. The laces had been removed from his trainers and he wore no socks. He was asked to state his name and address, and whether he understood the charges he was to be questioned about. Anna wondered if, like Orso, he would play out the 'No comment' strategy, but he leaned back in his chair, smiling. He gave his name as Eugene Camorra and his address as Orso's property.

'Did you know Carly Ann North?'

'Yes, very well: she was my girlfriend.'

'Could you tell us where you were on the fifteenth of November, last year?'

'Yes, I was at my house for most of the day; in the

evening, I was playing cards with four friends. If you want to know why I remember the exact date, it's because that was the night she was found murdered. It was a terrible thing, to be told that one of the men working for me, Idris Krasiniqe, had killed her.'

Langton and Anna listened as he went into a lengthy explanation of how shocked and distressed he had been, as he had loved her. He was stunned when they told him that Carly Ann had planned to run away with Krasiniqe's brother, Eamon.

'I gave that girl everything. When I first met her, she was out whoring on the streets; she was on drugs and I took her in and cared for her. I wanted to marry her — nothing was too much for me to do for her.'

'We will require a DNA sample from you.'

The man leaned forwards. 'I had sex with the bitch before she left me, so whatever you need my DNA for won't be any use. That's how she tricked me — she made love to me and then, as soon as my back was turned, she ran off.'

'Did you own a white Range Rover?'

'No, it belonged to Mr Orso's company. I never drove it. I've got a problem driving automatics — can only drive ones with gears — so I never used the car. One of my guys drove it: Rashid Burry.'

'Are you saying that you were never inside the Range Rover? You were never a passenger?'

'Could be. You see, I am trying to answer everything you ask me, because some of the charges you are trying to pin on me is just out of space, man. You got to under-stand, I work for Mr Orso; I am just employed by him.'

'But you admit that Idris and Eamon Krasiniqe worked for you?'

'In a roundabout way, yes; it's like they work for me but also work for Mr Orso, know what I mean? He sends me the brothers and they stayed at the house in Peckham.'

'Could you please list the names of the people you employed who lived at those premises?'

'Christ, I dunno; they came and they went.'

'Just start with recently: the men and women living at the house with you?'

It was like pulling teeth: each question, Camorra took lengthy explanations over, claiming he had a bad memory for names. He constantly threw in Rashid Burry's name and, each time, made him seem more important in the running of the house. The more he talked, the more he attempted to distance himself from anything to do with the house in Peckham. He claimed not to be aware that some of the people over whose heads he 'just gave a roof until they settled' were illegal immigrants. He could not recall meeting Arthur Murphy, but said that perhaps he had not been at the house when Murphy had called round. He denied knowing Vernon Kramer and constantly implicated Emmerick Orso, saying that he was just his employee.

'You gotta understand, I was more or less running a kind of bed and breakfast; there was a lot of traffic every week. I got someone cooking and doing laundry, but basically that's all I was doing – running the place.'

Camorra did not recall very much about Joseph Sickert: just that, at one time, Sickert had stayed at the Peckham house. He did not know anything about any arrangements Sickert had made with Mr Orso for his wife and family.

The more they questioned him, and appeared to

accept his answers, the more confident Camorra became. He made wide expansive gestures, at times appearing amused and at others times appearing to be concerned, as he gave some thought to their queries. He had laughed when asked if he was practising voodoo.

'Oh, man! As if! That's a load of shit those idiots believe in. Me? No way, man, no way – it's not my scene.'

Anna asked if he could give her an example of what his day-to-day routine was.

'Well, you know, I'd have to check the kitchen, see what we needed: bread, sugar, cleaning equipment . . . You'd be amazed at how much garbage we'd have – I used to get these big rolls of industrial black bin-liners. Some of these people that stayed had no English and shat on the floor. I'm not kidding – they was like animals.'

'Did you look after children at the house?'

'Sometimes they'd be sent over, yeah, but I'd get one of the women to see to them.'

'Can you give us a list of the children who were brought to the house?'

'Christ, I dunno. Like I said, they came and went.'

'Did you ever perform any kind of ceremonies at the house?'

'What?'

'Did you at any time perform ritualistic ceremonies at the house?'

'No way.'

'There is a cellar at the house, isn't there?'

'Yeah, but that was used mostly for keeping the dogs. You know, I am very worried about my dogs 'cos Mr Orso's not at home; who's taking care of my dogs?'

Anna said they were in the police kennels and being well looked after. At this point, Camorra licked his lips and said he was thirsty. Langton shrugged. The old station did not have any water fountains, so they had brought water in with them in a large plastic water bottle. This was now empty.

'Do you know a Doctor Elmore Salaam?' Langton asked.

'No. I'm really thirsty,' Camorra repeated.

Langton bent down and picked up a smaller water bottle from beside his chair; he unscrewed the cap and poured out some water for Camorra, then half-filled his own plastic cup.

'You have never been to him as a patient?'

'No – well, maybe. Name rings a bell, but I don't remember seeing him.'

'Have you ever practised voodoo?'

'Me? No way, man! Like I said before, I don't go with all that shit.'

Langton glanced at Anna, then turned back over pages of his notes, tapping his pencil. 'You have admitted that you had numerous people staying with you at the house in Peckham, amongst them children; we will need their names and forwarding addresses.'

'I dunno where they are; you know, they was just transient. Few days, sometimes a few weeks, then they was found work and moved on.'

'So you never kept any record of these people you say stayed?'

'Look, all I am is an employee of Mr Orso. He would arrange their work permits. They went all over the country.'

'Did you ever have Joseph Sickert's two sons staying?'

'I didn't even know he had kids.'

'But you knew his wife, Ella Sickert?'

'No.'

'She was working for Mr Orso.'

'Then I might have met her; like I said, Mr Orso would arrange his own domestics.'

'In the house at Peckham we found a printing press and—'

'I know it was there,' Camorra interrupted. 'Mr Orso had people come in to work, you know; you'll have to ask him about that.'

'Do you know what it was used for?'

'Well, we had to do a lot of copying – for references and so on.'

'You were aware that the people sent to stay at the house in Peckham were illegal immigrants?'

Camorra held up his hands. 'Okay, look – I admit I maybe suspected they was not in the UK legit, right, but I had nothing to do with bringing them in. Like I keep on saying, all I did was work for Mr Orso. I got paid well so, like, I didn't ask questions.' He gulped down the water and licked his lips. 'I need to go to the toilet,' he said.

Langton checked his watch and broke off the interview for a toilet break. Camorra was taken out by an officer; his solicitor remained in the room. Langton picked up his water and walked out into the corridor. There he lit a cigarette and used the beaker as an ashtray.

Anna leaned against the wall. 'Well, we've got no comment from Orso; Camorra's laying everything at his feet.' She hesitated. 'When do you start to put the pressure on him?'

Langton shrugged, walked over to a bin and tossed

the plastic cup inside. 'When he gets back, we go from the top again. I've just let him run. A lot of the other cases are linked to him; he was obviously doing more than just following orders, but you know what the reality is: the most incriminating evidence we have against him is the murder of Carly Ann, plus harbouring illegal immigrants and running a brothel.

Anna went to the cloakroom and splashed cold water over her face, then combed her hair. By the time she returned to the interview room, Camorra had been brought back. He was sitting next to his solicitor, but crouching in his seat, complaining of feeling hot.

Langton was already checking through the massive file in front of him and talking Camorra through his rights again. The tape was switched back on. Langton gave the time and date. 'Now, Eugene, you've been very helpful, but we will need to go back to questioning you about the murder of Carly Ann North.'

'I've told you all I know about her. I had nothing to do with her murder. That was down to Idris Krasiniqe, and you got him banged up for it. He admitted it; his brother was screwing her.'

'You have stated that at no time did you drive a white Range Rover.'

'I can't drive automatic, I told you this; I was never in that bloody car.'

'On the night of Carly Ann's murder, this vehicle was seen—'

Langton was interrupted. 'I don't give a shit who saw whatever – I wasn't in it.'

'You are lying, Mr Camorra.'

'I am not fucking lying: that Range Rover was used by Rashid Burry. I have never even been inside it.'

'We have a fingerprint that matches yours. You do recall that when you were first brought into the station, your fingerprints were taken?'

'Look, I might have been driven in it once or twice, but I told you: on the night Carly Ann was murdered, I got witnesses that I was with all night.'

Suddenly, Camorra whipped round in his seat to stare at the wall behind him; he brushed his shoulders frantically and then turned back to Langton, who continued.

'You have admitted that on the night of her murder you had sex with her: what time?'

'I don't fucking remember. She was my girlfriend, right? I had sex with her all the time.'

'We have a statement from Idris Krasiniqe that you in fact raped Carly Ann.'

'That is bullshit. She was my girlfriend! I never had to rape her.' Again, he turned in his seat and brushed at his shoulders; then he became very agitated.

'Mr Krasiniqe claims that you then forced him to have sex with her whilst his brother was injected with poison and made to watch.'

'I am not gonna listen to this, because it's all lies. Those two brothers cheated on me; that little bastard Eamon was screwing my girl. Maybe, if I—'

There was a pause. Camorra licked his lips. He had started sweating: it was dripping down from his hair and patches appeared under his armpits.

'If you maybe what?' asked Langton.

'If I maybe pushed that little bastard around, I admit to that – but she was my girl, right? I'm telling you, I could have had the pick of hundreds of them, but she—' He gasped for breath and licked his lips.

'Did you ever inject Eamon Krasiniqe with a poison called Jimson weed?'

'No, no! I never done anything to him but knocked him about: he was screwing my girl, in my own house!'

'So you now admit that the house in Peckham was your property?'

'No! I never said that – I wish, man, I wish. That was some place; I done all the decorations, but I didn't own it.'

'So you prepared the cellar?'

'What?'

'The cellar, Mr Camorra: do you need me to remind you of what it looks like?'

He was shown a photograph. He glanced at it and then turned away. 'I never went down there. I just told you, I didn't own the place.'

'Do you know the effect of Jimson weed?' Langton asked quietly.

There was a flicker in Camorra's eyes, then he laughed. 'No, I never heard of it.'

'So you did not prepare rock cakes containing the substance Jimson weed?'

'I don't know what you are talking about.'

'We have a statement saying that you passed rock cakes to a Mr David Johnson; he was instructed to take them to—'

'That is a fucking lie! What do you think I am? A cook?' Suddenly, Camorra stood up; this time, he made wafting movements with his hand, as if someone or something was behind him.

'Please remain in your seat,' Langton said.

Camorra slowly sat, but kept on turning back to look at the wall behind him; he constantly brushed at his sleeves, as if something was crawling over his body. By now, the sweat was glistening on his face; droplets fell from his hair and he breathed like a panting dog. 'I feel sick,' he said.

His solicitor asked if he needed a doctor. Camorra leaned forwards, clutching at his head. Langton waited; after a lengthy pause, he sat upright.

'Are you well enough to continue this interview?' he asked.

Camorra said nothing; spittle was forming in white, frothy globules at the corners of his mouth.

'Mr Camorra?' His solicitor leaned towards him.

Camorra cowered back. 'I don't want this man in the room with me,' he said angrily.

Camorra then pushed back his chair and began to rant at Langton and Anna that he did not trust either of them. He wanted to leave the room; he didn't feel well. It was quite obvious to them all that Camorra was becoming more and more anxious and his behaviour more erratic, then bizarre: he started to babble and curse, then lay on the floor. Officers were called in to take him back to his cell.

Langton ended the interview and suggested to Camorra's solicitor that he talk with his client; if he required a doctor, they would call one.

Camorra was running a very high temperature but no longer sweating. His speech was incoherent; he had a rapid heartbeat and he was screaming, saying he could see monsters coming through the walls of his cell.

His mood swung from confusion as to where he was, to almost a euphoric state, calling out for Carly Ann. He sobbed and kept on saying that he loved her; then his condition worsened, as delirium set in. An ambulance was called and Camorra was taken to the local hospital. Terror had overtaken his sobbing, and he cowered like a caged animal as they tried to persuade him to get into the waiting ambulance. It took four officers to help the paramedics. Camorra had his first seizure at nine o'clock. He then had two further seizures inside the ambulance and, by the time he was taken into the casualty department of the local hospital, he was in a catatonic state. At ten thirty-five, he suffered a massive cardiac arrest. Try as they might, they could not revive him. He was pronounced dead at ten forty-five.

Eugene Camorra's death certificate said that he had died from a cardiac arrest. As he had been held at the police station, a post mortem would be required by the IPCC, even though Camorra did not actually die in custody.

The investigation reported that there had been no suspicious circumstances. Camorra had shown very obvious signs of an oncoming heart-attack: sweating, disorientation and shortness of breath. His solicitor testified that, as soon as his client had shown signs of being ill, DCI Langton had terminated the interview and a doctor had been called. Camorra had had three seizures whilst attended by hospital paramedics. No one claimed his body; his lawyer attempted to trace anyone who wished to see him, but he had no relatives. When Emmerick Orso was asked if there was anyone who would wish to be informed of his death, he said, 'Try the Devil.'

Orso was refused bail and sent to Brixton prison to await trial. He pleaded not guilty to all charges but still refused to say anything, bar, 'No comment.' David Johnson remained in custody and agreed to become a prosecution witness against Orso.

The trial would take many months of preparation: there was an immense amount of paperwork to do. Anna and the team sifted through all the evidence, covering Orso's money-laundering frauds and his transportation of illegal immigrants. He had covered his tracks well, and they had no evidence linking him directly to the murders of Carly Ann North, Arthur Murphy, Gail Sickert, her daughter Tina, Rashid Burry, or the tragic child's body found mutilated in Regent's Canal.

As the trail was being prepared, Orso's wife applied for a divorce. She gave them details of various bank accounts and offshore investments. The millions he had accrued from his illegal transactions were exposed and Orso's accounts were frozen.

Another piece of uplifting news, especially for Anna, was that both of Gail Sickert's children were to be fostered by the same woman who had taken in Carly Ann: Dora Rhodes. Sharon and Keith would be cared for, and given every possible counselling to overcome the trauma and anguish they had both been subjected to by Camorra.

When Anna called to say that she could not think of a better person than Dora, Alison told her that no one else would take them both.

'I wouldn't allow them to be separated; eventually, I want to adopt them myself.'

Beryl Dunn, Gail's mother, was more than willing to allow someone else to take the responsibility: the adoption was in progress. It was the only good thing to come out of the nightmare case they had been working on for so long.

Idris Krasiniqe's legal team were preparing for a retrial. Langton had agreed they could be given access to the reports covering the time that the team had spent with Idris and Dr Salaam. Anna was making copies for them when she felt the first seed of suspicion.

She sat going back over all the data, returning time and time again to the statement made by Dr Salaam about the poison that he was certain Eamon Krasiniqe had been fed. This had then led to the interview with Courtney Ransford, who had been given poisoned rock cakes to pass to Krasiniqe, and culminated in the questioning of David Johnson, who had admitted taking the rock cakes into the prison.

Anna kept on studying the symptoms that Dr Salaam had listed for someone fed *Datura stramonium*, or Jimson weed: a dry mouth, dilated pupils, a high temperature and blurred vision. The psychological effects included confusion, euphoria and delirium. A higher dosage resulted in incoherent speech, impaired coordination and seizures, possibly resulting in cardiac arrest.

Anna went in to see Langton in his office. He gestured for her to sit down and continued a phone conversation.

He was asking someone if they liked their birthday present, then he laughed. 'So you've grown out of Barbie dolls? Well, listen, Kitty: you and me, we'll go and get them exchanged. Have you taken them out of the box? No? Okay, we'll get something else, all right?'

He listened and then laughed again. 'Well, don't let him unwrap them; besides, he's a boy!'

He looked very handsome: the haunted, dark circles

beneath his eyes had gone. He promised to see Kitty at the weekend and then finished the call. Not only did he look well, but he was also relaxed: seemingly, his knee joint was also less of a problem, as he jumped up from his seat.

'Barbie dolls are longer on the agenda; she wants a tape recorder that she can sing karaoke into!'

Anna smiled, loath to bring up something that might destroy his good mood.

'What is it?' he said, opening a bottle of water.

Anna explained that she was compiling the reports for Idris Krasiniqe's new trial. After rereading Salaam's evidence regarding the symptoms of Jimson weed, she was certain that Camorra had shown the selfsame ones.

'What?'

'Don't you remember?' she asked.

'Remember what, exactly?'

'Well, when we interviewed him, he was constantly asking for more water.'

Langton sat back. 'I'm not sure where you are going with this.'

'Well, Camorra had a cardiac arrest.'

'I know that.'

'He had food brought into the cells.'

'Yes?'

'Well, I wondered if it was possible that Emmerick Orso somehow got someone to doctor his food. If we did discover that he had, it would be yet another charge we can lay against him.'

Langton shook his head. 'Leave it. The bastard is dead; it saves us a lot of work. Right now, we have enough against Emmerick Orso to put him away for twenty-five years.'

'I know that, but don't you think we should look into it?'

'No, I don't. Just leave it, Anna; we've enough on our plate. We have a trial date, as of this morning.'

'If you say so.'

'I do say so.'

'Will they do a post mortem?'

Langton nodded. 'Already done. The IPCC have investigated the death and Camorra died of a heart attack, full stop.' He put out his hand for the reports. 'I'll see to these.'

Anna did as she was instructed, but asked Harry Blunt if he had seen the post-mortem report on Camorra.

'Well, there obviously was one. As far as I know, it was cut and dried. As nobody claimed his body, he'll be charred meat by now.'

'What?'

'Well, they can't keep him in the cooler for ever, can they? I think the Gov gave the go-ahead.'

'For a cremation?'

'Don't ask me, I dunno. All I do know is the bastard should have been strung up. I'd have pulled the lever myself. The day they bring back capital punishment is the day I'll celebrate. He's gone and it's over with. If he'd stood trial, he'd have been sent down for life: three meals a day . . .' Harry went on with his usual tirade about how many men were held in prisons and how, if he had it his way, he would have cleared out half of them. 'It was a good rock-cake job on Murphy; he was an animal. Eamon Krasiniqe deserved to be released just for getting rid of him.'

'Eamon is dead,' Anna said.

Harry shrugged. 'Don't mean anything to me. Idris raped Carly Ann, along with Camorra; whether or not he was forced into doing it is immaterial to me. He then tried to chop off her hands and decapitate her: whatever his new trial comes up with, in my mind, he's still an animal. All of them are sick. None of them deserve to walk away a free man.'

'But if he was terrified and forced to do it?' Anna said.

Harry put up his hands. 'Listen, if someone freaked me out, voodoo or not, it's no excuse. I'd let him spend the rest of his life banged up. You know the Gov has the big brass squeezing his balls about how much this case has cost?'

'We got the results in the end.'

'Yeah, and now we're all stuck here for how many weeks before the trial? It would do us all a favour if that prick Orso topped himself.'

Anna returned to her desk to plough on with all her work. It seemed that no one else was interested in the fact that Orso could have poisoned Camorra.

Orso's trial made headlines for days. Orso never took the stand; his battery of high-powered lawyers tried to throw out charge after charge as hearsay, but he was eventually charged with bringing in a network of illegal immigrants and using them as drug couriers. The charges of running a brothel also held, as did his fraud and drug trafficking. He was sentenced not, as the team had hoped, to twenty-five years, but to fifteen. There was only circumstantial evidence and hearsay linking him to any of the murders; those charges were dismissed. The team surmised that, with good behaviour, he could be released in twelve.

★

Langton threw an open bar at the local pub at the end of the trial. He thanked them all for staying with it, even if the result was not what they had hoped for, and praised them for their diligence and hard work. Now it was on to the next case. Whether they would be reunited as a team was uncertain, but possible; all he could say for sure was that he would work with every single one of them again.

Anna left the bar early, as she was driving home. She went up to Langton to say goodbye; he was at his most charming, asking if perhaps he could take her out for dinner one night. She was equally pleasant and said she would look forward to it.

As she turned to walk away, he reached for her hand, and drew her close. 'It's over, Anna.'

She knew he was not referring to their relationship. His grip on her hand was tight, and she looked into his dark eyes. 'Yes, and you seem to be really on the road to recovery.'

'I am, now. As I just said, it's over – do you understand?'

'Yes, yes of course I do. Let's have dinner one evening. I'll wait for you to call.'

He kissed her cheek, then released her hand.

Anna sat in the car park. She had such mixed emotions: she had no intention of starting any kind of relationship with him again and she could tell that he didn't either. His kiss had somehow felt like a threat, or a warning. For the first time since she had met DCI Langton, she was frightened of him. The mounting suspicion that had begun weeks ago persisted like a bad taste in her mouth. Anna was certain that Langton had murdered Eugene Camorra.

Chapter Twenty-three

With the trial now over and the incident room packed up, Anna had some time off before she would be assigned a new case. She organized her flat, cleaning and washing everything from the curtains to the bedcovers. She always did a marathon clean after a case was over: it was therapeutic. She did the washing and ironing, sorted out her wardrobe, treated herself to a haircut and a manicure, and worked out at the local gym. As she pedalled on the exercise bike, she thought constantly about her own jigsaw.

Langton was never far from her mind. He had not called. It was as if she was on automatic pilot. She had not wanted to let her suspicion ferment, but it had. She took out one of her notebooks from the case -- it had gone on for so long, she had filled three books -- and went right back to the start of the enquiry, to the murder of Irene Phelps. This had come after Langton's investigation into the murder of Carly Ann North.

His attack had occurred after Idris Krasiniqe had been arrested; he was then hospitalized and, due to his injuries, had been unable to be at the trial. She had made notes about the number of newspaper cuttings she had discovered at Langton's flat whilst she was caring for him. She also went over her notes on the private talks she had had with Mike Lewis: he had feared that Langton would, if he ever did recover, rope him and Barolli into acting like some vigilantes. Anna sighed; she could not blame Langton for wanting to track down the man who had caused his horrific injuries.

When Langton had described the attack, she tried to recall exactly what he had said. Langton had been tipped off by Idris Krasiniqe, who gave the names of two men he said were with him on the night of Carly Ann's murder and who escaped in a white Range Rover. Both the names were subsequently found to be false, but the address he had given was the one Langton checked out. Accompanied by both Lewis and Barolli, Langton had been walking up the stairs of the hostel, when two men came out onto the landing. Both men had escaped; one man, she knew, had been identified as Rashid Burry, but the man who had wielded the machete had never been identified. Langton had been taken to the Intensive Care unit at St Stephen's Hospital. She knew that he suspected that it had been Eugene Camorra.

Anna had then gone to Vernon Kramer's safe house to pick up Arthur Murphy; there she had, unwittingly, been confronted by Rashid Burry. Rashid presumed that the police were about to arrest him. Burry later found out that the officer who had been attacked was still alive, because Vernon Kramer had read about it in the newspaper in the patrol car. Kramer must have told either Camorra or Rashid that they were both being hunted down. This had to coincide with Joseph Sickert being sent to stay with Gail.

Trying to match the timeframe was making her head ache, but she kept coming back to Camorra. Camorra had forced Idris Krasiniqe to rape Carly Ann. Eamon Krasiniqe was held down and injected with poison. Both Idris and Eamon were then forced to watch Camorra rape and then strangle the girl. Idris pleaded guilty, but retracted the statement in which he said that the two other men had been party to her murder.

They now knew that Camorra and Rashid Burry had been in the Range Rover, from fingerprints. Semen samples taken from Carly Ann's body matched both Idris and Camorra's DNA. Rashid Burry's body was then later found wrapped in black plastic bin-liners inside the vehicle; they traced mud on its tyres to Gail's bungalow.

Anna closed one book and opened another. By mistake, she had jumped to her third book, which detailed the huge operation bringing the Krasiniqe brothers to the hospital for contagious diseases.

Reading her notes again, she was more certain than ever that Camorra had been fed poison: his symptoms were identical to those of Eamon Krasiniqe. Anna tried hard to think how someone could have got to him. If Camorra had been injected, then the autopsy would have noted the needle pinpricks; they had initially not noticed any on Eamon, but he had also ingested the poison via the rock cakes.

Anna lay on the sofa, eyes closed. She remembered the amount of water Camorra had drunk when they first interviewed him. Between them, they had consumed the entire contents of a large bottle.

Then she remembered that Langton had poured, from his own small bottle, a cup full for Camorra and a half-cup for himself. Camorra had gulped it down, and then shortly after, asked for a bathroom break. Anna now remembered standing in the corridor: Langton had put out his cigarette in his water cup and then he had tossed it into the waste bin! Langton, she was certain, had not drunk from the small bottle.

She was pacing the room: there was something else. At the time, she had thought nothing of it. Langton had mentioned that Camorra had ordered in steak tartare, when the officer asked if it was still permissible for him to order in food to eat in his cell. How did Langton know what he had ordered?

Anna called Esme Salaam to ask if she could talk to her, then hurried out to her car. The Salaams were back at their small practice in the East End and were just about to close by the time she arrived.

'I need to know how easy it is to detect Jimson weed in a dead person,' Anna said immediately.

Esme looked at her husband, who was taking off his white coat. 'To my knowledge, it isn't. It would require someone who was aware of the drug or who was privy to the symptoms. The drug would not be easily detected – though, of course, this would depend on the dosage.'

'Enough to bring on a cardiac arrest,' Anna said calmly.

Dr Salaam looked at his wife and shrugged. 'Well, if it was a cardiac arrest in suspicious circumstances, if the patient had severe auditory hallucinations or intense visual anxiety . . .'

'You mean like seeing things, or feeling as if something was crawling over them?'

'That could be a side-effect; as I said, it would depend on the dosage.'

'Say it was given to someone over a period of thirty-six hours?'

'Well, it would have to be a considerable amount. To

my knowledge, it is usually used in very small dosages
to control and frighten the recipient, by making them
believe that they are being taken over by another power.'

'How easy is it to come by?'

'It isn't; far from it – it is exceedingly difficult. I suppose someone, with the intention of acquiring it, could
grow it, but there is no antidote. It would be very
unwise for anyone to fool around with it.'

Anna accepted a cup of tea from Esme and sat down
as Dr Salaam excused himself, saying he had to make
some calls. As he went into his surgery, Anna tried to
think of the best way to explain why she was asking the
questions.

Esme made it easy for her. 'Is it connected to
Camorra?' she asked.

'Yes. Did he, to your knowledge, ever use it?'

'If he did, he would not have got it from here. We
only have a very small sample of it, and that is always
kept locked away. It is very rare for me ever to take
it out.'

'When did you last do this?'

'When we were at the hospital. My husband felt it
might be required, but as it turned out, I don't think he
ever showed it to anyone.'

'Is it in a bottle?'

'Yes: you can have it in liquid form or made into small
white tablets.'

'Do they have a taste?'

'No, they don't.'

'So they could be slipped into someone's food?'

'Yes, of course. Wasn't that the method they used
to feed that poor boy in the prison, the coconut rock
cakes?'

Anna took a deep breath. 'Yes, of course – I had forgotten. So Camorra would have had access to this poison?'

'Obviously, but he was instigating the importation of illegal immigrants; one of those poor souls might have been a carrier of it. They were also bringing in heroin and cocaine and marijuana, weren't they?'

Anna nodded.

Esme sipped her tea and placed her cup down carefully in the bone china saucer. 'Why are you asking me all this now?'

'Just tying up some loose ends,' she said quietly.

Esme nodded and proffered more tea, but Anna declined.

'Could I see the container that you brought the poison in?'

Esme hesitated. 'This won't have any repercussions for us, will it?'

'No, of course not,' Anna said firmly.

Esme unlocked a cabinet and took down a bottle with a red cross marked on the label.

'Did anyone at the hospital have access to this?'

Esme shook her head. 'No, it was in my medical case all the time. I only took it out to show DCI Langton.'

'Did you lock the bag?'

'Yes, most certainly. I always take every precaution and the bag was never out of my sight.'

Anna nodded; she then asked if Esme could check the contents for her, just to make sure that nothing was missing.

Esme hesitated, then pressed the cap down and un-screwed it. 'These are in tablet form: the seeds are crushed and then pressed into pills.' She carefully tapped the bottle to hold in the palm of her hand one small white pill. She held it out to Anna. 'So small and so deadly.'

Then Esme returned the pill to the container and screwed the cap back on. She asked very gravely, 'What loose ends are you so interested in?'

Anna shrugged. 'Oh, we were concerned that Camorra did show symptoms; we will need to verify that his death was by natural causes.'

'I see. Well, to be frank with you, the relief both my husband and I felt when we knew he was dead was considerable. He was a very evil, twisted man; who knows how many lives he had destroyed for his own sexual gratifications, including poor young children? I hope he died in great pain. He deserves no sympathy; sadly, there will be little retribution on behalf of those he damaged.'

At that moment, Dr Salaam came back in and apologized for not being available. He said he had two patients suffering from insomnia; he laughed and said that he himself very rarely ever had that problem as, by the time he was able to get to his bed, he was exhausted.

Anna thanked them both for giving up their time. The doctor shook her hand and walked with her to the door to show her out.

When she had gone, he closed the door behind her and bolted it both at top and bottom. 'What did she really want, do you think?' he asked his wife.

'Eugene Camorra might have been given some Jimson weed. I didn't press on it too much, but she said he had shown symptoms,' Esme replied.

'Well, I congratulate someone. If he died in agony and feeling the terror, then so be it.'

'Whoever it was did not take them from us; I was so careful.'

'Of course you were, my dear. Besides, the only people there were police officers, so I am sure she is not trying to implicate one of them.'

Esme kissed him and went upstairs to their flat to start dinner. Dr Salaam said he would be only a few moments.

After drawing the shutters, he turned to the cabinet. He stared at the bottle with the red cross over the label, then took it down. He shook it, then went over to the small reception desk and took out a miniature silver shovel. He emptied the contents and counted, sliding each pill across the silver shovel and back into the bottle. He then screwed the cap back on and replaced the bottle, locking the cabinet. Fifteen small white tablets were missing.

Anna returned home, dissatisfied; she had somehow thought that she would gain some answers. Her suspicions still lingered. Did Langton know that it was Camorra who had attacked him? She tried to recall his reaction at Orso's house when they had arrested Camorra; neither man had shown any sign that they remembered the other. Langton had never mentioned it during their questioning of Camorra.

Unable to sleep, Anna could not stop her mind churning over. She smacked her pillow to try and get more comfortable. So what if Langton did have something to do with the death of Camorra? He was a despicable human being; no prison sentence could be harsh enough for the crimes he had committed. Still, she could not rest easy, because Langton was a police officer; if he had taken the law into his own hands then it contravened all that they aspired to as upholders of the law. Break the rules once, and the next time was easier. Langton was known to be a risk taker: had he taken the ultimate one?

After a restless night, Anna sat drinking a strong black coffee. She was determined to get some answers. She made a shortlist of people she wanted to talk to. If they did not confirm her suspicions, then she would make herself bury them.

Mike Lewis was getting his young son into a pushchair when she turned up at his house. Like Anna, he was having a break before his next case; unlike her, he was enjoying his time off. Anna said she just needed to ask him a couple of questions. He shrugged and said he was on his way to the playground.

'Did you recognize Camorra as the man who had attacked Langton?'

He stopped pushing the pushchair. 'What?'

'Did you?'

Mike walked on. 'Look, it was a long time ago. To be honest, it was such a nightmare that it's kind of blank – but in answer to your question, no.' He stopped again. 'Maybe if Jimmy had said something I'd have thought about it, but if anyone was to recognize him, it would be him, right?'

'You know Camorra got meals sent into the station.'

'Yeah.'

'Well, I think someone got to him.'

Mike pushed his son harder in the pushchair. 'I dunno where this is going, Anna, but if someone did that, then it had to be Orso. What's your problem?'

'Nothing; just tying up loose ends.'

'There always are some on any case. I just don't quite understand where this is leading.'

'Never mind. You enjoy your time off.' She walked away.

Mike stood there, then turned and looked after her, before he continued on to the park to play with his son. Suddenly he felt uneasy, wondering what Anna was up to.

Barolli was also at home; although working on a case, it was his weekend off. Anna sat with him in a rather untidy lounge, as he chatted on about still being miffed he'd not been brought onto the investigation.

Anna took out the mug shots of Eugene Camorra. 'Is this the man who attacked Langton?'

'Could be,' Barolli said.

'But you were there – you saw him.'

'Yeah, but you gotta remember there was this big bloke in front to start with, then the bastard came out of nowhere. I dunno ... yeah, it looks like him, but I couldn't be certain.'

Anna put the photograph away.

'Why do you want to know?' Barolli asked. 'I know who that is, by the way – that's Eugene Camorra, right?'

'Yes.'

'So what's with you asking me about him?'

Anna said it was just tying up loose ends. She was surprised when Barolli tapped her knee and said, 'Your loose ends – or Jimmy's?'

'Mine.'

Barolli leaned back in his chair and shook his head. 'Drop it. Whatever you think you can gain by this, it is not gonna do any good, you hear me? Drop it.'

Anna felt the tears stinging her eyes. 'I can't.'

'Then let me give you some advice: whatever you are

trying to uncover will destroy you. If you keep going, it'll be down to the woman spurned.'

'That is not true,' she said angrily.

'Isn't it? Just drop this crap, Anna.'

'He's a bloody police officer.'

'So am I!' snapped Barolli.

'And so am I!' she retorted.

'Then drop whatever you are doing and get on with your life,' he said more quietly.

'So Mike Lewis called you, did he?'

'Mind your own fucking business. I mean it, Anna; now go on home. This is my weekend off.'

Anna drove out to the police station in the New Forest. They were surprised to see her. She asked to speak to the officers who were working the cells when Camorra was held.

She waited in an interview room for ten minutes before Officer Harris joined her. Anna was very pleasant, putting him at his ease, as she asked seemingly innocuous questions regarding Camorra and his arrangement to get food sent in. He said that DCI Langton had been privy to Camorra's requests, but was always warning them to check every meal tray.

'What about the time he ordered steak tartare?'

Harris shrugged. He had given Camorra a menu from the local Italian restaurant. He would choose what he wanted to eat and they would call the restaurant; it was delivered, inspected and taken to his cell. Camorra said they should take the money out of the wallet that they held when he was taken into custody.

'And DCI Langton approved this?'

'Yes, he often checked the trays personally.'

'Did Mr Orso ever have access to these trays?'

'No, he was locked up.'

'So only DCI Langton and yourself were overseeing these food trays?'

'No: whoever was on duty, ma'am.'

'Thank you.' She got up and, almost as an afterthought, asked if he had been around when Camorra was taken ill. He said that he was: in fact, he had been the officer who called a doctor.

'He'd gone apeshit, like he was seeing monsters or something coming through the walls. He was screaming and shouting that they'd come for him and he was trying to remove his clothes; said they were eating him. He was really crazed and his eyes were rolling back in his head, mouth frothing, really crazy.'

'As if he was drugged?'

'I dunno, ma'am; just he was crawling up the wall with terror.'

'Then what happened?'

'He went all quiet – stiff like – staring up at the wall. Oh yeah, when I looked in on him, you know, to check him out, he did this.' Harris lifted his hand and pointed with his finger, then made a circular motion. 'As if he was pointing at a clock.'

'So what happened then?'

'DCI Langton came down and said he wanted a doctor for him asap.'

'So, during the wait before the doctor arrived, what did Camorra do?'

'Nothing. He just lay there on his bunk staring up at the ceiling.'

'Like a zombie?' Anna asked innocently.

'Yeah, that's how I'd describe him.'

'Thank you very much.'

Anna drove away from the station. At least she had one visit she was looking forward to.

She had asked, as it was a weekend, if she could see Gail's children. Dora let her in, and said she was just about to make some tea. The children were in her jumbled lounge. Anna walked in to see the little girl in a rah-rah skirt, wearing Carly Ann's gold chain round her neck and playing with a massive dolls' house. Keith beamed at Anna; he was wearing a police helmet and uniform.

'My, you look terrific,' she said, as he pranced in front of her.

'I got the bad man,' he said.

'Yes, you did,' Anna said, sitting on a cushion. She turned as Dora brought in a tray of Coca-Cola and tea, with a plate of chocolate biscuits. 'I was just congratulating Keith on how he helped capture the bad man.'

'Yes. He's been given that uniform and all sorts of things, from handcuffs to charge sheets; he's a proper detective now. And he's going to be nominated for a bravery award. We also got lots of Barbie dolls and a Barbie house.'

Anna knew, without being told, who had bought the children their new acquisitions.

'James Langton – he's a special guy, isn't he?' Dora said happily.

Anna nodded. Dora asked what should be done with the jewellery left by Carly Ann. Anna said that, to her knowledge, no one was claiming it; as the children would need so many things, perhaps it could be sold to help finances.

Driving away, Anna knew she'd just bent the rules but she felt that, in these circumstances, it was acceptable. Yet again, her mind returned to Langton; although she had just done something unethical, she could hardly put it in the same league. She sighed. Do it once and it would be easier the next time!

As she let herself into her flat the phone rang. She dumped her coat and picked it up.

'Hi.' It was Langton.

She had to sit down. 'Hi, how's things?' she asked.

'Good, how about you?'

'Fine, just getting ready for the next case, whatever that may be.'

'Yeah. I'm off to France for a couple of weeks with the kids. I need a breather – well, not that I'll get that with Kitty and Tommy, but there's a health spa, so I can get some feelgood time.'

'That's great.'

'So, I was wondering if we could have that dinner? Maybe make a reservation now?'

'Yes, why not.'

Langton arranged to see her the day after he returned. He would collect her at eight.

'I won't be late,' he said, laughing.

Anna felt as if she could do with two weeks in a spa herself. Over the course of the fortnight, her suspicions became less of an immediate worry; in fact, she began to think that she should, as Barolli had suggested, put them to rest.

There was some good news: Ella Sickert's other child had been traced to a couple living in Birmingham. They ran a sandwich bar; the child was working for them and having very little schooling. The couple insisted that they had taken him in as a favour to his aunt, who had been unable to control him. The so-called aunt was tracked down: she was a known prostitute, living with a small-time drug dealer in a rundown high-rise block of flats. If the child had been used for sexual favours, he showed no signs of physical abuse; however, he was aggressive and abusive and, when the police arrived, he went into a frenzy. They finally discovered that, along with his brother, he had been taken to the house in Peckham. He stayed there only a matter of weeks before he was sent to his aunt in Birmingham. He had never seen his father as he was promised, and had not seen his brother after he left Peckham. It took a considerable amount of counselling and therapy before he admitted to being drugged and used by men who came to the brothel. There was a pile of fake immigration documents which, yet again, led back to Camorra and Orso. All others involved were arrested and charged.

After weeks of waiting, Ella was reunited with her son. It was never going to be easy. He rejected her totally and blamed her for all the abuse he had suffered. There would be a further lengthy period of legal paperwork before the deportation order came through for Ella and her son to return home.

The autumn weather was very warm, and Anna was still waiting to be assigned a new case. The two weeks flew past and she suddenly realized that she had agreed to have dinner with Langton. She was not looking forward to it.

Langton called to ask whether, as it was such a beautiful day, they could switch dinner to lunch. She agreed.

She dressed in a simple white suit and high heels; she'd

had her hair cut very short and the sun had brought out her hated freckles over her nose. She put a bottle of Chablis in the fridge. At promptly one o'clock, the doorbell rang.

Anna was taken aback. Langton looked fantastic; he was deeply tanned and was wearing a pale blue suit with a white T-shirt beneath it. He also carried a bunch of white roses.

'For you,' he said, with a mock bow.

He followed her into the kitchen as she took a vase and filled it with water. She arranged the flowers and took them into the lounge.

'I see you've caught the sun, or your nose has,' he joked.

'This is just from the sunroof in the car. I can't really sunbathe, I just go bright red.'

'Kitty is brown as a berry, even little Tommy. We had glorious weather, swam every day – sauna, massage. Did the trick – I feel terrific.'

'You look it,' she said.

'Right – you hungry?'

'Yeah. Where are we going?'

'As it's such a nice day, I thought we'd drive to Sunbury – you know, just before Shepperton? There's a lovely pub; they serve good food and we can sit outside and eat.'

'Sounds good.'

It was quite a long drive. Anna took the Mini. Langton sat beside her, complaining about the legroom, as always. They drove through Richmond, over the bridge, and headed towards Sunbury. He kept up a light conversation about the holiday and the food, saying he'd put on weight with the breakfast croissants, three-course lunches and then late dinners – the best food he'd ever eaten.

They went down the winding lane to the large pub, which faced the water. He chose a table outside and then picked up the menu.

'You want a salad? And they have good steak and chips.'

'Yes, fine.'

He ordered at the bar inside and came out with two glasses of red wine and a large spoon with a number on it, which he stuck into the pot provided. 'They'll call our number when it's ready.'

'You obviously know this place well,' she said, making conversation.

'Yes, it used to be a regular haunt when I was married.' He picked up his wine glass and tapped hers. 'Cheers.'

'Cheers,' she said quietly.

'So, Anna, what have you been up to?'

'Waiting to hear what my next case is; cleaning up the flat. I like everything all—'

'Shipshape,' he said.

'Yes, you could say that.'

He lit a cigarette, and gestured that it was okay as they were in the smoking zone. 'I've cut back and I'm going to have some acupuncture to give up.'

'Good.'

'So, what else?' His light tone had altered. He was very quiet, his eyes boring into hers.

'I went to see Gail's children, but you beat me to it.'

He nodded.

'Ella Sickert and her son have been reunited.'

'Immigration have such a backlog, they could be waiting for a year.'

'I think she wants to go home.'

'I don't blame her. This country sucks.'

Anna nodded and sipped her wine.

'So – what else?' Again she felt the undercurrent, and found it hard to meet his eyes.

'Spit it out, Anna. I know you paid a visit to Doctor Salaam.'

'I just wanted to find out.'

'I know what you wanted to find out; you also called on Mike Lewis and Barolli.'

'Yes.'

'Went back to the station.'

'Yes.'

'So, after this extensive runaround, what have you—'

They were interrupted as their number was called out; a waitress carrying their salads appeared. Langton held up the spoon.

'Thank you,' he smiled. He ordered two more glasses of wine to be brought with their main course, plus a bottle of still water. He picked up his knife and fork, and tucked into the salad.

Anna could hardly touch hers; her stomach was in knots.

'So tell me – what have you been so busy beavering around after?' He pushed his half finished salad aside and drank his wine.

Anna haltingly went over the facts she had unearthed for the defence team representing Idris Krasiniqe.

'Lemme tell you something: Idris Krasiniqe took the guilty plea over Carly Ann—'

'But he didn't kill her.'

His hand shot across the table and gripped hers tightly. 'Let me finish: we know he worked as Camorra's henchman/drug dealer along with his brother; we know they were both illegal immigrants. Christ, we are not even sure if that's their real name – right? *Right?*'

'Yes, I know that.'

'Idris was trying to decapitate her, trying to cut off her hands, so she wouldn't be identified, correct?'

'Yes.'

'Now, even if he was high on drugs, terrified of Camorra, afraid for his brother – whatever reason you want to give – he was still fucking involved in her murder. He said he saw Camorra strangle her after he had raped her and after he himself had been forced to rape her – so she was what? Tied up on that fucking stone slab? His brother was forced to watch, injected with that shit Jimson weed so he wouldn't know what time of day it was. You want me to go on?'

She nodded and picked at her salad.

'Okay: watching the attempted decapitation were Rashid Burry and Camorra. Idris gets picked up, the two guys piss off and the Range Rover disappears. You still with me?'

'Yes!'

Langton began to tick off on his fingers the next events: Idris Krasiniqe withdrew his statement; he said he did not know who the other two men were, and claimed that he, and he alone, killed Carly Ann. 'Now, you tell me, Anna: why would he do that? Why would he go down for a murder you say he didn't commit?'

'Fear for his brother maybe?'

'Eamon Krasiniqe was picked up for dealing drugs to kids outside a school. He resisted arrest and, at his trial, asked for eight offences of drug dealing to be taken into consideration, as well as one attempt to kidnap a fourteen-year-old girl.'

'Did it ever occur to you that both of the brothers were terrified of what Camorra would do to them?' Anna asked. 'At least locked up, they were free of him. As it turned out, Eamon was got at, and we know how.'

Langton shook his head. 'But Idris held back information; he held up our entire enquiry into Carly Ann's murder. If he'd given us Rashid Burry and Camorra's names at the start ... He lied: he had information and yet kept his mouth shut. Not until he was trying to save his brother, did he give up what he knew. Now, if you want to play runaround with his defence to get a retrial, go ahead; to me, the scum can serve out his sentence.'

'But he didn't kill Carly Ann.'

Langton snapped, 'My point is, for Chrissakes, that he knew who did!'

'So are you now saying that Rashid Burry and Camorra were at the hostel when you went there?'

'Yeah. If Idris had given up their names, look at the trail of death we might have stopped. Gail's kid was twenty-four months old, for God's sake – fed to the pigs! Does that sit all right with you?'

'No, of course not.'

'Then let Idris Krasiniqe rot in hell.'

The waitress called their spoon number again and brought over the steak and chips. She removed the dirty cutlery and crockery, and laid out two sets of steak knives and clean forks.

'Thank you, and the wine?'

She said it was just coming.

Langton picked up some ketchup and proffered it to Anna, who shook her head.

'Rashid Burry was murdered,' Anna said quietly.

'Yes, neatly wrapped in the trunk of the Range Rover that Camorra, because he couldn't drive an automatic – ha ha – never used.' Langton cut into his steak, and ate a large mouthful.

'So, Rashid – you recognized him, didn't you? The gold teeth?'

Langton nodded. 'That's pretty obvious; yes, I did.'

'Did you also recognize Eugene Camorra as being the man who attacked you on the stairs?'

He didn't look at her, but sliced another piece of steak. 'No.'

'You didn't recognize him at Emmerick Orso's house in Redhill?'

'No.'

'At what point did you . . .'

'Did I what?'

'Recognize him?'

'I didn't.'

Anna picked up the salt and sprayed a little over her chips. 'So Eugene Camorra was not the man who attacked you?'

Langton said steadily, 'Let me tell you: if, after what I have been put through, I came face to face with the man who had done it, I'd react. You can bet your sweet arse I'd react; I wouldn't be able to keep my hands off him.' He gestured with his knife. 'Your steak okay?'

'Yes, it's fine, thanks.'

Langton smiled at the waitress as she brought two fresh glasses of red wine and took their two dirty glasses away. He watched Anna as she picked at the steak. 'There's a rumour I'm earmarked for the corporate ladder. I'll have to do the friggin' homework, but Chief Superintendent sounds like it's about time. What do you think?'

Anna shrugged. 'Sounds good.'

He mimicked her. 'Sounds good.'

'Well, it does. I hope you do get promotion.'

He lifted the bottle of water to ask if she wanted some, then he poured another glass for himself and slowly screwed the cap back on. All the while he looked at her; until eventually she was forced to turn away. He was still the rakish, handsome man she had loved; she still loved his lanky body, his hands, the way he laughed. Tanned and fit, he was even more attractive than ever, but he was now, as he had often been, someone she didn't know. It was like dining with a stranger.

'I'm sorry, but I have a headache,' she said. 'I'd like to go home.'

Whilst Langton paid the bill, she walked to the car and sat waiting. She watched him strolling towards her and leaned over to open the passenger door.

'You go ahead; I think I'll just walk for a while.' He tapped the roof with the flat of his hand and walked past her, crossing in front of the car to head along the river-bank.

She saw him limp just a fraction. He seemed un-concerned, looking at the ducks, until she couldn't stand it a moment longer. She got out of her car and slammed the door shut.

She hurried across to him. 'I know how you did it!'

He turned to face her, frowning as if confused.

'I know Camorra attacked you. I know it was him. I don't know how you had the self-control not to want to get him by the throat and strangle him, but I do know, James. I know!'

Langton picked up a stick and hurled it into the water, then walked on a fraction to lean against a tree.

She followed. 'It was in his dinner trays. It was in the water you passed to him in the incident room.'

'What are you talking about?'

'You know what I am talking about, for Chrissakes: that poison, the Jimson weed. You used it on Camorra. He showed all the symptoms.'

Langton shook his head, smiling.

'I know you did it; I just don't know how you got hold of it.'

'Didn't you check already with Doctor Salaam and his wife?'

'Yes!'

'At first, I just thought it was your obsession and your inability to be, as I have warned you about, a team player. I presumed you were still trying to prove that Emmerick Orso was somehow involved.'

'He couldn't have been!' she snapped.

'Jesus Christ.' He shook his head and then stared at her. 'So now you want to implicate me, is that right? Is that what you've been running around raking up dirt on? Is it because I walked out on you, is that your problem?'

'No, it is not!'

'Then why? What in God's name are you trying to do to me? That I, shock horror, recognized Eugene Camorra as the man who almost killed me, then arrested him for Christ knows how many murders – and all I was interested in was taking my own revenge? What the fuck do you think I am?'

'You could have tampered with his meal trays.'

He suddenly reached out and grabbed her wrists. 'Listen to me: this is a crazy insinuation. You have not one jot of proof. I have been very patient with you, Anna, over three high-profile cases. You have made crass mistakes before, and I have overlooked one after the other, but this accusation . . .'

'It isn't an accusation: it's the truth!'

'If you have one shred of proof, then take it to the Commissioner. But if you do, then God help you, because I am going to have to do something that I have really, really tried not to do.'

'What?'

'I do not think you are a suitable officer to be attached to the Murder Squad. You have fouled up too many times. I will also have to bring into the equation the fact that I foolishly had a sexual relationship with you. It was a big mistake on my part, and one I really regret, because ending it has obviously turned you against me.'

'You can't get away with it like that!' she said angrily.

He drew her close, still gripping her wrists tightly. 'I got away with nothing. I have a crippled knee joint and constant problems with my lungs and my chest. I have got away with nothing but a life of excruciating pain and medication. If Eugene Camorra was the man who did this to me, I would have brought charges. Now, you had better make up your mind, Anna.' He released his hold. 'If you want to press these farcical charges against me, go ahead, but you will need proof – and you don't have it. But don't let that stop you. Go ahead, and take the repercussions.'

'Which would be what?'

He gave a soft laugh and then made a move with his hand, as if directing traffic, a smile on his lips; his gesture infuriated her.

'Do you think that this has been easy for me?' she cried. 'I've had sleepless nights! But you *can't* take the law into your own hands!'

She stepped back, almost afraid he was going to slap her, as he glared at her. 'I never have. Your furtive imagination has put two and two together and come up with a load of shite! Even hinting at your suspicions makes me unable to ever trust you again.'

Anna could feel the tears pricking at her eyes.

'One day, in the mound of illegal immigrants we are still attempting to trace, we'll find the man who almost killed me. When I do, and I intend to not let this rest, then you'll know about it. I did not, as you believe, find from God knows where this stuff to poison Camorra; in fact, by his dying, we lost valuable evidence we could have charged Orso with. I didn't want the bastard dead.'

Anna was shaking. She recoiled when he put his arm out and drew her back closer to him.

'Anna, I cared about you, but don't make me out to be the villain – you know we'd never have worked. I doubt if I'll ever be able to maintain a stable relationship but, without your care, I don't think I would have pulled through, and for that I will always be eternally grateful. Don't play these accusations out: the only person that will be hurt will be you. Do you understand what I am saying?' Langton gently brushed a curl from her forehead. 'It's over. Come on now, say it.'

She heard her voice whispering that it was over, like a chastised child. She looked up into his face. She had loved him so much; even now, she felt her heart beating faster, being so close to him.

'Forget it; that's what this is all about, sweetheart. Just forget it – I will. The case, thank Christ, is over. Anna?'

She broke away from him and forced herself to smile.

'Goodbye, Anna. You take care of yourself now.'

She nodded and turned her back on him, grateful he wouldn't see that she was crying.

Langton remained leaning against the tree. He watched her drive past but did not acknowledge her; instead, he turned back to the river, staring into the murky water.

He would begin working on tests for his promotion. He knew his physical problems would always be with him, and the rise in rank would mean a less hands-on role. He had also suggested that Mike Lewis be upped in rank; he deserved it but, like himself, Mike would have to sit the obligatory paperwork. He then turned from the riverbank and started to walk down the lane, calling for a taxi on his mobile phone. He could still not walk too far without the pain in his knee joint. The pain, he had told Anna, that would forever be a memory of the attack.

He smiled: revenge is always sweet, even when taken cold.

Anna received a call from Idris Krasiniqe's solicitor. They were still preparing for the retrial. They asked if she would be willing to assist with some of the documents that she had worked on. Anna agreed to drive to Wakefield prison to meet Idris and his solicitor.

She was shown into the interview room. Idris was being brought up from the cells, so she had a few moments alone with his solicitor, a Toby Freeman: a very pleasant and eager young man.

'It is not going to be easy,' Toby told her. 'We would have been looking at a reduced sentence, but now without his brother, without Rashid Burry and with no Eugene Camorra, I have to admit we are not in a very strong position. I try to keep his hopes up, but with two trials dismissed, the CPS require a lot more evidence.'

Idris looked fit; he'd put on weight and he seemed pleased to see Anna. He gripped her hand tightly, thanking her. It was a slow process; they went over all the statements Idris had made. When asked why he had not given details of the other two men involved in Carly Ann's murder when he had the opportunity, he shook his head.

'I was terrified of what Camorra could do to me. I knew he'd got to my brother. I was scared to ever come out onto the wing. They'd pumped him so full of crack and heroin and, Christ knows, that Jimson weed, he was out of his head.'

Idris bowed his head, crying, but they ploughed on. He repeated how Camorra had strapped Carly Ann down on the stone altar, stripped naked. He made everyone in the house watch: he wanted everyone to know what would happen to them if they betrayed him. Idris sobbed as he said he was forced to have sex with her whilst his brother – hardly able to focus, he was so drugged – looked on. He had watched Camorra strangle Carly Ann, but could do nothing to stop it: he was too scared.

Rashid had driven the Range Rover with Camorra beside him and Idris in the back seat; behind the dog rail lay the dead Carly Ann. When they stopped, Idris was instructed to cut off her hands and decapitate her. Camorra did not want her identified; as she had been arrested for prostitution, he knew her fingerprints would be on file. Idris was in such a state that he had only half-heartedly attempted to do what he had been told. Camorra, in a rage, had got out of the Range Rover with Rashid to do the job properly.

'He had picked her up by her hair, holding her body up to slice at her neck, when this cop runs up. He dropped her and they both ran. I couldn't get away: they picked me up, with blood all over me. I had the knife. I said I done it: I was too scared not to.'

Idris pleaded with Anna to help him; all she could say was that she would do her best. She told him that one of the charges for which Camorra was arrested was the murder of Carly Ann. Idris hit the table in anger: the man who could help him was dead. At this point, Anna turned to Toby Freeman and asked if she could have two minutes alone with Idris. He agreed; the guards opened the door and he walked out.

'Two minutes, Idris, that is all I have. I need you to answer me truthfully.'

'Yes, anything. You know me now, I'm telling you the truth.'

'Whilst you were held in the police station, you claimed you had not been alone, but with two other men: you gave two names and an address where they could be found.'

'Yes.'

'Did you call anyone from the station?'

'Yes. I called Rashid Burry to get me a solicitor, and I told him.'

'You then, after this phone call, changed your statement – is that correct?'

'Yes.'

'You claimed that you had been alone with Carly Ann, and that you had just invented the fact that two other men were with you – is that correct?'

'Yes.'

'Why did you lie?'

Idris bowed his head. 'I was told that Eamon was gonna die if I didn't. I gave the names of some blokes that had worked at the Peckham house; I just said the hostel, 'cos I knew it. They was really pushing me for answers; that guy Langton was hammering at me all night.'

'So let's just go back to the Range Rover: you said that you were driven there by Rashid Burry.'

'Yes, I've said this.'

'Who was the other man in the Range Rover?'

Idris shrugged. 'I have told you: the other man was Eugene Camorra. I can say his name now he's dead, 'cos he can't do nothing to me any more. He held her by her hair, lifted her up so he could cut her throat . . .'

Anna nodded. 'When you called Rashid Burry from the police station, did you tell him about your statement?'

'Rashid said I was a fuckin' idiot, 'cos they had guys there at the hostel and he didn't want the connection. I mean, I just said the first place that came into my head, right?'

Anna paused. 'What do you think happened after you had given the police this hostel address?'

Idris shrugged. 'I think Rashid got over there fast to get the guys out.'

'With Camorra?'

'I dunno. I guess so, yes.'

'But you can't be certain?'

'No. I did know that the cop who had been putting all the pressure on me was cut down.'

'By Rashid?'

Idris shook his head. 'He never showed up after that night. I was told he was dead.'

'Who told you that?'

'I don't remember, but it scared the shit out of me that Camorra could hack a cop to pieces and get away with it. I mean, I wasn't going to talk then, no way.'

'So you are certain that Eugene Camorra attacked the detective who had questioned you: James Langton?'

'Yeah. Camorra had a machete; he was always wielding it around, it was razor sharp. I'm telling you, Camorra was a madman; he boasted about it. It scared the shit out of everyone.'

Idris began to sob again. He blubbered about a little boy and what Camorra had done to him: he had kept his skull and hands until they were black and shrunken, and then wore them like a necklace.

The door was rapped on: their time was up. Anna collected her papers.

Idris tried to reach out for her hand. 'Please get me a retrial, ma'am – please. I never killed that girl.'

Anna clicked her briefcase closed. 'You watched Camorra kill that little boy?'

'Yeah, yeah – we had to; if we didn't obey him, he would turn on us – he . . .'

He never got to finish; the officers gestured that it was time for Anna to leave. She walked out, hearing Idris still calling her name, saying that he was innocent.

In the car park, Toby Freeman approached her. 'Do you think we'll get a fair crack at a retrial?'

Anna wound down her window. 'I really couldn't say.'

'Well, look, thanks for your help – I really appreciate it. Way I see it, basically Idris is innocent and was too terrified to admit the truth.'

Anna merely smiled and drove away. She felt drained and couldn't wait to get home and shower: get rid of the stench of the prison; get rid of the images Idris had conjured up; get rid of the animal Eugene Camorra, who